The Cassandra Curse

Fiorella De Maria

The Cassandra Curse

Progress PRESS

(Member of the Allied Group)

Published and Printed

by

Progress Press Co. Ltd
341, St Paul Street
Valletta, Malta 2005

ISBN 9909-3-076-7

Contents

I

For those of us who were born in the wrong country, at the wrong time or under the wrong circumstances, to feel at home can never be a comforting feeling. We do not tell strangers to make themselves at home when we want them to feel secure, we do not expect them to feel at ease with their environment. For those of us who were meant never to belong anywhere, to be at home is to feel unsettled, to feel unsafe, to feel not quite welcome but not entirely rejected either.

"Ask a silly question."

I had almost forgotten that he had ever asked me a question. His dry comment, made without opening his eyes, snaps me back to life like the voice of conscience. "I suppose I do feel at home here when it comes to it," I tell him, though I know he thinks I am talking in riddles again. "You can make of that what you like."

Sitting back in his chair with the sun making pleasing patterns against his face, Benedict looks like a sleeping child. He survived the first panic of arriving in a strange country, straight into the arms of a gaggle of noisy foreigners, and coped remarkably well for a man who had never travelled further south than Cornwall before boarding the Air Malta flight. By now he has been plied with food, interrogated about his job prospects, learnt and forgotten the names of every conceivable family member I could think to introduce him to and memorised Maltese numbers up to ten.

"It's not exactly what you were expecting me to say, was it, darling?" I know it wasn't. I think he imagined a warm sense of belonging, a feeling of being at peace with the world and for the first time he looks a little alarmed, as if there was some rule being broken somewhere.

"Not exactly, no." He does not lean back and close his eyes again. I have made him nervous and now he is going to try to hide it. "It doesn't matter. I'm not marrying you for your predictability."

Thank God for small mercies; poor Benedict could never predict any of this. He is like an English version of my father: softly spoken, impeccably mannered and one of those rare things – a truly innocent man. *Innocent in every sense of the word.* A man who has never wilfully broken a rule in his life. From our vantage point, I know that he sees beauty everywhere. A sky to make a man believe in eternity; palm trees and dusty rock formations; the Mediterranean Sea, cool and inviting, as silent as the grave.

"As silent as a mass grave."

"Erm - pardon?"

"Nothing." It makes no sense to him, he is not given to letting his imagination run riot. I know that the Persian traders, British sailors, Barbary pirates, Turkish galley slaves, all lying together on the seabed in their shipwreck coffins, do not cry to him across the centuries. We only ever see reflections of ourselves in the world around us and Benedict has a keen eye for beauty, which is all very well.

"Don't you have any ghosts in your cupboards?"

"I think you mean skeletons." I am not sure I do. I had always thought of memories as ghosts before. Impossible to capture. Real and not real creatures that came back to blot out the sun if the world became too lovely. "You have to understand, my love. Nothing remotely exciting or tragic has ever happened to me before."

Heavens, what a privilege! I hide my shock. "Oh well, don't feel too badly about it. I think I can provide enough brooding tragedy for both of us."

He picked the wrong moment to start asking me questions about home and family - right in the middle of a family party. Downstairs in the patriarchal house there are cousins, aunties, uncles, parents, children, all gathered together to celebrate Easter. Three generations of Maltese under one roof. Everyone eating and drinking, the men talking politics, the children squabbling, the women laughing together in the kitchen. "Marija, but what a lovely young man he is!" "What a perfect English gentleman, wherever did Kristjana find him?"

"I like your family," says Benedict, oblivious to the discussion going on in a language neither of us is so familiar with. "They'll be my family soon. I want to get to know them better." Well, he did say nothing exciting or tragic had happened to him before... So I will take him by the hand and drag him into the warm, noisy heart of my family, as long as he doesn't envy our liberated emotions too much. In the midst of all this familial revelry that he is so entranced by - the jokes, the laughter, the good food - he cannot have wondered for even a moment whether it is not all an act of drowning out. Drowning out, burying, shouting down. And how very much we have to bury that no outsider knows about, that Benedict with his innocence and his complacent belief in human goodness is too good even to imagine.

I try to say as much, but the words sound too theatrical spoken aloud. How many voices we have to silence, how many moments we must pretend to forget. Old feuds, heartbreaks, betrayals, curses, guilt, secrets, but old families as distinguished as ours always have more skeletons than cupboards in which to hide them. "Are all families like this?" I must be a little more specific. I ask aloud: Does your family, my love, contain such a rogue's gallery of tyrants, child abusers, fraudsters, bastards, madmen, refugees, saints, heroes, dissidents, aristocrats and wayfarers, all held together in glorious discord? Does it? Does it contain even one of these?

3

"Well, I suppose every family has one black sheep..."

I actually thought he might say yes, but he is laughing now. I knew he would react like that. It all seems too much like a melodramatic Mediterranean dream, a thriller with a hint of the exotic about it. A little too apocalyptic to be real. And perhaps that is what it is, in this heady, sun-dazed land where pagan temples and baroque cathedrals stand side by side in a vortex of history and where seven thousand years lie stretched out like the map of eternity, spiralling into darkness. Perhaps this is a dream of mine, of my people, of my family, but a refugee has nothing else for a dowry, so I must be sure that he will take it. *Tread softly for you tread on my dreams...*

Where to begin? When can a family story be said to 'begin'? If I am to be the storyteller here, I must use my authority and pick my moment to bring a little circle of long dead lives into being. The twenty-first of May in the year of Our Lord, 1939. And the place? Mdina, the old capital of Malta. Appropriately known (by the greatest of all fiction writers, the tourist companies) as *a city of dreams and memories.*

For the world outside this little country, it was a time of hopeless optimism and broken promises. In Britain, Mr Chamberlain was busy making desperate and wholly futile attempts at averting war, whilst in Germany, the concentration camps were full, the press stifled and the expansionism that would soon plunge the world into chaos was well underway, though no one appeared to have noticed just then. A little closer to home, Mussolini was stirring up trouble that would eventually consume even sleepy Malta. But all that was to come and on that particular day, in that particular city, the world looked a considerably more cheerful place than it really was. I say city but I really mean citadel, because the historic capital of Malta, with its sumptuous Norman architecture and its maze of narrow, shady streets is smaller than any English village; a peaceful, inward-looking little world secure behind protective walls and ramparts. The only sound to disturb the morning was the chiming of a church bell.

As Edward Sant'Angelo stepped out of his family home, he was greeted by all the joys of a sunny May morning in his native land; gentle sun, clear, cloudless sky and the slightest of spring breezes. In a book about identity crises, Edward is a good person to start the ball rolling, with his English Christian name (in honour of his English mother who died in childbirth apparently) and his Maltese surname that must have been Italian once. Family folklore had it that he was descended from the Normans on his mother's side whilst all manner of rumour and legend surrounded his father's roots. The Turks, the Knights of St John and Italian merchants have all been accredited with a part in this noble family's beginnings, but Edward's father had a knack of changing his lineage depending on the politics of the moment. Italian was certainly not in vogue just at that precise second, so the Italian merchant line had been temporarily disconnected.

Anyway, it was Edward Sant'Angelo's wedding day and he cut a dashing figure in his very best clothes, curly black hair carefully groomed to show a bronzed, aquiline profile. There were very few women who would not turn to look at him on this day more than any other: he really was a fine figure of a man. He must be seen like this for a moment, young and striking before the years descend on him like waiting vultures. I need to see him like this, if only to be reminded that, had I lived at the start of this family fiasco and not been condemned to view it all from retrospect, I too might have found him irresistible. It stops me from reproaching my grandmother too much for marrying a monster, because he was not always a monster and monsters are seldom ugly.

5

This monster or monster-to-be was a very handsome, benign-looking gentleman with a sound academic record, a decent inheritance coming his way (or so he thought) and a bright future. A closer look would reveal a slightly haunted expression in those heart-stoppingly lovely eyes. That is another family legacy - we are a haunted people. My mother's expression is exactly the same and it will be all his fault when it comes. I have even seen it in my own reflection but I have no excuse, except perhaps it is the inherited terror of looking back. Edward had good reason to look the way he did, having had an unhappy childhood of his own. Little as Edward knew it with his optimism and good intentions, his father had already given him the skills necessary to destroy his own children's lives and was about to commit his most terrible act of all.

As Edward climbed down the last few steps, he turned back to the door for his father's blessing. Old Leonardo Sant'Angelo was where he should have been, standing in the doorway of the family house, as huge and terrifying as Edward's nightmares recalled him and he struggled to suppress a spasm of panic even then, when he was a grown man far stronger than his father. For perhaps the first time since his wife died, Leonardo was stone cold sober and he fixed a steady, steely gaze on the son he was about to disown. There are some who would have said that Edward had a nerve expecting the customary paternal blessing under the circumstances – he was marrying a woman of whom his father disapproved, into a family his father despised. *Romeo and Juliet* for the ten thousand millionth time, but Edward did not see it coming.

"My son," said Leonardo, all well and good, but there was something funereal in his voice. Silence, a long, heavy intake of breath. The world stopped to hear what Leonardo Sant'Angelo had to say to his son on the morning of his wedding. "My son. I put my curse on you. I curse your wife, I curse your marriage and I curse all your descendants, to the last of your race."

With that, he turned his back on his only son and stepped inside. He caused a scandal by not attending his son's wedding and by forbidding his daughter to be present. They never spoke again. I will leave Edward Sant'Angelo there for a moment, shaking in spite of the sunshine, as the door to the family home slams shut for the last time.

II

"All families are like this, aren't they?" I should not keep asking, I am beginning to sound desperate. There can be no question about it anyway, I am in no doubt at all. All families are like this. All families contain evil, embittered old men who are prepared to condemn their own sons to indescribable misery over a family disagreement. All families live under ancestral curses.

"You don't believe in curses, do you?" Benedict's voice is all laughter. He might as well be asking: "You don't believe in Father Christmas, do you?"

The question makes me shiver but he does not understand why yet. "Don't take that tone with me, you haven't the faintest idea!"

"Kris, you've got a degree."

"What's that got to do with it?" I suppose he imagines that Leonardo's worst failing was a rather perverse sense of humour. Or perhaps he needs the reassurance that I am joking about my great grandfather's words, because normal people just do not say such things and actually mean it.

"You make too much of it, that's all." He is placatory now, reaching out a hand to touch my arm. "Once upon a time, a nasty old man cursed his son because he didn't like his choice of girl. People say stupid things all the time."

"Of course, of course, I forgot. Just my superstitious Catholic imagination running away with me."

"My love, my love, I didn't say that -"

"I know that's what you're thinking."

I imagine that I understand Benedict perfectly. His delicate little liberal mind cannot cope with the notion of a curse. It does not square well with a man from the land of Brunel and Fleming. Well, perhaps it is a little mad but the strange and terrible thing is that Edward's marriage *did* seem to be cursed. For whatever reason – and there are many possibilities - Edward's life went steadily downhill from that moment and it pulled down everyone else with it – his wife, his children, his grandchildren. Not one of us has entirely escaped injury.

I suppose that it might have been supernatural forces – "Complete and utter *rubbish!*"

"Well, for all your sweating and squinting in laboratories, can you really say you've disproved any of that?"

"Your accent changes when you're angry," he comments to the world in general, "you're turning into a Maltese matriarch."

"Am not."

"A good psychiatrist could put your mind at rest in a minute."

I suppose he could. The shrinks would say that the idea was planted in Edward's mind right from the beginning that there was a curse on him and it changed him slowly into the monster his father wanted him to be. Of course, if the geneticists are right, it might just be that the evil simmering in Old Leonardo Sant'Angelo's blood, trickled down into his son's veins – and further? No, forget 'all your descendants', poison cannot last that long. Filtered down through the generations, diluted, mutated, it must have dissipated long ago. And anyway, as my affianced one tells me, there is no such thing as a curse. I really need his clever English ways to bring me back into the twenty-first century at times like this. Let me keep saying it, there is no such thing as a curse, there is no such thing as a curse. There was no curse that day, there has never been a curse hanging over my family, none of the terrible acts that have maimed and scarred us like bullet wounds ever happened. It was a dream, it was all a terrible, terrible dream...

It is time to introduce my maternal grandmother, as she waits nervously in the narthex of the church. It is difficult to believe now that she was a society beauty at the time of her marriage. Cancer has thinned her white hair and left her frail and withered when she was once rounded and peachy-faced. Her gold eyes - and they really are tiger-gold - have been almost blinded by diabetes. The wartime photographs of the two of them when they were a young married couple do not really do her justice. Men in uniform retain their appeal somehow and my grandfather in his RAF uniform, reclining in a caddish posture with a pipe in one hand in the style of Douglas Bader, might be any mysterious stranger on the silver screen today. Nanna Antonia though, with her hair tortured into what was the height of fashion then, make-up just a little too garish, looks like a porcelain doll. I suppose it is still beauty, but it is not entirely real, lost across the generations.

When Edward saw her on their wedding day, dressed in soft blue-white satin, her auburn hair covered in lace and tiny flowers, Antonia Bonnici-Cardona must have seemed worth the absence of a father and the weight of ten malicious curses. He thought her perfect in every way. She had beauty, elegance, refinement. Better than that, she had her father with her. A normal father, who led her gently by the hand, smiling and whispering to her with the easy affection a father ought to have towards his own. As she floated to his side on a wave of scent and swishing satin skirts, it did not occur to him to be afraid. He thought, 'to hell with him. I am getting married all the same. I have my own family to create and care for. He is the one who will be alone.' There is something pleasingly noble about making sacrifices for love, particularly when the sacrifice looks so much greater than the young man in question thinks it is. He did not feel cursed at that moment, kneeling at the altar before God and man. He did not feel cursed as he placed a ring on an expectant finger. Twenty years on, he would be too cursed to know it anymore.

And there was revelry there too, to drown out the sound of a father's voice. The Silent City erupted with noise for the afternoon with food, wine and dancing. Flowers were scattered, musicians played, the bride and groom were lifted onto the shoulders of the guests and carried amid shouts of '*Busa! Busa! Busa l-Gharusa!*' (Kiss, kiss, kiss the bride!) When they came together, he was caught in the spell of her scent and stooped forward - blushing desperately - to kiss her.

"But, my goodness, do you suppose he really meant it?" asked Antonia, as they lay together a little awkwardly in their wedding bed. He should have had other things on his mind after the delight of watching her coming to him, hair flowing free, an array of lace and embroidered flowers. She had slipped into his arms as easily as if she were playing a part she had rehearsed in her mind for most of her short adult life. He felt the delicious sensation of her hands cradling his head, heard the rapid, shallow patter of her breathing near his face. She was warm and lovely against his body, still richly scented and he knew that if he was distracted at that moment, he was truly lost – but he was distracted and the sound of a father's curse cut through his desires like a discordant orchestra.

So it happened somehow that instead of making love to his new wife, he found himself telling her what had occurred that morning. He had some notion that if he could just get it off his chest he would feel better, and he joked and chuckled at every word to show her that it was nonsense. And Antonia was not a clever woman, certainly not an educated woman, but she knew his humour was mirthless.

Edward was disturbed to feel her body shaking against him, starting a nervous wave effect along the layers of her lacy white nightdress, but he remembered that he shook violently enough when he heard the words for himself.

"It doesn't matter if he did," Edward explained, tracing a finger gently down the contours of her face. "It doesn't mean anything. You don't believe in curses, do you?"

"No." It was the first lie of their marriage. It would soon become a habit.

"There you go then. Let us just forget all about it."

Antonia pretended to be reassured, but he could feel the aura of fear hanging over her, conjuring up an invisible barrier between them when just hours before they had sworn to be one flesh, never to be put asunder. He should not have told her, he thought, wondering if she would have fallen for a more mundane excuse for his father's absence. Fathers disinherited sons without cursing them as well. He need not have told her immediately that they had fallen out at all; he could have said his father had been taken ill. That would never have washed with her. News spread like wildfire in those close, restless communities and any other man would have been carried into church on a stretcher rather than miss the wedding of his son and heir.

I put my curse on you. I curse your wife, I curse your marriage. It sounded too terrible, like something out of a Gothic horror story, Dracula or Frankenstein, except that it had been the other way that time – man-made, monster-son cursing father. What were the exact words? *I will be with you on your wedding night.* As Antonia's little shivers turned to icy resignation in his arms, it seemed to Edward that his father with his curse was doing just that. He was visiting them on their wedding night, standing in the room showering fear like poisonous flowers over their bed.

Young children are supposed to bounce back from a fall like cartoon characters, their soft bones not yet entirely ossified take the impact of a knock without breaking. The same perhaps with young couples. The morning after Edward Sant'Angelo fell asleep and dreamt that the Frankenstein monster was strangling his bride, he woke up with a jolt to discover his Antonia lying beside him, sleeping peacefully with her chest rising and falling reassuringly. Curses never seem quite so threatening in the light of the early morning, particularly for a man lying next to a beautiful woman. He drew her close to him and was relieved to find that she curled up against him without a hint of resistance. The night terrors had apparently disappeared.

And the newly-weds had every reason to pretend that Edward's father wished them well as they embarked together on this new chapter of their life. They had a new home in a fashionable part of Valletta and if Edward now had no prospect of an inheritance, the threat of war had one tempting advantage to it – respectable employment. Shortly before the first bombs rained down on unsuspecting Maltese heads, Edward walked effortlessly into the bosom of the RAF where he was to remain for much of his working life - though, sadly, without becoming the great flying ace he thought he might become when he enlisted. When they did go hungry, it was Hitler's fault not Edward's.

I should write about the few months when they were happy, to compensate somehow for the rest, but there is little more to say about them for now. For the moment, Edward is still handsome, caring and sober, and Antonia has managed to conceal her growing sense of alarm that she has married into a cursed, thoroughly peculiar family. Imagine them together for the moment, affectionate and happy, going about their daily business in a house that will soon become a battleground. Enough said. Time to take you to another part of the island and another family with troubles of their own.

III

Carmelina Buhagiar sat on her doorstep, stitching the seam of a cocktail dress. The dress was not for her; she was making it for one of her clients, an officer's wife who had heard about her from another officer's wife. She was already a popular seamstress among the English community, known for her fluent if slightly comical transatlantic English and her skill in copying the very latest in Paris fashion. She would arrange appointments in her sewing room whilst her mother made tea for her customers and showed them pictures from the fashion magazines she subscribed to.

She preferred fittings – they were more creative and she was a natural artist. If Carmelina had been born into another class, perhaps in another country, her sketches and paintings would have been on display in art galleries around the world. As it turned out, she used her talents disguising rolls of fat with free-flowing panels of cloth cut across the bias, and varicose veins behind tasselled hems. Ornaments held all kinds of promise in the right hands – beadwork and silk flowers to enhance or distract attention, a bow hovering on the shoulder like a butterfly, a length of soft piping to trace an attractive neckline.

As the summer approached, she would work late into the night – all night sometimes – to complete her orders in time, kneeling before a gaudily dressed mannequin with her cotton reels and papers all over the floor. Her mother would come in early the next morning with breakfast to find Carmelina curled up asleep or blearily hanging up a new creation and send her to bed for a couple of hours whilst she put the room to rights in time for the day's clients. Then there would be a knock on the door and Carmelina would find herself kneeling at a customer's feet with her mouth full of pins, outwardly as fresh as a daisy, whilst inwardly she tried to remember how she had got there in the first place.

It was not a bad life, she said much later, when she had wrecked her eyesight and her hands were crippled by arthritis. She was her own mistress, earning her living in her own home now that there was just mother and her. She had a reputation of sorts. It was surely better than eking out a living cleaning other people's houses or burning out in a factory. And she liked the ladies she worked for and came to know them better than they realised. Her second role as a maker of extravagant clothes was similar to that of a priest in the confessional. All sorts of worries and secrets poured out as she tacked and measured her way around a subject, nodding and making sympathetic mumbling noises to fill in the pauses. Whenever they began by saying: "Well, I wouldn't expect a nice girl like you to see it this way of course, but..." she took it as a cue to rummage in her basket for an imaginary needle, the soul of discretion.

"Those English girls are filling your head with rubbish!" her mother complained, when she hovered at the door in time to hear that some girl was wildly in love with the husband of her best friend. "It's bad for you." But Carmelina needed her head filling with something, even vacuous gossip, to keep her from thinking about her father too much.

She was busy distracting herself as she sat on her doorstep that evening, whilst her mother and Mrs Grech from next door chatted about the news they had just heard on the BBC World Service. Something about the invasion of a country called Poland, but she was too lost in her own thoughts to care very much what it was called. It was fortunate that she was so absorbed in her work, as the name would have given her a terrible jolt.

She surfaced from her musings briefly to register that the two older women had stopped talking about world politics in favour of talking about her. "I thought she was getting married, Liljana?"

"She is, I told you before. You know Lawrence Falzon – Michael and Anna's boy. He's a sailor, it's hard with him away so much."

"They should get on with it. How old is she now?"

Carmelina bristled. She was only twenty-one which was no age at all, though she was far too well brought up to say so. She would have seemed older than Antonia, every bit as lovely, but evidently from a different class altogether. A wild flower, plainly dressed without a trace of make-up and she was a little too dark to be considered elegant. In spite of long hours sitting inside over a sewing machine, her large black eyes glanced out of a tawny Madonna face. *Like a peasant from the fields,* Mrs Grech would have said but even she had some sense of when to keep her mouth shut. Against the wishes of her mother, Carmelina had given in to fashion and cut her long hair into a curly, unadorned bob and she wore no jewellery except a small gold cross, given to her at Confirmation, and an inconspicuous engagement ring.

Carmelina was what her mother's friends would have regarded as a sensible girl who had made the best of a bad job. Her clients would never have guessed it, largely because they were not interested in her, but her life to date had been badly unsettled. Six years before, she had been an American schoolgirl living a few miles away from Niagara Falls, punctuating her prosperous existence with trips to the movies, picnics and chaste convent school parties. She had learnt to speak and think in American English. She had not really been American at all; her school friends had made that quite clear, but after seven years there she had almost forgotten what it was like to live anywhere else. She still felt homesick for Niagara Falls.

It had been a time when the world's destitute and persecuted seemed to be heading for the New World by the tens of thousands. Her father was one such man, taking the freedom boat alone when she was five years old – she thought she could still remember him leaving the house – an unemployable man, illiterate, unskilled, searching for goldmines like the first pioneers. Unfortunately, he ended up wandering into Canada by accident because he could not read any of the signs and, coming from an island, could not quite believe in the concept of land borders, only to be unceremoniously deported after three months working as an illegal immigrant. He settled a few miles from the Canadian border, refusing point-blank to learn to read and write in spite of being given the opportunity – *what would I want to write my name down for? Do you think I'm likely to forget it?* Too proud to return to the classroom, he found himself working in a factory exposed to the most dangerous carcinogenic chemicals known to man. By the time Carmelina found herself sitting on her doorstep on Blanche Street, he had died a terrible, lingering death of bowel cancer, aged only forty-three.

He could not have known at the time (and probably never knew) that the Land of Opportunity was killing him at the same time he was enjoying whatever aspects of America's new affluence had cared to trickle down to his level. It was the Roaring Twenties and America was the only place to be. When Ġorġ Buhagiar had established a home for himself and was sure he could keep his family adequately (or thought he wanted to), he summoned his wife and two children, Salvatore aged eleven and Carmelina aged nine, to cross the world for him. It was that moment, the moment when the letter arrived via Freddie the Postman that

Carmelina remembered as she finished the cocktail dress.

She had been busy stuffing her schoolbag full of half-finished homework and textbooks glued back together many times over when her mother passed her the letter to read aloud. "Quickly, quickly! Tell me what he has to say!"

As a pupil of the Sisters of Saint Dorothy, Carmelina could read very well, and the friend in America who wrote the letter for her father had a neat enough hand. She muttered her way through the lines of swirling black ink, searching for the point of the whole thing before landing on it in the penultimate paragraph. "He says to come to America," she explained, expertly, too young to be surprised at the command.

She looked up and found that her mother was staring at her as though she had written the bolt out of the blue herself. "Come to America." Just like that, not even a suggestion of sounding out her feelings on the matter before asking. An order to uproot and travel across the world, issued in between putting away the breakfast things and packing the children off to school.

As soon as the children had left the house, Mrs Buhagiar stormed down the street in search of someone who would make it all make sense to her.

"Just like that, father!" she exclaimed in a stage whisper, fanning herself with the edge of her mantilla. The confessional was hot and stuffy at that time of year and she had received absolution only yesterday, but it was the only place she could think of to have what she imagined to be a really quiet word. "He pushes off for years without so much as a by your leave and now he wants me to leave Malta and everything to go to him – I mean, is that nice?"

Father Cini sat in respectful silence on the other

side of the grille, knowing perfectly well that she was not actually asking him a question. "I mean *America*, father! Where on earth is that anyway? And how does he expect me to get there with two little ones? He's out of his little mind!"

"Did he send you the money for your fares?" asked Father Cini, thinking that Ġorġ Buhagiar might as well have told her to find her way to the moon. She had never left Malta before and as far as she was concerned, other places simply did not exist. They were mythical lands made up by the hazy voice inside the wireless set or the drunken creations of off-duty British soldiers. "Have you enough money to get there?"

"Of course he sent me money, father, I can't even use that against him!"

He tried enthusiasm. "Come on, Mrs Buhagiar, America is an exciting place. There are many people who would give anything for the chance to go. He has made a home for you there. Think of how happy you might be."

"But *America!*" The name already had a slightly ominous ring to it as far as she was concerned. "It's full of men in stupid hats shooting at each other! It's full of fat men with cigars – what do you call them? – *Guuunsters!* And-and" she was on a roll now, quite unstoppable. "I don't even speak American, and what about my mother? She's old and frail. Who will look after her if I go far away? Tell me that much?"

"Don't worry about your mother, we will all look after her," he said, thinking that this was the least of her problems. "She will be perfectly safe and comfortable until you come back, I promise."

There was some hope in that at least, he had thrown her a lifeline without realising it. "Do you suppose we will come back again? He must get bored of the idea some time or other, I suppose."

"Of course you'll come back," Fr Cini assured her, "many Maltese go away for a few years to earn their money and then come home to retire." And by the time you do come back, he thought but decided not to share it, you may not even want to come home. The wandering Maltese, like the Wandering Jews found homes everywhere and nowhere. "You must go to the immigration people in Valletta. Tell them your situation and they might be able to help you. Would you like me to ask Filomena to help you pack?"

So, suddenly it was all decided. Mrs Buhagiar bought three single tickets to Never Never Land, Carmelina wrote to the father she was not sure she could remember to tell him that they were coming and Filomena, Fr Cini's fat, ancient, dragon-with-a-heart housekeeper came to nudge them all into order. Their belongings filled two small suitcases and three paper bags, a somewhat sorry sight on the Buhagiar family doorstep but Filomena reminded them of the wonderful things that would probably be waiting for them in America. Mrs Buhagiar imagined her husband waiting for them at the dockside laden with presents and stoically clung to that picture throughout the final preparations to stop herself from regretting the whole escapade. She was too old for adventures, she thought, but she also knew – with a certain amount of tired resignation – that no one ever really picked their adventures. Her brothers had not thought that they would spend the last years of their youth in a foreign country fighting an enemy they had never met before for that matter; and they had never complained. It was a strange time to be alive.

The day before they left, a friend paid for them to have a family photograph for the old mother who was to be left behind in the now quiet family home. Her friends from the parish attended to her with great care and diligence until she went to her Maker, eighteen months before her family returned to Malta.

Dressed in their best, Salvatore in a borrowed suit that was clearly made for a thinner figure, Carmelina in her much extended and adapted First Holy Communion dress, they stare together out of a faded monochrome photograph, casting reproachful eyes in my direction. As if to say, 'we are the family you have forgotten about, the good, respectable ones who were forced abroad by poverty. We have nothing to hide. We are not the ones who threw away the silver spoons in our mouths to consort with tyrants and monsters. We are not the family who cursed and destroyed one other. There are no secrets here to make you blush. Throw in your lot with us.'

They would not need to ask. I find it impossible to let them go. This is my heritage too, the farewell Mass at Sacro Cuore church, the emotional good-byes. The heartbreak is still fresh even seen through the faded glass of many years. Whatever the hope of return, none of them knew if they would ever see their old friends and the family home again, yet somehow this is bearable. This is the harmless sorrow felt by a tiny community for one of its families, nothing more. Pain without guilt. Tears without shame. No one is being irrevocably hurt by the action of leaving.

They travelled across the Atlantic as steerage passengers, crammed below decks in third class cabins like rats to be quarantined and kept safely out of sight. All the children remembered of it afterwards was chronic, gut-wrenching seasickness and the stench of bodies living in close proximity for far too long. Mrs Buhagiar remembered trying to stop her children from hearing the men swearing and blaspheming as they grew bored and quarrelsome. It was not the way Hollywood would have it remembered; no one drank Guinness or danced jigs to pass the time of evening, parents telling stories about fairies to their curly-headed kiddies were distinctly wanting. Sentimentality has its benefits when it comes to remembering when the memories belong to someone else, but if there was nothing to alleviate the misery of this journey they at least stumbled onto dry land at the other side.

Perhaps the details are not even important. If any image is worth remembering at all it is the first moment of leaving, as the three of them stood on the boat to Sicily and looked back at the shores of Malta for the last time. Mrs Buhagiar had tears in her eyes and the last sliver of Malta she saw was blurred and elusive as it disappeared into the sea. We have all been there, except that those of us who came a little later watch Malta fading into the distance from far above, the last fragment of coastline snatched away by cloud or heat haze. And there are murky windows to press the face against so that other passengers cannot see our sentimental, unsophisticated reactions. A haunted people, a mourning people. Exiles, whatever age they belong to, whatever evil they are fleeing, can never be sure that they will return.

IV

My country 'tis of thee,
Sweet Land of Liberty,
Of thee we sing!

Land where my fathers died!
Land of the pilgrims' pride,
From every mountainside –
Let freedom ring!

Or so the patriotic poem goes, capturing the spirit of the age. It was not my country – or even theirs for that matter – and though my fathers have succeeded in getting themselves killed in every conceivable place, only Salvatore is buried in this particular land and he was certainly not a puritan pilgrim. Little Man Salvatore, buried next to his Italian wife Irena at the age of eighty-seven, after a lifetime of smoking, drinking and working in the same factory that killed his father. The little boy who didn't want to go home. There are kindred spirits everywhere, even in this Wild Card, but there will be more said about him at a later hour. For the moment, the Buhagiars have arrived at their destination – *America! America!* Land of Liberty, Land of Ford cars and jazz and skyscrapers and flappers and speakeasies and moving pictures and backless dresses and the American Way and laissez-faire and parties and money... and the Ku-Klux Klan and segregation and people-swallowing factories and the dust bowl and poverty, but there is no room for bitterness or politics here. Little Carmelina Buhagiar stood at the gateway to the happiest years of her life and she would live off that time until she was too old and confused to remember her own name. Heartbreak and disappointment await her in her motherland but that must wait until she has grown up. When their boat came in, she crawled out onto the dockside, dishevelled, dizzy, extremely dirty, into the cold, crisp air of the New World.

After cramped days at the bottom of an ocean liner, nothing felt sweeter than the first long, deep breath of American air. Air and light. There was light everywhere, bright artificial lights that made them blink and shield their eyes. They had arrived in the early evening, just after sunset. They would see their first American dawn huddled in a train, shivering with the cold, but Mrs Buhagiar had not quite understood the travel arrangements at that stage and found herself in a bewildering conversation with a Maltese American who had got off the same boat.

"Have you far to go?" he asked. He was a short, flabby man who spoke with an accent Mrs Buhagiar did not care for.

"No, somewhere called Niagara Falls," she answered. "Do you know which way I have to walk? Do you suppose I might have to take a bus?" She thought of how heavy the cases would be to carry even a short distance. "Oh dear, I'm not sure I have enough for the fare."

"*Walk*?! Did you say Niagara Falls?" He actually took a step back. "But that's practically in *Canada*!"

Mrs Buhagiar was nonplussed. "Oh, so you think I should take a bus, then?"

"Dammit, woman, don't you know how big this place is?" He thought that she looked rather pale and realised that he must have offended her. He lowered his voice, ashamed. "You've got a good long journey before you get to Niagara Falls, *Sinjura*. What was your husband thinking of?"

"I thought he would be here to meet us," she offered by way of explanation, *after three years apart*, she would

25

have liked to have added, but it would not do to be bitter about her own husband in front of a stranger. The aforementioned stranger noticed her two children sitting scruffy and dazed on the family suitcases, then looked back at Mrs Buhagiar, who looked terribly fragile and beautiful and ready to burst into tears if she was upset any further. His heart sank. "All right, don't worry. I'll put you on a train just as soon as you're sorted with immigration. How much money do you have?"

She held out a handful of coins and notes that meant absolutely nothing to her. Under the circumstances, it would perhaps have been nice if she could have read the words on the dollar bills saying, 'In God we trust'. Fortunately, she had been sent a guardian angel all of her own, who took one look at the sum total of her worldly effects and began milling around the other Maltese passengers for cash. A strange kind of an angel, unshaven and looking as though he had just escaped from Alcatraz but she was wise enough to know that goodness came in all sorts of unexpected shapes and sizes. Just before they were dragged kicking and screaming through the ordeal by Ellis Island, he approached them holding out what looked to Mrs Buhagiar like a small fortune.

"I'll hang onto this until you get through," he promised. "I'll be waiting for you." Mrs Buhagiar never thought to wonder why he was able to slip around the terror of being questioned in a language he did not understand, the distress of being temporarily (and at least in their case it was only temporarily) separated from other family members, not to mention the humiliation of being prodded and manhandled by doctors on the off chance that they were not quite physically fit enough for the Land of the Free. But he was as good as his word. When the three Buhagiars emerged from purgatory, chastened and thinking some fairly dark thoughts about the inhabitants of their new country, this enterprising stranger whose name they never knew was waiting to escort them to their train.

And there they left him, waving at them from the platform. As the train pulled away, he disappeared from their sight and their lives forever. They always remembered his kindness and that of the other passengers who helped them on their way, but as Carmelina grew up to explain, we have all been helped and rescued by strangers. Our lives are nurtured and held together by people whose names we never learn and whose languages we do not speak.

"How does it feel never to have been alone?"

The question takes him by surprise. "Is that a real question?"

"Did I get the inflection wrong?"

I don't know what possesses me to speak to Benedict like that. He hears an interruption in the story and cannot tell where I am going next, so he is confused. Carmelina could only just remember her father. Or at least, she thought she could remember but wondered whether it was just her mother's stories that made her think that. So when she met him at the house in Niagara Falls, she was being introduced to him for the first time. I know something of what it means to be separated from loved ones but Benedict has never been wrenched from his family before, certainly not against his will.

"Ben, have you ever been cast adrift before?"

He pauses for a moment. "Does boarding school count?"

"No, it doesn't."

"I don't see why not," he persists, "its terrible being dumped in a strange building full of psychotic sadists at the age of eight."

Perhaps it is, but I tell myself that it is not the same. "Have you ever looked at your father and wondered who he was? Have you lain awake at night trying to imagine what he might be like?"

"No, it doesn't really work like that." He looks awkward, put out. "You know, you are very good at making me feel guilty for not being miserable. How am I supposed to know what it feels *not* to feel something?"

I should not have made him feel guilty. It is hardly his fault that he does not have a family absolutely determined to destroy itself – or who were just a little unfortunate. There are absent and estranged fathers in every generation of this family, through no one's fault in particular, but none of the children left to bear the consequences knew it at the time. Carmelina did not feel any reason to warm to her estranged father when she finally met him and made no attempt to play-act the overjoyed child. Not only did Ġorġ fail to meet them when they arrived, when they reached Niagara Falls he was still nowhere to be found. When his poor wife – whose nerves by that stage were balanced on a razor-sharp edge – finally managed to make herself understood long enough to ask directions to his home, he answered the door minus his shirt with shaving foam all over his face. He had forgotten which day they would be arriving.

Some time later, when Ġorġ had pulled himself together and finished shaving, he kissed his wife and showed her her new home. Carmelina, feeling distinctly unwanted, put herself to bed under the kitchen table and Salvatore attempted to make a break for it altogether. Unfortunately for him, when he was halfway across the kitchen floor, his mother caught sight of him. "Salv! What do you think you're doing?" Oh dear, the timeless matriarchal reprimand. "Come and greet your father properly like a good boy!"

Salvatore glanced at the father he remembered, but as he looked at him, he had the sense that he was shrinking. He remembered that *he* had been the man of the household whilst his father was away, whilst his father was busy having adventures and freedom and a jolly good time. A usurpation was taking place but at the advanced age of eleven Salvatore was still a man and intended to be treated as such. Standing as straight and tall as he could make himself, he reached up and shook his father stiffly by the hand. She told him to greet his father properly. She never said he had to look as though he was enjoying the moment, which was just as well. A moment later, he was out in the alien street alone, blinking at the terrifying precision of the smooth, stone, orderly sidewalk and the towering houses and shops.

After a week of rest and recuperation, Ġorġ sent Carmelina and Salvatore to register at St Anne's School, three blocks away, run by the Sisters of the Sacred Heart and they could become children again for a little while. Things did not get off to the most wholesome of starts. When Salvatore and Carmelina found themselves ushered into the office of Sr. Bernadette the Principal, there were more communication problems than they had previously anticipated. Both children were more educated by now than their parents and spoke some English, but their names did not translate.

"I'm sorry, my dear, what did you say your sister's name was?" asked Sr. Bernadette with a benevolent smile, beginning to wonder if the boy might have marbles in his mouth.

"Her name is – " Salvatore paused wearily, knowing that saying 'CAR-MEL-INA' slowly for the fourth time would not make the blindest bit of difference. He made a unilateral decision. "Her name is Clara."

"Oh, *Clara*," repeated Sister, writing it down in her impeccable, florid hand. "What a beautiful name! And yours?"

"Sam," said Salvatore, quickly.

"I see. I presume that's short for Samuel?"

"Erm – yes, but everyone calls me Sam." Salvatore took the sweets Sr. Bernadette offered him and wondered how on earth he was going to explain this to his parents.

"That's fine, Sam. Now, would you take Clara to the first classroom on the left? Your class is the third on the right when you get to the top of the stairs."

"Those weren't our names, you great *Nit*!" complained Carmelina, as soon as the door closed behind them. "What do you think you're playing at? What will Mama say?"

"You're not going to tell her," he answered, giving one of her plaits a sharp tug. Just a gentle discouragement. "They don't understand, we're in a new country now, we have to be like everyone else. You're Clara here, understand?"

"As if they'll never find out!"

Another tug. "I said you're Clara. Got that?"

"But – stop that! You're hurting me!"

"Understand?"

"Yes," came the crestfallen reply, because she rather liked being Carmelina but was too young to realise the significance of what was happening to her. "All right. *Sam*."

So, Carmelina felt herself becoming Clara as they walked the few paces to her new classroom, a change from which she would never quite recover. Identity crises on both sides of the family, just to keep things balanced.

V

How quickly the years pass when we are happy! In the dying light of that September evening whilst the world held its breath, Carmelina remembered the years when she was Clara. Clara running to school with homework and a doughnut stuffed inside her satchel, Clara shaking the freshly cut grass and blossom petals out of her hair after a day in the country, Clara stepping into the school playground on the first morning she ever saw snow, wrapped up to the ears in woolly hat and scarf and bright green gloves her mother knitted for her. Clara winning the spelling cup for the third week running, Clara tobogganing down the hill with Sam, gasping and shrieking with laughter. Clara dancing around a bonfire of fallen leaves in November, Clara and Sam going paddling in the summer, Clara ice-skating. If there was anything wrong with the world at all, and she could hardly bring herself to imagine it, it was that it was too big. There was too much to do, too many feelings, too many good things waiting for her. During her short years of growing up, it seemed to her that she was never still for a minute unless she was in her bed, sitting at her desk or indulging another passion: the picture show.

Mrs Buhagiar never quite got the hang of going to see a movie. On the one and only occasion that she went along with them, it ended, if not in tears, in recriminations. As soon as the lights went down, Clara and Sam quaked with embarrassment and pretended she was with someone else as she whispered, 'Ġorġ!' And it is not quite a whisper. 'Get me out of this dark room! I can't stand it!

"It has to be dark, *qalbi*," he whispered in her ear, "otherwise you won't be able to see the picture."

"But I don't want to, I want to go home!"

Something about the darkness and the flickering screen upset her and they were not even watching a horror film, so whilst the rest of the audience laughed uproariously at a tramp with a moustache clowning about all over the place, Ġorġ had to escort his wife off the premises. He tried not to be cross, but this and the hat episode were making him wonder whether she would ever get the swing of things when it came to living in their new country.

The hat, a beautiful new hat he saw in the shop window on his way home from work and just thought, 'I have to buy it for her.' A hat with silk ribbons and tiny roses woven intricately into a little crown. She was a pretty woman even then and he glowed with pride to see other men eyeing her from the other side of the road, knowing that she belonged to him. It was her clothes that caused the problem. She had refused to buy herself anything new since her arrival and turned her nose up at the loose-fitting, brightly coloured frocks of the younger women, calling them unseemly and coquettish.

Do you want me to go flaunting my body like a – like a – well, you know what like?! All that flesh hanging about all over the place, I wonder they don't catch cold!

She cannot disapprove of a hat, he thought, watching as the shop assistant packed it away in a large striped hatbox. Why, it was positively modest for a lady to cover her head and these hats were just the thing at the moment. She could wear it when they went picnicking at the weekend and he could show off his beautiful wife, not yet past her bloom, adorned with flowers and ribbons.

Well, at least she did wear the hat, but whether it could be called the same hat he had bought with so much pride is another matter. Two minutes after taking it out of the box, she had torn off the ribbons – *Marija*, Ġorġ, what do you want me to look like, a merry-go-round horse? – and pulled the fine weaving of flowers to fragments – *really*, dressing me up above my station! Have you no pride?

Yes, poor Ġorġ Buhagiar had pride, but not the gritty, stubborn defiance of a working class woman determined to remain what she had always been. There was an inverse snobbery in her disgust at Ġorġ's social climbing materialism and in all the years they were in America together, his love of the garish, the novelty, the slightly risqué, his desire to belong to this mysterious glitzy noisy world they have found themselves in... simply did not rub off on her. If Clara and Sam took to their new names and their new life like apartments on fire, Mother Buhagiar was a Maltese housewife and she would remain one; defiant, unchangeable, like the essence of the Maltese spirit itself. She learnt to pay for her groceries in dollars rather than pounds, she learnt enough English to be able to eavesdrop on her children when they came bouncing home from school chattering in a language that they soon thought of as their own and yes, she did enjoy watching them getting to grips with it all.

Mrs Buhagiar somehow managed to avoid the trap that so many parents fall into of resenting their children for thriving in an environment they do not appreciate. She enjoyed watching them develop new skills and habits she did not understand. She bought them pumpkins when they requested them to cut faces into on Halloween and let them drag a wet green tree into her immaculate sitting room on Christmas Eve. She laughed at the latest in technological genius that Ġorġ brought home for them periodically – a Nativity scene with imitation silver doors that opened and shut to the mechanical chime of *Silent Night,* an alarm clock in the shape of the Statue of Liberty that played *Stars and*

33

Stripes Forever to wake up the household every morning – but these things did not belong to her world. She watched them from a distance like a curious but slightly unsettled tourist watching a bizarre ritual being enacted from the safety of the tour bus. When they returned to Malta in 1933, she alone would slip back into the old life as if she had never been away, because in many ways she never had been away.

When they returned. It was at that moment in her remembrance that Carmelina Buhagiar – because she was Carmelina again and America was a childish dream – felt grateful for the failing light, gathered up her work and stepped indoors. Not all her happy childhood memories would obligingly rush past her like landmarks from a high-speed train. Some events hung suspended in memory, waiting for her to look at them again and she had almost given into the temptation.

She had so nearly started thinking of her first kiss, sitting behind the orange boxes in Adolph's father's grocery store, amid the packages and bottles and the smell of Jan Senior's fermenting Moonshine. He was almost a man by then and his face felt prickly against hers. And he had even said he loved her, giving her a cheap metal ring that her father later made her take off. She had thrown it over the side of the ship on the journey back, knowing it was all a nonsense, but for a moment, Carmelina thought that she saw his face again, so clearly that she could have reached out to touch it. If she stopped remembering now, it might never happen. She could pretend she never left.

She went carefully up the stairs in the dark because they had not yet had electricity installed and they would no sooner wire the place up when the Luftwaffe would be gracious enough to put them out again. She found her way into her sewing room – her father's old room and the room where her son would be conceived on a love-scented wedding night to come – and took out the pieces of her wedding dress. It would cheer her up to think of her wedding, even if it was a little far away.

By the glow of the gas lamp she touched the soft white cloth and was relieved to find herself thinking of Lawrence. Tall, strong gentle-giant Lawrence, standing at the door in his pristine Royal Navy uniform, holding out a hand to her. He did not have the gentleman's hands that Edward Sant'Angelo would have had, they always felt rough as they curled around hers, calloused with the work of a sailor like Adolph's were calloused by years of dirt and splinters from the store room. She longed for the touch of them now all the same. Lawrence would be in Gibraltar for the next three weeks then home for a lengthy leave. It seemed like a long time, even for a girl engaged to a sailor, and they were very far apart. He was in Gibraltar and she was still in America. Home is where the heart is, or so she had read in a schoolbook once, so she would have to give him a carbon copy because even the promise of marriage could not tear her away from the Land of the Free.

Whilst her fingers deftly pinned panels of material together, she found that she was running down the chilly streets dressed in school uniform and lace-up boots, past all the landmarks of home – Jan's grocery store, the *Hair So Fair* hairdresser, the *God Bless America* coffee bar (coffee served in the front room, liquor in the back) – names and slogans jumping out at her from glowing store signs, snatches of music drifting out as shoppers opened and closed the doors.

Brrrring! 'Evening Clara!'

'Evening Mrs Klepacka.'

"You do something to me, something that simply mystifies me…" 'Hello there Clara! Nice day at school?'

'Yes thank you, Harry, our team won the basketball.'

Straight into the bosom of a quarrelling family

home. Clara was not used to loud arguments. They had never really had them before, managing to live together in relative peace most of the time. This was all very different. As she stepped through the doorway, she heard the tail-end of Sam barking "what do you mean, we're going home?" He was a real man now, tall and gangling with a position at the factory and a weekly pay packet. And a voice deep enough to silence any row – or almost any. "We are home."

"I mean that we're going back to Malta." Ġorġ began to explain the situation as if his son had asked him a real question. "I've saved enough for us to live comfortably back home, understand? Oh, come on, that's gratitude for you! You're supposed to be pleased!" She thought he looked oddly cornered as she caught sight of him, as if he had not expected hostility and did not know exactly how to react. She was right; he was utterly bewildered. The boy was supposed to be grateful – all exiles longed to return home, it was the most natural instinct in the world. He thought there must be something wrong with his son, because no one, simply no one would choose to be far from their natural habitat for longer than they needed to. "I always wanted us to go back and now we can. What's the matter with you?"

"And what about her?" asked Sam, pointing at a dumbstruck Clara standing shivering in her school coat. "She's fifteen, she's still got another year of school before she graduates. You can't pull her out of school now."

"She doesn't have to go to school.   She's old enough, she's learnt plenty already."

"She's fifteen."

"Precisely. Time she stopped dressing in a pinafore pretending to be a little girl. She can read and write. I managed with less than that." He looked across at Clara and panicked at the sight of tears suspended on her eyelashes. "All right, all right, she can go to school in

Malta, can't she? They do have schools there, you know." Anyone would have thought I was committing some terrible cruelty against them, he thought, unable to express how hurt he felt. He was giving them his greatest dream. He had expected celebrations, excitement, not tears and angry questions.

"I want to stay at *my* school," came a very small voice from Clara's direction – she had not inherited her mother's strident tone and had seldom disagreed with anything her elders decided for her. Rebellion had never been necessary before, but the idea of leaving St Anne's just when she was almost in the class where they had their own common room and green bands on their sashes and a leavers' party with pretty dresses and music and dancing – well, it was quite impossible to contemplate. And how was her father to know that she was top of the class in everything and the darling of the teaching staff? Ġorġ had never taken any interest in his daughter's schoolwork before, saying that it was a foolish waste of time, but if he had taken the trouble to speak to her teachers, he would have found that his growing child knew the Catechism backwards, received top grades in history (that's because we have one and they don't, said Sam) and had an extraordinary talent for needlework. If he had gone as far as to meet with her principal, he would have discovered that Clara wanted to be a teacher herself when she had finished school, a profession that even he could not have objected to.

But he had never visited her school and Clara found herself standing in the void that was left when her friends and plans, the pleasant little American life she had built for herself, had been torn out without a thought. No one had asked her if she wanted it when the letter came and they went on the big boat across the sea. She would hardly have chosen to be plucked from the cosy familiarity of her home, the school and the friends she had known all her conscious life but she had not complained. It was just that now he was telling her to do it all over again and this time she did not think she could bear it.

"What are you going to do, stay here on your own then?" came the sneering reply. Clara signalled for Sam not to interfere and got up from the table. "Where do you think you are going?"

Clara looked at him steadily for a moment, contemplating whether or not to make a reply, but she could not bring herself to answer back even with her happiness hanging in the balance and she moved slowly out of the room. Silent children are always more threatening to adults than the noisy ones who cause scenes and are patently incapable of concealing anything. The silent ones are inapproachable, immovable, startlingly isolated from the adult world of dependence. The air chilled at the slight sounds of Clara stepping out into the blustery street and the door closing softly behind her.

She knew where she was going. Like her mother years ago, hurt by an unexpected male decision, Clara needed the presence of people to make things make sense. She hurried down the road to Jan Wisniewski's food store, or rather to the flat above the shop where Jan was enjoying dinner with his family; Zosia his wife – *she laughs too much and too loud,* said the neighbours, *and if she gets any fatter, they'll have to find a bigger shop* – and his four children, Adolph, Jan Jr. and the twins, Emilia and Petra. Clara and Sam had been friendly with the family for years, long before Clara had become keen on Adolph and forsaken Sam's company for his whenever she had the chance. Their parents had encouraged it, as they belonged to the same social circle, attending the same school and the same parish church Sunday after Sunday. To Clara, they were a second family. They were the kind of quasi-relatives people create for themselves when they are used to big extended families and find themselves away from their own. So it was the natural place for Clara to go when her own family was in a state of mayhem.

As soon as Clara appeared, white-faced and shaking in the doorway, Zosia pushed the children closer together and made a place for her at the table. Before Clara could explain her situation further, Adolph had taken her coat and sat her down on a spare tea chest and Zosia had placed a bowl of soup in front of her. Clara blushed lightly at the attention, causing an indulgent smile from Jan. She was only just beginning to understand why he encouraged their friendship and her father positively fumed at it – *of course I want you to be friendly with them, they are a nice family but just you make sure you're friendly to all of them exactly the same way.*

So Adolph was a rival of sorts then, a rival to Malta. Someone to hold her to a country her father had seen as a kind of transit camp or playground for him to make his money in and leave by the earliest boat. If that was the case, it was all the better that she should be with him now, feeling his hands holding her carefully by the shoulders until she was safely perched on the box. He wore a cheap cologne that his mother disapproved of but it was a reassuringly masculine smell at such a moment. She plucked up the courage to speak. "We're going away," she said, "Papa wants to go back home to Malta."

There was a sympathetic silence and Clara only realised afterwards that they might already have known. Then Jan felt compelled to break it and said, "I see. That's too bad, darling."

"I don't want to go." Clara fought tears for the second time that evening and won again. She half-thought that if she told them everything, they could maybe persuade him to drop the idea. "I don't want to go, I haven't even finished school and Sr. Gillian wanted me to be a prefect next year."

Adolph positioned himself next to her like the Arabian warrior in *Love in the Desert* he had seen last week. She ought to have had a veil fluttering around her face to finish the effect, but the pose was pretty good anyway. "She should stay with us," he said. "She's practically one of the family. We could make space, couldn't we Ma?"

"You shouldn't encourage her to go against her father," said Zosia, throwing her a round of bread, but the idea had already crossed her mind. "If he wants to go back, she really should go with him."

"She could always go back later. He wouldn't mind if it was just for a year until she graduates." Adolph was secretly thinking at this juncture that if she stayed until she graduated, she would be free to stay for as long as she liked. Her father would be safely deposited on the other side of the world and she would be educated enough to look after herself until he could take care of her. Clara's smile prompted him into calling for further support. "Come on Papa, you could talk him round, couldn't you? You're old friends."

Jan looked at the two faces smiling inanely in his direction and could hardly help smiling in return. More was at stake for Clara than just another year at school and they all knew it. "Well, it's all rather sudden. Let me have a little think about it then I'll go and speak to your father – how would you like that Clara?" Clara grinned, knowing that the rest of the family were on her side and that he would not be given a chance to think about it.

"Absolutely out of the question." She had known that would be the answer the second she stepped into the room to see how Jan had got on. She had heard raised voices as she hid in her room, listening against a glass pressed against the floor and placed her last hopes in her own persuasive abilities.

40

"It would just be for a year."

"I'm not leaving you here in a house full of young men."

"Two young men."

"I said no. It's too much of a responsibility for them, caring for a strange girl…"

"But I'm not strange to them. I'm like one of the family, they said so. It would just be for a year."

If anything, it looked as though poor Jan had made things even worse than they had been to start with. He was on a warpath and she was in the way. "You're still my daughter, whatever else they've been telling you. It's a big responsibility to look after someone else's child, and what if you suddenly decided you missed us? What about when you wish you'd come home with us and it's too late? You can't just pack up and pop off to Malta on your own you know."

I won't regret this, she wanted to say, but her courage came to her in very small packages and she knew she had lost. And part of it, which she only admitted to herself many years later, was that she had truly not wanted to leave her family any more than she wanted to leave America. The conflict of desires paralysed her, leaving her helpless and floundering.

"Go and pack, hanini. We won't say any more about it," he said. She did not yet know that he could never have let her go – Sam had just informed him that he would not be returning to Malta with them under any circumstances and he was a free man, he could do as he pleased. If Ġorġ had lost a son to America, he had to keep his daughter.

And there was nothing left to be done. Three months later, laden with considerably more luggage than they came out with, the Buhagiars left one home to go back to another. Clara said good-bye to her school friends and the nuns who had coaxed and cajoled her through her lessons, sadly to no avail. On the evening before they left, she sat at the dinner table with the Wisniewskis for the last time and made herself believe when it came to it that it did not hurt to walk past the grocery store where she had spent so many hours sitting behind stacks of tins and crates, talking to Adolph. Their plans meant nothing anymore and she pretended that she could not see him glancing out of the shop window at her as they walked past. To look at him would be to break the spell of indifference she had conjured up and she would need it for the journey ahead.

Farewell Adolph. She joked for the rest of her life that it was lucky her first love came to nothing, because it would never have done to have a husband with such a preposterous name just in time for the war to start. Farewell ice-skating and the picture show and picnics and running down the sidewalk after school and trams and dollar bills and pumpkin pie. Farewell Niagara Falls. Farewell America. Farewell Brave New World... and farewell big brother Sam, never to be Salvatore again. His promise that he would 'join you all in a few years when I've made my money' was a touching untruth to ease the pain of parting. The family would never meet together under the same roof again.

When he had got over the shock of seeing his family leave, however, Sam settled down to a long, happy life, blessed with a devoted wife and children who grew up to make him proud. Even his youngest son, who found himself called up to fight in Vietnam, managed to be invalided out of the fighting early enough to escape the worst horrors that the war produced. There was happiness to be found for some members of the family but only in the act of walking away.

Clara survived the voyage back to the beginning again, the spell of indifference keeping her quiet in spite of sea sickness again and regrets and any little resentments she might have been feeling. By the time the ship neared Malta, the rains had come and she saw the motherland she was supposed to love under a faint drizzle. "Look!" called her mother, pointing at the spectre of the Grand Harbour slowly drawing them in. A mouth, the great carnivorous mouth of a predator – she would not be drawn in, she would not be drawn into it.... "Oh look, Lina, look! Malta! We're really home at last!"

The sound of her old nickname broke the spell. For a moment, she seemed to be nine years old again as if the film of her life had run in reverse and America and all its joys had never happened. As if she had always been standing here, shivering on the deck of a ship travelling nowhere at all. She covered her face and wept.

And so Carmelina found herself in her sewing room alone. No Maltese school would take her because she had never learnt Italian and they were too petty at the time to make an exception for her, so after the death of her father she took up sewing. Not much else for her to do with her life but she turned out to be rather good at it and her wedding dress was very chic indeed when it was ready.

Her wedding was a hasty, wartime affair. They exchanged vows in Sacro Cuore church, celebrating union whilst the island was torn to shreds around them. The bombers were kind enough to stay away on their wedding night and there were no father figures to curse them and drive them apart. Ġorġ Buhagiar (God rest his soul) would have wished them well if he had been there to lead his daughter down the aisle. And at some point during that night, Carmelina conceived her first children, but it is not the moment for any more introductions. I will step back respectfully and leave Carmelina – now Carmelina Falzon – lying in the arms of her husband. For the short time they are together, they think of no one and nothing else.

VI

The urge to linger is almost unbearable. There is nothing to be ashamed of yet. I could freeze time now and leave Carmelina and Lawrence to enjoy their numbered nights together without the thought that he must go to his death because he was born in the wrong age. I could make it turn out another way, but I am a creator of words not lives. There should be no fear in the telling of a story. The past is as it is whether or not it is remembered, but I am still afraid of it.

In early 1942, Antonia Sant'Angelo received an unexpected visit from her doctor. The Sant'Angelo house in Valletta looked a little more like a house under the influence of a curse already and the doctor's presence in the kitchen hardly helped. It was not quite as bad as a policeman or the telegram boy but Doctor Saliba was clearly not there on a friendly visit and he was not taking any nonsense from a protesting Antonia.

"I'm just asking you a simple question, Mrs Sant'Angelo, that is all," he explained for the hundredth time. "Where did you get that?" He had found a bruise on her arm when she rolled up her sleeve so that he could take her blood pressure and he had already formed his own theory about where it had come from.

"I fell," explained Antonia, using the lie women have always used to protect abusive husbands, but this time there was at least some truth in it. "I was blocking his way when he wanted to go out. He pushed me aside, that's all, and I fell against the stairs. It was my fault, he had a right to go out if he wanted to."

"And I suppose he stopped to help you when he realised he had hurt you?"

"He was in a hurry. He would have stopped."

"And where was he going?"

"I'm sure I don't know, I was just worried that there might be a raid. I hate to think of him getting caught out somewhere far away from a shelter. I'm sure you understand." Her voice had become pert and defensive, but only because she knew she was lying – it was *precisely* where he had been going that upset her so much. Doctors did not need to know such things.

"Mrs Sant'Angelo, you are pregnant. I need to be absolutely sure that you and your baby are safe, that is my only concern. There are quite enough dangers with the present situation as it is."

"It was an accident, he apologised afterwards." Antonia felt her face becoming hot. It was all too humiliating. "Anyway, I don't care if he does go out drinking with his pilot friends, I just wish he wouldn't drink quite so much. They can take it, he isn't used to it like they are."

She blushed even deeper as the lies came. She knew that Edward's father had become an alcoholic after his wife's death and that Edward had grown up in a house filled with the stench of spirits and vomit, and the clatter of empty whisky bottles. He knew as a child what it was like to be afraid of drunken feet thundering into the house at some ungodly hour, just as he made his own wife afraid now when he came careering through the front door spoiling for a fight. It was just the curse passing itself on as they both knew it would, but the doctor would not understand about that.

Under the circumstances, it would perhaps have been better if Dr Saliba had found the time to talk to Edward, but there was very little time for a doctor in a war zone to concern himself with the habits of a burgeoning alcoholic. It was almost certainly too late anyway, as Edward's inability to communicate with anyone, particularly his wife, had been a major factor in his change of behaviour. That and the age-old rule that wars test people and bring out the best – or the worst – in them.

Edward failed the test. At a quieter time, a weak man cast out by his family might have muddled through life without hurting anyone but Edward lived out the early years of his marriage whilst the world was falling to pieces around him. The short walk home involved dodging falling masonry from bomb-shaken buildings and praying that his own house would still be standing when he turned the corner. He would have liked to have taken Antonia to a safer place. Mdina would have been perfect, an old fortress town far from anything of strategic value, but the war had not brought about the smallest possibility of a reconciliation and they would never be welcome there again. So they lived instead in the one of the most vulnerable civilian targets in the world, the capital city of an island under siege, conveniently close to the most coveted natural harbour in the Mediterranean.

And in case Edward did not feel helpless enough, he had discovered in under two years of marriage that there were certain things he simply could not tell Antonia. In fact, he could not tell most things to her and he bitterly regretted that he had told her the first secret of their marriage. She had never said it to his face but he knew she did not trust him and he had only himself to blame. Not even his father. He could have told her *anything else*! Could he not have been forgiven for telling her one little lie, just to keep her head together? He need not have even lied to her, silence would have been the best remedy. Too late, far too late already.

Edward could ignore her poorly concealed nerves and furtive, suspicious glances when he had nothing else to worry about. There had even been something remotely comical about the whole affair, knowing that the poor little thing believed in such nonsense. He had joked to his friends that she must think a witch on a broomstick was going to come and get her on a stormy night and the Maltese lads had laughed good-naturedly and the English ones felt a certain amount of pity for these poor unenlightened natives. He only felt her mistrust now that he had something he desperately needed to confide in her, something he needed to confide in *someone.*

How could he tell her what it was like to send young men out in planes patched up with newspaper to do combat with Stukas and Messerschmits and have to watch them being blasted out of the sky minutes later. Seeing the list of fatalities growing larger and ever larger and all of them so young – Frobisher, aged eighteen, Darrington, aged nineteen – Englishmen, Australians, Canadians, families upon families in Suffolk and Toronto and Queensland having their lives shattered by a visit from the telegram boy.

How could he tell her about working in the war rooms, hearing calm public school voices breaking into screams as flames ripped through the cockpit and there was no way out? How could he tell her what it was like to hear a boy, because they were only boys, crying for help before the radio cut for the last time? What would she say, he wondered, if she knew that his voice was the last sound some of them ever heard, that he heard words heroes were not supposed to shout? *Don't be so silly, Edward, Englishmen don't cry for their mothers when they're falling to their deaths, when they're burning alive! What an idea!*

Could he risk telling her that he was afraid of leaving her in the morning, knowing that he might come back at night to find her dead among the ruins of the house? Could he, when she might think that it was all his fault? Could he say that he had nightmares that they would both starve to death, or that the day of capitulation would come – because it seemed so inevitable that it would – and they would see Nazis goose-stepping through the streets of Valletta and prison camps and reprisals and carnage... He was afraid, that was all, just as she was afraid. A pair of frightened children and he did not know about the third child yet.

If there could be no solace for him in Antonia's company anymore, there was plenty to be found in the smoke-filled cavern of the officers' mess. Cries of distress could be shouted down in smutty jokes and improbable anecdotes, fears drowned out with glass upon glass of Scotch and gin-and-tonic. Shouting down and drowning out. Our haunted people are good at covering our eyes. It is one way to deal with the crisis when it comes, except that this family does not live through single crises, which explains why they have to shout louder and drink deeper than everyone else.

I do not have the imagination to excuse his behaviour any further than that, nor can I give sufficient justification for his treatment of his wife or the catalogue of offences he committed in the years that followed. A greater man would have dealt with the terrors and miseries of living under siege with dignity – many thousands of others did so. I doubt that the boys he watched soaring to their deaths relied on alcohol or violence to get themselves into the cockpit. But before I judge him, how am I to say how I would have responded to the sight of my people being dragged bleeding from rubble or the choking, panic-inducing experience of sleepless nights cowering in underground shelters? Perhaps I too would have become a monster to be ignored or explained away by my descendants. *There go I but for the grace of God.*

Antonia walked down a wide, rubble-strewn street in Sliema – Dingli Street, to be precise. A bystander might have asked what she was doing straying so far from home with the bombers coming to visit every five minutes, wasting her precious energy resources when food shortages and a hidden child of three months were making her dizzy with hunger. Antonia would not have answered anyone: she was on a secret errand of her own. It was probably very wicked. She judged the rightness and wrongness of most things on the basis of what her Nanna would have thought and she was sure she would have disapproved of this, but she told herself over and over again that she was just shopping. She certainly intended to purchase a little food but not exactly at legal market prices and not from the usual places. And the establishment she was searching for was not too particular about ration cards.

"Desperate times call for desperate measures," she rehearsed, thinking that she might come home with an egg or a slice of horsemeat, not to be sniffed at when whole families were living on an ounce of rice here and there. If her children had ever asked her what it was like living through a siege (which they didn't, having rather more to worry about at the time), she could never have explained it except through metaphor. She might have compared it to the Great Siege of the sixteenth century, when the Turks encircled Maltese forts and reduced the inhabitants to eating rats and the leather of their boots. She might have spoken about people starving, collapsing in the streets, or of children gunned down by dive-bombers whilst they queued for a mug of kerosene, because the kerosene was too precious to be abandoned even at the sound of the siren. If they could still bear to listen, she might have described children being enticed to their deaths by pretty cracker toys, presents from enemy planes that hurled them into eternity the moment they picked them up. And air raid after air raid, days on end spent shivering in darkness only to emerge into the blinding light to discover that a whole street had disappeared.

And the worst had not yet happened. As Edward convinced himself that they were all doomed and Antonia fondly mused that it would all be over very soon, forces that neither of them could see were preparing for an assault against the island that would result in Malta suffering the equivalent of the Coventry blitz every eighteen hours for thirty days. Like the early Christians, they would be driven deep underground, into caves, catacombs and vast maze-like shelters, struggling with madness and starvation and the greatest horror of living in small, dirty, overcrowded places – disease.

I cannot tell the full horror of it, but neither could those who saw it. Even if Antonia had had an audience, she could never have described it. Her reminiscences would dutifully stop when Malta's war started and begin again after the eighth of September, 1943. This was the war that it took fifty years to be able to commemorate without bitterness, the war whose dead were not spoken of or recorded on cenotaphs until my own generation reached adulthood. This is the war my grandmothers would never talk about for more than a moment.

My grandmothers met that day for the first time, though they would never know it. It was the only time they ever met, even when their children, a baby boy and a girl whose bones were still being knitted together in darkness, grew up to marry and have children of their own. Antonia's pregnancy had only just started to show, but it was conspicuous enough that she had to tell her husband about it, particularly when the morning sickness could no longer be concealed by phantom food poisoning. She had not expected tears of joy.

"What do you mean you've got yourself pregnant?" *Crash*! "What a time to have a baby!"

"Well, you had something to do with it," she muttered, ignoring the sight of a broken teacup lying in a ring around her feet, "or had you forgotten about that?"

"We can't start a family now!"

"I'm sorry, but it seems we already have."

"What a clumsy thing to do. You should let me use those—"

"Over my dead body. You might be wearing a British uniform but you don't have to pick up all their bad habits as well." Antonia had never thought she could have an argument before, it was certainly not the way she would have spoken to her husband just a few weeks before, but her pregnancy seemed to be turning her into a matriarch. The silent, frail little life she was carrying needed an advocate with a strong voice and who else was there to reason with this angry, overgrown schoolboy? She cleared her throat to finish things off – she was about to say something quite shocking. "Stop talking about it as if it were a nuisance – it's my baby. If you're doubting it's yours, you will just say so, won't you?"

That put the knife in, he backed off immediately. "My love, my love, I wasn't suggesting that, for heaven's sake!" She refused to allow her reproachful look to soften. "Oh come on, of course I don't think it's a nuisance. It was the shock, just the shock..." and then of course there had been tears and embraces and apologies, and the row was forgotten about, by him at least. Of course he wanted the baby, they would be all right, they would manage somehow, he could look after them... She knew he would change his mind before long but it was very nice to have him his old self for a little while, holding her and telling her he loved her and wanted to protect both his treasures. It was those moments of fiction that gave her the will to live.

The air raid siren brought Antonia back. She looked

around for somewhere to shelter and made a dash for the swarm of people who had gathered a little further along – where there's a crowd there's cover, she thought. A great deal of pushing and shoving was going on, causing her to hang back a little, more afraid of being trampled on than blown to Kingdom Come. As usual, it was a stranger who took her hand and helped her down the steps, realising the condition she was in. Someone made a space for her so that she could sit down. Someone else offered her a blanket because she immediately started shaking and they thought that the dripping wall behind her was making her cold. The concern for the two of them touched her, particularly because she could not help feeling already that Edward would not be overly grieved if she was convenient enough to have a miscarriage, in spite of his extravagant promises.

She barely felt the cold but it she was afraid. The tedious familiarity of the underground chamber and its sounds and smells had not stopped her from wondering just what it would be like if they took a direct hit. She had a powerful imagination and the picture flashed repeatedly into her mind of an almighty explosion and the stone ceiling crumbling in on them. She imagined the sensation of dust and grit hitting her face and the last desperate struggle through fire and smoke whilst heaving bodies screamed and choked all around her.

Morbid nonsense, her Nanna would have said, but her Italophile Nanna had not lived quite long enough to see her beloved little island come to such a pass and would not have believed it. *The Italians would never do that to us, they are our friends. I will not have you listening to this nasty British propaganda…* It was the effects of being with child, Antonia told herself, blinking away tears. It seemed to her that the last years before the war had been the last age of innocence the world had ever known, when elegant old ladies could happily believe that there was such a thing as friendship and that any nation could be trusted. A world in which there was still such a word as 'never'.

Someone in the thick of the group took out a rosary and began to pray aloud. *In the name of the Father and of the Son and of the Holy Ghost...* A gentle echo of voices to calm her. She glanced up at an old lady carrying a toddler, who had entered the shelter at the very last minute and looked ready to drop with exhaustion.

"Mama, where is Pawlinu?" called a young woman, holding another toddler which Antonia realised must be the twin brother. "Where on earth is he?"

"He wouldn't come!" choked Mrs Buhagiar, struggling for breath after a long, frightened run carrying a child. "Lina, I tell you, he's doing it on purpose, he's trying to kill me!"

"It's all right. He'll be all right."

"I actually had to repeat myself! And he still wouldn't come! What sort of a child is that, my goodness?"

"When we get back..." Carmelina trailed off, refusing to consider the possibility that when she got back he might not be there to bear her anger. The little boy she carried began to cry, distracting her for a moment. That is my father, a troubled little boy called Nicholas, and the child trying to remove the brooch from his grandmother's blouse, my most favourite Uncle Gregory. The noise of falling bombs and shattering brickwork sounded a little closer than usual, which distressed even children who were used to hearing it as a constant background murmur.

Antonia instinctively held out her hand for the little boy to take. She noticed that he had his mother's black eyes, striking in a baby's white face. "Were his eyes always that colour?" she asked, absently.

"Always," Carmelina replied, "since he was born." She looked up at the now closed entrance to the shelter on the off chance that Pawlinu might have found his own way, but the raid was roaring overhead and she knew he was caught in the thick of it.

"Are you waiting for your other son?" asked Antonia, feeling as if she ought to ask something like that to fill up the silence.

"No, he's the son of my husband's cousin in Vittoriosa," Carmelina tried to explain, but she had told the story so often now that it was beginning to sound like something she read in the paper. "His parents were killed in a raid six months ago and he's been living with us. A troublemaker, I'm afraid. I think he wants to be a soldier but he is only twelve and he's as blind as a bat." It had, in fact, occurred to her that the poor child might be so distraught he might actually want to die, but it was too wicked a thought to contemplate and she thought it unworthy of her. "I think this is his idea of braving danger," she added, reassuring herself. "Oh, I *do* hope he is all right!" Her change in tone upset her dozing son and he began to cry again.

Pawlinu was not all right. In fact, to say that Pawlinu was in trouble at that particular moment would have been to make a heartless understatement, if Carmelina had only known. The moment Mrs Buhagiar left the house, calling upon the entire communion of saints to preserve him, he ran up the spiral staircase to the roof so that he could get a good view of the planes. The attraction was irresistible to a fidgety boy who had found himself trapped in a claustrophobic female household where he was desperate not to be welcome. Watching a dogfight was as close to a gladiatorial duel that someone of his era could ever hope to glimpse: two young men, one British, the other German, circling and tearing at each other with bullets, merciless, exact, fighting it out to the death. And there would almost certainly be death for one of them and for whoever was caught in the carnage on the ground.

It was the first thrill of an instinct he was too young to understand yet – terror, agony, the need to be unsafe. The sound of bombs falling all over the arena warned him that even the spectator might not be spared but it was a game, a blood sport and from his rooftop vantage point he was caught invincibly between the battle in the skies and the desolation on the ground: fire, smoke, dust beneath his feet and the cries of those too slow or too foolish to find cover in time.

I saw the heavens filled with shouting, and there rained a ghastly dew,
From the nations' airy navies, grappling in the central blue.

Not so invincibly. It was only when Pawlinu looked across the bay and saw the seafront alight with incendiaries that he realised which way the bombers were going that day. Something tightened in his chest. The thrill of the game could not touch him for a moment, he only looked ahead of him, aware that all was not as it should be. They should not be so close. He should only know that he might die, not that he would.

"This is a problem," he said out loud, watching unblinking as the houses two streets away were pounded to dust under his nose. He felt the impact of the blast and curled up instinctively into the brace position, feeling an unfamiliar urge to burst into tears. Could it have been the memory of his parents' deaths such a short time before and in such similar circumstances? Was it perhaps a little concern for the families who might have been killed as their homes fell around their ears?

His fears were a little closer to home. "God!" he whimpered, struggling for breath. "Somebody help me!" In the few seconds it took for him to stand up straight again, he knew that he was trapped. He realised that he could not possibly reach the air raid shelter now, the bombers stood between him and safety, and he was beginning to doubt whether he could risk leaving the house when shrapnel would surely be flying about the street already. But if he stayed and the house was hit he would be killed for certain.

Carmelina had done him a disservice: he had no wish to die. No matter how terrible the circumstances, life never seems so very miserable when it is about to be lost. It was simply that as the roar of planes became deafeningly near, he knew that he would certainly die because that was what it meant to be trapped during an air raid. Either he would be blown to pieces as he cowered in the house or he would be torn to shreds when he ventured into the street … or they might drop more incendiaries and he would burn alive. Terror gave way to an insane panic. They were doing it on purpose, he told himself, the might of the Luftwaffe was out to get him personally today. Somewhere in Berlin, some beefy Nazi boss was commanding his fighter pilots not to come back until little Pawlinu Caruana was out of the way and they could begin the land invasion.

Pawlinu's first temptation was to stay on the roof and jump up and down shouting, "come and get me, you vampires!" like men did in war films when the game was up and they wanted to show they were not afraid, but Pawlinu was absolutely terrified and cared very little now who knew it. He ran to the top of the spiral staircase and put his foot on the first step. Better to hide under the dining room table or in a doorway as they had been taught at school. *That will be a lot of help when the house falls down!* some joker had shouted from the back of the class, earning himself a rap over the knuckles. He had not even found the comment funny from the safety of the schoolroom.

Pawlinu could not entirely remember afterwards what happened, but there was a flash of light from somewhere and he seemed to have been hit on the back of the head. Whatever it was, he felt himself falling. He could hear himself screaming as his body crashed against the sharp edges of the steps and the dizzying sight of the world going round and round as he somersaulted into oblivion. Nothing. A resounding silence.

It did not make sense. None of it could be explained, the haze and confusion and far away noises. He had some notion that he was being carried very carefully through a darkened street. He could feel himself pressed up against a warm body, his face brushing the edge of a woollen shawl. He thought he heard a woman's voice, familiar, reassuring. Then he was falling again, dream-like, through swathes of smoke and heat haze, knowing that he would never find an end. Nothing was clear, nothing around him had a definable shape or purpose, not even himself. But then, he did not need to make sense of it. He let himself drift, knowing that he had no alternative.

When Pawlinu jolted awake, he still seemed to be in a dream. The world was still an undefined haze and he was still confused, but he had lost his bottle-top spectacles somewhere and would have been bewildered enough even without the bump on the head. He was aware that he was cold and stiff and that he was lying at the bottom of the stairs in a crumpled heap, though he could not for the life of him remember why. His forehead felt wet but before it dawned on him that his glasses had fallen off and smashed during his fall and that he had cut his head on the slivers of glass, he heard a terrible noise overhead as though he was being attacked by a swarm of insects. He remembered that he was caught in a raid.

All of a sudden, his mind was as clear as a bell and he forced himself to his feet with a huge effort, trying to ignore the fact that the floor was shuddering beneath him. The house would not come down. He would not be so unlucky, these things happened to other people...except that he had already seen his home destroyed once and knew that he had to get out, even if there were dangers waiting for him in the street.

He felt his way as far as Carmelina's sewing room, knowing that it was the quickest way to the stairs, but all the doors and windows looked the same to him now and he could not find his way. He turned in the wrong direction and accidentally reached out of the now-broken window, brushing his fingers against something soft and delicate. He would have screamed with fear if the breath had not been mysteriously knocked out of his lungs again but he had been frightened by too much to even register his panic now.

Pawlinu knew what he had touched, the sensation had been quite unmistakable. His fingers had brushed the fluttering white mushroom of a parachute falling just outside the window and it would not be any old parachute either. He was not a small boy with a fascination for things that went bang for nothing. A mine would be dangling from it, he had seen them before, just a hair's breadth away from the wall he was leaning against. He had a second, perhaps two, the slightest fraction of a moment or he knew there was no chance for him...

He took a flying leap across the room, a split second too late, and felt the impact of the explosion lifting him off the ground, hurling him into the opposite wall.

Another blow to the head and this time he was too stunned to notice the haze of unconsciousness creeping over him. As the world swam and swirled around him, he reached out for something to steady himself with and found his hand curling around the great big Sicilian crucifix that had fallen across the floor. With something resembling a wry smile, Pawlinu could not help thinking that his mother would have liked him to have died like this and he closed his eyes in what was almost relief.

Little Pawlinu Caruana slept. He was not destined to make a good death yet but no one knew it then. When the family returned, the house was still standing and Pawlinu was out for the count, stunned, bloodied but ready to fight another day. Rather like Malta in 1942. Mrs Buhagiar was the person who found him and her screams brought her daughter and half the neighbourhood crashing up the stairs, where Pawlinu lay apparently lifeless in a pool of blood, his hand still curled around the crucifix so that he looked like an icon of a child martyr.

She fell to her knees in the full paroxysms of grief, cradling his limp body in her arms as if her own warmth could somehow bring him back to life, sobbing: "No, no, not yet! Not my little boy, not yet!"

She was convinced afterwards that Pawlinu had in fact been dead as she held him and that her plea for him to be spared caused the sudden ripple of life and a cough from the dusty, bloodied head pressed to her bosom. She held him away from her for a moment and saw a pair of myopic eyes opening to stare straight through her. A rasping voice said: "I don't think I feel very well."

She was almost annoyed, as though he had played a heartless trick on her, or should have at least thought of something a little less ridiculous to say in front of all those who had watched his return to life. She might almost have shown it if he had not remembered what had happened and burst into tears, overcome with relief and the beginnings of pain.

Not that it spared him from the recriminations that were bound to follow. As soon as the house was cleared with promises from friends to help repair the damage, and Carmelina had declared the boys' room safe for habitation and put them to bed, Pawlinu found himself being unceremoniously relieved of what was left of his ·clothes and dunked in a tin bath of cold water.

"If you weren't put on this earth to spare me Purgatory I don't know why you are here at all!" she blustered, as he shivered and whimpered in the darkening water. "From now on, you stay with me when the siren goes off, understand?"

"Yes," promised Pawlinu, the picture of miserable compliance, though it came out more like "*yee-eeee-sssss!*" because he was sure he was going to freeze to death and had begun to think that going to His Maker would have been the soft option.

Mrs Buhagiar cared very little at that precise moment if the child was uncomfortable. "Wash that blood out of your hair! My goodness, you look like you fell out of an abattoir!" she shouted from the kitchen.

"I didn't cut myself that bad," he promised, when she re-appeared with a bottle of iodine. "I'll be all right."

"If you get gangrene on your face, your head will fall off," she retorted, holding a wet rag against the gash on his head. The world swam again but he felt himself being helped to his feet and wrapped up in a warm towel. "There, it's all right my little darling," she said, putting her own slippers on his feet so that he would not be cut by the tiny slivers of glass that still remained.

She had to guide him to his place in the big bed with the twins because he could not see the length of a room and it would be a long time before they could get hold of another pair of glasses for him. He was not sure he minded, wallowing in the delicious sensation of feeling wanted for the first time in so long. He let himself be dressed in a massively large night shirt belonging to Lawrence who was away at sea and wouldn't miss it and fell effortlessly asleep, exhausted beyond measure.

Mrs Buhagiar sat at his side for many minutes as he slept, feeling a sense of unease that made her want to watch over him. It was as though she thought that the war would still kill him, that he was marked out somehow for a violent death and his escape had been a mere postponement. She had said 'not yet' after all, not 'not at all.' During the hellish months that followed, she kept him under her special care, keeping as close an eye on him as she could without arousing his suspicions, praying always: "Let me die first, let me die before he does".

Carmelina thought her unsettled by the shock but old Mrs Buhagiar was right to think that the war would kill her charge sooner or later, but not when she expected, not even in her lifetime. Thirty years later, when Mrs Buhagiar had long gone to join her fathers and the toddler Gregory was a much-loved parish priest, Pawlinu took his children to the beach for a swim. There was no warning at all that time, nothing could have looked more innocent as that stretch of rocky ground and the murmuring, barely moving sea. As his sons rooted about for sea urchins, they found a rusty metal ball, spiky like a sea urchin but much bigger than that and infinitely more exciting. Big enough to climb on in the water and float. And Pawlinu with his short sight would understand what they had found only when he was too close for safety and too late to tell them not to touch it. There was smoke and dust and blood again, but he did not live long enough to notice this time. By the time Fr Gregory and the doctors arrived, there was little left to save either way.

But all of that was yet to come. Gregory standing on the beach in his cassock and purple stole, weeping like a little boy – for the moment, he was still a sleeping infant, curled up next to the friend whose requiem he would one day have to say and Pawlinu too was safe under old Mrs Buhagiar's watchful gaze. The war took them all, even those who danced on VE Day thinking that they had survived, even the ones who thought that they had forgotten all about it. No one has escaped untouched, not even us, Benedict and me and all our generation living our complacent little lives. We have been changed and conditioned by events we do not remember and pretend we care nothing about. But for all the pretences, I suppose I must confess to being touched by all of this somehow, these war and peace memories; moved, inspired, frightened, a little saddened by it all. A mourning people, a haunted people...

VII

"It must have been somewhere near here then," Benedict suggests, stepping over a sudden gap in the rocks. We have the beach to ourselves now that it is not quite warm enough to swim. In July we would be tripping over lobster-coloured tourists sunbathing themselves out of their hangovers but it looks romantically deserted this afternoon. He is on a hunt for a clue. "Wouldn't there be a little shrine to him at the place? Isn't that the custom?"

He has seen the little crosses and icons marking the places of fatal accidents along busy roads and wonders why we cannot find one to Uncle Pawlinu. "I don't know exactly where it was," I protest, only just truthfully, "none of the family ever came down here again afterwards."

Well, that much is true, they never did. But nor did they ever want to remember it and that is harder to explain to a person who has never known the meaning of an unspeakable memory. The War does not count, for all its carnage and misery. If anything I have lingered on it too long, but the strange truth of it is that it is one of the more peaceful periods of my family's history. The history books say that the war ended in 1945, even earlier for the inhabitants of southern Europe but the war did not commence at all in one particular Valletta household until peace had broken out all over Europe.

A very personal war, a civil war between two people united by blood began in a smart Valletta house in the autumn of 1947, as a young couple sat at table having a quiet disagreement. A little girl called Alexandria, the child Edward Sant'Angelo had to keep pretending he wanted, had just discovered the desire to be a grown-up and was making her first tentative steps into No Man's Land – though she did not know it at the time.

Happily unsuspecting, Alexandria wobbled gingerly across the marble kitchen floor in her mother's dress and a pair of red high heels, her face smudged gaudily with lipstick and powder. Then she stood still and listened, suddenly aware that the grown-ups were having a serious conversation.

"It's only for a couple of weeks," Edward explained to Antonia for the hundredth time. Neither of them noticed Alexandria's presence as they sat sipping coffee together. They thought she was out in the yard minding her brothers – Mark aged three, who had been in the process of trying to strangle the cat last time she saw him, and Anthony, who at six months had not yet wrestled himself out of the cycle of eating and sleeping. Antonia did not wish to be convinced. "We all have to go through training some time. It's just two weeks in England flying planes and things like that. I have to go."

"Why aren't all the others going for that long then?" demanded Antonia, letting her cup drop into its saucer with a little too much of a clatter. "Why is your training two weeks long when the others are only there for six days?"

The situation was getting complicated. Antonia had been chatting with other RAF wives. The story would have to expand a little. "The others aren't supposed to know, but they're thinking of promoting me. That's why they're keeping me back a bit longer, to give me some more advanced tests."

As if to confirm to the two of them that the story was childishly implausible, a tiny giggle like a patter of wind chimes closed the conversation. Alexandria, who had been listening intently to every word, had also been listening intently to her father's telephone calls. She knew he was lying and was dying to tell them both what she knew. It did not occur to her that her mother might not have known as much. "Pull the other one!" came the response that Antonia would dearly have liked to have made herself.

At five years old, the words were meaningless, just an expression she had heard people in the street use when they knew they are being given a tall story. The insolence of it went over her head. For a moment. "She's only a child," Antonia pointed out, as he rose from his chair with murder on his face. "She doesn't know what it means." Playing the advocate again, for one of the last times – devil's advocate, Edward would come to say – all to no avail.

Alexandria, who was too young to feel threatened by a raised hand, stood watching him impassively as he advanced on her, refusing to take the hint and run away. The impact of the blow when it descended on her head knocked her off her high heels and sent her skidding across the marble floor like a rag doll. She would be the wiser next time, but it was the power of it that she remembered afterwards far more than the pain, the sense of being completely helpless at an age when all children are helpless but seldom know it.

"Who teaches this child these things?" The roaring voice sounded too far away for her to bother shrinking away from it and it did not occur to her that he might hit her again. What really hurt and it was something she never forgot, was that he did nothing else. She glanced up from the floor, staring bewilderedly at her father's figure swinging from side to side with the rest of the room and waited for him to bend down and pick her up. She would have to wait a long time because he stepped over her as though she were not there at all and walked away. Better to be a threat that had to be knocked down than not there at all.

Then, even worse, her mother's reaction. After a short pause, Antonia was still too surprised to do what any other mother would have done automatically. She felt like the witness of an unfortunate accident, desperate to disappear from view before the police turned up. So she rose to her feet and stepped quietly and apologetically out of the room. A word would have been enough to prove that the child had not suddenly become invisible to the grown-up world; but this was a silent declaration of war. Alexandria heard the door closing softly and knew that she was alone. She pressed her face against the cold marble and noticed that it felt a little better, but she was still alone.

There were many children in 1947 who felt alone, orphaned or abandoned as children always are in the aftermath of bloodshed. Whilst Alexandria discovered the sensation of being unloved, a seven-year-old boy called Nicholas sat on a balcony, watching the street below. A man in a gleaming white naval uniform had just left the house. He saw the white circle of his flat cap and thought for a moment that it was his father. Now he remembered why he was there. Gregory had taken Rosaria out of the house so that she would not disturb their mother. They were not really supposed to go out, the house was in mourning, but a four-year-old could not be expected to respect that and her merriment upset everyone.

Pawlinu, well goodness only knew where that reprobate had hidden himself. Five years on and he still seemed to feel the need to absent himself from family affairs whenever he could. He had at long last got into the habit of calling Mrs Buhagiar *Nanna* and Carmelina *Mama,* but a stubborn sense of belonging elsewhere kept him back whenever he began to feel too familiar with them. In all honesty, Carmelina and Mrs Buhagiar did not greatly care where Pawlinu was at that moment and the fact that he was in the process of being sacked from his job delivering telegrams for *Cable and Wireless* would have been of minor importance under the circumstances even if they had known. Something about forgetting to tell his boss he could not ride a bicycle.

Telegrams caused rather a lot of grief to the Buhagiar family in those days. Two weeks before, a slip of paper had arrived telling them that Lawrence had had a fall during a storm off the coast of France and was in a hospital in Toulon. It said that he had suffered a brain haemorrhage. Carmelina had known the moment she read it that she would never see him again but the boys did not know what a brain haemorrhage was and thought that it meant he would be coming home on an extra-long leave, like sailors who broke an arm or got appendicitis and were unfit for service for a while. They were more shocked than their mother when the news came telling them that he had been certified dead. Well, she did not break it to them quite like that but those were the words she had read.

Some one came to visit them with his personal effects: a leather wallet containing a ten shilling note and a handful of foreign coins, a series of photographs he had taken to show them when he came home on leave, the remains of a rosary that seemed to have snapped when he fell. And there was an explanation about what they thought had happened, except that no one saw the actual moment and they could only guess.

There was something particularly painful about him dying so far away. Nicholas could hear his mother crying in the next room, "but he was my husband! Why won't they bring his body back home? I want him buried here where I can be near him!"

And dear old Mrs Buhagiar, comforting her that she did not need to be near his grave to be near him. He was in Heaven, he would always be with her. But Carmelina would not be comforted. "I don't want him in Heaven, I want him *here!*" The promise of eternal life, which should have comforted her, had quite the opposite effect. She did not want to think of him invisible, purified, watching over her with the distance of time and space between them. She did not want a guardian angel; she wanted him as she had always known him. It was hardly something she could have told her own mother, but she wanted the pressure of his arms holding her against his body, the moist, delicious sensation when their lips touched, the reassuring feeling of his fingers smoothing her hair. She wanted the sound of his baritone voice calling to her from the foot of the stairs when he arrived home on leave.

"He got through the war, he got through all those years to die in some stupid accident!" And it was a cruel irony that a man who spent the war years navigating the treacherous waters of the Mediterranean (which was particularly hungry for shipping and human flesh at that time) should have died because he lost his footing when the ship listed with unexpected violence and he fell heavily onto the deck. But then, who was to know that his health had not been invisibly weakened by the terrors of those years – the endless cigarettes he smoked, the heartbeats he missed when they had a particularly close call. No one could rightly say afterwards whether the fall had caused the brain haemorrhage or whether he had the haemorrhage first and fell unconscious to the ground.

However it happened, his ship had left port before his funeral took place and none of his friends and companions for so many long journeys were present to see him off. The French priest prayed for him with just a representative from the Royal Navy and a couple of charitable old ladies who made it their business to stand by those who died far away from their families, laid in unvisited graves. And his grave was entirely unvisited until my father, at the age of fifty-five, made the journey to France with his brother and they paid the family's respects. It was a long, emotional homecoming when it happened and perhaps a little absurd. When they arrived in the cemetery, they discovered that their father had been buried in the wrong place and that his name was written on a memorial commemorating soldiers who died fighting for the French Empire. Thus, the British Crown's faithful subject, who died in His Majesty's loyal service, found himself laid to rest under a French Flag.

"I thought you said he was a hero." Benedict again. It is almost a nuisance having an audience.

"Come again?"

"You said he died doing something 'terribly heroic and terminal.'" Did I put it quite like that?

"Well he did. What do you suppose he was doing so far off the ground if he wasn't trying to help save the ship? Hmm?" My accent slips at moments like this. "Do you think he decided to do a little climbing in treacherous weather conditions for fun?"

"That wasn't exactly what I meant..." He could have found somewhere else to argue about my seafaring grandfather's death than standing at the edge of the shore with the rippling waves behind him. "I thought he died fighting."

"Oh I'm sorry, I suppose risking his life to help save his comrades from going down doesn't count then."

"Yes, of course it does. I meant–" I sense a guilt complex at work. "I just mean that it was his job. He was trained to do that."

It is ridiculous to feel so indignant in defence of a man I never knew, but it rankles. Except that I know he would probably have looked at it like that if he had had the chance for reflection and perhaps it was just an unfortunate accident. Perhaps the medals they awarded him which he would never show off on parade were just compensation of a kind – a few metal stars and coins with the king's head stamped on them, each one bearing its own striped ribbon – to make us proud of him and to make us all believe that his death was not a criminal waste. "You are an unspeakable cynic. Leave the dead alone."

The only redeeming detail is that I know in the end that he did not have to do it. He was not a conscript. Not one of us has the right to sneer without asking whether our lives will ever add up to more than his did, whether we will have anything more to show our Maker when the day of reckoning comes. It might be that a clean conscience, a few pieces of ironmongery and a wife and children who loved you will seem like great treasures by comparison, when you discover that you do not have quite so much to offer as you had intended.

"Sorry."

"Whatever." An uneasy silence descends. "Was I ranting?"

"Yes." I feel the touch of a welcome kiss. "Why don't you carry on?"

There seems so little to say. Whatever happened in decades to come, in 1947, Carmelina was still weeping. "Why could I not have gone to him? I went to America, didn't I? That was further away than France. Why wouldn't anyone let me go?" The information that there would have been little point in her making the journey – he was in a coma throughout his brief stay in hospital and by that stage would not have recognised her even if she had appeared at his side – cuts little ice with a woman widowed so young when she was still very much in love. "France is a cold, wet place! They should have brought him back to Malta where the rain and snow wouldn't touch him." It is hard to want to protect a loved one who no longer needs protecting.

So whilst the women wept and Gregory silenced Rosaria with ice-cream and Pawlinu picked up his one and only pay packet from *Cable and Wireless*, Nicholas sat alone, watching the street below. Part of him still believed that he would see his father turning the corner and running towards the house like he always did when he came home on leave. He half-wondered whether there might not have been a terrible mix-up somewhere and he really might come back, then he could have his father and some other family could have the tragedy. Exiled by death in his far away grave, Lawrence would have understood why his son felt so alone.

Here's to absent fathers. We have all been lonely children at one time or another – Alexandria my mother, Nicholas my father and me, Kristjana, the problem child, the exile, the naturalised Brit, the Maltese girl who understands Chaucer better than her own relatives. I have lain awake at night trying to imagine that I was back at home with my parents instead of at the boarding school God forgot. Alexandria lay awake at night wondering what it would have been like to have a different father altogether. She thought a cross between Mr Portelli the baker and Uncle Tom from her English reading book would be nice. On the many more occasions when she found herself curled up on the kitchen floor, she created in her child's mind a father of her own, tailor-made to suit the imagination of a little girl growing up at the end of the nineteen forties.

Consequently, he was tall to command her respect but thin so as to have no weight to throw around, calm, mild-mannered, excessive only in all things good. So he never lost his temper, but when he appeared at the door at the end of the day (always standing straight and able to speak coherently) he would rush forward to sweep his wife and children into his arms, saying something like 'my darlings, I'm so glad to be home!' as caring fathers always said in the sentimental, harmless films on which Alexandria grew up. As to habits, well, he smoked a pipe that sent fruity curls of smoke about the room in the evening, wore a panama hat in the sun and braces rather than a belt (think about it, whoever managed to seriously injure a child with a pair of braces?) His accent resembled Lawrence Olivier.

It must have been her early fantasies of an olde Englishe father figure that gave her such a disastrous interest in Englishmen, but as the Sant'Angelo family grew, Alexandria's imaginary father grew in stature. Very soon, he was protecting her from the pretend father who lived in the house, rocking her in his arms and singing softly to her when her body ached too much for her to drop off to sleep on her own.

And what of little Nicholas, sitting alone in the balcony seat? He was unique, he remembered his father before the absence, but memories are easily confused by children struck by an unexpected blow. It was not very long before the memory of what his father was like had muddled itself with the memory of the dead that inevitably presented itself in a house of mourning. Lawrence still enjoyed some sort of a life in the house. His photograph hung in the hall framed by black crepe, the scent of votive candles burning in his memory penetrated the atmosphere every moment of the day, his medals and papers and rosary lay about the place as though he were going to walk in at any moment to gather them up. And in every room, the souvenirs and artefacts he bought on his many tours of duty mapped out the course of his short career – a statue of Our Lady of Mount Carmel bought in Haifa, bottles of heady perfume, musk, rose and sandalwood bought in Egypt, little wooden boxes embossed with mother of pearl, bartered for in a Palestinian market.

But was this really him? I can hardly say. I can think of him only as Nanna's dead husband or my father's dead father, not as someone I should have known as something other than a slightly stern face on a monochrome photograph. Nicholas had to learn to forget until he was fifteen years old and too grown up to grieve in public. I cannot get over the cruelty of a good father dying whilst a bad father across the bay is alive and kicking (amongst other things), but what on earth am I suggesting...

The Royal Navy paid for Nicholas and Gregory to go to two excellent schools, where Gregory was happy and successful and Nicholas was academically substandard and thoroughly miserable until he left. And as their academic adventures began, Alexandria, quite unsuspectingly, had the pleasure of getting her own back.

VIII

Teatime at the Sant'Angelos. Auntie Josephine, Edward's indomitable older sister, had arranged to meet her brother and his family for the first time since the door to the family home slammed shut so ominously eight years before. She had come with the news that Old Leonardo Sant'Angelo had had a heart attack and was currently floating indecisively between life and death. "That's his problem," came Edward's emphatic answer. So much for the notion that time was a great healer.

Beefy, acid-tongued Josephine was having none of it. "I'm not telling you to go and see him, he wouldn't want to see your ugly face anyway. I just wanted to be sure you would be at the funeral when it comes." She was impatient to get her message across; she had bigger fish to fry than the impending death of a relation neither of them had ever loved. "We don't want a family scandal, do we now?"

"There *has* been a family scandal," answered Edward tartly, and he had a point. "It's called my father not deigning to come to my wedding. I suppose you remember that, or did he drug you on that day, just in case you took the initiative for a change and turned up?"

"You know perfectly well I could never have come, don't get bitter with me."

Edward was slightly in awe of her, even now. At a discreet age just past thirty, Josephine was already a confirmed, self-determined spinster with a rotund figure and a singularly unattractive face to match. She was the sort of woman who had deliberately forfeited the chance of marriage to take up a career as a nurse and she had been more successful than he would have liked. As a military sister she ranked higher than him and her very presence in the house, dressed up to the nines in navy blue uniform, complete with a bleached white starched cap trimmed with frills and an expensive blue and red cape, triggered his inferiority complex. His military career had not yet allowed him to command such respect or such a beneficial salary, nor was it ever likely to. *Looks like bloody Florence Nightingale*, he would mutter for weeks to come. "He cursed me to hell, Jo," is what he actually said and it was impossible not to feel a little sorry for him. "He even cursed my children and their children. What sort of a man does such things?"

Josephine felt an old fraternal warmth at the sound of her nickname. He was still as handsome and bewildered as she remembered him, it was hard for her not to be swayed a little by the memory of his banishment from the house – she had been distraught enough about it at the time. As the only female in the house, the task had fallen to her of stripping down his room, emptying it of everything that made it his; pictures, his gramophone, his books, bits and pieces he had collected over the years but never found a use for. His clothes and the rug he had bought when they were travelling in Italy were gathered up and burnt before he could write to ask for them. It had been unhappily like stripping down a room after the death of the occupant, but then he *had* been dead and she had mourned his passing even though he was living in a town no more than seven miles away from her own.

She tried to forget all of that as she watched him, the wronged son rejected by a tyrannical father. She had come to the house to do more than warn him about his father's forthcoming funeral. Military circles were close, claustrophobic environments at the best of times and gossip travelled fast. A particularly unpleasant piece of gossip about her estranged brother's domestic affairs had reached her ears and she intended to get to the bottom of it before it began to affect her own reputation. After all, it could hardly help her standing if she shared a family name with a… innocent until proven guilty, she reminded herself. It helped her case a little that his handsome features were already being polluted after a comparatively short time. If she looked at him closely with her medically trained eyes, she could see that his skin had discoloured with the endless smoking, his eyes bore the telltale redness and swelling of excessive alcohol consumption and there were hard grimace lines creeping around his mouth and forehead. There was no doubt in her mind at all – he was precisely what they were all saying he was.

She tested the water. "If you ask me, brother," she said, knowing perfectly well that he would never ask her anything of the sort, "you are not the damned one in this little equation." He snapped to his feet. First point to her, he had understood the accusation immediately.

"If you've come here to interrogate me about my private affairs…"

Too weak for words, she thought. She said: "Nothing of the sort, I promise. Just make sure I don't find out that *you* are the hate-corrupted demon dropping curses on his children." She had thought that might make him run, he never could outstare her even when they were children. She watched him turning his back on her, half-tempted to remind him to salute her as he left, but she let him go without another word. He had spoken in his own prosecution.

There was a short pause, then she turned to Alexandria, who had been sitting as quiet as a mouse next to her at table, hands folded in her lap as they had taught her at school. She was wearing her short blue school pinafore that fell just above the knee whilst she was sitting down and exposed her swinging baby-fat legs. Josephine took one look at the red marks running in little horizontal lines where someone had clearly been at her with some offensive weapon or other and passed her a plate of cheese pastries by way of condolence.

"Who did that to you, *sabiha*?" she asked, as nonchalantly as if she were asking the time.

"Daddy did," replied Alexandria, obligingly, too young to feel the need to protect a criminal. It had not dawned on her yet that this was the work of a criminal or even that his behaviour was slightly inappropriate.

"Did he indeed? Is there anything else you would like to show me?" Josephine instinctively began to unbutton her yellow school shirt. She was not a nurse for nothing and knew exactly where to look for further evidence. "And while I'm at it, Alex, what about your brothers? Do you suppose they'd mind me taking a look at them too?"

Alexandria compliantly showed her the bruising on her shoulders, the cigarette burn on her wrist and various other pieces of incriminating evidence imprinted on her flesh, blissfully unaware as she explained exactly where she got them and why, that she was lowering herself and her brothers into extremely hot water. By the time Auntie Josephine had helped her to get dressed again and poured her a nice cup of milky tea, showing the sort of care and attention that she had never received from anyone else before, Alexandria had forgotten to ask why Auntie was so interested. It hardly seemed important now, Auntie seemed rather keen for her to go out and play in the yard for a bit whilst she caught up with Daddy about this and that. Alex jumped down from her chair and left her to it.

Josephine said many years later that the biggest mistake men made about women was to underestimate their ability to be angry. It was a mistake Edward at least failed to make a second time. As soon as the child was safely out of earshot, Josephine bellowed for her brother. When he failed to respond, she realised that he had scuttled out of the house like a cockroach and knew exactly where he had gone. So be it, she thought, rising from her seat like an avenging angel. If Edward thought she looked like *bloody Florence Nightingale*, she looked more like the Lord High Executioner as she stormed down the street, a face to put the fear of God in a man, nursing cape flowing behind her like something from a ham horror film. She did not slow her heavy, determined stride until she reached the entrance to the officers' mess. If he would not confront his domestic transgressions in the privacy of his own home, she was quite happy to make them a little more public.

Fortunately for him considering the state she was in, the mess was empty except for the barman and an extremely edgy Edward smoking a pipe in an alcove. The barman looked up in surprise at the sight of a symbol of gentleness and patience standing among the empty tables. She looked fit to kill a man at ten paces. "Were you looking for someone, love?" he asked, when he had intended to ask her to leave.

"Edward!" she barked in her brother's direction like an enraged sergeant major. *"Edward!"* At least the second shout forced him to turn around, just in time for him to see her marching towards him, vast and terrible, retribution without end. "Edward," she said, furious still but hanging onto her self-command. The words came out in an angry flood. "If I ever find that you have mistreated those children again, I will report you for assault and battery and I won't rest until I've seen you court martialled. Do you understand me?"

Edward took a guilty look about the room, half-expecting to find his superiors watching the sorry spectacle, noting down her every word. "So, the little brat's been telling you stories, has she?" and he tried his best to sound light-hearted when he was really wetting himself.

"Stories? It's all over the barracks, you stupid boy!" This was big sister talking now, "and she didn't have to tell me anything, it's written all over her body, you *bastard*!" Silence for a moment, as the three of them took in the shock of such a word coming from a nursing sister's mouth. There was worse to come. "I'd like to tear you limb from limb, you unspeakable coward! She's a defenceless child, a baby and you of all people! You know what it's like to be at the receiving end, we *both do*!" She found to her surprise that her voice was cracking and she was not given to crying, but Alexandria was little more than herself many years ago, violence passed from father to son like a – well, like a curse.

Perhaps that is what a curse means. Perhaps Leonardo Sant'Angelo could see all that would come to pass: a son who seemed so handsome and benevolent but whom he knew was corrupt and cowardly. Perhaps he even saw that Edward and Antonia were ill-matched, that their marriage should have never taken place and was doomed to failure. Perhaps Edward was like that from the beginning, curse or no curse. It may even be that there are no heroes to speak of at all here and that I must simply walk away. I can tell myself that my family is big enough that I can disown large parts of it without feeling any sense of loss.

But then what about my mother? What about little Alexandria Sant'Angelo who came into existence because of the two people I would so gladly wash my hands of? What about me, for that matter? Am I to disown myself as well? There are still some ways of escape.

"Where are we going?"

"I don't have to explain." I am the author, I am the guide. I do not have to account to anyone. "Just get on the bus." I know he is afraid of the buses and is trying not to show it.

"Couldn't we take a taxi?" Not a tremor of fear but I am not fooled and drag him onto the first step.

"Not worried about our sturdy British buses, are

you? You went to a public school."

"They must be sixty years old." He sits down and clings to the seat ahead. "What does that sign say?"

"Which one?"

"The one over the head of the driver." The driver has taken his hands off the steering wheel to light a cigarette.

"It says 'No Smoking'. Just ignore the driver." We lurch around a corner. "Look at the nice shrine to Our Lady up there."

He is green by now and sweating lightly. "I suppose that's meant to be reassuring."

He brightens up when we get off, straight into the sunny streets. This really is a beautiful country. The Romans called it Melita – Latin for honey. A honey land then, golden earth and stone and a honey-sweet people with a gentle, sensuous language and a culture built on the best that East and West could offer. On January mornings, cycling through the bitter, misty Cambridge streets to lectures, it is difficult not to feel a little homesick for this land, in spite of bullying and cajoling and the demands to 'obey – assimilate!' The feeling usually lasts just until ears and nose and feet have thawed, but it is telling enough.

We are outside the Catacombs of St Paul. Shades of green appear again. "I hate underground more than buses!" protests Benedict, the picture of misery.

"I'll explain later." The need to tell the story has made me heartless. I cannot explain yet why it is necessary to bundle the man out of bright sunshine into the gloom of an underground burial chamber but I feel more at home underground and some stories can only be told underground, buried far away from human civilisation. I feel closer to the past down here and not just the far away past either – St Paul sheltering in a cave after his shipwreck, the first Christians gathering underground to pray in secret, the war generation hiding from the Luftwaffe. And closer to home, my mother. She is also underground at this present moment, locked in the much-neglected wine cellar under the Sant'Angelo house. I want to keep her company for a while, she is terribly young to be left alone behind a locked door.

It was six months after Auntie Josephine's visit to her brother and Edward had just returned from another training visit to England. No, I do not know what he was doing. The RAF are very thorough with things like that, aren't they? No more interruptions. Who is the author? Is it you or me? In that case, I decide what gets told and what gets tactfully forgotten. You have plenty of material here to indulge your morbid curiosity, I can't think why you should want anything else. You ought to have emotional indigestion with it by now.

That is where we were. Edward had just returned from training in England and found the house in chaos. And it was at least part, if not all Alexandria's fault. To start with, he stepped into the yard and found that all the baby turkeys he had bought just before he left had mysteriously died. Then he reached the fishpond at the bottom of the yard to find that someone had pinched the thermometer from the water as well as all his tropical fish. And what on earth had become of Bonnie the dog? He knew who would have the answer. "Alexandria! Alexandria! Come out here, you thieving little cockroach!"

The turkeys really were not her fault. She went out with Mark to feed the fish only to turn her back for five minutes and discover him drowning – sorry, washing – them in a bucket. He really was washing them, apparently, but they did not take kindly to being held under water whilst he scrubbed them and they collectively expired. She tried to convince her father that there was a turkey disease that came and killed them in the night but even after he had thrown her down

81

the stairs, she could not be persuaded to blame anything else for their mass murder.

As for the thermometer, that was Mark too on another day of disasters, but he was only trying to take Bonnie's temperature like he saw the vet do and he was egged on by cousins David and Lela from the end of the street. It was just that Bonnie did not appreciate his medical intervention and ran off with the thermometer clattering along the ground behind him, neither dog nor thermometer ever to be seen again. After that they had all been in rather a blind panic and it was the least she could think of doing to make a little campfire and roast a couple of fish, just like schoolchildren did in England apparently.

A merry evening it had been, eating half-cooked tropical fish garnished with a lemon picked straight from the tree, then campfire songs that David and Lela learnt at the Brownies and the Boy Scouts - *Gin gan guli guli guli guli watcha!* and *I love to go a-wandering along the mountain track*. She was sure she had not fished out all of those fish but they must have been hungrier than she remembered and there was not much flesh on them. To be quite honest, by the end of it she had been rather hoping that her father might get lost in the big big city of London and never come back. Fat chance.

"Oh dear, what a mess I've made of you," he said, finally giving up on getting any kind of an explanation from her. There was a small trickle of blood coming out of her mouth where a tooth had broken but she was so completely punch-drunk that she would not notice the sharp edge under her tongue until much later. "We can't have Auntie Josephine getting a look at you now, can we?" And with that, she found herself locked in the cellar among the dust and the cobwebs and the – oh God – rats.

If this were a fairy story, the rats would be cuddly intelligent creatures who would talk to her and snuggle up to her and possibly gnaw an escape route out for her.

Unfortunately, this is not a fairy story and the rats were just rats. Disgusting, disease-ridden vermin with big sharp teeth and long tails who have smelt blood and fear coming from a suitably vulnerable source. And there was no fairy godmother here to keep the tragic heroine from harm.

I cannot take another step. I do not want to say anything else and stand, rooted to the spot, waiting for Benedict to cradle my head in his arms and tell me very quietly that I am a liar. A liar or a woman fantasising. There are things they can do about a sick mind inventing horrors, nothing that they can do about horrors. We are stuck with them. They will hang about me forever if he cannot persuade me that I am what he knows I am not. It will not do. Tears and darkness calling across time.

IX

I wanted to remember something else, a happy event in the Buhagiar house of mourning when the spirits of Carmelina and her unhappy family were lifted by the arrival of an unexpected visitor. But there are no ways out of here, I cannot extricate myself from this place. When it comes to it, I am afraid to leave my mother alone, knowing what is about to happen to her. There is no such thing as the worst thing, there is always something worse that can happen. Even something worse than a beaten child fighting for breath in an airless, disease-ridden dungeon worthy of the Tower of London. Even worse than the encroaching circle of rats and the touch of filthy, matted fur and sharp claws against purple-dappled flesh. And teeth, yellow vampire teeth.

Alexandria began to scream. She could never remember opening her mouth to scream, just the realisation that she was screaming and the thought that she could never stop, an alarm call of distress roaring out of her like a convulsion; spontaneous, violent, quite against her will. There are many frightened children in this book, but this was worse than an air raid or an angry male voice or even hospitals with their monsters in white coats prowling around. This was the fear that made grown men collapse with heart failure. Vision growing hazy with terror, grainy like an old television screen, then black then bright white until she thought she could see red eyes everywhere. She *could* see them, the red eyes of rats, demonic, penetrating, a childhood terror that she could never wake from. Her blood roared in her ears and she went on screaming, hysterical, unstoppable, filling the room and the rest of the house with the tortured, desperate animal noise of battlefield despair. And all of this coming from a child not yet seven years old.

So runs my dream: but what am I?
An infant crying in the night,
An infant crying for the light
And with no language, but a cry.

And in the kitchen, Antonia was trying to get the key from her husband's closed hand. "She'll have a heart attack, she'll have a seizure, and then what will happen?"

"She'll die. Good. Then we might all get some peace." He knocked her hand away from his wrist.

"You don't mean it. Let me get her out!"

"There's nothing wrong with her if she can make that much noise."

She tried a different tactic. "I think they can hear her in the street. What will the neighbours think, I wonder?"

By the time the key turned in the lock, Alexandria had started battering and hurling herself at the door, so that she almost flew out, covered in grime and still screaming, like a Victorian chimney sweep popping onto a rooftop on the tail end of a fire. Before anyone could restrain her, she hurtled through the house and out of the open front door, not stopping until she reached the end of the street and the home of cousins David and Lela. Overpowering sunlight forced her to cover her eyes but she knew the way and ran blindly to sanctuary.

Into the fire, actually but she was not to know that yet and thought, 'thank goodness, safe at last,' as she pushed open the door and stepped into the cool calm of the entrance hall. A comforting smell of dusty carpets and heavy wooden furniture greeted her and she felt her heartbeat slowing down healthily. A grandfather clock ticked irregular seconds from an alcove.

"Hello?" called a man's voice from upstairs. "Who is it?"

She tried to answer but she was still hoarse and breathless from screaming and the words would not come. Her chest ached with the exertion as though her lungs were lined with sandpaper. She waited, wheezing and gasping, until she saw Uncle Luigi walking down the stairs before she tried to speak again. "It's Alexandria," she announced in a thin, careful voice, unaware of the fright she had just given him. "Where – where are David and Lela?"

Luigi struggled to maintain his look of calm reserve at the sight of a little girl with filthy hands and torn, dirty, blood-stained clothes and a face that was already beginning to swell. She was a child whom Charles Dickens might have created in a particularly dark hour, who had somehow found her way into his sane, civilised, twentieth century politico's home. "They're on an outing with their mother," he managed to say. "I'm sorry, I'm really very busy. I've got a speech to write. Why don't you come back later?"

In his mind he imagined her compliantly backing through the door, without stopping for a second to think that a child looking like that could not compliantly back out of anything easily. Alexandria did step back, two or three paces so that her face fell into shadow, and began to cry, knowing perfectly well that she could not go back to the home she had just fled in panic. Who could say what might be waiting for her if she did? Another stint in the cellar with the rats and who knows what other nasty creatures? Her father, ready to break every bone in her body for displaying herself in such a state outside the house? The prospects were too appalling and she was too tired. She leant against the cold white wall, leaving a lasting stain across it, and choked with exhausted, half-strangled sobs. It was as though she had reached the welcoming border of neutral Spain after days of climbing and danger only to find the Gestapo waiting to drag her to her death.

Luigi was at her side in a moment, stooping down to pick her up. Many years later, when his own children were long grown up and gone away, he stood in the same spot and discovered that the faint smudge of blood she left there when her head pressed against the wall was still there. Then he sincerely wished that he had left her alone, precisely where she was, damaged by someone else.

But at the time it did not seem to him that he was doing anything wrong. He was a liberal-minded, soft-hearted man who dreamed freedom and republics. He told himself that he was helping her, that was all, as he rocked her gently in his arms, not a little like her imaginary father. "There now, there's no need to cry, my poor little one, it's all right, it's all right."

He felt her arms tightening possessively around his neck and took it as an invitation. He would tell himself afterwards, when he had cleaned her up and given her almond cakes for tea, that it really was what she wanted. Then he would make himself believe that it was not such a terrible thing to do to a child who had already suffered so much. It was a gesture of love in a way, was it not? Not like what that sadist of a father did to her. Had he not been the one she had run to? Had he not been the good uncle who had dried her tears and been the most compassionate of nurses and felt the greatest most heartfelt outrage at her suffering? For the moment, all he felt was the baby-soft brush of her lips innocently touching his neck and he carried her gently up the stairs.

"I could have told you anything, couldn't I?"

An arm slips carefully around my waist. "You're shaking."

I know he wants me to say something, but there are no more words. I wonder if I could have simply lied, told him that my forefathers were philanthropists or social reformers or anything, anything other than what they actually were. I know that I should end it all here whilst there is still some hope left in his heart. "I want to stop this."

It would not do to tell him what Luigi did when he returned to the room where he had committed his crime and, for a life-changing series of empty minutes, almost accepted the evil that he had done. How he frantically changed his clothes and the bed linen to hide any evidence that she had been anywhere near him. How he had looked up and seen his wife's icons of the Madonna and Child and St Dominic, and the great Gothic crucifix facing him wherever he looked and realised that his actions had been witnessed. It should have been a moment of grace, the realisation, terrible and awesome, that God was in His Heaven, seeing and knowing everything, even the life of an insubstantial figure in a country that could not be seen from space. But instead of feeling remorse at that moment, he felt only anger and mad panic. He became convinced that the faces were actually moving, that they must have turned to glare at him as he held her in his arms, condemning him for exploiting her innocence and desperation to be loved. And in a final act of defiance, he hurled himself around the room, tearing the pious images down from the walls so that they could never watch him again, hating the sight of them for reminding him of churches and confessionals and guilt.

My head rests against a comforting shoulder, but I realise it was Benedict, not me, who was shaking. I cannot explain what it feels like to be so weary. I imagine, with something verging on hysteria, that we can step out of this nightmare and occupy our time in some more innocent way. We could go on a tour of the Neolithic temples, step far back into a time before history, before memory, we could take a boat trip around the harbour. I could take him to Valletta so that we could walk the ramparts together and I could hurl this bundle of secrets into the waiting sea where secrets belong. *I'll drown my book.* Then we can go back to England and I will reinvent myself, make myself a new identity. Refugee turncoats are good at doing that; I will take a leaf out of Uncle Sam/Salvatore's book. I remind myself that most people think I am Spanish or Italian or Lebanese – I will take my pick, choose a national heritage like a new set of clothes and no one will be any the wiser.

"You can stop if you like, my love," I can hear Benedict telling me with what is almost relief. "Tell me what you want." But his voice sounds so distant. I wonder, if I go on much longer, whether he will be able to reach me any more. I cannot explain to someone who has lived all his life in the same green country what it means to be so *lost*. I wonder if he would be shocked to hear me say out loud that leaving your country is like leaving a bullying, manipulative mother. You might hate her but you owe your life to her all the same and no action or word you speak will not have been spoken by her first. And we have come so far.

I am in blood stepped so far, that should I wade no more,
    Returning were as tedious as go o'er.

I doubt that even the Mediterranean could drown out these voices now, but at least I did not shed the blood I am swimming in. But if we must go forward, there is a little hope left somewhere, in a quiet house in Sliema where a period of mourning is about to come to an abrupt end.

Uncle Sam arrived on his sister's doorstep without a word of warning. After two years of writing consoling letters that were clearly having no effect on his widowed sister, Uncle Sam, Salvatore that once was, decided to take matters into his own hands and burst into their lives like Americanisation personified. Carmelina and her mother cried, Mrs Grech and the neighbours rushed to greet him with 'my goodness, how you've grown!' and '*Marija,* but it seems like yesterday that you were this high!' whilst the children took one look at the grinning, larger-than-life Father Christmas figure before them and fell at his feet.

It helped that his suitcases looked like something out of Aladdin's Cave of Wonders: candy, brightly-coloured clothes, balloons, crackers, toys, posters of cartoon characters, comics… there seemed to be no end to the treats he had to offer them. After a long two years, the house filled with light again. The black crepe came down. He personally folded it up and helped his mother to store it away for the mourning period of the future which she would not have to keep, the family exchanged their black clothes for an array of reds and blues and greens and thanks to the gramophone Uncle Sam brought with him, the house was filled with crooning American voices. *It ain't a-gonna rain no more no more…*

"Uncle, this sweet's really hard to swallow."

"You're not supposed to swallow it, honey, it's bubble gum."

"Oops."

A-B-C-D-E-F-G-H-I gotta girl, in Kalimazoo! I don't wanna boast but I know she's the toast of…

"Which way round does this go?"

"Buttons on the front."

Heigh-ho, heigh-ho, it's off to work we go! Heigh-ho heigh-ho heigh-ho heigh-

"I hope Irena doesn't mind you being away so long."

"Course not, it was practically her idea."

I'm dreaming of a white Christmas, just like the ones

I used to know. Where the treetops glisten, and children listen...

Admittedly, things did get off to a slightly awkward start. Tucked away in Niagara Falls, Uncle Sam had remained blissfully oblivious to the sufferings of Europeans during the war and its aftermath. He saw the pictures of Auschwitz with its wasted, staring survivors and the piles of rotting corpses. He remembered watching footage of war-ravaged, bomb-crunched London with children playing in the hazardous shells of burnt-out houses and men tearing at the piles of stones in search of their families, but they were just grainy images on a screen. Not so very different to the horror films that made your spine tingle and maybe gave you nightmares once or twice if they were really bad. It was difficult to believe that it was all true.

So, when Uncle Sam tried to run a bath and found that there was no water in the tap, he was more than decently indignant. "You have to leave the tap on all night," Carmelina explained, when he called her to see if she knew what the problem was. "It drips all night and by the morning there's enough to wash in." He was even more outraged by her placid acceptance of this appalling state of affairs and vowed to take the matter into his own hands, ignoring her apologetic assurances that there really was nothing to be done. It was fortunate that she decided against following him all the way to the town council to make his complaint or she would never have been able to show her face there again.

"What's wrong with this place?" he boomed in broken, Americanised Maltese, in the direction of the terrified clerk he found waiting compliantly behind a desk. "My sister's got an old mother and four children to care for and she ain't even got running water! What are you going to do about it?"

"Fix the pipes, sir," came the humble answer, amid

a rustle of papers.

Sam hesitated. The man was not supposed to give the right answer but he was not thrown off course for long. "Great. When?"

"Some time in the next year or so, I hope." It was quite amazing how frightening jocular men like Uncle Sam could appear in moments of temper. Even the people waiting outside the office quaked at the roar that followed.

"What?!!" Oh this was bad. This was very, very bad. "The war's been over *four years* man!"

"We are having to reconstruct everything, sir," explained the clerk, covering any sense of nausea he might have been feeling with a trained clerical tone of quiet patience. "We were bombed out of existence – look at the ruined buildings everywhere, the rationing, the poverty. It will be years before the work is finished." Then, quite unable to restrain himself, he added, "I'm afraid you will have to put up with shallow baths for the duration of your stay, sir. I hope it will not spoil your holiday too much."

Holiday. 'The duration of your stay'. That took the wind out of his sails. Uncle Sam went home a chastened man. All the ruined buildings the clerk referred to seemed to be rumbling his name and not his American name either. *Salvatore! Salvatore!* The little boy who sold his heritage for a weekly pay packet and the American Way. The man who lived his comfortable little American life whilst his mother and sister starved.

Hang your head in shame, Salvatore Buhagiar and I will call you by that name for just a moment. I hope you had a comfortable war, I truly hope you did and that you never lay awake at night wondering what it was like for your family to live in an island under siege. I'm sure you never gave it a second thought.

But before I indulge in any manufactured bitterness, I cannot imagine how it would have particularly helped

Sam/Salvatore's Maltese relatives if he too had been trapped in misery during those years. He escaped nice and early, long before anyone could have dreamed that Malta would be subjected to such an experience. What was done was done. And no one could have pretended that his decision to stay in Niagara Falls was made selfishly. It was made when Sam/Salvatore was still a young man and in his heart he still believed that it had been the right decision. As he walked back in the direction of Blanche Street, he thought of his wife, Irena, he remembered the family, the life he had made for himself across the Atlantic, then glanced slowly round at the familiar-unfamiliar landscape of his boyhood. It was so heart-rendingly tragic precisely because it belonged to his childhood. He could not entirely make the connection with it, like a key that had become too rusted to slide into the lock it was built to open.

When I was a child, I spoke like a child and thought like a child,
But now that I am a man, I must put all childish ways before me.

He would make it up to them, he thought, planning the five weeks he intended to spend with them. The twins would celebrate birthday number nine soon and he would see to it that they celebrated in style. More music, more colour, more laughter. On the afternoon of their birthday, he blew up the sausage-shaped balloons he had brought with him and twisted them into animal shapes, little dogs and giraffes and snails, then threw them down over the side of the balcony when the children came running down the street after lessons. This was Christmas, this was Carnival come early. Screams of delight as multi-coloured balloon animals floated down from heaven into waiting hands. They were even more delighted when he leant his head out and they discovered that he looked just like Charlie Chaplin. He really did, curls of black hair and a trim little moustache to cover the scar from a childhood accident. And Uncle Sam smiled, knowing that it was this new generation of Maltese children who would teach their parents to laugh again.

Happy days with Uncle Sam. Uncle Sam taking them on outings, Uncle Sam playing practical jokes, Uncle Sam spoiling them rotten. Carmelina woke up in her lonely bed in the morning to find big brother standing in the doorway with the breakfast he had made for her, Nicholas endured the miseries of failing his third Latin test in a month, knowing that Uncle Sam would be waiting when he came home. It was a long time since they had all been so happy.

There had to be a catch somewhere, didn't there? It was called Pawlinu. As the oldest male of the family since Lawrence's death, it was his business to provide for everyone else. Unfortunately, Pawlinu's academic excellence at school had not translated very well into practical work and he had been unable to hold down a decent job for more than three months at a time. It was not entirely his fault. He not only had the confused demeanour of a professor without the possibility of ever becoming one, he was as short-sighted as ever, overly tall for a Maltese boy and gawkily self-conscious with it. When Pawlinu's 'problem' came up at the dinner table, halfway through Uncle Sam's stay, he had just been sent packing by the General Post Office.

"He is a good boy, a clever boy," promised Mrs Buhagiar, handing Uncle Sam a bowl of *minestra*. It sounded as though she were speaking to a nervous fiancée who was having second thoughts. "He just can't settle."

"I just haven't found the right thing for me yet,

Nanna," said Pawlinu, for the hundredth time that month. "Give me a little more time and I'll find something."

"You should come to America," suggested Uncle Sam and it was out of his mouth before he had considered how his mother would feel about this generous invitation. "They'll employ anyone there – look at my father and I! Thick as two..." Mrs Buhagiar glared across the table like the Maltese Falcon Feminised. Uncle Sam was five years old again and forgot how to finish the sentence.

"He is not going anywhere," she said, in a voice that should have ended any argument. "You're not carting him off with you."

"It's all right, Nanna, I wasn't thinking of going anywhere."

"Must I give up all my children to America? Answer me that! Must I?"

"Nanna, I'm not going to leave you." But Nanna's ire was focused on her natural son and Pawlinu might as well have been swearing his allegiance to the pepper pot.

"If that's an accusation, I didn't choose to go to America in the first place – we were sent for." Nicholas and Gregory had not yet heard Uncle Sam angry and stared down at their soup bowls in embarrassed alarm. "Remember that? Remember the letter? I just made the effort to make something of my life there, that's all."

"Yes, promising to come back in a few years. What happened to that promise? You *knew* you were never coming back." And the guilt trip had hardly started yet. "Your father died and the most we got from you was a letter saying pretty things. Your sister had to be the man of the family because there was no one else to support us. I suppose you're grateful you missed it all."

Years of unspoken resentment bubbled nicely. Uncle Sam dealt with the problem by ignoring it and turned his attention back to Pawlinu. "You could come and work with me, they always need more people. Think about it, you'd have a better standard of living." (Possibly the lack of running water was still rather grating on his nerves).

"That's it, Pawlinu," Nanna Buhagiar interjected, "go and feed the factories of America, just like my husband did. He paid enough for a few years of 'better standard of living.'"

"His death had nothing to do with that!" He really was angry with her now for trying to scare the poor kid out of it. "Look at me, I'm alive. It hasn't done me any harm." He turned back to Pawlinu. "Come on, son, what do you say?"

Pawlinu exchanged glances with Nanna, if it could be called an exchange. It was an awkward situation. A young man with few prospects who had never had the chance to travel could not help but be attracted by the idea of going abroad. He also knew that he might never be offered another opportunity and looked with horror at the prospect of years and years spent floating between menial jobs that would never satisfy him, never venturing further than a mile from his front door (and not even his own front door either for that matter). But then he thought of Nanna Buhagiar's kindness to him and how it had always hurt her that he could not bring himself to think of her family as his own. And here was Uncle Sam, taunting his mother over the dinner table but not in his usual harmless way – no respectable Maltese boy would ever raise his voice to his mother like that. It marked the man out as an outsider, a position that he did not occupy for once. It was the perfect opportunity to set the record straight.

"Thank you," he said, in an uncharacteristically grave voice, "but the family need me here. We are still recovering from a death."

Uncle Sam would not be derailed that easily. "You

can send money to support them from America, that's really not a problem. At least if you come with me you'll have something to send them. You have to think about your happiness as well, you know."

"I don't measure my happiness in dollars." Uncle Sam winced at the contempt in his voice. It was as if the young man knew exactly where to burn him.

"My offer stands, you've plenty of time to think it over."

Well, of course he ended up going. Could anyone really doubt it? In the end it was Nanna Buhagiar who persuaded him to go. It was also Nanna Buhagiar who packed his bags for him and made him up a new suit to travel to the New World in. She would have paid his one-way ticket there as well if Uncle Sam had not insisted on covering the cost himself. Only Carmelina was not surprised, knowing more than anyone else that she had too much of a heart to hold him back when it came to it, however she felt about losing him.

There were more good-byes at the dockside. "I'll come back in two years, I promise," said a somewhat guilty-looking Pawlinu with masses of humble pie to eat. We've heard that before, haven't we, Mrs Buhagiar? She just smiled and pressed a little gold crucifix into his hand, resigned to the fact that she would never see either of them – her son and her adopted son – again.

They misjudged Pawlinu. He surprised everyone (including Uncle Sam) by proving to be as good as his word. Two years later, with a tidy sum of money saved and a plethora of happy memories, he waved good-bye to both Uncle Sams and came home to Malta, only to find the house decked out in black crepe again. In the interim time, Nanna Buhagiar had tripped on the hallway rug and suffered a massive heart attack. A painless, instantaneous death and burial next to her husband in a quiet corner of the cemetery. Not a bad end to a life that took her from sleepy Sliema to Roaring Twenties America and back again.

Joy and Woe are woven fine,
A Clothing for the Soul divine...
And when this we rightly know,
Thro' the world we safely go.

Joy and woe in varied measures, but we will say a respectful farewell now. After letters from America and transatlantic voyages and cinema pictures and vandalised hats and nursing a sick husband and running for her life and gossiping with Mrs Grech and comforting a daughter and losing her sons and laughter and tears and prayers and Masses and friendships, old Mrs Buhagiar rests peacefully under an olive tree.

X

Alexandria closed her eyes and desperately tried to remember the words to the song. Sr Therezina from school said that you should always say a prayer or sing a song in moments of fear – like when you went to the dentist or were sent to the headmistress – to help you take your mind off it. For a child who spent most of her waking hours trying to take her mind off things, she had an appalling memory for words.

Heaven, I'm in Heaven.
And my heart beats so that I can hardly speak!
And I seem to find the happiness I seek
When we're out together dancing cheek to cheek.

But Alexandria was not in Heaven, she was hanging feet first from the third storey balcony of the house, rocking dizzily in midair above the empty yard. This was torture that left no marks, the threat of ending her life broken into small pieces on the stone ground hundreds and hundreds of miles below, never to grow up and run far away.

"I didn't do it," she whimpered, feeling perspiration seeping out of every pore. She knew she should not have allowed that to happen, but she couldn't help herself. It would make her slippery and he would drop her, even if he never meant to. "Please don't drop me, I didn't look at anything." But in her imagination she had already been dropped and fallen and been pronounced dead on the scene at least four times. Her mind was becoming clouded with fog. Roaring darkness again like in the cellar but worse now, so close to death, with a man shaking her just in case she was beginning to feel safe dangled by him like a laundered shirt.

Holy Michael the Archangel, defend us on the day of battle, be our safeguard against the wickedness and snares of the devil, prayed the child who was already caught in one. She did not realise she had spoken the words out loud or that her father was what the ladies described in whispered dismay as *lapsed.*

"I really am going to drop you now, spouting that nonsense at me!" He opened his hands a little so that she slipped down maybe two or three inches. It was enough to make her believe for a split second that he really had let her go and she started screaming and writhing in his grip.

"Let me go! Oh please let me go!" It took all his strength to get her back onto terra firma without actually losing hold of her. He threw her onto the tiled floor of the balcony instead with the clinical detachment of a camp commandant. She did not even cry out, relieved just to feel solid ground beneath her.

"What were you doing among my papers?" She could not understand why he hissed the words at her as though he were afraid of being overheard. He was never usually so fussy. "How many times have I told you to keep your filthy little paws away from my personal things?" It was not his 'papers' that he was worried about her touching, it was more the magazines he had found her leafing through nonchalantly when he stepped into his study. "If your mother finds out about this, I'll crucify you head down and I don't care who you tell!" She was limp and unresisting as he picked her up and threw her with considerable force against the glass top coffee table, unperturbed by the crash of shattering glass and the thought of what such a collision might do to her. "Go and show yourself to Auntie Interfering-too-good-for-the-rest-of-us-Josephine now!"

It never occurred to him in his enraged panic that he was the one who ought by rights to be apologising to her, but he was more worried about what she might blurt out than what damage that sort of material might have on an impressionable young mind. She struggled to catch her breath. Every inner voice told her not to say a word but there had been something about one of the images that sent searing needles into her stomach. She had known it was bad, it must have been for him to hide it away like that, but it had seemed horribly familiar. "Does Uncle Luigi read things like that?" she asked, without a whisper of accusation in her voice.

She noticed her father flinch though he quickly covered it up. "What did you say?" He was still angry, she thought, but surprised and a little curious. "What do you mean by that?"

She hesitated, trying to anticipate how he would respond. Her life was made up of these guessing games; she ought to be more proficient at reading him by now. It seemed to her that she might be able to reach him if she could only say it right, that he might not blame her this time. She took her life in her hands and opened her mouth to speak, but a second later Anthony and Mark came running to the doorway. The noise of her crashing through the glass table had been heard all over the house and they wanted to know what the commotion was about. Mark was eight by now and saw himself as quite the gallant female defender, running past his father to where Alexandria lay covered in slivers of glass. "Alex, Alex, are you all right?"

A wave of irritation swept over her, partly because she knew his intervention would aggravate their father, just as she had been hoping he might relent, and partly because it was such a ludicrous question to ask her when her life's blood was ebbing away. "Go away!" she hissed in his ear, but the troubling thought of a minute ago had already slipped from her mind. "Disappear!"

Her annoyance had the effect of fortifying Mark to prove himself and he turned back to his father, demanding: "Why can't you leave her alone?"

"I told you to disappear!" she insisted, trying to pull her hand away from his. She was the older one, this was her job. "Just go away, you silly boy!"

Mark held her hand a little tighter to prove his loyalty then saw his father advancing on him and jumped to his feet, losing the plot comprehensively. She covered her ears as he ran out of the room to deaden the sound of two pairs of feet thundering down the stairs and cries for help and cursing and blasphemies across the house. She felt mildly guilty that the first thought to enter her head was, "oh for heaven's sake Mark, I said go away not run away!"

When silence descended and Mark was almost certainly locked in the boys' bedroom on the other side of the house and Anthony had hidden himself in his mother's wardrobe, Alexandria stood up giddily among the carnage of the battle scene. She would have felt even more wretched if she had known how close she had come to turning her unhappy life on its head, but she told herself when she was a woman that he probably would not have believed her in the end anyway. Or he would have said it was her fault.

For the moment, she was absorbed in assessing the damage done. Her hands had taken the brunt of it because she had covered her face as she fell and her arms would be raw in the morning after dragging through the sharp edges of the frame as she broke through. Auntie Josephine certainly would have had something to say if she ever saw it, but he need not have been so concerned about that now. It said something for his paranoia that nearly three years after Auntie Josephine issued her ultimatum, Edward still believed that she was watching the children.

In fact, Auntie Josephine for all her good intentions had been notably absent since her outburst in the officers' mess, though not through any lack of good intentions. It was just that work busied her more than she would have liked it to and time passed almost without her noticing, and by the time she was able to visit the house again, Alexandria had reached the top of a steep learning curve and would not let her anywhere near her.

"It's all right, Auntie, it's all right now." Oh she had learnt a lot – what it meant to be embarrassed and ashamed, what things should and should not be seen. She had become defensive.

"I just wanted to make sure that no one's hurting you, *qalbi*, just let me have a little look at you," but the child had slipped out of her reach before she could take her by the hand.

"Don't worry, Auntie, really, it's all right since I changed school."

Josephine had to concede that she looked contented enough or rather she wanted to concede that much. She realised later – far too late – that she had never seriously believed that Alexandria was safe and that she could easily have pursued the matter. Except that at least part of her wanted to believe that it was all right. She liked to think that her furious intervention had counted for something. More than that, she wanted to believe that she had nothing further to concern herself with, that she did not have to deal with the sheer messiness of rescuing a tormented child.

And Alexandria for that matter could never have explained afterwards why she felt such an aversion to being touched or undressed. In the cruel, twisted little world of her childhood, what Luigi did to her did not yet seem so horrific, her mind could not understand how a man who smiled and embraced her could also be doing her irreparable harm. And unlike her father, who would maintain until the bitter end (and it was a very bitter end when it came, hastened by years of smoking and alcoholism) that he never did anything to be

103

ashamed of, Luigi's latent Catholic guilt complex would eventually get the better of him. One day, when Alexandria was a grown woman, he stepped into the confessional after years of absence and begged for absolution. It was only a short step from kneeling behind the grille to begging his victim for forgiveness and even a woman with some justification for hating everyone could not bring herself to hate him anymore.

For the time being, though, a smaller miracle had happened to Alexandria and she found herself in a situation that could almost be called happy. Just when she was reaching the point in her life when she was seriously beginning to wonder why she was alive at all, she fell straight into the vast and welcoming bosom of the Sisters of the Sacred Heart. She would remember it as a land of polished floors and echoing corridors and angelus bells and sport and needlework and chalk dust. For a few precious years, it would offer her something very like an ordinary childhood.

So she was not lying completely when she said that changing school made everything all right, though it did not mean what Auntie Josephine took it to mean. Home life remained what it had always been, but from the age of seven to the age of ten, she was out of the house all day every day of the working week having the time of her life. Things only proceeded to get better, because when she turned ten she became a weekly boarder, taking to the sanctuary of school like a duck to water.

School offered her something else – an outlet for her burgeoning talents. It was no good disguising the fact that Alexandria was a difficult child. She may even have been difficult if she had not had such a miserable start to life. She was what is known as hyperactive, long before the word had even been thought of and from the moment she went to school, it became clear that she was extraordinarily gifted.

And there lay the tragedy of it. It is a natural assumption that every parent must want a gifted child who will win scholarships and make them proud by being musical, artistic or athletic. Most believe that their children are gifted even when they clearly are not, but very few consider the implications of having a talented child. Such as the endless patience needed by a family in order to cope with the debit side of a child prodigy temperament.

Alexandria seldom passed a school exam with less than ninety-five percent. She could add up four five figure numbers in her head whilst she waited for the school bus. Whilst other children grappled with the Italian verb *essere*, she was reading Dante's *Inferno* in the original and debating with the teacher about the theological complexities of Canto 13. And her parents barely noticed.

They did not glow with delight at her achievements or show any inclination towards stimulating her growing mind. She was a nuisance, a mistake, and her excessive amounts of mental energy, left unappreciated and unoccupied, only made her more of a nuisance. By the age of six, Alexandria felt the need of no more than four hours sleep at night. She would sit up for hours reading and if there was nothing to read, she would get herself into scrapes trying to find something else to do.

On one occasion, she climbed on top of the wardrobe to try and reach her mother's fashion magazines, only to find that she could not get down again and the floor seemed considerably further away than she remembered. She sat wedged between the top of the wardrobe and the ceiling for over an hour, willing herself to be safely back in her bed again. She realised with a growing sense of doom that even St Jude could not get her out of such a mess and she was finally reduced to calling for her father. It showed how seriously scared she was of the drop to call for his assistance but he got her down all right. He did not bother to ask for an explanation.

On an uninspiring autumn evening, she decided to explore the grandfather clock to see where the noise was coming from. She did not actually tamper with the clock, but made the mistake of closing the glass door behind her – only to find that she was locked in. Calling for help, even her father's help, was not an option that time because the sound of her voice was drowned out by the enclosed space and the maddening bong of the pendulum. It was only when her mother came downstairs for a glass of water and saw a ghostly little face pressed against the glass, staring at her with the remorse of a lost soul, that the alarm was raised. Fortunately her father was out drinking on that particular occasion, but it was discovered that someone had lost the key. Alexandria did not think it the appropriate moment to mouth through the glass that she had buried it in a corner of the yard to see if she could grow a key tree and Antonia was eventually forced to break the glass at considerable risk to her daughter stuck against the other side of it.

The two hours she had lain under the bedclothes waiting for her father to come back and find his priceless clock in ruins were like something out of the Agony in the Garden. Cold sweat, tears, frantic prayers and not even an angel to offer comfort. The problem was that she could not decide what to pray. One moment she was praying that he would not come back until as late as possible, then she was praying that he would come back quickly so that she could get it over with. Next she prayed that the glass would mysteriously repair itself or at least that he would not notice the great jagged hole. When it occurred to her that there was no way he could possibly not notice, even if he was desperately drunk, she prayed for courage only to discover that she was actually praying that she would not need any. She was almost relieved when he came and dragged her out of bed like a startled cat.

On a sultry summer night, she climbed the yard wall so that she could try and touch the moon. Little Alexandria Sant'Angelo alone in the midnight garden, reaching up at a silver-white circle that seemed small enough to hold in the hand. Tiny hands hungry for the touch of ice suspended in the black, forbidding sky – she was sure that the moon would be cold to touch, especially on a stifling summer night. The trees hissed in conspiracy against her, the lights of the houses taunted her with their welcoming, unreachable promise of happy families in happy homes and she stretched up, precarious at the brink of a fall.

By the time Mr and Mrs Fenech next door had extracted her from their grape vines (they heard a crash and found her hanging upside down three feet in the air, the branches holding her helpfully by the ankles) she had managed to persuade them not to mention it to anyone – particularly a certain you-know-who. They sportingly joined in with the conspiracy, doing their very best to get the leaves out of her hair and to remove as much incriminating evidence as possible from her white nightie. Then Mr Fenech deposited her on the right side of the wall and wished her luck getting indoors.

It would have been perfectly all right if the back door had not been locked in the interim, forcing her to slip inside via the kitchen window. Someone had obligingly left it open just wide enough for her to reach through and loosen the catch. With a few twists and turns the window was wide enough for her to squeeze through, feet first – straight into her father's waiting arms.

A demanding child, and that was only before she went to sleep. Even when she finally nodded off, she would not be able to lie in bed until later than three or four in the morning and they could lock the doors of the house as carefully as they liked, but she would somehow find her way out into the empty streets and freedom.

"Have you ever walked the streets in the early morning, Benedict?"

"I gave up on mornings when I became a student," he answers. He looks a little brighter now, either because he is finding the subject matter a little less distressing or because he has simply got used to it.

When I look back on my incarceration in a Dorset boarding shool, I seem to remember the early morning having a certain magic to it. There was a sense of mischief in the act of slipping out of bed whilst the rest of the boarding house slept. In summer, it would already be getting light and the birds would be singing the Dawn Chorus and the air would smell fresh like a ripening fruit by the time I stepped outside.

In winter, the streets would still be in darkness and the crunch of ice under my feet would be there to greet me. Then there was the sting of the cold air against the face and the reassurance of gloves and scarf and heavy overcoat, that illegal feeling that the dark streets and the silent school buildings gave to the most innocent of wanderings.

Alexandria knew what it meant to need the cover of the early morning to shelter her. Her early morning excursions took her on a zigzag path down to the sea. She would smell bread baking and the inviting aroma of coffee percolating in the little bars where the fishermen and bakers and hunters had their breakfast before they started their work. This was a community all of its own, a band of nocturnal workers who slept by day and missed the bustle and noise when the capital city roared to life. A friendly community too in its own way, intrigued by the presence of a well-to-do little girl wandering the streets alone, but she was perfectly safe in the hands of those strangers.

At a time when children were not afraid to talk to

adults they did not know, she talked to anyone who would talk to her and let them pet her and share their breakfast with her. She quickly became a member of the family and like any child deprived of love at a young age, she revelled in the attention she received. Smiling faces, gentle hands lifting her up onto fat, comfortable laps so that she could sit and watch whilst some of the men prepared their nets and others loaded baskets with freshly baked bread.

The women used to take her to five o'clock Mass and she sat throughout the service in the black folds of old Mrs Scicluna's *ghonella,* a great big black tent of a traditional dress with a stiff headdress and a sweeping veil. Perfect for a child who enjoyed the security of being hidden away. They took her under their wing – *literally, and not always a particularly sweet-smelling wing at that*, she said much later – but it kept her out of mischief for at least part of the day.

But something was wrong with her that no amount of night-time excursions could prevent. Shortly after Alexandria's seventh birthday, members of the family noticed the appearance of tiny scratch marks suspiciously positioned at about the height of a small child, along the whitewashed walls all over the house. Even Edward could not quite bring himself to blame her for them, unable to imagine how they could be connected with her. Then months later, he heard a noise that sounded like a small animal clawing around on the upper floor and ambushed her at the top of the stairs, gnawing her way through the outside corner of one of the landing walls.

"Of all the disgusting habits this child could have picked up!" he roared to Antonia, as though she could offer some kind of an explanation for their daughter's mad habits. "I mean *biting the walls*, is she completely loopy as well as everything else?"

It was many years later when she sat in the doctor's

consulting room being diagnosed with osteoporosis that she realised she had been suffering from calcium deficiency on top of everything else. A little detective work would have revealed that the whitewash used at the time contained calcium residue and her body instinctively sought out a badly needed mineral. A hyperactive child who got herself trapped in grandfather clocks, wandered the streets in the early morning and tried to eat the walls. There is one in every family.

Whilst Benedict tries to work out the exact scientific process by which a child could have subconsciously deduced that whitewash contained calcium, I will remember Alexandria's happy school days. I will imagine what it must have been like to be top of the class at everything, showered with praise and encouragement wherever she went. Her only failing was needlework – quite a social flaw at the time, particularly for a convent girl, but she could be forgiven for that.

Well, not quite her only failing. In fact, when virtually anything happened that was not meant to, like a nun finding herself unable to move after divine office, only to discover that her belt had been interwoven around the back of her pew whilst she was in prayerful reverie, they always knew whose troublemaking hands had been responsible. And it had to be admitted that Alexandria took a while to fully understand what nuns actually were, which a young teacher of English discovered to his cost on the one morning when nothing was meant to go wrong.

"Right, girls," Father Bartoli began, "let's start with a nice easy question." He was nervous because he had only been teaching English for six months and there was an inspector sitting in the corner of the classroom, monitoring his performance. His pupils were diligent enough children but rather unpredictable, particularly when they noticed he was a little on edge. So he picked on Alexandria to answer a question, knowing that she would almost certainly get it right. "Alexandria, my dear, give me an example of male, female and neuter words in English, if you please."

Alexandria obliged him by giving a warm smile, feeling very special for being singled out. "Certainly, father. Daddy, Mummy and Nun."

The inspector stifled an unprofessional giggle in his handkerchief. "No, you know that's not right," Father Bartoli explained, feeling the beginning of unmitigated panic creeping up on him. "You know that 'nun' is female. Try again."

Any other child would have thought up another word to put in its place but Alexandria would have none of it. She just *knew* he was wrong. "Oh but father, they're not you know."

"Yes they are." A faint crimson tinge had appeared across the young priest's face. He had a nasty feeling he knew where this was going and made a pathetic attempt at saving his class. "How about 'bucket'?"

"But father, they can't be." Then, in a conspiratorial whisper, as if she had discovered some piece of top-secret information she was being generous enough to share with him. "They don't have any legs."

By this stage, the inspector had bent doubt gasping for breath, the other children were joining in the argument and Father Bartoli's lesson on gender in the English language had died a very sorry death. "Alexandria," he said with considerable dignity given the circumstances, "nuns are ladies, just like I am a man."

"Yes, I know you're a man," she said, with a dismissive wave of the hand, "I didn't say you weren't, but nuns..."

Her moments of mayhem were not usually so indiscriminate. Shortly after she became a boarder, it dawned on her that she could use her propensity to make trouble as a weapon in her campaign for self-preservation. The rules were very simple. If you were a boarder, the very worst thing that could happen to you if you misbehaved was to be grounded for the weekend, unable to leave the school premises and go home to the delights – good food, soft beds, doting parents, possibly even hot water – that would normally be waiting on a Friday night. For Alexandria though, the prospect of not going home was too good to be sniffed at and when she was practically given an invitation to be grounded, she just could not help herself fast enough.

It all started one Friday morning when Alexandria, for want of anything better to do, left a large rubber spider sitting demurely on the teacher's desk just before morning lessons began. Sr. Jacinta walked in, screamed and dropped what she was carrying, scattering the week's essays into a flurry of disordered papers. It took half an hour for the class to sort out whose work was whose (to be fair, it would have taken ten minutes if it had not been so much fun to prolong the start of the lesson) and, as always, Sr. Jacinta knew precisely who was to blame. "Put one toe out of line and you're not going anywhere tonight!" she warned in her heavy Portuguese accent.

"Hooray! Is that a promise?" cheered Alexandria, literally jumping out of her seat. And no, she was not being sarcastic or precocious, she was genuinely excited… which was lucky as the remark constituted putting a toe out of line.

After that it all seemed so incredibly easy. All she had to do was deliberately get herself into trouble on a Friday morning and she would not have to go home. At least it would have worked if the sisters had not rumbled her so quickly. It dawned on them before many weekends had passed that there was something a little odd in the timing of her bad behaviour, not to mention the lack of an obvious motive. She had always been a practical joker certainly, but she would do silly, disruptive things that were far too clumsy to have come from her imagination. She would be rude when she was normally impeccably mannered or she would perform spectacularly badly in a test when they knew she was bright enough to have passed with full marks – and always her Friday morning tests, never any others. It was not long before she found herself summoned to Mother Eugenia's office to offer some sort of an explanation and the whole story came out in a flood of tears and apologies and pleas for the reason to be taken no further than the door.

It was already too late for that. Unknown to Alexandria, the truth behind her unhappy home life was already widely speculated in the small, talkative environment of the boarding school. Classmates noticed her scars when they changed for games in the locker room, teachers raised eyebrows when they stood over her to glance at her work and she shrank away in alarm. Some suggested that something should be done, except that no one really knew if anything could be done. If Alexandria had not found herself in Mother Eugenia's office, ensuring that there was no doubt whatsoever about the matter, it is likely that she would never have been helped out of the predicament. But amid cups of tea and clean handkerchiefs they reached an agreement and Mother Eugenia found herself entering into a conspiracy. There was to be no more bad behaviour. If things were going very badly at home and she really could not face going back when the end of the week came, Mother Eugenia would send a message to her parents to say that, for some particular reason, Alexandria would have to stay at school for the weekend. They would think up some good excuses – a play rehearsal perhaps, extra tuition for exams, preferably things that were not entirely untrue or likely to make them think she was at fault in any way.

Edward must have thought she was being recruited or something, but fortunately he felt no great sorrow at her absence for long periods of time and the arrangement suited everyone, including the nuns I suspect. She became such a familiar feature feeding the birds in the convent garden or sitting with the sisters at teatime that she began to feel as if she belonged to the place. The feeling increased one day early in the school holidays when she was too frightened and wretched to stay at home any longer and ran away to school.

Running away *to* school. That just about sums up the Sant'Angelo family's ability to look after one another – children reduced to seeking sanctuary in an institution most children are desperate to spend as little time in as possible. It had been something to do with only getting seventy percent in a school exam, or at least Alex thought it was, but by the time she found herself cowering and shaking in the corner of the study feeling like there was no air left to breathe, she did not greatly care what the reason had been. She had only one thought in mind: escape by the safest exit.

This was easier said than done considering the condition she was in by then. She lay very still, listening hard for the slightest evidence of a human presence near her before struggling to a sitting position. She knew she could not stay where she was. In this little house of horrors, no experience was brutal enough to be final. She knew that it might have been simple exhaustion that made him relent when he did and he might come back to her later if he had still not calmed down, but she felt as though her limbs were tangled up in heavy weights.

A thunder of footsteps on the stairs sent her stomach lurching, but she still could not move. There was no point anyway. Even if she could haul herself to her feet in time, there was no way out and she would hit the ground again in an instant.

Shades of the prisonhouse begin to close
Upon the growing boy

Her mother hurried into the room. "Quickly, get up," she ordered, barely looking at her. "Hurry!"

"I can't," answered Alexandria, entirely without self-pity. "Everything hurts."

"Don't be silly, do get up." Antonia reached forward and helped her daughter to her feet, apparently unmoved. "Let me look at you. Well, your face doesn't look too bad. No one will notice if you keep your head down."

"Who is there to notice?" This must be what it is like to be old, she thought to herself, leaning back against a bookcase for support. Always stiff, always aching and limping, every movement a struggle. She was puzzled to feel her mother pressing a coin into her hand as though she were paying her off. "What's this for?"

"It's a bus fare," her mother explained, yanking her towards the door. "You must get out of the house before he comes back."

Alex flinched with pain and surprise. "What do you mean? Where do you want me to go?"

The response was impatient. "How should I know? Do you expect me to think of everything? Just go as far away as possible. What are you shaking for? I'm trying to save your skin."

Too late, thought Alex, tripping and stumbling down the stairs. "But shouldn't I change my clothes? Don't I need to pack a bag or something?"

She had never run away before, but she was sure it was not supposed to happen like this, walking out of the front door in the crumpled clothes she stood in without so much as a clean change of underwear. "I'm telling you to disappear for a few days. Are you stupid?"

Alex quaked in the haze of the summer evening. She was the first refugee of her family, owning nothing and with no place to go. She turned to ask what her father would make of it when he discovered she had gone, but the door closed softly behind her and she found herself alone in the street. It was almost a prophecy of the way in which she would one day leave the family home forever. She felt the first stirrings of anger and forced herself to walk away as quickly as she could

She did not think of herself as a refugee as she walked to the bus terminus. She was a resistance fighter, a secret agent out on a mission with the secret police pursuing her at every turn. It quickly occurred to her that if her father was at large, they might meet and her mother's plan of spiriting her away would have been for nothing. Why doesn't she just throw him out? She raged, bracing herself to move more quickly. Why doesn't she dump him in the street with a bus fare in his hand?

It was as she stood in the queue that she thought of where she could go but panic was at her heels again. If he knew she had run away, this was the most natural place to look. She was a resistance fighter with only one adversary but she had not covered her tracks properly and was sure she could see him everywhere. Little noises like the clatter of the ticket inspector's machine or the screech of brakes on the hot road set her nerves on edge.

It was just another of her mother's ridiculous plans anyway. What was she thinking of sending her out alone like this? He would find her and drag her out of the queue in front of everyone. She would kick and scream, begging the world and his wife to intervene, but nobody would because they would think it was her fault.

Alex glanced across at the city gate and saw a man her father's age walking along holding a child by the hand. They were laughing at some shared joke like two grown-up men sitting in a bar, their hands intertwined so naturally she wanted to go and force them apart. She knew they were taunting her, with their happy affectionate little show but it was all just a show and she took some comfort from the thought. The old never really loved their young, who came into the world just to annoy them. The child walking contentedly beside his father, talking incessantly in a way she would never have dared to, was probably as bruised as she was beneath those nice neat clothes and that cheery smile. She was not fooled.

"Are you getting on this bus or what, sabiħa?" called the bus driver. She scrambled inside, handing over her fare, but she only believed she was actually leaving Valletta when the bus jolted into motion. "Where are you going?"

There was no respite. She had fallen into enemy hands. "San Ġiljan, of course," she said, evading nicely. She knew he wasn't interested in that.

"Yes, but where?"

The man was a spy. He probably recognised her from somewhere and would take any information he wormed out of her straight back to her father. She sat back in her seat, wishing there had been place for her anywhere other than right at the front where he could keep her talking. It did not occur to her that her attempts to look nonchalant and relaxed were unlikely to cut any ice with him when her left cheek was swelling noticeably, her hair had been yanked out of its ribbons and there were bloodstains on her lilac summer dress.

"I'm going to my Nanna," she answered finally. "She is expecting me." She was sure she had been told once that if you absolutely had to lie to save your life it didn't count as a sin. Anyway, she had always liked the idea of having a Nanna, some fat cuddly old lady in black supplying sweets and wisdom like the other children had. Except that Alex's Nanna, if she had lived to be a Nanna, was English and she would have called her Grandma.

"Where does she live?" But at that moment the bus

lurched round a corner and stopped abruptly to shed a few passengers. Alex took advantage of the divine intervention and slipped to the back for the rest of the journey.

When Sr. Therezina went to answer the door, she knew something was wrong when she was still at the other end of the building. The bell would not stop ringing. Whoever it was who was standing at the door was so determined to be let in that they were tugging at the rope relentlessly, unsettling the whole house. "All right, all right, I'm coming!" she shouted, quickening her pace, whilst heads poked out from behind doors in search of an explanation.

She flung open the door and jumped visibly. She had thought it might be a drunkard in search of something to eat or some old lady in need of urgent spiritual guidance (because the more mundane the request, the more urgent it always was) or at the very worst, perhaps an accident in the street or someone taken ill. But there was Alexandria Sant'Angelo, all alone and looking ready to collapse. She took her hand and helped her inside without a word being exchanged between them

"Well of course she'll have to stay," said Mother Eugenia, when Therezina had bundled her into an anteroom whilst she sorted things out. "What was her mother thinking of shutting her out of the house like that?"

"Thank you. I'll get a bed made up for her." Therezina felt the excitement of a child who has been allowed to keep a stray kitten. "Can I let her sit in the parlour?"

"Yes. And you'd better find her something to eat. I don't imagine she's had any dinner." It was the worst moment the child could have found to burst in on them, between vespers and compline, and she felt unusually flustered. "And I suppose we ought to find her some clean nightclothes to borrow. Did you say she brought *nothing* with her?"

"Nothing at all. She said her mother gave her enough for a bus ride and told her to 'disappear for a few days' or something like that." Therezina hesitated before broaching another subject. "I don't suppose she could have a bath, could she? She's really rather a mess."

And so it was that after a bite to eat, Alexandria found herself running a warm bath. Sr. Therezina had handed her a bottle of lavender oil to put in the water but it had no label and she could not make out how much she was supposed to put in, so she walked back into the parlour in her petticoat to ask for guidance. The community was enjoying a little recreation time before bed and looked up in unified alarm as she appeared in the doorway. "Excuse me," she asked politely, "am I supposed to put the whole bottle in or just a little bit? There seems to be rather a lot." A row of normally placid faces stared back at her in silent horror. "Have I done something wrong?"

What she did not realise was that she already looked as though she was covered in oil. Her whole body appeared to be streaked with petrol that had made patterns of black and purple and yellow and blue over every inch of her flesh, so that it was impossible to imagine that she had ever looked any different. The scanty covering of an elegant lacy petticoat that should have made her look like a properly brought up little girl, only served to make the sight more disgusting.

Therezina remembered that she was supposed to be responsible for Alexandria and found her voice. "Let me help you with that, darling," she said, leading her quickly out of the room.

She returned when she had deposited Alexandria safely in the scented bath. "I don't want to alarm anyone, but I think you might have to call a doctor," she explained, in a voice that was trying unsuccessfully to be pragmatic. "I really don't think she's very well."

Mother Eugenia had no desire to involve more people than was necessary. The situation was awkward enough as it was. "You're the school nurse, Therezine, can't you deal with it?"

"I don't think so." She swallowed, keeping the sight firmly out of her mind. "She has a burn on her knee that's festering. I could dress it but there are other things. I think she might need stitches. There's an injury on her shoulder I don't like the look of. I'm not really equipped…"

Therezina got her ready for bed and stayed with her all the time the doctor was there. She promised Alexandria on the soul of her mother not to tell anyone anything that happened, particularly that Alexandria had turned out to be afraid of needles and was reduced to biting the ear of an abandoned teddy bear whilst the doctor made no fewer than three stitches in her shoulder. He had had the annoying habit of telling her each time that it was the last one in a bid to reassure her until she was sure the ordeal would never end. But Therezina barely remembered that she had shown fear. She was used to dealing with terrified girls trying to worm their way out of vaccines or nasty medicine and would barely have registered it if it had been anyone else. What really struck her was how passive the child had been even when she was quite obviously in pain.

"You don't have to keep quiet just to please us," she promised, but it seemed to be force of habit. Ironically it made her difficult to treat. The doctor had to rely on the slightest of whimpers and intakes of breath to discern that a rib had probably cracked or a muscle strained in the act of falling badly. For a normally boisterous child the silence was chilling. She would not even answer their questions and the doctor eventually

120

gave up getting any information from her and gave her a sedative, knowing that she would never be able to sleep without help.

"I've never seen anything like it in my entire medical career!" he thundered at the sisters, as though it had been all their doing. That was not entirely right. During the war he had pulled a child out from the ruins of a school and she had looked about as battered as that, but she had been quiet because she was in shock. "If it had been much worse I would have had to have her admitted to hospital." His air of gentle paternalism had evaporated the moment after he had ruffled Alexandria's hair and wished her sweet dreams. "I don't suppose an explanation might be in order?"

They told him all they knew, not just what Alexandria had told them but what they had heard from the other girls, from outside staff, the rumours and fragments that were bandied about in the playground and staff room. "I suppose it should be with the police," Mother Eugenia acknowledged, when they came to the end, "but apparently they already know about it. No one seems interested."

"They should be, she's not safe in that house!" The doctor thought of the number of cases that went through the courts involving men being sent down for months at a time for getting into fights with other grown men and yet he could not see how this situation could be repaired. Even if the man were convicted of a crime and went to gaol, the only real victims would be his family left without a breadwinner and in eternal disgrace.

"I don't think I could be easy in my mind if I left this place without having some assurance from you that she will be taken care of. Can she stay here?"

"Of course. She practically lives here in term time anyway. It's just that..." Mother Eugenia trailed off. "Well, it's just that if she decides to go back or he comes for her, we will have to let her go."

The doctor allowed himself to be reassured. "Well, why would she choose to go back to such a home?" he asked. Mother Eugenia wondered whether he had any understanding whatsoever of the way children formed their loyalties and ideas. She knew even if he did not that Alexandria would choose to go home long before her father thought to claim her.

I remember a house where all were good to me

For the moment Alexandria had no thought of going anywhere. She woke up early next morning after a long dreamless sleep, eased into waking by the feeling of the sun filtering through the grey curtains onto her face. Whatever it was the doctor had given her, she felt more than usually comfortable after such an experience, as long as she did not make any sudden moves. The sound of women's voices singing made her wonder seriously for a moment whether she might be dead. It was not so much the sensation of being comfortable, rather the sensation of feeling very little that made her think that... and the fact that she felt so safe.

It slipped her mind that they were all early risers in this house and she imagined that it must be late in the morning for them all to be up at prayer and she struggled out of bed. That hurt. The moment her feet touched the cold floor she felt the familiar sensation of juddering nerves and twisted muscles. The sudden cold made her gasp for breath, starting up a sharp pain in her ribs. She half-contemplated trying to get back into bed again, but curiosity won as it always did and she made her way to the door, wafting out into the corridor in an absurdly oversized nightdress.

It had not occurred to her to get dressed first, but then she could not have done if she wanted to. Her clothes had been hurried to the laundry for emergency repairs and she had nothing else to wear except this tent, which she thought must belong to someone about Mother Eugenia's size. She fluttered down towards the sound of singing and got as far as the chapel door before a hand touched her arm, sending her spinning round in alarm.

"Sssh, it's only me!" whispered Sr. Therezina, pulling her away from the door. "What are you doing out of bed? You're supposed to be resting."

"It's late," Alexandria explained, trying to ignore the sinking feeling that she had done the wrong thing again. "I thought I should be up."

"It's very early and you certainly shouldn't be up." Alex let herself be led back to her room with not a little regret. "I want you to get back into bed, then when we've finished prayer I'll get you some breakfast. Are you in pain?"

"Yes," Alex responded matter-of-factly. "Can't I go in with you?"

Therezina imagined her in a downsized habit for a moment and smiled. "I don't think so, darling, it's definitely not for you." She helped her into bed and changed the subject. "Try not to move about too much. How's the shoulder this morning?"

"Fine, absolutely fine." Actually, it felt as if a large spiky insect had attached itself to her, but she was wide awake by now and felt faintly irritated to be back in amongst the bedclothes again. But then, it had not occurred to Therezina, as the image of Alexandria the nun flashed through her mind, that little Alex had been imagining exactly the same thing, though she saw herself striking a rather more romantic pose in elegant layers of black and white, walking down the silent corridors in pious reverie.

Over the months and years that followed, Alex became a regular guest at the convent. She would appear out of the blue, wounded in battle, and wait for

Sr Therezina to come to the door and rescue her. In spite of the name she had chosen at her profession, Therezina was Irish and Alexandria came to associate her easy-going Irish lilt with safety and comfort. For years afterwards, the sound of a County Cork accent brought back memories of pious stories, sweets, holy pictures and a comfy bed with sheets smelling of starch and lavender oil. She came to long to be a part of this secret, peaceful little world she could only know as a visitor, where there were no raised voices and where she never felt afraid, where time hardly seemed to pass.

She would stay as long as she needed to stay, for several weeks at a time on some occasions, but as Mother Eugenia had predicted right at the start, she always found herself going home in the end. She would think of Mark and Anthony and the others and know that they were living in fear in the house without her to take the brunt of it all. And the real tragedy for her was that a violent home was still home and a tyrannical father still the only kind of father that she would ever have. So she would go back and be beaten into the ground again and run back to the sisters and they would patch her up and nurse her back to health, then she would go back home again, on and on in a cycle of suffering that was to last until she was a woman.

"I can't make sense of it." I know I should be able to somehow but I am not sure it is meant to make sense. It gives me a feeling of safety to say it, as though only a psychopath or a saint could find a reason for all of this misery. "You're a scientist," I remind Benedict, in case his years of study had disappeared from view. "Give me reasons. Give me answers."

He is very quiet. I wonder for a moment if he has fallen asleep but he opens his eyes very slowly. "I wish people were that simple. Why did she go back?"

"I told you."

124

"That's what doesn't make any sense. She had a place to stay – why did she go back?"

He is puzzled by a question I barely think relevant. "Because she couldn't help herself, I suppose." Irritation takes over again. "Oh come on, were your parents never desperately unhappy at home but couldn't bear the idea of leaving?"

"No, not at all. Not like that anyway." He sounds appalled at the prospect, which annoys me even more.

"Oh come on, Benedict, don't give me that!"

"What?!"

"Don't tell me your parents had completely idyllic childhoods, because no one has. It can't have been all beach holidays to Blackpool and boating trips on the Norfolk Broads and candyfloss and fairgrounds and roaring fires and cottages with rose creepers?"

"Well, funnily enough – " He looks faintly embarrassed, as if he needs to apologise for having a family who were charmingly normal. "I don't know how you manage to say so much in one breath."

"It's all right, your family couldn't help being unsportingly happy," I explain, rescuing him, "they didn't grow up under a curse."

"Oh no, not this again." He still doubts it after all I have told him, but there is plenty of time yet for him to understand.

It was fortunate for Alexandria that she never thought to share her dreams of a vocation with her father, or we might have a murder to recall as well as everything else... except that I would not be able to recall it. She told no one, weaving her little dreams in secret. She was going to be a nun. More than that, she was probably going to be a saint. She was St Therese, the Little Flower. She would enter the convent when she was fifteen and die of consumption by the time she was twenty-four. Or she might be a little more militant,

125

travel to some war zone somewhere to be a missionary sister in a sub-Saharan field hospital.

As her thirteenth year drew to a close, she plucked up the courage to broach the subject with Mother Eugenia, who at that time was struggling through a backlog of school reports. For obvious reasons, however, she always had time for Alexandria and called her into her study expecting the worst. "Is everything all right? Are you in trouble?"

"No Mother, not at all," she answered, but now that she had taken the plunge and knocked on the door, she was having trouble getting the words out. "May I sit down?"

"Of course. Whatever is it?" Alexandria had many problems, but being tongue-tied was not normally one of them. She reached instinctively for the pile of clean handkerchiefs she kept in her top drawer behind the bottles of ink and paperclips.

"I wanted to talk to you because – because I've been thinking a little about my future." That sounded grown up, she thought, she will be impressed with that poised, impeccably constructed sentence.

"Yes?"

She rushed straight in. "And I think I might have a vocation. What's it like to be a Mother Superior?"

Mother Eugenia stifled a chuckle. It would not do to laugh at the poor child but she was the most unlikely vocation since Moll Flanders. "You can't have a vocation to be a Mother Superior, dear. You might have a vocation to the religious life and be called upon later on in life to be a Mother Superior. It works in that order."

Alexandria looked somewhat crushed. She had never realised there was any evolutionary element to the religious life. She had somehow got it into her head that girls entered at a particular level and just stayed there: some were called to be novices, others a little

126

higher up and a select few were called to run the place. "You mean if God's calling me to be a Mother Superior, I can't jump the queue even then?"

Mother Eugenia stared down at the cluttered surface of her desk and conquered a brewing fit of the giggles with true Christian valour. "Alexandria, we have a vow of humility in our order."

"Oh, I'd be a humble Mother Superior, don't worry about that." But the prospect of having to be a postulant and then a novice and then a nun and then maybe after years and years a mother superior was rather off-putting. She had not anticipated the time scheme or the possibility that, after all those years of waiting, she might never get the prize of a place on the front pew in chapel or being in charge of everyone else.

"Don't look so disappointed." She had not anticipated that the girl would be so crestfallen. "You are welcome here whenever you need us but you will never be one of us." Where is the consolation in that? thought Alex, feeling the beginnings of bitterness. *I will belong, I know I will.* "You feel that you belong here because you feel safe and everyone loves you, but that doesn't mean you're meant to stay here." It sounded too harsh, she thought, the child couldn't take it. "Listen, please don't take this too badly, you'll be glad I said this to you one day."

"I have nowhere else to go," she answered, turning to look out of the window. She was speaking the truth of the matter without realising what it meant. "I don't feel right anywhere else."

She looked out at the distant view of the trees and the great grey sky stretching to eternity over the convent walls. She knew it ought to be telling her something, but all she could see was the little convent garden with its shrine and its bird table and the rows and rows of plants she had taken such care of when she had stayed there. She felt the ache of rejection. "Don't take this badly, Alex, I would like nothing more than for you to stay here but I don't think you will even stay in Malta that much longer."

Mother Eugenia wished fervently afterwards that she had stopped herself in time, because Alexandria had been startled and it was too difficult to explain that it had just been a teacher's intuition. She had simply known, watching the girl growing up that she was meant to be somewhere else. She was too unsettled, too restless. Even her mischief-making when she ought to have been too brutalised to stick her head above the parapet, had the hallmarks of a person desperately seeking out new territory.

I suppose I owe it to this person that I ever came to be born. But just to make things extraordinarily complicated, at around the same time Alexandria was being persuaded that the religious life was not for her, Nicholas was being persuaded that it was.

XI

Nicholas did not think of his school as a sanctuary. In fact, by the time he had battled through his first year, he was sure that Evelyn Waugh's belief that *'anyone who has ever been to a public school will feel comparatively at home in prison'* was quite correct. Not the British public school system that Waugh was referring to, though, the made-in-Malta equivalent and a boy whose Papa was not a doctor or a barrister was in for a rough time. Carmelina's inability to donate large sums of money to building work and restoration projects was a persistent source of hassle throughout her son's unremarkable academic career at – well, he called it Colditz. Added to that were his humble origins. His father could just about be excused for being dead and unable to attend prize-giving or parents' meetings, but he had been a sailor, barely able to read and write, not even a proper officer or anything.

And as a final insult, the horrors of Colditz – fear and cold showers and assembly and detention and bullying by boys and teachers alike and failure and the general crushing of the human spirit – were not even particularly exceptional at the time. It would have been a bit too much if Nicholas had had a happy family life and a happy education though and at the end of the day there was the bus ride back to Sliema and the short walk home. Out of the topsy-turvy worlds my parents inhabited in their early years, I know which one I would have chosen, had I had the unfortunate choice between being tortured at home and tortured at school. His school experience could at least be blamed on the climate of the times or words to that effect but it is impossible to find sufficient excuse for a childhood more violent and traumatic than that of many children who grew up on battlefields.

Nicholas had another escape as well, right on his doorstep – the youth club for boys run by the Salesian fathers. After school, he and his brother would take the short walk to Don Bosco Street, where a recreational world of sports fixtures, catechism and the boys' brigade awaited.

On a particularly significant afternoon in Nicholas's life, the Oratory was its usual hive of activity. Boys gathered in groups around the hall, talking and playing games. There was plenty to do; football and pinball machines, a snooker table and a wireless set in the corner where the boys could listen to the Hit Parade. Behind a counter, Brother Kevin from Kerry was selling bottles of pop and packets of crisps, and outside in the playground, another young brother was making shambolic attempts at organising a game of football. Gregory was vying with Simon Borg to play goalkeeper, whilst the other potential members of the team became distracted by a bird that someone had caught in a trap and left the concrete pitch altogether. It turned out to be a homing pigeon and they had to let it go. Anyway, Fr Francis took his patron saint's sentiments to heart and didn't approve of such things. When the pigeon was safely airborne again, the cardboard box propped up by a stick attached to a length of string was unceremoniously confiscated and thrown into the dustbin with the food wrappers and vegetating apple cores.

In the meantime, fourteen-year-old Nicholas sat in Fr Jonathan's office concluding a meeting that would change his life. He was drawn to the same sort of life that Alexandria had dreamed about in her unhappiest hours, but it was no such safety blanket for him. In fact, it had been Gregory's idea to start with, suggested during one of their many whispered conversations when they were supposed to be asleep.

They had joined a group of aspirants to the priesthood for a year, meeting every week for discussions, talks and prayer. They were not committed to anything, many lost interest and dropped out once the novelty wore off, others joined them and a year on, after much discussion at home, Nicholas put his name forward to join four other boys, including Gregory, to go to England after his O-levels and begin preliminary studies for the priesthood.

There was only one question Fr Jonathan had asked that he hesitated to answer. "You are sure you're not doing this to be near your brother, aren't you?"

"Of course," he answered, but the question had hit a nerve. "Why would I do that?" It was an occupational hazard of being a twin, particularly an identical twin, that it was deemed impossible to be an individual. One was always thought to be following the other, one living in the other's shadow. "I've made my own mind up about this, father."

"I'm sure you have." He half-regretted asking, knowing that the boy must seldom have been credited with doing anything for himself. "I had to ask. You need to be thinking about these things in the years to come. It's all about discerning what God is calling you to do."

"I know." Nicholas had a reputation for being a pious child and he looked particularly angelic then, a little diminutive in size, his expression characteristically bewildered. "I want to do the right thing."

Fr Jonathan smiled at his tone. "Well, that's good enough for now, isn't it?" But as Nicholas left the room, his confessor found himself thinking that the boy was almost too innocent to be a priest. He had come to know him through his involvement with the youth club and the aspirants group and knew that he had no guile in him at all. He was that rare thing: a person who saw goodness everywhere and who was himself so delightfully transparent that he could not hide any fault in himself even if he had the desire to do so. Whether he became a priest or not, Fr Jonathan had the unhappy feeling that Nicholas would be badly hurt one day and he sincerely hoped that he would not indirectly have been a part of it.

Years later, when Nicholas had indeed been hurt by life, it seemed to him that it had been a mistake to go to England, but a mistake that he would have made all over again if he had had the chance. Because he also knew that he could never have watched his brother go far away on such an adventure without him. They were inseparable, sharing the many details of their growing lives without even realising it: education, sport, household tasks, dreams, spirituality. They had been baptised together, confirmed together, tested one another on their catechism.

"Who made you?"

"God made me."

"Why did God make you?"

"God made me to know him, love him and serve him in this world and be happy with him in the next."

"Forever. Careful Nick, you always forget that word."

"Sorry. It's a big word – forever. I'm not sure I like it."

"Who cares if you don't?"

"Big things are difficult to get the head round."

"Everest's big, space is big. Not liking it won't make them disappear."

"Fr Jonathan told you that, clever dick."

They had argued together, served at the altar together. So it had seemed quite natural that they should have gone to the junior seminary together. Even if Nicholas had not been drawn to the priesthood – and he could never deny that he had, even in his darkest moments – it would have been unquestionable for him to do anything different.

And it all felt so right. With his ticket to England booked, Nicholas began performing better at school, driven by the need to do well in his exams if he was to take up his place. But beyond that there was the promise of a world he had only ever glimpsed in books and the nostalgic memories of ex-pat ladies who came to the house to be measured for ball gowns. A world of green hills and country cottages and cream teas and red, noisy double-decker buses and cricket on the village green and tormented poets.

Oh to be in England, now that April's there!

He could not yet see that the end of his happy family life was also in sight and that when he and Gregory returned to Malta after a five-year absence, they would feel like visitors in their own home. He had never travelled abroad before, except on the ferryboat to Gozo and could hardly help the urge to explore. It was an instinct in all of them. Wanderlust, the call of the sea, the yearning for the big wide world beyond the bay. The Wandering Maltese could never be still. Even Carmelina who had lost a husband, a brother, an adopted son for a time and even her father who signed his own death warrant in an American factory, knew that she must surrender the boys she loved to England now. It was their turn to join their fathers and make a home far away from her, and it was some consolation that they were going away to consecrate themselves to God, even though she could not understand why they had to go to a godless country to do it.

There were lots of things she knew she would never understand. She had the sense that she was getting old, watching them pack their things – such a few things as well, but that was in keeping with a family tradition too. It seemed like yesterday and a hundred years ago all at once since she had to read the letter to her mother summoning them abroad. More than a hundred years, another life. There were careful preparations to be made again and a tearful farewell Mass but they would not have the long arduous journey she had. No cramped transatlantic liners for them, no Ellis Island, no trains and donated money for tickets. They would be flying to their New World in the very latest in long-distance transport. There would be people to meet them at their destination, it had all been so perfectly organised. They had it easy, she would like to have said, as everyone always says of the younger generation. Then she remembered that they would be travelling without her.

The night before they left, they said the family rosary together as they had done every night for as long as the boys could remember. Pawlinu swallowed his macho pride long enough to hold Rosaria's hand because she was taking the departure of her brothers worst of all and he had to keep saying the prayers for her when it was her turn to lead because her eyes filled with tears and her voice broke. There was already one empty chair sitting poignantly in the corner, still smelling faintly of Nanna Buhagiar's lilac water. Meetings and partings, the essence of human existence – especially for this migrant people – but Rosaria was too young to understand that yet and was still struggling to get to the end of the mystery of the Incarnation without a hiccup.

Carmelina did not cry. Later, when the boys had both gone to bed, she stood in the doorway of their room and watched them sleeping. She had seen them like that so many times that it was a struggle to take in the enormity of watching them sleeping in her home for the last time. Gregory had still not grown out of the habit of sleeping with both his feet sticking out from under the bedclothes and she covered them up, wondering whether schoolmasters in England would think of doing something like that for him when they walked up and down the dormitory at night. She suspected not; he would have to wake up with the cold.

"Better send them plenty of food, Lina," a neighbour had warned when she heard the news. "English boarding schools are barbarous places. They treat them like little soldiers."

Carmelina had done her best to dismiss the warnings her friend gave her, which were extremely graphic and lifted almost entirely from *Tom Brown's Schooldays*. It was not how she had been told it would be and she comforted herself that they would at least be together if the worst came to the worst. Nevertheless, she wasted a good deal of time in the months after they left, attempting to read between the lines of their letters home for warnings of ill-treatment.

When she went to wake them on the morning of their departure, she was stung to find them already up and dressed, checking through their provisions for the journey (paper bags again but it was more convenient for them that way). There was a callous lack of sentimentality in their behaviour. They were even talking as though it were just another morning and they were preparing for a school day or an outing to the beach. It did not occur to them that she had desperately wanted to wake them up herself that morning, to kiss their sleeping heads as they lay curled up under the bedclothes. She stifled the disappointment of a lost moment and made their breakfast with an inordinate amount of care, watching them eating and talking as though her concentration might hold back the ticking clock.

The setting of Luqa Airport made for a less moving farewell than the dockside and Carmelina stood with the glum group of mothers as Gregory and Nicholas joined up with the boys who were to be their classmates for the next five years – Victor Bonello, Lawrence Scicluna, John Attard, Guze Debono. They waved back as they climbed aboard but neither party felt as if it was really good-bye. Carmelina would have plenty of time to think of that when she went back to a house with two more empty chairs and two empty beds and mugs and plates and books without owners.

The boys, on the other hand, had not felt it yet. They pressed their faces against the window to catch a last glimpse of mother and Malta and they felt a tremor of emotion to watch the last square of land disappear (like grandmother like son like absolutely un-thought-of-at-the-moment daughter of the future) but the excitement of soaring thousands of feet into the air and being steadily engulfed in cloud deadened the pain of separation.

Now is the hour, when we must say good-bye,
Soon you'll be sailing far across the sea.
While you're away, oh please remember me...

Or so the old song goes, capturing all the poignancy of the boat passing out of sight into the deep. Being whisked away into the deep blue sky was too shocking for young first time travellers. But they did remember the mother they left on the dusty ground and may even have spared her a thought when they arrived deep in the organised chaos of London. And if it was not quite Wordsworth's London, it all looked terribly exciting, seen through the murky window of a bus. Fortunately for them, their first day in England proved to be a sunny afternoon and they were only a little chilly by comparison with the Mediterranean island they had left behind that morning.

The jovial mood of the twins only began to ebb when the journey showed no sign of ending. Like Mrs

136

Buhagiar before them, they had no notion of distances and were of the opinion that Yorkshire was perhaps five or six miles outside the airport. Three hours into the journey, Nicholas was beginning to wonder whether the whole journey was not some sort of theological exercise. Maybe the endless roads and chimneys and green fields and that persistent rumble of wheels beneath them was meant to give them some notion of what eternity must be like. The true horror of hell might be that it was full of longed-for exotic things, greenery and wide open spaces, but they could never end and then the mind would begin to numb and sicken at the sight of them. Mother's provisions, all so distinctly Maltese – *galletti* (crackers) with peppery cheeselets, Maltese bread packed with olives and capers – disappeared through boredom and hunger and seemed suddenly to contain so much more pathos than the action of stepping aboard a plane. When would they ever eat an olive again? When would they next feel the tough, crackling texture of Maltese bread between their teeth or the spicy sensation of curdled cream and black pepper at the backs of their mouths? They huddled together in the chill of the school bus, silently aware of a chapter of their lives slamming shut.

Long after darkness fell, the bus came to a reluctant halt. They had slept for the last part of the journey and could not remember exactly where they were, staggering sleepily outside where they were greeted by the unexpected cold of a late summer night in England. Whilst the big Scottish priest who met them at the airport moved towards the building they had huddled near, promising to get the doors opened and to check that everything was ready, five very sad Maltese boys stood together in the darkness, feeling the discouraging sensation of icy rain pattering against their faces.

The schoolhouse, which they presumed was the name of the ghastly building beside them, looked about as welcoming as Castle Dracula in the rain and darkness, a vast crumbling structure towering over them like a metaphor for the human condition. Victor forgot propriety and began to cry but Nicholas felt too completely bewildered and empty to be moved. The outside world simply could not be real. The previous evening, he had been sitting in his warm, honey-coloured house, praying the rosary amid the smell of candles and Nanna Buhagiar's lilac water. By some hideous twist of destiny, he was standing on wet grass, damp curls of hair falling into his eyes under a canopy of darkness, about to make his home in possibly the most unhomely place he had ever seen in his life.

"Why am I here?" he whispered to Gregory, feeling sure he would have an answer.

Gregory had slipped into sardonic mode to muffle his shock. "Well," he said. "First, I think there were the dinosaurs, then other forms of lesser life. Homo Sapiens appeared on the planet in around…"

"No, no, I mean, why am I here?"

"To love and serve God and to be happy with him…"

"But why do I have to be happy with him *here?*"

"Oh I see. Isn't there something in the Gospel about taking up your cross? I think you might have to offer it up." Nicholas glowered at him, unable to enter the game for perhaps the first time in his entire life. Gregory did not miss a beat. "If you don't think you've sinned enough, you could offer this up for someone else's soul."

And with that, they were shepherded in silence through the front door.

XII

No one – for better or for worse – ever forgets their first morning in a new country. Nicholas and Gregory certainly never forgot. The first sensation Gregory was aware of as the layers of sleep unwrapped themselves from around him – or rather, the first non-sensation – was that he could not feel his feet, whilst Nicholas opened his eyes and thought he must have been arrested in the night. The ceiling was all wrong. He knew that there should be a crack down the middle where Gregory's shoe had struck it during a game of indoor football and it should be whiter with a patch of soot in the corner from the nightlight.

As the rest of the dormitory came into focus, he received his second shock. Whatever had become of Nanna Buhagiar's hefty old furniture, the chest of drawers, the wardrobe with the broken mirror, the ottoman box? What about the mannequin covered in a sheet that his mother used to work on but which they had always thought was a ghost when the nightlight burnt out and they were still wide awake? Instead, he was surrounded by rows of beds on either side of him, each one exactly the same – metal frame, horsehair mattress, striped sheets and a slightly varied shape and colour of head slumped on each of the uniform white pillows.

He closed his eyes again and thought that it might all be a bad dream, but the encroaching cold of the morning had started prickling its way through the insufficient bedclothes and he shivered. No, this was definitely not home. He was too cold. He was stiff and uncomfortable from sleeping in a hard, unfamiliar bed, and instead of the sound of his mother pottering about the kitchen or the whistle and rumble of John the milkman and his cart, there was an eerie silence punctuated by discordant snoring.

"Gregory?" he whimpered, peering out from under the sheet for the second time. At least his brother was still lying in the bed next to him. If he had been accidentally transported into the world of *Nicholas Nickleby* overnight, he at least was not alone. "Gregory!"

"Ssssh!" Gregory had curled up into a heap of linen and stuffed his head under the pillow. He too was trying to pretend that he was hallucinating.

"Gregory? Greg!"

"No, I don't know the answer and I can't think of anything funny to say. So don't ask."

Nicholas sat bolt upright, ignoring the chill. A horror too terrible to name had raised his blood pressure enough to warm him. "Listen, we can go back, can't we?" He had suddenly remembered the time span involved in this enterprise, the endless mornings he would wake up cold and uncomfortable, far away from the heavenly sights and smells and noises of that idyll he had so recently and unresistingly left. "We can just tell them, can't we?" There was a way out. There was always a way out.

"Don't be daft," came a mumbled reply. "We're in England now. We can't go back just like that."

Nicholas felt panic and outrage welling up in him. To think, he had walked to that plane like a lamb to the slaughter – like a lamb to the *freezer*! He could have locked himself in his room, he could have kicked and screamed and fought to keep himself at home where he belonged... in fact, now that he thought about it – and this *really* made him cringe with fury – he could have just said 'I'm sorry I don't want to go', quietly and politely and that would have been that.

"Gregory, why am I here?"

"*Marija,* not again!" Gregory slammed his hands

over his ears, but he was not to be allowed any peace. A moment later, the ringing of a bell jolted them out of bed and they found themselves joining a queue of reluctant, yawning boys at the end of the dormitory, waiting to wash. "Lordy, what hairy legs this lot have got!" chimed Seamus O'Reagan, a blonde Belfast boy in the second year, as the Maltese posse huddled around the sinks. "I hope you brought plenty of shampoo with you." There were peels of laughter all round.

"Sorry, how embarrassing!" answered Gregory, casting a pointed glance over the rest of the group, "I didn't realise we were in the girls dormitory." Well heigh-ho for multiculturalism.

Nicholas was simply glad of the diversion. Moving around meant having no time to think. There was some comfort in the scrambles into uniforms that chafed with newness, the futile searches for combs and socks and other bits and pieces they were so sure they remembered packing. Then breakfast in a vast refectory, toast and tea already cold by the time they had found their way down two flights of stairs and three almost identical corridors.

The question only rose in his mind again when they were sitting down, but then his attention was distracted by the sight outside the large bay window in front of them. On the other side of the glass, the spell of the early morning fog was breaking slowly and they could make out the garden with its flowerbeds bulging with late summer flowers and the rows of trim hedges making paths everywhere. The path they had been driven down late the night before was lined with beech trees (though they did not know the name yet) and in the distance, there were green fields, vast, freedom-making tracts of land rolled out at their feet like an invitation.

If Nicholas was still hankering after limestone houses and palm trees and the sun gold-dusting the sea, he at least thought for a moment that he needed enough time to explore the place properly, so that he could tell his friends back at the Oratory what it was like to run barefoot through green grass and climb trees like *Swallows and Amazons* and wade in rivers. He gave himself a week, just for the experience and failed to notice his brother stealing the last slice of toast from his plate.

"You always get like this when you're about to talk about your mother's family," comments Benedict, turning back to look at me. He has been sitting with his back to me so that he can sit with his legs dangling into the sea. "Don't think it's not obvious."

"I'm sure I don't know what you mean." I could have come up with something a little more original than that.

"You're in denial."

"I am not in denial." There is no point in trying to argue with a statement like that. Either I agree and he wins or I disagree and he still wins, because it proves that I really am in denial. I denied it. I try the pretentious artist approach. "I'm tired, that's all. It is too much of a strain on my creative energies to describe sixty years of history all in one go like this."

"Yes, but like I said, only when you're describing your mother's family. You gallop away with the story at other times."

"So I do, clever of you to pick up some method in my madness." When I take that tone, he knows he has won, so I change tack again, like an actor slipping from one mask to the next. "Method. Of course, that's the problem. I lack routine with all this moving about. Too many questions and interruptions. I can't work like this."

Benedict looks incredulous. "I have hardly said a word! If you're tired, stop for a bit."

He has said that before, as though it were that easy, but I cannot stop now and hope to take up the threads again later. The story has me by the throat and I cannot simply put it down. It must put me down when it has the power to do so and that will not come yet. Not just yet.

Nicholas and Gregory must be left to their own devices for a while and learn to live their new lives unrecorded. By the time they enter the narrative again, they will feel as though they have lived in an English boarding school for years. I would like to stay there, reliving every tiny detail of their first few months in this startling new world, but find myself called back against my will to a house in Valletta – a house in which Robespierre would no doubt have felt at home – where Alexandria Sant'Angelo was coping with the trials of growing up.

The transition from childhood to adulthood is popularly a difficult time, even for young people living out their lives in relative safety. For Alexandria, it was almost impassable. At fifteen, with the fifties drawing to a close, youth culture was in the process of being invented. It should have been a good time to be her age – except that she was not allowed to wear make-up and her father periodically threw her lipstick and rouge out of the window. That would have been a minor consideration, but she was rarely allowed out either, had no option about the clothes she wore and her choice of music was enough to send little bits of black vinyl flying across the room.

"Bloody English rubbish!" her father would roar, shouting an English swearword in English as he cursed English cultural influences. And his almost post-colonial identity crisis had barely begun. "As if we don't have a culture of our own!" *Crunch!* There would be none of her favourite music left. "Not satisfied with good Mediterranean music, eh? Have to look to London for your entertainment!" *Crunch! Crunch!* "We are the people of Puccini and Verdi and – and- "

"We're not," answered Alexandria quietly. Another

crunch of splintering record, this time over the back of her head. There was only so much violence a growing child could take before the threat of it ceased to be an issue of much importance. He would have done it anyway. "We're not Italian either." She ducked out of the way as the last remnants of her music collection spun in her direction. She stood and watched impassively as he proceeded to throw her record player against the wall and stamp up and down on it. *Bloody, bloody, bloody English rubbish!* As shards of metal flew out from under his boots, she spared a thought for Mark who had put up some of the money for this pitiable machine, but the sight of his white face peering in from the doorway assured her that he would not be angry. Not with her for provoking her father for the umpteenth time, certainly not with their father whom he would only defy when the old man was floating in and out of consciousness in an intensive care unit, too weak to threaten any of them any more.

Gentle Mark who by some ugly twist of the family curse would find no way either of reconciling himself with his father or of building a life away from him. Mark who wet the bed until he was fourteen and who stammered and hated to sleep without the light on. Looking at him wavering in the doorway, caught between the desire to run from the scene of carnage and the outraged duty to defend his sister (and his record player), it would have been impossible for Alexandria to believe that he would grow into an embittered man whose only strength was in his ability to hate everyone and everything. Impossible to think that one day, when the phone rang summoning him to the hospital, he would shout down the line at the same girl he had once felt such impotent pity for: "I will *not* take part in some obscene bedside reconciliation! I *will not* give that man the luxury of a peaceful end!"

Alexandria on the other hand felt her rage at the

precise moment she had cause to be angry. By the time Alexandria was to be seen having her most prized possession (and her attempt to live the harmless happy-go-lucky life of other girls her age) smashed to smithereens, she, Anthony and Mark had been joined by Joseph, a delightful baby brother whose existence served only to show how different things might have been. The four of them were a reminder that a well-to-do family living in a more than comfortable house with plenty of room for children to play in might have been idyllically happy. The 'if onlys' and 'might have beens' trace a path to a house filled with the sounds of children laughing and playing, to a model father, tall, strong and handsome whom they could so easily have adored... but then, Edward was a cursed man who bore cursed children or just an evil man plain and simple whose children never stood a chance. So instead, his children grew up to hate him and they ran away one by one. The prison house in Valletta where children cried lies almost empty now, empty of the children who should have come to visit with their spouses, empty of grandchildren, empty of a tyrant's presence. A faded old lady destroyed by cancer sits alone in the house where the children she loved but did not have the power to defend will never return.

Defence was Alexandria's job. Alexandria the eldest, the miniature matriarch, the human shield, the nurse, the litigant. Alexandria who pushed them in their prams, washed them, dressed them, did their homework for them, pushed them about, took the blame for them because she was stronger than them, she could take it. Well, that much was untrue and Alexandria was closer to breaking point than she or anyone else in the family realised, but for the moment she was about to forget her ruined record collection and sneak out of the house to an illicit party.

It should not have been illicit, it was a perfectly

respectable cocktail party held aboard the yacht belonging to one of the officers' wives, but Edward had taken a dislike to the hostess ever since he and her husband had a falling out over something neither party could exactly remember afterwards. Nevertheless, it was enough to ensure that Alexandria and her mother were invited without Edward... and that the invitation was swiftly filed away.

Alexandria had other plans. How she actually imagined she would get away with going to a party in secret when half the people her father worked with would be there did not bear thinking about, but she answered the invitation in secret and made her plans. She felt sufficiently confident of Mrs Digby Royston's discretion to ask if it would be all right for her to get ready in her house, knowing that she would understand why. She might have been singularly lacking in tact to deliberately exclude one family member from an invitation, but Alexandria was sure the lady must have some sense in her head.

So, on the afternoon of the party, Alexandria slipped out of the house carrying her new make-up set, an elegant frock made of blue cotton and her favourite new acquisition: a hat with a white flower at the side and a trim little veil that slipped over her eyes and most of the top of her face. She knew she would almost certainly get the third degree when she returned if she could not think up a decent alibi in the intervening hours but it hardly mattered just then. Out in the crowded streets she was free and secure at the same time, keeping to the crowded areas the way an escaped convict might do to avoid arousing suspicion.

An hour later, she stepped out of Mrs Digby Royston's guest room, looking like the heroine of a pre-Raphaelite painting. She was growing up beautiful like her mother with the same striking auburn hair and porcelain skin but scarred like a sculpture covered in hairline cracks.

"My dear, you do look exquisite," cooed Mrs Digby Royston, helping her to put on her little white gloves. Alexandria smiled, thinking that she was just being polite. No one had ever told her that she was beautiful before except Uncle Luigi and she simply refused to even think about him. Her brothers were the striking ones, like little dolls with their rosy cheeks and tiny white teeth and soft baby curls, but her skin tanned easily and she had to be kept indoors not to look like a peasant. Then her father said she still did, white skin or not. "Nasty vulgar features. Can't think where you got them from. Scrawny like a rat and eyes too big and the wrong colour."

She was touched that her hostess was trying to make her feel at ease and followed her gratefully to her car. "I've never been on a boat," she whispered, as they settled down on the comfortable leather passenger seats.

"A Maltese girl and never been on a boat? What a sheltered life you've led, my dear."

"In a way."

"It's all right, you'll love it," said Mrs Digby Royston quickly, seeing the look of discomfort on her face. "There will be lots of young people I'm simply dying to introduce you to and Augustus and I will be there to make sure you have a good time."

She did have a good time. In fact, when she arrived home and realised that her father had found her out, it hardly seemed to matter, even if she was a little bewildered by his reaction at the time.

"I'm going to knock you through the wall, you scheming little liar!"

How on earth does he know? She wondered, putting her hands out to stop herself as she lurched in the direction of the wall. It was a tactical error, her wrists jarred with pain. "Carousing with your English friends! I'll soon put an end to that!"

"But I was only at Caffe Cordina with David and Lela!" she protested but she was on the floor by the time she had thought up an alibi, scared that her head was going to be kicked in. "Ask them yourself!"

"Lie to me again and I'll ram red hot chilli peppers down your throat!" Stars and planets spun out of orbit through the room. "It's written all over your face!" He lifted her up by her now disordered hair and dragged her in the direction of the nearest mirror. "Tell me you were at Caffe Cordina again!"

Oh dear, she really had caught the sun dramatically, standing outside in the middle of the afternoon with the light coming at her from both sky and sea. A faint crisscross of white lines had appeared across the top half of her face, stencilled in by her beloved and much admired hat-with-a-veil. A tiny trickle of blood came out of her nose. She blinked at the absurd reflection of herself and began to laugh. She really did look too ridiculous for words; even the blood and the patches that she knew would shortly become bruises looked like the make-up of a clown.

He would have done far worse to her if he had known what else had happened at the party without his watchful gaze to keep her away from all possible avenues of happiness. It would have upset his almost post-colonial identity crisis even further if he had known that she had been introduced to and immediately fallen for an Englishman that afternoon.

Mrs Digby Royston had not been exactly motiveless when she thought to invite Alexandria to the gathering in the first place. She was such a dear little thing, so refined, a real convent girl – definitely in need of a suitable young man. One of the first things she did when her husband had pressed a gin and tonic into Alexandria's nervous hand and commented on the fine weather for the time of year was to introduce her to a young officer called James Carlisle. Mrs Digby Royston was a keen matchmaker in the absence of anything more meaningful to do with her life and it seemed to her that Alexandria would be perfect for such an ambitious, entertaining, well-off and handsome young man. To give her the benefit of the doubt, she may not have realised the danger of what she was doing, regarding it as a delightful game to pass the time of day. At best she was simply irresponsible, at worst… well, who can say?

She watched with middle-aged glee as James took Alexandria's hand and gave her a courteous little bow – the two of them seemed to have hit it off immediately – thinking what an attractive couple they made, him tall and dark in his immaculate uniform, her delicate, aristocratic, an array of spring colours. But all Alexandria was aware of at the moment of meeting was the aroma that hung around him; he smelt of clean linen and expensive cologne. She did not know why she found it so comforting but it was also a novelty. The only security she had known before had been female – Auntie Josephine's prim, matronly presence, Mother Eugenia and the sanctuary of the convent – never anything like this. Then, almost as if he had known what she was thinking, there had been the grip of his hand when she had slipped off her glove and offered it to him, just tight enough that she knew he was powerful and yet meant her no harm.

The rest of the gathering could be forgotten about. The two of them talked avidly all afternoon as if no one else was there, discussing everything and nothing – ambitions, dreams, likes and dislikes, a little politics here, a little religion there but even these forbidden topics of polite conversation seemed to draw them closer together. A great deal of conversation was devoted to the subject of England and travel, because Alex had never been anywhere before and here was a man who had seen the world. She bombarded him with questions. In all honesty, she was only now beginning to believe that such a place as England existed, listening to James Carlisle with his so soft accent talking about double-decker buses and hiking in the Lake District and how terribly it had rained on Coronation Day.

By the time the day drew to a close, Alexandria and James were standing together watching the sun slipping beneath the sea as if they had watched the sun setting together every night of their lives. Mrs Digby Royston was ecstatic that her plan had worked but that was nothing to what was going on in Alexandria's tortured child's heart. James was as enchanted as she was, drawn by her beauty and the peculiar air of guarded playfulness she exuded as if she wanted to laugh a little more, share a little more with him but was held back by some magic spell he could not see. Like a princess trapped by a curse, he thought without a hint of irony at that time. He thought that it was just a cultural convention that made her so irresistibly reserved whilst allowing him a wide enough glimpse into her character to know what was waiting for him if he returned to her.

So Alexandria went to bed content that night, knowing that if her father hated her, there was a man on this little island who had spent hours talking to her and fussing over her, whose only contact with her had been a gentle touch of her arm to make a point or the curling of warm fingers around her hand in greeting. A man in whose presence she had been unafraid, even when they were almost alone and there was no one else keeping an eye on them.

And in the morning a vast bouquet of flowers was waiting at the breakfast table, filling the room with the perfume of love. The card caught in the green stems read: *to the girl with the beautiful eyes, your humble servant J. C.*

"Pity he didn't notice your nose," remarked Edward and he spent the rest of the day sniggering at the shameless sentimentality of the message. If Alexandria had a single flaw in her appearance it was that a close look would reveal a slightly crooked nose, the only visible sign of the twenty-seven fractures she carried around with her without knowing. She failed to react to his nastiness, which he took quite rightly to be a bad sign for him. Instead, she picked up the bouquet and took it upstairs in case he decided to poison the flowers or something, emerging a short time later with a white carnation pinned in her hair. "Where do you think you're going?"

"You must let me thank Mrs Digby Royston for having me," she insisted, too high spirited for words. "It would be very rude of me not to."

"You can't go outside looking like that."

She hesitated, lifting a hand to her face. There were tender patches around her nose and both her cheeks. Questions would be asked and she would have to tell lies about unfortunate accidents coming down the stairs again. She refused to be dispirited. "I suppose I will have to wear that dreadful hat-with-a-veil then," she volunteered.

Oh Love, Love, Love, Oh withering might!

Little Alexandria Sant'Angelo, whose head was still buried in trigonometry homework and the poetry of Alfred Lord Tennyson, was passionately and unashamedly in love.

XIII

How do I love thee? Let me count the ways...

Alexandria in love. At the time she thought of it as the happiest experience of her life. And the most frightening. It was perhaps her first adult insight – that falling in love was frightening, even for a girl who had survived the rat-infested dungeon, hours hanging over the side of a balcony waiting to fall to her death and so much violence that she thought it normal to be permanently covered in cuts and bruises. In spite of her history or even because of it, the act of surrender was unbearably painful and fraught with dangers. She had dedicated so much of her life to building a protective wall between herself and the rest of the human race, particularly men, and now she found herself willingly climbing it.

It might have been that the racial divide actually helped them, because he was a stranger, or it might simply have been that he was a strong, charismatic enough character to break through the years of fear that would otherwise have hardened her against him. Whatever it was, Alexandria took to James Carlisle with the trust of a child who had grown up in a happy home.

Whatever was waiting for them over the horizon, he brought her happiness. I will risk being a voyeur and watch them together. I need to see her happy, involved in a tender moment so that I can remember that there are such qualities as gentleness and love. I would like to see them on another visit to their matchmaker friends, so that I can hear James declaring to Alexandria that he loves her, as though that could somehow wipe away everything else that we have seen.

It was the first time since Alexandria had met James that she had been given paternal permission to attend a social function. She was shocked to realise, as she stepped onto the bus, that she was growing into a cynical creature. It was just that she knew her father was up to something. Not only had he agreed to let her accept the dinner invitation but he had gone as far as to allow her to stay the night at Mrs Digby Royston's house. There must be some unsavoury reason why he let me go, she thought, adjusting the choker her mother lent her. He probably wanted to drown her siblings in the bath whilst she was away, or perhaps she would come back in the morning to find that he had made a bonfire of all her personal belongings. She stopped herself from guessing; it didn't matter. For whatever reason, she was going to enjoy herself for a whole evening and nothing was going to stop her.

Edward had not trusted her at a formal dinner since she ruined his own dinner party, but that fiasco had hardly been her fault. Even if it had been, she had been bleeding so profusely by the end of it that there had really been no reason for him to be so heavy-handed about it after the guests had politely taken their leave. She probably should have realised it was coming, but then Alexandria could not really help getting herself into ludicrous or dangerous situations if there was a quieter way.

"Please tell me this isn't about what I think it's about?"

"And what might that be?" Benedict's face has flushed a little and it is not sunburn. "It wasn't her fault that her body decided to go careering from girlhood to womanhood whilst she was sitting down to dinner, was it?"

"Oh God."

"We don't use that expression."

"Why is this necessary?"

"Because this is all about my mother growing up," I explain like a school librarian, "and let's face it, there aren't a great many laughs to be had at this stage in the narrative."

It is quite amazing the things men can get embarrassed about. Those who witnessed it made far more valiant attempts not to be, more for the sake of Alexandria's mother than for her. And she was wearing such an attractive pink silk dress, settling herself at table alongside her father's squadron leader, several other RAF sorts, a barrister and a Jesuit whom her father was careful to seat at the other end of the table.

Halfway through the main course, Antonia prodded Alexandria in the ribs. "Look at you, you stupid girl!" she hissed, pointing at her skirt. Alex looked down and instead of seeing her napkin draped carefully on her pink lap, she found that her napkin had slid to the floor and that her pink lap was stained with blood. For someone who was quite used to bleeding, she overreacted monumentally, went into a blind panic and screamed.

"*Ġesu Marija*! I've cut myself!" The gentlemen stared politely into their wine glasses, knowing perfectly well what was happening to her. Natalino Fava SJ complimented Antonia on the seasoning of the chicken, offering Alexandria the perfect opportunity to drop the subject. She failed to grasp the lifeline, too shocked by far. "Mama, I have, I've cut myself!" She added insult to injury by addressing her mother with the Maltese word. Could she not have remembered to call her 'Mummy' in front of this distinguished company? It mattered very little by that stage anyway, considering the fact that she was menstruating copiously in front of the aforementioned gathering and there was simply no way of concealing it.

"Would you excuse me for just a moment?" enquired Antonia, with admirable deportment, pulling her daughter out of her chair. Alexandria was almost relieved to be propelled in the direction of the downstairs bathroom.

"I'm dying!" she bleated, wondering exactly how long she had before she keeled over and ended it all.

"You stupid girl!" She felt her head being knocked against the door. "You stupid, stupid, stupid girl!" I certainly will be after this, she thought, as three sets of stars spiralled before her eyes. My brain cells are falling out of my ears. "Don't you know what's happening to you?"

"I'm bleeding to death!" wailed Alexandria, "that's what's happening! I've got a tumour! I'm having a haemorrhage! I've probably got cancer as well!"

"You know perfectly well what this is – don't the nuns teach you anything about growing up?"

"I think they expected you would," and it was honestly not meant as an accusation. It was taken as one.

"You're not dying, you stupid girl, you've got the curse!" Well, she certainly had that, but it was the first she had heard of it.

There was none of that girly indignity to worry about now, her entrance into the Digby Roystons' drawing room went without a hitch. The elegant room was filled with little groups of beautifully dressed people, talking in huddles with their pre-dinner drinks. "Ah, Alexandria, how wonderful to see you!" Mrs Digby Royston took her by the arm and led her in the direction of the drinks cabinet. "We were worried you mightn't make it on time."

"I'm so sorry, one of my brothers was taken ill." That was a flat lie. One of her brothers, namely Anthony, was certainly rather the worse for wear now but that was only because one of the neighbours had told their father that he had seen him smoking behind the public lavatory. At least Anthony would never tamper with cigarettes again. In fact, she thought it likely that he would have a morbid fear of fire for the rest of his life.

James Carlisle appeared at her side, giving her a pleasantly squirmy feeling inside her. "You do look stunning," he said, offering his arm. "Let me introduce you to some people."

"It is very kind of you to say so," answered Alexandria, happily distracted from the vision of Anthony choking and gasping for breath on the floor of their father's study.

"I'm not being kind at all, you look beautiful." He saw the cynicism on her face and felt faintly irritated by it. "If I wasn't a gentleman, I would think you were fishing for compliments, looking at me like that."

"And I would say you were telling me a naughty fib," she explained, so matter-of-factly that he knew she meant it. "All the good looks of the family got passed on to my brothers."

"Who told you that rubbish?" Their voices were a shade louder than they ought to be in such an environment and he nudged her the opposite way he had intended, into a quiet corner of the room. "Who on earth could be so stupid?"

"My father." There was a hint of annoyance in her voice, and for once she was not annoyed with her father. The rest of her speech was chillingly deadpan. "He said it's a pity that I inherited my mother's capacity for thought and not her looks because at least she's stupid and beautiful."

Alexandria noticed James reddening slightly and thought it was the heat of the room or the alcohol. "You know, this is a dreadful thing to say, but the more I hear about your father, the more I think I hate him." She signalled for him to be quiet, a moment before a waiter came within earshot. They were silent as James had his glass replenished. "I mean it, you know. What an evil thing to teach a child. What else has he made you think about yourself?"

"If you don't mind, there are more pleasant subjects of conversation." She was stoically determined that her father would not crop up for the rest of the evening or she might as well have stayed at home.

The timely sound of the gong summoned them to dinner. James and Alexandria walked together into the dining room. They sat down at table in front of a silver candelabra glowing with encouragingly dreamy light. And Alexandria glowed, thinking that this was what it was like to be a proper couple. It was almost worthy of the nostalgic settings of girly books about knights in shining armour and beautiful damsels in distress – and he *had* said she was beautiful, so maybe she was after all and they were not all being polite, James and Mrs Digby Royston and all her friends. Maybe she was beautiful in this languidly love-inspiring environment of candles and fine wine, and maybe the man sitting beside her was desperately in love with her and only just restraining his feelings.

James's thoughts seem to have been travelling in a similar direction, because halfway through the starter, whilst Alexandria picked her way through the mussels arranged artistically on her plate, he said: "This is like something out of *Brideshead Revisited.*"

"What's that?" she asked, hoping it was not something that would make her look incurably ignorant for asking about.

"It's a very elegant tragic love story about an unbelieving Englishman who gets mixed up with an old Catholic family."

"Oh." This was not particularly reassuring, but he gave a light laugh and slipped his hand onto hers. She felt the pressure of his fingers caressing the soft flesh between her knuckles and a shudder of pleasure rushed through her body. He felt her tremble and squeezed her

157

hand a little tighter, looking up at her face to see the reaction.

Alexandria was already looking at him and their eyes met. "I think I'm in love with you," he whispered, lifting her hand to his face. A murmur of a past nightmare emerged and then subsided: his cheek was clean-shaven, smooth like writing paper under her fingertips. "Do you understand, Alex? I love you." He heard her give an almost inaudible sigh then the waiter spoilt everything by coughing behind them, giving them time to pull themselves together before he reached over to clear their plates away.

Alexandria did not mind. The untimely interruption only added to the air of subdued passion and mystery surrounding the whole experience and he had told her everything she wanted to hear from him. As the different courses were laid before them and they fulfilled the obligation of making small talk with the guests on either side of them, Alexandria and James held hands under the table. By the time the crème caramel arrived, Alexandria was having quite a bit of trouble concentrating on Mrs Chesterton-Finch's description of their new Persian cat's eating habits. A peculiar transformation was taking place in her. She seemed to be floating, pushed out of her seat by an invisible impulse she could not explain. She was drawn up over the heads of the good people dining, caught in a bubble of liquid light. She was giddy, she was breathless with a fear that was too like ecstasy to be fought.

From the highest point in the room, she looked down and watched the meal drawing to a close. And whilst she watched, she was unaware that she was also watching an era coming to its end. In a few short years, the close circle into which she had stepped would leave the Maltese Islands bound for their motherland and a hundred and sixty years of colonialism would finally pass into history. They were all captured in Alexandria's heady dream vision as they were for those few short hours, sitting at the round mahogany table with its white damask cloth and flickering centrepiece, talking and sipping their coffee.

Marcus Jefferys, whose dinner suit skilfully disguised the rolls of fat he carried around with him, was caught in a somewhat strained discussion about the Independence movement with Miss Gertrude Thornton, the editor of a newspaper of which he heartily disapproved. Gertrude Thornton, with her earnest blue eyes and carefully tamed blonde hair, talked animatedly about progress and the wind of change, hands spread in front of her in a gesture of openness and immensity. She and her husband-to-be were the only people around the table who refused to be scared off when their compatriots fled the island in droves. Their children became Maltese nationals.

Gertrude Thornton's husband-to-be, Piers Berkeley-Temple, was listening with admirable patience as Captain Owain Lloyd related the entire unexceptional contents of his son's last letter to him. Piers Berkeley-Temple like Alexandria was moved by the heady, amorous atmosphere and only snippets of the conversation penetrated his reflections on Gertrude and how much he would like to be alone with her at that precise second in time. *Fisher House beat Southwell House to win the inter-house rugby cup last week...* oh Gertrude, stop talking to that tiresome old bore and look at me! *Roland Flynn stole my bag of mint humbugs, so I left a pool of ink on his chair just before we went in for Algebra...* who cares about this and that movement, just look at me across the room like lovers are supposed to do! *Someone dropped a frog in my gumboot the other day. I am hiding it in a box under my bed ...* Gertrude, Gertrude, I'm going to die of boredom – can't you faint or something? Then I can rush to your side and carry you in my arms *outside*.

And of course, from her vantage point, Alexandria saw herself sitting next to James and saw their hands linked in secret under the folds of the tablecloth though from her bubble she could feel nothing. She watched their heads coming closer together to exchange a few words, a raised eyebrow and a conspiratorial smile here and there from other guests who noted the affection in their body language. And finally, James breaking the rules and abstaining from port and cigars to join her out in the garden.

James and Alexandria walked in the garden together. It was the midnight garden of her childhood, full of mystery and wonder but she did not reach out to touch the moon now. The light bubble had burst, she was flesh and blood again held securely in James's arms. They walked past the fountain with its statue of Pan standing in the middle of a shell-shaped pool, spouting water in an arc from his mouth. Her hand idly swept through the water as they moved towards the tunnel of vines at the end of the garden. They were being called out of sight of the house, covered up by green leaves and heavy bunches of grapes, fresh and ripe for picking. There was shelter there in plenty as they stood face-to-face, wide-eyed, overwhelmed by the intensity of this thing without a name.

"What's happening?" murmured Alexandria, feeling her body shaking violently – a little too violently - against his. "Tell me what's happening to me!"

"It's all right, don't be frightened." He was a little alarmed by her reaction, afraid that she would try to fight him off. "Don't be frightened, you're with me." But Alexandria was not afraid; she was confused. The world was swirling around her so that she could hardly stand up, but she had never felt such euphoria in her entire life.

Our spirits rush'd together at the touching of the lips.

A single kiss wiped away the pressure of Uncle Luigi's unwanted kisses, but a great many memories would be wiped away in that unexpectedly chaste encounter. James's fingers running through her hair, so much gentler than hands reaching for her in darkness, but everything he did was gentle even then, every gesture tender, affectionate, carefully considered. They stood perfectly still, faces pressed together, letting invisible waves sweep over them. And he asked nothing else of her. When she remembered the evening afterwards, she remembered the black sky behind his head as she reached up to cradle his face in her hands and the flickers of light reminding her that they were not alone.

XIV

It was time for Alexandria to begin living out her brief, danger-fraught, painful-wonderful double life, meeting James Carlisle in secret. If Malta lacks anything it is hiding places and Alexandria and James spent much of that long summer seeking out the few they could find. They could not be seen in public together if at all possible as it would take just one innocent remark from a neighbour or relative to finish the business once and for all.

Their favourite hiding place was the cinema, whenever Alexandria could persuade Lela to enter the conspiracy. Lela would arrive at the Sant'Angelos done up to the nines, the two girls would leave the house together then Lela would clear off for the evening the moment they arrived at the cinema. After the film, she would meet them again, James would disappear after a private good-bye and the girls would walk home together. They picked their films at random, absolutely any film from *Richard III* to *Around the World in Eighty Days* would do – though they were almost thrown out when they saw the latter one. Alex had to explain to James afterwards that the name Passepartout sounded like the Maltese word for tea strainer, which was why she had burst into fits of giggles every time David Niven said it.

It was one of the few moments James had genuine reservations about what he was doing, realising how young she was. She was not much younger than him but there were times when there seemed to be a generation gap between them, when she seemed to be caught between ages, an infantile adult or an old child. But he was too shallow to let a little rankling guilt overtake him and he could let himself be distracted by her girlish precocity. At least part of him could make believe that it was a delightful pretence, a woman play acting a vulnerable schoolgirl when he knew what she really was.

On most of their illicit cinema visits, they barely noticed what was being said. It was only a front after all and they were usually too busy kissing and cuddling and making plans in nervous whispers to notice what was going on on the flickering screen. He would take her to England, they would marry and settle down together far away from her family, he would look after her and they would be happy forever. They would walk together along the White Cliffs of Dover, they would live in a tiny cottage by the sea, they would be free. No more hurried meetings like this, no more lies and alibis to keep angry fathers out of the way.

When they wanted to meet during daylight hours, Alexandria would take one of her younger siblings on a shopping trip, send them to buy ice cream two or three miles away if possible and meet him in the back room of some bar or other. The streets of Malta were safe enough places for small children to roam, it was not such an act of neglect on her part and she could never risk any of them meeting him in case they accidentally let something slip.

They had to give up on the Digby Roystons as a safe haven because Edward's quiet political turn around was almost complete by then and the mere sight of an invitation from a colonial family was enough to send him into an apoplectic rage. "Toadying to your little English friends again?!" *Slam!* "Get it into your thick little head, these people just want to use and oppress you!"

But in James's presence, Alexandria felt free. She was too young and preoccupied to care about the political implications of dating an Englishman or her

163

right to self-determination. She barely noticed that Malta was moving ever closer to full independence and that the world she was so attracted to was an anachronism about to disappear altogether. The only oppression she knew came from her father and she was finding his behaviour harder and harder to understand. Here was a man who until four or five years before had forbidden his wife and children to speak any language other than English in the house so that they found it almost impossible to express themselves in their own mother tongue. Suddenly, almost overnight, he turned into a champion of Maltese nationalism, smashing up their English records and banning the younger children from joining the Boy Scouts on the grounds that 'they're brainwashing you! There will be no saluting her Britannic Majesty in my house!"

But Edward Sant'Angelo saluted her Britannic Majesty whenever he was on parade, he dressed in a British uniform, worked for the Royal Air Force and if he was no longer a loyal subject of the British Crown, he still looked to it for the salary that supported his family. He knew no other life than the oh-so-English military world he had walked into back in 1939 and when he cut himself off from the social circle that surrounded his work as a show of pro-Independence solidarity, he found that he had no other circle to join. Any other man might have tried to reach a compromise but the Sant'Angelos have never been very good at compromise, being among the most stubborn, stiff-necked people in the entire Mediterranean – and they were up against some pretty stiff competition. So Edward Sant'Angelo surrendered himself to the spiralling decline of premature old age; bitter, isolated and filled with hatred though he could never tell exactly why and to whom.

"I don't know why you are looking at me like that,

darling." I haven't seen Benedict smile for a while and know it must be at my expense.

"Nothing." He stifles a laugh.

"I'm not like that if that is what you are insinuating."

"Of course not."

"I am not in the least bit stubborn and stiff-necked – there are just certain things *I am not prepared to compromise on so don't ask!*" He laughs without any attempt to hide it.

"No, of course you're not."

I have reason on my side. "Laughter is not an argument – did they not tell you that at Oxford?" Well, if he would go to the wrong university for his first degree. I am not stubborn and I am not like that. I can find refuge in my beloved's scepticism. There is no such thing as a curse and so I cannot resemble that creature in any way. "I am not like him," I declare to the world in general, and no longer care what answer I receive.

There is an invincibility to being in love. Even when Edward did find out that his daughter was lying to him about where she had been or they were careless and someone spotted her walking arm-in-arm with a man – and an *Englishman*, Edward, in his uniform and everything! No shame that girl has at all, absolutely no shame! – his cruelties simply did not affect her any more. Alexandria could endure anything knowing that, sooner or later, she would be in some new hiding-place being held very carefully in the compassionate arms of a man who loved her.

The imaginary father was relegated to childhood history with the appearance of James into her life. He would caress her as she pressed her face against his shoulder, reacting sometimes in anger – 'let me get my hands on this bastard! I won't let him do this to you, Alex' and 'why won't you let me sort him out? He'd never lay a hand on you again…' – sometimes in sadness, rocking her back and forth with tears in his eyes, whispering, 'my poor love, my poor baby, don't cry. I'll make it better, I'll look after you. I promise, when we're married, no one will ever hurt you again.'

Kind words, reassuring words and she believed him. The thought of marriage strengthened Alexandria, particularly when she sat her exams and had to leave the school where she had found something resembling peace throughout her childhood. Then, the day she turned eighteen, James plucked up the courage, with her permission, to ask Edward Sant'Angelo for her hand in marriage.

It would have been easier if they had just eloped, but I may actually have something to be grateful to Edward Sant'Angelo for. I may owe my existence to the fact that, having been most unadvisedly included in Alexandria and James's plans, Edward refused to give James Carlisle permission to marry the girl who grew up to be my mother. Not that he appeared at a first glance to be refusing James anything.

When he stepped inside Edward's study, leaving Alexandria listening fearfully outside as he popped the question, her father could not have been more polite. "I think you know why I have come to see you, sir," James began, and he almost sounded as though he respected him.

"Yes, of course I know, my dear boy," answered Edward, using the most ludicrously English expression with barely a trace of an accent. "Do sit down."

James found himself sitting in the comfiest easy chair with a cigar in his hand, half-wondering whether Alexandria had been exaggerating to him. He went straight to the point. "I would very much like to marry your daughter."

He watched for a change in the man's expression, but Edward gave him the warmest of smiles. "It is very kind of you to offer," he began, and there was not a hint of malice in his tone. He sounded warm, congenial, a little concerned if anything. "And you must not think for a moment that I do not want you to marry my daughter. I have no doubt that you are a fine young man with good prospects."

James felt his pulse quickening, hearing the creaking of an invisible trap opening before him. "I expect to be promoted within the year," he said, pressing his knuckles against the arm of his chair.

"I'm sure you will be, but it is hardly a life for a young woman who has led such a sheltered life, is it?"

"Sheltered?" He swallowed the accusation, hoping he could make it disappear altogether. "I – that is, I know it will be difficult for her to leave Malta, but she wants to come to England with me."

"She is far too young to know what she wants," and Edward's voice was all smiles. "She has no idea what life would be like in a foreign country. And you will be often away at sea. She has always hated being alone."

I've a better idea than you of what she hates, thought James, pressing the arm of the chair a little harder. "If you would only trust me…"

"You should not ask me just yet, she is not ready for this." James felt a hand patting him on the shoulder and wavered between resignation and anger. "It would unsettle her terribly."

The scale tipped. "With the greatest respect, I don't think I could possibly unsettle her any further than you have." No one ever claimed to have the greatest respect for people they really respected, but James knew already that Edward would never agree to him marrying Alexandria and all he wanted was to tear the ridiculous mask off his face. "Why do you hate her so much?"

It was a question Edward might have asked himself if he had ever had a functioning conscience, because at least one side of him knew that his behaviour towards his eldest daughter was unreasonable. But he had started to loathe her so early in her life that it seemed perfectly natural now. He had hated her before she grew up to be beautiful, so he could see no beauty in her. He had hated her before she had been brilliant, so he could think of her as stupid and ignorant. And he was too vain a man to imagine that he could make such a serious mistake as to cause a lifetime of misery to his own flesh and blood without good reason. "I don't think I understand what you mean, young man."

James stood up. "What can you possibly lose by letting us get married? You've never loved her. I love her. I'll take her out of your way. Surely it's the most practical solution all round?"

Edward looked pained. "I don't know who you have been talking to." (He knew perfectly well who he had been talking to) "But you cannot tell me what I feel for my own daughter. I have always loved her, in spite of everything she has done."

He sounded so dignified that James had to fight a doubt again before asking: "What do you mean by that?"

Edward sat at his desk, unable to meet James's gaze. It was fortunate for Alexandria, eavesdropping outside, that he lowered his voice in apparent shame for the next part of his speech and she was unable to hear the slander that followed. "I do not want in any way to lower her in your eyes, but she would make you terribly unhappy. She brings men home all the time. You have a word for such women, I think."

James felt his stomach lurching. "Are you trying to say that Alexandria is a – tart or something?"

Edward looked genuinely horrified. "That is putting it more starkly than I would like... but you I think understand my dilemma..."

"Why don't you just say no?" Suddenly, Alexandria could hear everything that was being said on the other side of the door as clear as a bell. "I'm a military man – do you think I don't know what such a woman looks like?"

Edward tried to stand up but his legs seemed to have turned to cotton wool. "Now see here young man, I was only trying to help you…"

"Do you realise I actually thought they were all exaggerating when they said you were the most poisonous little despot to ever walk God's earth?" said James, advancing on him. "That child is the only pure thing to come out of this Godforsaken family of yours and don't think that the rest of us don't know it. Our relationship was entirely honourable, neither of us suggested that it should be otherwise."

Edward managed to scrape his moral outrage together. "If you are going to speak of my family like that, I must ask you to leave. We all produce one bad apple, you just happen to have chosen it…"

"What?!" All propriety forgotten, James hurtled around Edward's desk so that there was nothing for him to hide behind. *"You dare speak to me of bad apples? The son of a shameless philandering murderer and you speak to me of bad apples?"*

Silence. Horror passed momentarily between the two men to have said and heard such a thing. The cicada orchestra outside made nervous music. "My mother died giving birth to my younger brother," explained Edward, finally, but his voice quavered with the effort. James was no easy sight to deal with, huge and uncharacteristically angry. And he had said what he should not have said; it was too late to go back now. He might as well see the thing through to its unnatural end.

"Of course she didn't, no one believes that old fiction, least of all you. She couldn't have died in childbirth because *she never gave birth to that boy.* He only grew up in your household because his real mother had a brain between her ears." White with rage and panic, Edward tried to leave his chair only to slump back into it again with the effort. It was a long time since he has been the powerless one and he was relieved

169

to see his adversary turning on his heel and marching out of the room. Alexandria would be considerably easier to deal with.

"What sort of a man was he?"

"A cursed man," I reply with venom, "a cursed father with cursed children. Only a man who was no man at all by that stage in his life could have lied about his own daughter. Families used to try to hush things like that up…"

"I meant his father," Benedict persists. "He said – well, he didn't really kill his wife, did he?"

I am not sure whether Benedict is more frightened of me or of my story. "Not exactly. He didn't actually kill her with his bare hands."

"But why would he say that? He said 'murderer'."

He must wait for me to get Alexandria to safety. She did not know what he meant either and there would never be enough time for James to explain. When he stormed out of the study, he almost fell over her, sitting on the landing with her head buried in her hands. It was the sight of her like that more than anything else that made James realise the hopelessness of it all. She was a child, and for a moment she was not even an adult child. Her plaits hung glumly over her arms as she sobbed and hiccupped like a child from a Red Cross advertising campaign. "Come on, my love," said James, quietly, coaxing her to her feet. "Quickly. I'm taking you away from here."

It should have ended another way. After an angry scene of chivalric outrage when the dashing young officer had defended the honour of the lady he loved, he should have picked her up in his arms and carried her into the sunset so that they could both live happily ever after. But if James Carlisle seemed like a hero to Alexandria, he was a hero who fell short, and he was to fall much further than she could possibly have imagined at the time. He swept her up in his arms and led her to the only place he could think of where she would be safe until her father had calmed down – to the door of the convent.

The anticlimax nearly killed her. They sat miserably together in a private room at the back of a club James knew, trying to find a way to say goodbye – or in Alexandria's case, accepting that it had to be that way at all. "Take me! I'm eighteen, he can't stop me getting married. If you thought I was too stupid to be your wife, you might have said so to start with!"

He held her as tight as he dared as if he were trying to squeeze out all the hurt he had caused. "You're not stupid at all, my love. You're wonderful, I meant it when I said I loved you but you're just a girl. I've no right to do this to you, you're just too young."

"I'm eighteen, for heaven's sake!"

"I know. It doesn't really have anything to do with age." It dawned on him that he had never seen her upset with him before. He wondered whether he would ever be able to put right what he had done.

"I thought you said it did! Why are you saying this to me now?" She felt sick with outrage. Never once in her life had she been considered too young to get hurt or too young to be held responsible for something she was supposed to have done, but now that happiness was staring her in the face she was too young to be granted it. There was no justice for her anywhere in the whole world, not even from James Carlisle and the little English heaven he had promised her. "I'm not a child, I was never a child! You know that."

"I know, I know. That's not what I mean." He kissed her forehead, swallowing a nagging regret every time he thought that he would never feel her touch again. "I know this hurts, but you'll be glad it ended like this one day." Her outcry was stifled in the coarse fabric of his jacket.

They held hands all the way to the convent but James already felt as though he was holding a child's hand to stop her running into the road. His rejection of her had drained the gesture of any other significance. "Do you want me to come in with you and explain?" he asked, misunderstanding Alexandria's shaking again – it was not fear or euphoria this time.

"They'll know why I'm here," she answered tonelessly, "you can go."

"Alex, please don't hate me for this." He needed her forgiveness or at least the hope that she would not think ill of him. A look from her would be enough, he thought, but she turned to face the gate.

"I do hate you." She did not want to watch his retreating figure walking out of sight. "Just go."

He reached forward to touch her arm but drew back, knowing it could only be a cruelty now. "You don't mean that. Don't let's end it like this."

"I didn't end it." Her voice was so blank it almost sounded sleepy. He knew she was in shock. "But I don't suppose I mean it. If you're going, please go."

She closed her eyes and listened until his footsteps had faded out of hearing. It was a long time before she had the energy to reach up and ring the bell.

A record needs to be straightened. Leonardo Sant'Angelo did not murder his wife. He may have been a man malicious enough to stand and curse his own son on his wedding day, but even he could not have committed such a crime against a woman he loved. And he did love her. When she was alive, he had been capable of love and he had loved her, but she did not die in childbirth and it is in this fragment of an almost forgotten life that the origins of the curse may be found.

Edward had always known the truth of the matter, though he claimed all his life that he did not remember anything of the events he witnessed as a very young child. Whilst Alexandria sat in a corner of the parlour, unmoved by the tray of *pastizzi* and tea they put in front of her and whilst James made arrangements to return to England as quickly as possible, we must travel back to quiet, sleepy, unchanging Mdina. We must go back to where our story began but we must go a little further back this time, to the night of February the fourteenth, 1920.

It is not the only cruel irony of the story that the pretty, delicate English wife of Leonardo Sant'Angelo would have her suspicions about her husband's infidelity confirmed on a night that would one day be associated with lovers. It all happened as Lady Elisabeth Wilson sat in her bedchamber staring into her looking glass. She had already sensed her husband's coldness towards her. It had been increasing steadily over the past six or seven months and she found herself searching her reflection for the reason why.

Twenty-seven is not old, she reminded the flawless white face glancing back at her. Not a trace of a hard line anywhere, even around the eyes and she had had plenty of sleepless nights alone, wondering who was taking her husband from her. Her eyes were still the same shade of blue – 'like the sea and the sky, my darling, like eternity!' – her hair the same silvery blonde it was when he met her and said that she looked like a fairy princess, but he had not spoken of her like that for a long time. After eight years of marriage, she asked herself, was she truly any different to the woman he had once claimed to love madly, passionately, above all others?

She touched the gold band around her wedding finger, pressing on the vein that was supposed to lead straight to the heart but she did not know for certain if it did. Frankly, she did not greatly care, at a moment when the love of her marriage seemed to have dwindled to nothing and she could not even tell why. Something compelled her to remove it, inching the ring slowly and painfully over the knuckle. It did not want to come away, but then she had never tried to remove it before. It had sat uncomplainingly on her finger all that time since the day in Mdina Cathedral when he stood with her at the altar and put it there. It resisted her efforts to be taken from its natural place, sliding back whenever she let go but she would not be stopped. He put it there of his own free will. He must have loved her then, he must surely have thought that he would always love her. A flush of half-forgotten tenderness rose in her for a moment, extinguished only by the light thud of metal falling onto the embroidered covering of her dressing table.

Am I mad that I should cherish that which bears but bitter fruit?
I will pluck it from my bosom, though my heart be at the root.

The slightest of noises above her head jolted her to her feet. Draping a shawl over her shoulders, she slipped out of her room and hurried up the winding stairs to the servants' quarters, a sickening sense of dread mingling with the suppressed excitement of an imminent ambush. Eavesdroppers never hear good of themselves, snooping wives seldom witness their husbands performing admirable acts. It did not therefore come as a great surprise to Elisabeth that she reached the top of the stairs in time to see Leonardo slipping out of her lady's maid's bedroom in a state of some dishevelment.

"Good evening, Leo." The situation was so appallingly reminiscent of a French romantic farce that she had trouble suppressing a giggle. She wondered whether he would have tried to hide in a cupboard or under the bed if she had burst into the room. Instead, Leonardo stood rooted to the spot, looked about ready

174

to drop through the floorboards but there was no escape for him anywhere. She had seen him in a situation that could not have been more incriminating if she had walked in on him in bed with Inez Balzan. "I wish you would leave my maid alone. I do not like her to work night and day shifts in succession like this."

There was more than a slight regret in Leonardo's mind as he glanced shamefaced at the grave, shadowy figure of his wife, so much more exquisitely beautiful then the woman he had just betrayed her for. He always remembered her as she looked just then, standing still in the half-light framed by yards of white lace, hair spilling over her shoulders like a reproachful reminder of what he had willingly thrown away. Something in the steely look she gave him warned him that she would never let him near her again.

"Woman, why in heavens' name are you spying on me?" he demanded, as if she had somehow wounded his dignity. "Creeping about after me like a snake in the grass. I will not live under your suspicious eye!" He could have apologised but it proved easier to assume an air of moral superiority and lay the blame for his indefensible behaviour at her door. It was too late anyway, no apology could have taken away what she had seen and he lacked the humility to sincerely beg his own wife for forgiveness.

But if it was any consolation to him, he would not live under her suspicious eye after that. It was the cold eye of knowledge that regarded him from then on, across the room, from the other side of the dinner table, but he would soon escape from even that. For the present, she turned her back on him and walked with considerable gravitas back down the stairs.

Cruel ironies were to be the undoing of Elisabeth. In mid-April, Inez Balzan gave in her notice and left very quietly for an apartment in Victoria, the capital of Gozo, paid for by Leonardo Sant'Angelo. Elisabeth hired a new and conveniently ugly lady's maid and tried to banish from her mind the memory of the girl who had served her and ruined her life. Throughout the stifling, spirit-sapping summer that followed, Elisabeth threw herself into her charitable work by day and locked her door at night, deaf to the calls of her husband to let him in. At first he knocked plaintively at her bedchamber, doing his best to coax and cajole her into unlocking the door, then with remarkable speed he would demand that she open the door or he would break it down, battering at the wood in an attempt to frighten her into submission.

She would not give in. She was from a stubborn people too, with a lineage stretching back to the Catholic recusants who had gone to the gallows rather than conform to the Elizabethan establishment. She could handle a man. The door was a strong, solid one and no amount of maltreatment would persuade it to open. When it showed signs of weakening, she called in a carpenter and a locksmith to make sure that it really was impregnable. On one occasion, he took her by surprise as she walked downstairs in the morning to have her breakfast, but she was not as fragile as she looked and kicked his knees out of line. *He was fortunate I did not kick anything else out of line!* – the servants heard her shouting in a rare outburst as he was carried into his bedroom, screaming and shouting obscenities, to await the appearance of a doctor.

Then, on Armistice Day – the second anniversary of the outbreak of peace throughout Europe – Inez Balzan reappeared in Mdina carrying a baby boy. She refused to uphold the status quo that insisted upon illegitimate children being given the mother's name and registered him – Sant'Angelo. As James Carlisle said, she had a brain between her ears. By publicly acknowledging Leonardo Sant'Angelo to be the father, she was not only preventing the head of one of the wealthiest, most prestigious families in the Maltese Islands at that time from denying his part in her disgrace, she was ensuring that her son would want for nothing. The Sant'Angelos were legally obliged to take him in and he grew up the son of a nobleman; wealthy, educated, comfortable – hated, despised, rejected, ridiculed. It was through the persecution of this child, whose only crime was to have been born, that Edward first learnt the meaning of cruelty. Fortunately for him, by the age of eleven, Leonardo was unable to bear his presence in the house any longer and he was packed off to boarding school in England, far away from gossiping tongues and the guilty hatred of a man who would never know the blessing of his wife's forgiveness.

And what of his wife? What of Elisabeth and her heartbreak and her shame? It was a pity that the two women were pitted against one another, because Elizabeth and Inez shared the same defiant spirit. Except that Inez won their only contest and like gladiators there could be only one survivor. As with every action of her short life, Elisabeth's escape from her humiliation at her husband's hands was made quietly, barely noticed by anyone. Whilst Leonardo attended an Armistice Day ceremony in her place to remember the war dead and to pretend that nothing untoward had happened, she stood in the vestibule of her house, calmly putting on her coat, hat and gloves. If they had ever found her body, they would have found the stub of a candle and a matchbox in her pocket. Three-year-old Edward watched from behind the clock as she stepped out of the house and closed the door behind her, too young to know that he would never see her again. He paused for a moment in the empty hall then ran upstairs to the nursery. Whilst the rest of this domestic tragedy was unfolding, he was fighting with his sister over a red building brick he suddenly could not live without.

Elisabeth walked through the streets of Mdina, listening to the gentle tap of her shoes touching the limestone pavement, then out of the citadel in the direction of the sea. By the time Leonardo arrived home and raised the alarm, she had walked all the way to Ghar Hasan, a place where no one who knew her would have thought to look. A couple of villagers later reported that they saw her walking towards the cave, but she was too much of a lady for them to think of asking her what she thought she was doing and they were the last people to see her alive.

In the entrance to the cave, she lit her candle and began her journey into darkness, welcoming the feeling of being hidden from the world of the living where she no longer belonged. She recalled the cave from her childhood adventures, knew that the light from the open cliff-face at the other side would reach her by the time her flame went out for lack of oxygen. She did not pause for a second, walking steadily in the direction of the stream of light coming from the stone doorway out of the world. The light grew brighter, she felt the warmth of the sun against her face until she emerged into daylight. She had reached the end.

Far below her vantage point, the sea waited to take her. She hesitated for the first time, but she was alone and there was no one to tell her it did not have to end like that. She stepped off the stone platform into nothingness. Before she lost consciousness, she saw the world outstretched beneath her, stark and beautiful. A blue world made of a blue, unblemished sky that met the sea with nothing to break it. *Blue like the sea and the sky, my darling, like eternity.*

She was dead before her body came to rest on the seabed.

They shall not grow old, as we who are left grow old,

Age shall not weary them, nor the years condemn.
At the going down of the sun and in the morning,
We will remember them.

But Lady Elisabeth Wilson was not to be remembered. There was no funeral, no body to bury in unconsecrated ground, no mourning and no memory. Leonardo never spoke of her again. Any object connected with her, down to her powder compacts and hair ribbons, was stored away and forgotten about and her children pretended that she had never touched their lives. They never dared to speak of her, afraid of what would happen if their father overheard.

The sea gave her a burial of its own, down amid the rocks and barnacles and shards of other forgotten lives. And the Mediterranean can always be trusted with a secret.

XV

I am afraid. I am afraid that I am enjoying the process of unsettling him. There is a certain power in a troubled past, as if knowledge of the worst that a human being can do gives me the advantage in some unspoken game between us. If it is a game, I know that Benedict has lost the will to play. "Are all the men going to be like that?" he asks. I should have known that was the real problem. "All the men in your story are adulterers, drunkards or sadists. And you're wrong, he did kill his wife."

"Lawrence, Pawlinu, Sam..." I know this does not exactly count. All the good men seem to emerge from the Buhagiar side of the family, which practically proves his point but I hope he will not notice. "They were all perfectly decent men with happy marriages."

"Yes, and two of them died young." That is not a fair criticism, they could not help it. I cannot help the world into which they were born. "If we carry on much longer I'm going to lose my belief in humanity."

"Didn't think you had one."

We glower at one another, but there are no hiding places left, even in our manufactured irritation. "Take me somewhere else. Tell me something that makes you happy."

"I knew you would ask me that." He has given me a ticket to freedom. I can pretend that I am escaping for his sake. "Come along then."

I will take him to the nineteen fifties, to two rapidly growing boys who will join the ranks of decent men leading ordinary lives in an age where death would not call them too soon. I will give him a glimpse of lives going right, of happy children having a whale of a time in case he has forgotten that there ever was such thing as a happy child.

It was late November and Gregory and Nicholas had been billeted in their Yorkshire school for nearly three months. They had acclimatised to their new environment slowly, getting used to one new obstacle after another: the itchy blankets, the perpetual cold, the revolting sliced bread the texture of soggy cotton wool and the plethora of accents that made them wonder whether anyone had ever taught the English to speak their own language.

It had not been exactly plain sailing for any of them. They had all lost weight and many of them had battled with head colds and screaming diarrhoea in their early weeks there, but they had emerged without bearing any serious ill-effects and even Victor, who had been positively determined to be miserable after their disastrous arrival, succumbed to actually settling down. The twins, too proud to admit after the first fortnight that they had ever entertained the idea of escape, came to regard every mishap as a learning experience and they were careful to omit any unhelpful details from their letters home. Grown-ups were delicate creatures and the first rule they learnt when they began their lives as boarders was to mention only the happy and the mundane to a parent who was too far away to be of any earthly use:

Dear Mama,
Fr Liam took us on a nature ramble yesterday and we saw a hedgehog.

Gregory had also succeeded in getting stuck in the mud, right up to his knees. It took four of them to haul him out and he shed crumbs of dry mud for days afterwards, but she didn't need to know about that.

Dear Rosaria,
We went exploring with Seamus yesterday and found
a winding staircase leading to a tower. It was just like
something out of a ghost story.

They knew she would like that, she had always had
a slightly morbid side to her and well, it had been
exciting and rather scary creeping up the dark spiral
stairs, hearing the patter of their boots touching the
blackened stone and wondering what lay around the
corner. Unfortunately, Fr Mackay happened to appear
behind one such corner on his way down to a lesson.
They succeeded in scaring one another silly and the
three boys had been kept in an hour after lessons to
write out 'I must not wander out of bounds' a hundred
times. Rosaria didn't need to know that the staircase
had not led them to a dark tower after all, it led to
nothing more interesting than the quarters where the
staff lived. 'And we weren't wandering, we were
exploring,' Seamus chimed in, when they had handed in
their papers and watched them being thrown straight
into the wastepaper basket.

"Well, explore somewhere where you won't give me
a heart attack, you shamrock-waving Irish leprechaun!"

Then one day in mid-November, the boys woke up
feeling more than usually bitterly cold. Nicholas tried
wrapping his bedclothes right round him for extra
comfort because they had just learnt about insulation in
science and he thought it might help, but something
other than the cold bothered him. It was far too quiet.
Every morning since the end of their first week, he had
woken to the sound of the two boys on milk duty
clattering about under the window with the milk pails
whilst the staff got breakfast going, but there was no
sound today.

"They've overslept," he thought out loud. "Now there will be no milk for breakfast." But immediately he started imagining all the other things that could have happened. Maybe they had suffered some misfortune on their way to the gate to meet the farmer, had a fall perhaps or been kidnapped. Or perhaps something had happened to the farmer. His horse might have injured himself or the farmer might have had a heart attack, because he was very old and should not be travelling those winding lanes alone in the early morning at his age. Whatever it was, he thought he might be the only one who had noticed and should raise the alarm.

It was amazing how out of control the imagination could get first thing in the morning. It did not occur to Nicholas, as he clambered out of bed and hurried in the direction of the wash basins, that he could not possibly be the first up and that if there really was an emergency, he should forego the usual morning rituals, but Nicholas had been dreaming all night and was still caught in the hinterland between sleeping and waking.

There was no water in any of the taps. It was worse than he thought. In Nicholas's mind, the absence of water was caught up with vague memories of the war and its aftermath rather than the first frost of winter. They were under siege.

He would have caused chaos if Fr Mackay had not appeared in the dormitory at that moment to wake everyone up in the absence of a bell. There was white powder stuck to his cassock. "What are you doing out of bed, Nicky?"

Nicholas sincerely wished afterwards that he had not had such an audience to hear him explaining how it had been all quiet and he thought maybe something had happened and there was no water, which meant that there was a war. He was bewildered by the peels of laughter. "The pipes are frozen, son," explained Fr Mackay over the noise, "and I could hardly send a couple of kids across the fields in all that snow now, could I?"

The news that there was snow on the ground caused a diversion greater than Nicholas could have hoped for. The boys made a dash for the window. "I don't suppose you Maltesers have ever seen snow before?" asked Fr Mackay.

"It's like a great big Christmas card!" giggled Victor, when they had picked the ice off the inside of the glass enough to look out, because the familiar outdoor world of green fields and trees had turned white overnight. A thick white fleecy carpet of cotton wool had been unrolled across the gardens whilst they slept, the trees were still trees but eerily black against the white ground, branches glistening with fine stalactites of glass.

"Can we go out, Father? Just for a minute? Please?"

"Ah, well…"A cluster of smiling faces appealed to him. "Oh, I suppose so. After breakfast, but only if you can borrow some warmer clothes. You'll freeze to death like that."

Been there, done that, they might have said, but instead they gobbled up their toast and tea and ran riot in the dormitory until they had enough scarves, gloves and overcoats between them. "You look like a bunch of street urchins," was Fr Mackay's comment, when he looked at the bizarre assortment of clashing and ill-fitting clothing they had thrown over themselves. Gregory had a vast scarf wrapped awkwardly around his neck, no doubt knitted by some poor child's doting grandma, but then he had never worn a scarf quite like it before and was not entirely sure how to stop it from strangling him. The sleeves of Victor's borrowed overcoat partially concealed the green-and-red striped mittens bulging off his hands and as for Nicholas and the others, they were fighting with hats that covered their eyes, gloves put on the wrong hands and gumboots that forced them to walk like penguins. It was one of those

184

moments when he wished he had a camera. Instead, he made a mental note of the clothes the foreigners would need to get them through the winter. "Coming?"

In a world of new experiences, there was nothing quite like the feeling of stepping into snow for the first time. As Fr Mackay heaved open the door, they felt a blast of frost-laden air hitting them straight in the face and staggered back. "Actually, I've changed my mind!" gulped Victor, feeling as though icy cold marbles had just been rammed up his nose and down his throat.

"Don't be such a chicken," Fr Mackay gave him a shove that he thought hearty and Victor thought bullying, so that he flew out face first onto the fleecy white blanket that no longer seemed quite so cosy. The others ran straight for the big drifts of snow beside the hedges, screaming with cold and excitement as snow began to fly in all directions. By the time Victor had pulled himself together and caught up with them, they were drenched and red-faced, shaking the melting snowballs off their borrowed clothing like husky dogs.

"Look over there!" Nicholas ran to the wall where a row of perfectly formed icicles hung beneath a layer of snow four or five inches thick. He reached up on tiptoe.

"Careful!" called Fr Mackay, watching in a mixture of horror and amusement as Nicholas pulled an icicle away in his hand. "That snow's not…" A second later, Nicholas had caused a minor avalanche and been almost completely buried in snow. "Right lads, back inside before I have to send rescue teams to dig you out!"

For a few surreal minutes, back in the hinterland of a dream, Nicholas lay completely still, feeling the crisp snowflakes prickling against his face and his breath coming out of his mouth in little puffs of smoke.

A long day of lessons, praying that the snow would last until after tea and the Angelus and freedom. More snowfall during Classics kept their hopes up and thoroughly distracted them from Fr Liam's commentary on the extended metaphors in Homer's *Odyssey*. It seemed to Nicholas, never the most diligent of classicists, as though the clouds were breaking into pieces and falling all over the grass – 'what do you mean, "why does Homer keep talking about the *wine-dark sea*? They drank a lot of wine in those days, all right? People would have known exactly what he meant, not like you puritanical Englishmen scared to death of enjoying yourselves...' – he had always imagined snowflakes to be like the pieces of paper they threw at the feet of the procession during the *festa*, solid, substantial, not quite these delicate curls of thread that were landing in their thousands on the other side of the glass.

'Yeeees, but that's not quite what I had in mind. These examples are merely metaphors, 'wine-dark sea', 'rosy-fingered dawn', I wonder whether someone could tell me what...' – and so many of them. The sky and land blurred with the flurry of snow so that he could barely tell which was which. He was a visionary, a dreamer seeing the mysteries of creation in a winter miracle. '...and if a certain Mr Falzon does not stop staring aimlessly out of the window and PAY ATTENTION, I am going to wrap this book around his ears. Ah, good evening, glad you could join us.'

Nicholas sat bolt upright, frantically trying to remember which page they were on. He always knew when Fr Liam was talking to him because he was the only priest in the school who pronounced his name as if it were a pasta sauce.

"Sorry, Father." He was not long enough out of Colditz to have stopped being afraid of being singled out. He looked steadily down at his book as though he had been following the class all along.

"Page fifty-two, Nicholas." Nicholas scrambled through the book but he felt as if the world and his wife was watching him and he had somehow forgotten which order the numbers came in... "It's all right. If the snow stops in time, you're all allowed out tobogganing after class. Nicholas, I suggest you take a shovel with you." Raucous laughter, but at least it cut nicely into what would otherwise have been the most boring class on the timetable.

During the winter of his first year, Nicholas got himself quite a reputation for getting buried, submerged and generally overwhelmed by the elements in this startling new world in which he had found himself. A week after the snow arrived, the football pitch was still inaccessible and the boys were beginning to tire of snowball fights, sledging and skating. "I dare say it's time to be getting back to normal," declared Fr Jennings the gym teacher at lunchtime. "If the boys can't play football, I'll take them on a cross-country run."

"Is that wise?" asked Fr Mackay, taking a look out at the none-too-promising sky. "Some of the foreign lads won't be used to running in this weather."

"Then it's about jolly time they toughened up a bit, isn't it? I'll tell them to be ready by one thirty." Fr Mackay, who amongst other things ran the school sanatorium, started weighing up the risk factors. They would be running just after eating a stodgy meal, it was bitterly cold, the ground was treacherously slippery in places... he made a mental list of all the extra provisions he would need by the end of the afternoon; bandages, splints, painkillers, honey and lemon, a hot water bottle or two wouldn't go amiss...

"Do we have to persecute them like this? It's not as though we were a public school."

Nicholas had to be given credit for surviving most of the way around. He was a good sportsman in spite of being a little small for his age and was unfazed by the hidden roots of trees trying to trip him up, the terrors of skidding several yards across solid ice and the struggle for breath because the air was dense like a wall and it was a long time since he had run five miles all in one go. It was only when he came to cross a stream that things started to go badly for him. He lunged straight in, knowing that if he hesitated for a second he would lose momentum and probably his nerve as well. The water came up to his knees and was painfully cold, making him cry out as though he was being kicked repeatedly until he managed to scramble out onto the opposite bank.

Then when he attempted several more steps he felt his legs giving way altogether. "Hey, Nicky – you all right?" called Seamus who had been running behind him and was just in time to see him crumpling up on the ground. "Jesus! Bruiser, would you stop a moment, we've got a problem here."

Bruiser, so-called because he was the most aggressive tackler in the history of English football, hurried to the scene of the accident where Nicholas was writhing on his stomach, screaming, "*My legs, I'm dying!*" He had never experienced pain like it. He was sure that it must have been just like this to be turned on the rack, the muscles in his legs seemed to be stretching to tearing point then tying themselves into knots.

"Lordy, look at that," Seamus pointed at the backs of Nicholas's legs which looked as though several ping pong balls were trying to escape from his calves. "Father! Father Jennings!"

It was unfortunate for Nicholas that by the time Fr Jennings had run back from the front of the group, the muscle spasms had subsided a little and Seamus and Bruiser had managed to heave him onto his feet again, holding him up between them. "We've got to get him back to the San, Father," explained Seamus, "he's got terrible cramp."

Fr Jennings gave the three of them a look to strike

down the devil. "What a convenient moment you've chosen to get unwell, Falzon, right at the foot of a hill." Seamus felt Nicholas slump slightly against his shoulder in desperation.

"Father, he's really unwell. We saw him."

"How tragic. I suppose that means the two of you will have to go in with him then."

Seamus opened his mouth to reply but he felt Bruiser nudging Nicholas forward and the three of them skidded back in the direction of the school building without another word. "I don't like that at all," murmured Nicholas, who was by now feeling distinctly light-headed.

"Just ignore him," snarled Bruiser, kicking up a minor snowstorm in front of them. "It's his own stupid fault for sending us out running in this weather anyway. Mad git!"

Fr Mackay was thinking something very similar by the time Nicholas was carried through the door of the sanatorium. Nicholas did not have to look far for the reason either – he was the last of the Maltesers to fall in battle. Victor had lost his bearings, confused by the glare of the sun on snow and run straight into barbed wire – not a pretty sight to say the very least – Lawrence and John had both tripped over the same concealed hole in the ground and sprained their ankles, Ġużè looked like a lobster and had something resembling windburn – he would be shivering with fever by the morning, just to add insult to quite enough injury – and Gregory was laid out on the bed next to Nicholas with concussion.

"Are you all right?" asked Nicholas stupidly as Fr Mackay covered his mangled legs in what felt like hot bandages. Gregory's forehead was swollen to Frankenstein proportions and he stared vacantly up at the ceiling.

"I can't see anything," mumbled Gregory, but he sounded drugged.

"It's all right, son, he just got a nasty knock on the head," Fr Mackay explained, when Nicholas began trying to get out of bed. His brother was blind, Fr Jennings had blinded his brother... "He slipped on the ice and went straight down on his face. Lucky not to break his nose."

"Lucky?!" spluttered Nicholas but the warmth enveloping his legs brought on a sudden violent spasm and he shrieked with pain. *"I'm dying, no really,* I'm going to die!"

"There now, I don't think you'll be needing the consolation of Holy Church just yet. Close your eyes and think of... well, think of Malta, I suppose." Fr Mackay handed him a hot water bottle and walked off down the corridor to tend the walking wounded, muttering, 'I don't know what he was thinking of...' every step of the way.

Nicholas closed his eyes and thought of Malta.

Alexandria sat in her room, positioning herself so that a pleasing draught fell across the back of her head. With her eyes closed, she thought of England or at least she thought she was thinking of England. A particular place in England – Portsmouth, where she had found out that James Carlisle had been sent. It was fortunate for her that she had never seen Portsmouth before. It left her free to imagine it as a slightly wetter, greener version of the Grand Harbour and its surroundings. She imagined James walking, alone and tormented by the memory of her, under the shade of palm trees and lilac trees swaying together against a brilliant blue sky. Life held many disappointments for Alexandria.

Alexandria had a gut feeling that their paths would cross again before long and it was a comfort to her to believe that she might be out walking in Valletta one day and he would approach her from the crowd or she would be woken one morning by a knock on the door and he would be standing there waiting to take her away. To *properly* take her away this time. He might even write and send for her.

We'll meet again, don't know where, don't know when
But I know we'll meet again some sunny day.

Her instincts were right, they were destined to meet again before many years had passed, but it would certainly not be a sunny day when they did and they would both wish it had never happened. But that was yet to come. As Alexandria sat in her room, dreaming about a country she had never set foot in, she was just a few days away from starting studies for a degree in mathematics at the University of Malta. She hoped the excitement of it all would distract her from brooding on her ill-fated romance, but she very much doubted that it would. It all felt so fresh, in spite of the events of recent weeks.

She had stayed with the nuns for two weeks after James left her at the gate. It was harder to leave that time because the convent was a place where he had never belonged and it had no painful associations with him. She could go back to the way she had been before he had come crashing into her world and made her feel as if she was drowning and burning at the same time. It was a world sealed against the taint of men, good or bad and she felt liberated by it, wondering perhaps whether Mother Eugenia had not been wrong in her prophecy. Maybe this had all been God's way of telling her to renounce the world and all its fickleness. She saw herself a tragic, shadowy heroine, unhappy in love, greeting the veil and its promise of perpetual solitude with dignity and grace. She saw herself walking up and down the silent corridors, taming her restless spirit with prayer, fasting, self-sacrifice. She would be a saint, she would live a quiet holy life for a year or two then die very courageously of consumption in the odour of sanctity.

Then her father ruined everything as he always did by sending a message to Mother Eugenia summoning her home.

Tell Alexandria to pull herself together and come home.
She starts at the University next week.

Just like that. She had not even known she had applied for university, but she struggled home somehow and found a new set of clothes waiting for her and a pile of stationery and books. She was suddenly a student. Eighteen years old and a student.

"But I wanted to study Law," she declared in a small voice, as she and her father sat in the Rector's office.

Her father threw her a filthy look. "That is not a job for a woman," he answered – they had been through this before – "all that fighting and arguing." He had never thought that arguing and fighting was the wrong occupation for a woman when she was trying to dissuade him from doing permanent damage to her or her brothers – or perhaps he *had* thought that. She should have capitulated immediately and saved her female dignity even if she was not entitled to save anything else...

"I hope you understand now that you are no longer at school," preached the Rector. He was slightly perturbed by the rainbow hair slides and snowman earrings she was wearing. "You are clearly an exceptionally clever girl, but that does not mean you have the maturity to settle down into university life. We will be keeping a close eye on you."

There's a novelty, she thought bitterly as they stood

up to leave. I am going into the big adult world of university and there is *still* some man watching out for me to put a foot wrong. And who told them she was immature anyway? They stepped out into the corridor. The second the door closed softly behind them, Edward took Alexandria by the wrist and pushed her into a corner. "I thought I told you not to bring that up again!"

"What am I going to do with a Mathematics degree? Mathematicians are so *strange.*"

"You'll be a teacher if I must allow you to work at all!" He knocked her head against the wall. "And don't go causing me any embarrassment or I'll break your scrawny little neck. Understand?"

Oh, Alexandria understood. Unfortunately though, even the distraction of a leather attaché case and a whole array of new books and notepads to put in it were not enough to quell the rebellion stirring in Alexandria. Particularly when her course quickly degenerated into a pattern of extremely dull lectures given by lecturers she was quite sure were actually dead but no one except her had noticed yet.

She could not be entirely blamed for the mayhem she succeeded in causing during her short, sadly curtailed university career. There were only so many betrayals of trust that a girl could take and James Carlisle had opened a floodgate by abandoning her, whatever his pretext of loving concern. He had had a power over her that her father and Uncle Luigi had never had – he had loved her and she still loved him. He had shown her during their brief love affair how things should be done, never making demands on her, never intimidating her or deliberately hurting her.

For the first time in her life she felt angry and restless, but her emotional development was so stunted that she had no way of expressing it constructively. So she got herself into mischief that was as harmless and childish as the pranks she had played at school, but whereas her minor naughtiness had fitted the image of a bright, charmingly precocious convent girl, her behaviour jarred in an environment where students were expected to be a little more responsible for their behaviour.

She earned her first dressing down in her first month because she happened to notice that the rector's office was right next to the Ladies Cloakroom and acted on an irrepressible temptation to swap the sign reading: 'Rector: please knock' with 'Ladies'. It took no more than three or four young ladies to walk into his office adjusting their underwear before the rector realised what was going on and he knew exactly who was responsible without the need of any evidence. It was fortunate for Alexandria that when he was telling her off about it he had not yet found out that the Governor had come on an unofficial visit that day and been ushered very politely straight into... well, she had hoped they might see the funny side of it at a later hour.

It was when her displays of mischief made the national newspapers that her father grew restive. She always claimed afterwards that she had been put up to it and she probably was, but during the Christmas holidays when she and a group of her fellow students were working on the restoration of public monuments, she somehow found herself giving the statue of Queen Victoria in Valletta a good scrub. They removed the bird droppings, accumulated dust and graffiti, and as Alexandria was the smallest and most agile she climbed up onto Queen Victoria's crown to finish the job.

"You'll break your neck, my girl!" called a passer-by, as she shinnied up Queen Victoria's right shoulder blade, but she felt secure enough and then one of the gentlemen produced (it does not bear enquiring from where) a large pair of white underpants spotted with red love hearts. It was an innocent enough wheeze and she slipped them over Queen Victoria's head, securing them at a jaunty angle among appreciative giggles from the others stationed safely on terra firma. It was just a pity that she was unable to clear the area before the papers arrived, but her descent was hampered when she realised how far off the ground she was and panicked. She finished up on the front page of the papers, sat in the lap of her Late Lamented Majesty wearing Dennis Attard's underpants.

Jangle of cups and saucers smashing against the wall. "Defacing a public monument – I think there might be one or two people on the island who don't know about it!"

"But they weren't my underpants!"

Thud! "Walking past the newsstand with all the old biddies smirking and tutting – and your picture all over that ghastly rag! I thought I'd die of shame!" He should have been delighted at his daughter's apparent rejection of Imperial rule, but he had just shown his cultural independence by using the word 'ghastly' in a perfect Etonian lilt. "It'd serve you right if they threw you out of that university with a flea in your ear!" There was certainly something jangling in her ear now but it felt more like a tiny piece of broken china. "You'll destroy this family's name! You'll drag us into the gutter!"

We're in the gutter already, you idiot, she thought, then quaked with fear, convinced he had heard her thinking. But it was probably her lack of a political motive that annoyed him more than anything. It was plain from the expression on her face when he shouted the article at her word for word that she had thought of the incident as nothing more than a few friends larking about, something slightly naughty that would make the oldies shake their heads and mutter and the young ones giggle conspiratorially. The idea that it could have been used as a political statement was entirely beyond her understanding.

Her friends knew though. They all knew.

That was the whole problem. She had finished with being an adult child. Now she was a childish adult, with a child's impulses and tastes and a mind that saw everything in black and white. People were either bullies or they were nice people who would never lead her down the garden path. And they *were* nice people, the circle of Maltese students and English servicemen's children she became a part of, witty and clever and welcoming. In the absence of the convent, she adopted them as her family.

The feeling of affection was mutual. They liked her for her prim convent manners and quick temper and wide-eyed innocence. The English boys particularly loved her because she was so quirkily old-fashioned and spoke comical English fraught with double entendres she never made intentionally. They realised just how far they could stretch her when Jeremy Parkinson brought in a box full of strange, sausage-shaped balloons to show her.

It came as only the smallest surprise to any of them when she picked one of them out and started blowing it up. "How charming!" she said, as she dealt with the difficulty of securing it at the top. "But why are they all the same colour?"

"The Navy's a bit stingy like that," Jerry explained, his face admirably deadpan, "always buy the cheapest of everything to entertain the men."

"Oh." And by the end of the afternoon, Alexandria had aided and abetted the Anglo contingent in blowing up hundreds of the aforementioned sausage-shaped balloons and floating them across Grand Harbour. She was right, they did look pretty in a surreal kind of way, fluttering daintily on a light breeze then disappearing under the water or into the distance. And there were more photographers to capture the naughty antics of apparently rebellious students, though they only caught the back of her head for the front page. It was enough.

196

"Is there any other institution you would like to offend?"

Alexandria had discovered the self-defence potential of the corner of the room. If she sat as far into it as she could it shielded quite a lot of her. "But they were only a few balloons…"

"Don't you dare play the innocent with me!"

"But they were!"

"You know perfectly well what they were!" But she truly had no idea. It did not help when he produced the offending article – they seemed to be describing a quite different event. Who were these rabid, over-sexed lefties they were describing? And why did they describe them as 'angry'? They had had a very jolly afternoon of it, laughing and joking their way through that great big box. "I will never be able to show my face in church again!"

She was even more confused. When she was pious and talked nothing but choirs and convents, he attacked her for being a superstitious fool, lecturing her on how to be a good anti-clerical. Now he was Pius the twelfth. "But you haven't been to church for years. You said it was all about money and power…"

"I never said any such thing!"

"But you did, and you said that the Church was run by…" but she was accusing him of being a liar again and she could not hide enough of herself. If she pressed her knees up against her chest her legs were exposed but if she wriggled onto her knees she could not protect her front. She wished she had chosen a cupboard to sit in before arguing with him.

This is ludicrous, she thought, at the same time as she resigned herself to wearing long sleeves and skirts for the next fortnight. Why am I letting him do this? James had told her it was illegal but the idea of going to the police about such a private matter was too revolting to bear thinking about. She still did not know exactly what had passed between her father and Auntie Josephine all those years before and at the back of her mind she doubted whether they would believe her if she did talk to them.

So she continued to live at home, knowing that if she could finish her degree, she could find work and a home of her own. She was wasting her time and patience but did not know it then as she fought her little corner. She would never get her degree and she would never make a home for herself in Malta. Before much more time had passed, she would walk away without ever intending to.

XVI

We have ventured into Sliema's Independence Gardens. We walk across the ornamental bridge, listening out for the sound of stray cats fighting noisily in the dusty hedges, and find a seat near the fountain. "When did she run away?"

"Shortly before Malta gained independence. She just beat her country to it." I want her escape to have some symbolic value, but all it really meant was that she fled the country on the same flight as a large number of Englishmen going home. "She shouldn't have gone," I add, knowing how he will respond.

"I thought she'd never go." He looks put out. "I can't believe she stuck it so long. How could running away make things worse?"

Because things can always get worse. Because I know what awaited her when she arrived in England and because it was only youthful madness that made her imagine she could escape so easily.

Do not seek to escape your troubles by running away,
for no matter how far you travel,
you will find them waiting for you at your journey's end.

Or so the Greek philosopher said. I long to be able to stop her. I know that Alexandria is heading unwittingly into even murkier waters than the ones she has been fighting against all her life and yet I cannot prevent her. But then, like all the life-shattering moments in Alexandria's life, her escape was not planned or it would probably never have happened.

Alexandria's eyes opened to the possibility of escape when she restored the sight of her ten-year-old brother Joseph because her father was too blind to notice that anything was the matter. He had noticed that his son was very clumsy but just thought that he was more than usually stupid. His writing was appalling and his teachers frequently complained that he ignored the lines on the page completely and that his letters often ran into one another or that he missed out bits of words he should have known perfectly well.

At home he found himself left out of his brothers' ball games because he simply had no coordination whatsoever and when he was not missing the ball by miles he was tripping over loose paving stones and bits of furniture. It was only when Alexandria watched him colouring in a picture he had drawn that it occurred to her what was going on.

He had drawn a picture of a cat to decorate *The Owl and the Pussy Cat* which he had copied out for school. Without even looking at the text, something was obviously amiss. The body parts simply did not match up. There was a space between the head and the body and there were five paws instead of four as if he had drawn four then forgotten how many he had drawn and added an extra one just to make sure. He had tried to colour it in with grey pencil, but had gone outside the lines like a four-year-old.

"How would you like a trip to the shops, Joseph?" she asked, the afternoon the penny dropped. "That's it, up you get. We'll go and buy cakes for tea."

She could easily have passed for his mother, walking hand-in-hand with him in the direction of the Optician's. She knew just how to gain his co-operation, chivvying him into the dingy shop with more promises of cakes and possibly an ice cream when he froze outside the unwelcoming glass door. "I just want you to meet this nice man in here," she said. He flinched at the dull clank of the bell over the door warning Dr Vella that he had customers. It felt as welcoming as a mortuary.

There was a muffled, "yes?" then an elderly gentleman half-fell into the room where they were standing. "Can I help you?"

"Yes," answered Alexandria, seizing the moment, "I wonder if you could test this child's eyesight for me – quickly?"

Dr Vella narrowed his eyes at her request, but he could not imagine why the little woman should want a quick eye test for any sinister reason and he let the query pass. "Of course. Take a seat. Come with me, son."

Joseph found himself sitting in a big black chair feeling quite the centre of attention. "Now son, do you know your alphabet?"

"Of course I know my alphabet!"

"Very good then. What is the smallest row of letters you can read?" Joseph looked ahead of him for some considerable time without speaking before he began to make small distressed noises. "It's all right, all in your own time."

"But there aren't any letters, sir," he bleated, convinced that this was all some sick joke meant to get him into trouble.

"The letters on the card," Dr Vella explained, but the boy was facing the right direction.

"What card?"

Ten minutes later, Dr Vella came crashing out of the room holding Joseph firmly by the hand. Alexandria jumped out of her seat and instinctively drew back, knowing that a fight was coming. "This child cannot see a thing!" he roared, too angry to notice that Joseph had slipped his hand away and covered his face, braced for an attack. It was all his fault, he should have made something up. Now they were both in hot water and it was all his fault. "What sort of a mother are you? He is practically *blind!*"

"He's not my son, he's my brother and it's not my fault!" she shouted back, hurrying across to where Joseph was cowering.

He was taken aback – where were the boy's parents? Were they too ashamed to face a professional with the son whose sight they had neglected? Did he perhaps have no parents? "All right, all right." Heavens, he really had succeeded in frightening them both, a pang of conscience sent him off his usual impeccable balance. "I'm sorry, but-but this really... this really is very bad. There now, my dear, I tell you what..." He placed a hand on Alexandria's shoulder and helped her into a chair, gathering his nerves together in the interim. "I tell you what, why don't you two disappear for the afternoon? I'll make up his spectacles straight away and they'll be ready for you when you come back. How does that sound?"

So Alexandria took Joseph out for a treat and bought him Kinnie to drink and as many sweets as she could risk giving him without making him sick, Then they walked around the Upper Barrakka gardens to make up the rest of the time. He remembered his last afternoon of living in a haze with unhappy fondness, recalling what it had been like to run around in a whirl of spring light in the company of his sister. It was the last time for many years that he felt love for her, because she had not done the worst thing yet and he still knew with certainty that he could reach out and find her.

Alexandria wondered how she was going to explain all of this to her father. It dawned on her on the way back to Dr Vella's shop that if he had not noticed that his own son could hardly see, he might not even notice that he was suddenly wearing a pair of shiny new spectacles. Except that she would have to slip him the bill sooner or later.

Joseph was about to leave the vaporous wilderness of his childhood. All his life he had lived in a world of undefined shapes and swimming splashes of colour. Without realising it, he recognised people, even immediate family, by their outlines or by the shape of the shadow their voices came from, perpetually listening for a monster to come leaping out of the whirlpool of fuzzy images. Joseph did not even have the benefit of a short warning before he was struck down and he had spent much of the time since he learnt to walk creeping about the misty rooms and open spaces of the house waiting for the worst to happen. He never believed in monsters lurking behind the wardrobe or things that went bump in the night because he never needed imaginary monsters to frighten him.

Standing in Dr Vella's shop, all that was about to change. He was told to close his eyes whilst a pair of plain, round, steel-rimmed spectacles were placed onto his nose and curled around his ears. They felt heavy and cold against his face. "Perfect," said a satisfied male voice. "Now open your eyes."

Joseph opened them a little too quickly and flinched with shock: the world had appeared out of nowhere. He was standing in a room with clearly defined boundaries, there were hard lines and right-angles everywhere. Alexandria's blue dress was covered in tiny pictures, there were prints of mountains and green places and the sea all over the walls. The two people on either side of him had faces.

He ran to the doorway to see if it still worked outside but the sight made him dizzy. Instead of the now reassuring watercolour of soft, furry-looking objects that had made up his world until that moment, the street was harsh and precise like gold glass, full of people like Alexandria and the optician, so busy to look at, so full of detail – and horses and shop signs and steps everywhere. That was why the pavements had felt so strange under his feet! They were not pavements at all they were staircases following the road up and down and far away, as far as the world went from now on.

"Well, do you like them?" asked Dr Vella, following Joseph out into the street. "What can you see?" But from behind the thick, bottle-top lenses, Joseph was silent. The world was suddenly alarming, exciting, terrible, wonderful... but he had no words to describe how he felt. With the help of two pieces of glass, the world had snapped into focus.

"I'm not sure I fancy telling Daddy about this," Joseph confessed as they walked home. He stopped to watch a *karrozin* clattering past. "I didn't realise the horses had all those straps attached to them. That's how the cab keeps up."

"It's all right, I'll think of something," Alexandria promised, pulling him away from a shop-window cluttered with sweetie jars. "He probably won't even notice."

"I hope he won't break them."

"I'll deal with it, you don't worry about a thing."

"You're nervous, your voice has gone all hard."

She was nervous, but when they reached the house she found that their father was nowhere to be seen. Antonia was bustling about the kitchen preparing dinner. "That's what she looks like," said Joseph out loud, marvelling at the sight of a lady he had never met before who glanced down at him with startling *mandorla* eyes and jumped with shock.

"What is he wearing those for?" she demanded, thinking it was a practical joke. "He looks ridiculous." Oh, it really was his mother after all.

"I took him to have his eyes tested," Alexandria explained. "Dr Vella said he needed them urgently, so he made them straight away."

"But I can barely see his eyes through those lenses!" She was appalled. The child had such a sweet face and now Alexandria had gone and ruined him.

"The lenses are thick because his eyes are very weak," she said. "He could hardly see a thing before."

"Well, you might have told me something!" She forced herself to look at the son she barely recognised. "I suppose if he needs them it can't be helped, but he really does look a mess."

"You'll get used to it," promised Alexandria. She thought he looked rather adorable in his bottle-top spectacles, more studious and vulnerable than ever. "I don't suppose you could hand over the bill, could you?" Alexandria placed it on the table in front of her mother, who gave a small yelp. "I'm sorry, he did promise a good price, but they had to be done so quickly. Where is Daddy, by the way?"

"Fortunately for you he has a little function on tonight." Thank God, thought Alexandria, he'll have a few pints inside him by the time he returns. "I shall broach the subject when he is nice and comfortable."

Alexandria knew it would not be that straightforward, but she had no idea just how complicated it was going to be for her. She could barely eat a thing over dinner, and would have had even less appetite if she had known it was the last meal she would ever eat in her home, but it was better that she never had any warning. The hours of the evening slipped slowly away, punctuated by nervous glances towards the door and the endless mental rehearsal of every possible reaction they might have to deal with. She seemed to remember afterwards trying to teach Mark how to play chess just so that she could beat him every time. He did not have a tactical mind at all. Joseph's nerves were drowned in the novelty of being able to see. He walked around every room, studying the paintwork, the furniture, the pictures on the walls. Antonia had to keep stopping him from reaching up to the ornaments sitting in a squat row on top of the mantelpiece, because he had

205

never seen anything so lovely and intricate, swirls and bubbles of colour trapped in glass figures.

Alexandria went up to bed eventually and slept very badly, waking every half hour with a growing sense of trepidation. And that should have been all there was to it. A nervous evening that concluded at some point in the night or following morning with a violent confrontation – nothing unusual about that. Except that this time, when Alexandria woke with a start and realised that her father must be home, she knew that something was different. It was difficult for her to understand what it was, but she was different. She woke up knowing that trouble was coming to her as it had so many times before, many more than she could even have counted, and for some inexplicable reason, she found herself getting up and going out to greet it.

She tiptoed out of her room and stood in the corridor outside her parents' room. A growling whisper assured her that her father was awake. She could hear him talking to her mother. "What do you mean she just took him there without a word?" An inaudible retort from Antonia. "Didn't she at least ask you?"

Another murmur, this time fainter. "There's nothing wrong with his eyes! Do you suppose I wouldn't have noticed if my own son was that blind?" Alexandria held her breath, waiting to be brought up in the conversation. He never failed. "Why must she always interfere? Have you seen the size of that bill?" Anyone would have thought that she had been squandering his money on a life of riley. "I'll make her wish she'd never been born!"

Astonishing to say, but never in her entire life had Alexandria wished that she had never been born. She had wanted to curl up and die many times, but that was hardly the same thing. Only one person wished she had never seen the light of day in her family and she was listening to him detailing exactly how, leaning flat against the wall with her ear pressed against the edge of the doorframe. She thought that she was glad she had come into the world if it was only to get her own back. There, she knew what was wrong now. She was not afraid.

She would normally be shaking by now, trying to guess how much time she had to brace herself or make a run for it, but she could not hear the blood roaring in her ears or feel the sickening lurch of her stomach turning somersaults. She found that she was standing up straight, taking her weight firmly on both feet. Something momentous was taking place inside her and she seemed to be growing in stature like Alice in Wonderland, filling the house with her strength. "No you're not," she thought and found herself crossing the landing with a silently determined tread. For the first time in her life, Alexandria Sant'Angelo had other plans.

> *It seemed that out of the battle I escaped*
> *Down some profound dull tunnel...*

She listened for sounds of movement but it was all quiet now and she forced herself to open the door to her father's study. She knew what she had to do; it seemed so straightforward that she could not imagine how she never had the nerve to do it before. It was not as though anything worse could happen to her now, even if her father woke up and her plan was rumbled. She could still go, he could not stop her. She was a woman.

She made for his desk, knowing that in the bottom drawer there was a stack of family passports, among them her own and his emergency supply of cash. It helped that he came from a generation of hoarders, perpetually ready for the next national emergency. Even she did not know what that fear felt like, she just knew that it was the one part of him that was vulnerable to attack. A memory of broken glass visited her for a moment, causing her to falter. She was not robbing him, she told herself, it was her passport. She leafed through the wad of banknotes she found, swallowed a rumbling conscience and took it all. She was not robbing him, she told herself, she was just taking her reparation money.

She only began to tremble when she was back in her room, changing into clothes suitable for travel, but it almost felt like a game, cramming a small suitcase with whatever she thought she might need. She did not need to pack much and avoided anything that would remind her of home. She was emigrating, she was leaving everything behind; she should not even allow a grain of Maltese dust to cling to her feet as she boarded the plane. He would provide for her – had he not said over and over again that he would look after her in England and protect her?

She stepped out of her room with her case and lingered outside her brothers' door, shaking off a sickening thought that she was betraying them. She knew that she could not wake them up. They would wake up in the morning to the murderous wrath of their father without any warning at all and discover that it was all her fault, that she had left them without a word. But if she spoke to them, she knew that she would change her mind and it was better for them to hate her than for her to remain. That was what her reason said anyway. Her emotions said something quite different and she cringed against the wall, choked with the pain of their presence so near to her. They were the reason why she had always come back, even when the nuns had begged her to stay away. But this time she knew that she would not come back. The surge of grief passed as quickly as it had come, leaving a dull ache that was to remain with her until she had a child of her own. She walked down the stairs and out into the quiet street.

Alexandria was never told that, after she had left, Joseph took to sitting on the doorstep of the house every day for a year watching the planes coming in from faraway London, believing that she would be on the next one... or the next one... or the next. Hope is said to spring eternal, particularly among the young, but even he had to accept after 365 days of waiting that she would not be coming home.

We can see plenty of planes coming and going as we talk, even on a public holiday. Every time I see the lights blinking overhead, I cross myself out of force of habit. "They won't fall out of the sky, you know," Benedict reassures me.

"A priest told me to say a prayer every time I see a plane," I explain and feel like a five-year-old convent girl, "because there is always someone on it who doesn't want to be." It is no good explaining to him that travel is an unnatural state of affairs; he enjoys it, like Englishmen who find the desert romantic because they have only ever known green places. There is nothing more terrible than being in a state of transit; it is like a *memento mori*, so much coming and going and passing so quickly.

"It's lucky for you that your mother went to England," says Benedict, "or she would never have rescued your father from the priesthood. You owe your existence to that escape, you know."

"Who said he never became a priest?" Oh the things I have not told him about. Have I really not told him that my father was a priest? I never knew what the word 'blenched' meant until I saw Benedict's face, though I cannot think why he is so shocked about the breaking of rules he never believed in. He must think I was conceived in a presbytery cupboard, but it is almost a pity it was not quite as sensational as that. "Oh dear, have I shocked you?"

"But you're a... you know..." he points at the rosary ring attached to my wristwatch as though it were a medical advice tag.

"Yes I know, but you would be fairly committed if you had a priest in the family." He is wondering why my unorthodox origins have not turned me into a dungaree-clad, muesli-eating feminist. "Look, someone had to rebel into Catholicism, didn't they? Lapsed Nannu, lapsed uncle, lapsed mother…"

"I thought she wanted to be a nun?"

"Dropped it all like an old coat the moment she left the country." That is a little harsh, they all came back eventually except grandfather who was too scared to believe in a just God by the end. "Anyway, you're a lapsed atheist."

"I prefer 'resting atheist'. When are they going to meet?"

"Not yet."

It hardly mattered that they were in the same country, there was no way yet for their paths to cross. My mother went to Portsmouth, my father was still in the north and they might have been in different countries. Nicholas remembered England as the Arcadia where he learnt to milk cows and toast marshmallows on bonfires on chilly autumn evenings, but it was a long time before Alexandria could look on the country with such charmingly rose-tinted spectacles.

It started to go horribly wrong for her before she had even left Malta as the manner of leaving was quite contrary to tradition. She was an émigré after all – where were the hoards of weeping relatives, the heart-wrenching farewells, the promises of letters and prayers and speedy returns? Why did she sit alone, dry-eyed without the slightest shadow of a regret that she was leaving her home indefinitely, waiting for the flight as though she were waiting for the bus to school? Why was her only source of unease the terrible possibility that her father might discover what she was doing and drag her all the way home before she had the chance to make her escape?

He did not think to look for her there. According to Sr. Therezina when they met again many years later, he was convinced that his daughter had simply run off to the convent again and it was more than three weeks before he contacted them to ask why she did not come home. He refused for months to believe that she was not with them or that they had played no part in her disappearance, leaving them desperately worried about what had actually happened to her.

The journey continued to go wrong. "Have you got a coat, madam?" asked the stewardess, as the BEA flight neared London and they began to prepare for landing.

"Oh no, it's quite all right," Alexandria explained with a superior smile. "I'll manage."

"I think you might find it a little cold," persisted the stewardess, taking in the girl's flimsy cotton dress and bare arms. "I don't suppose this is your first visit to England, is it?"

Alexandria was unperturbed. She was quite able to cope with bitterly cold days when the temperature plummeted to twenty degrees Celsius. She dismissed the stewardess with a knowing smile and waited to catch her first sight of green fields far below. It did not occur to her to ask why she did not see a single patch of green as she descended over London. The plane landed with a bump, she scrambled to the opening doors and... seemed to be floating down the steps of the aeroplane. Somewhere between the stuffy warmth of the aircraft and her first breath of English air, she seemed to have walked straight into a wall of solid ice. Her head pounded with the cold blast striking her face... her feet in their sandals wafted over slippery iron steps... and somehow or other, choking and gasping for breath, she found herself standing motionless in the bracing frost of an English February.

She could barely stand opening her eyes and felt tears coming. It was like a bitter reproach. "This is

England, you ignorant little girl," the icy cold, miserable world around her seemed to be saying, "you have not come to a dream world, you have not stepped inside a book. This is a real country and you are welcome to it, but you must take all of it. You cannot pick and choose." She stood in real England paralysed with shock, feeling the tips of her fingers and nose being stabbed with cold needles. She began to shiver. 'I'm going to die,' she thought, certain that her blood was freezing in her veins along with everything else. Didn't people die of the cold in places such as this? *The late Alexandria Sant'Angelo met her end in a London blizzard and will not be sadly missed by anyone.*

"Can we help you, my dear?" a voice whispered from the end of a tunnel. She felt something warm wrapping itself around her body and blinked. A smiling old lady had covered her in a heavy fur coat smelling of mothballs, someone else, her husband she assumed, appeared to be stopping her from falling. "Are you on your own?"

"I am a foreigner," she bleated – in case that fact was not entirely obvious – but her bilingual abilities seemed to have been curtailed somewhat by her descent into the Arctic. But of course the deepest darkest circles of Dante's Hell were full of ice not fire...

"We'd better get her indoors," said the voice at the end of the tunnel. "She's going to die out here, the poor soul." Yes, poor soul! She thought, poor lost soul! *Abandon hope all ye who enter here...*

Mr and Mrs Blake helped her inside. She remembered nothing afterwards of passport controls or of collecting her suitcase and only began to feel compos mentis again as she sat with her rescuers in front of a mug of steaming coffee. They seemed worried about her, pestering her with questions. "What brings you to England? Are you a student?"

"Not exactly. I'm – I'm looking for my boyfriend."

She did not understand the looks they exchanged and it only occurred to her when she was a parent herself that they probably thought she was pregnant.

"Oh, is he coming to meet you?"

"He doesn't know I've come yet. He's in the Navy."

"Oh dear." She did not understand that tone either, but then she did not see herself as just another naïve little native who had been led up the garden path by a member of Her Majesty's forces.

"I have to go to Portsmouth. Is it far from here? Do you suppose I will have to take a bus?" Some things never changed about the Maltese abroad. She waited whilst the Blakes excused themselves from the table and conferred out of earshot, allowing her time to slip back into a comfortable trance before they returned. It was probably all a dream anyway.

"My dear, we've been thinking," said Mrs Blake. "It's really too late for you to be taking the train to Portsmouth tonight, you'll arrive in the dark. It wouldn't be very safe for you. Why don't you come back to our house for now and we'll put you on a train in the morning?"

So, Alexandria went home with the Blakes to their comfortable if tiny suburban home, where she sat with them for dinner and Mrs Blake noted her pleasingly quaint table manners. Whilst Mr Blake made careful conversation with her, attempting to find out as much about her background as possible, and Alexandria was the epitome of courtesy, addressed him as 'sir' and declining to give him any useful information whatsoever, Mrs Blake made up the spare room.

Alexandria slept soundly, too exhausted and bewildered to feel homesickness yet, waking up whilst it was still dark. She had no watch and drifted in and out of consciousness, waiting for sunlight to poke through the gap in the curtains. The night refused to make way for morning. She lay still in the darkness hour after hour, waiting for the dawn, but the night sprawled out and she began to think that she was sleeping, dreaming that she had been abducted and imprisoned in a night without end.

The nightmare only came to an end with the gentle sound of Mrs Blake knocking on the door. "Lunch in ten minutes if you would like to eat."

Alexandria leapt out of bed and scrambled into the first clothes she could pull out of her suitcase in her panic. Had she said lunch? She tore open the curtains and stared outside. It was dark. The sky was a deep grey, no sign of a sunrise anywhere, no sun to rise, in fact. The windows of the houses on the other side of the street glowed with artificial light. And it was lunchtime, halfway through the day.

"It could be worse," she whimpered to her reflection in the windowpane. "I could be curled up in a sunny room with my father throwing pieces of crockery at me." She thought of that and the prospect of meeting James again and hurried downstairs to apologise to Mrs Blake. She was very relieved when they found it so funny and realised that she was not a lazy good-for-nothing who spent half her life lolling in bed. "You'll have a long wait if you want to see the sun at this time of year!"

After lunch, Mr Blake searched telephone directories and telephoned friends until he had found her the number of the correct Naval welfare officer to track down the whereabouts of James. Then he telephoned him for her because she was crippled by a sudden bout of nerves in case it turned out that his ship had sailed to Hong Kong or somewhere like that in the interim. Of all the nightmares she could think of, finding herself in England without the security of James was too terrible a fate to contemplate. She had no contingency plan if he was not there for her. She could not afford the flight back home and in any case, she did not dare go back now. Even if her father did not throw her out for fleeing him in the first place, she was too proud to have to grovel to such a man and admit she had made a mistake. She could just hear him saying: "See, I told you your English friends were just trying to use you... that's what happens when you go running after them, you lose everything." Anything rather than that.

"He's in the Hasler Naval Hospital – nothing to worry about, just a sporting injury by the sounds of things, but he'll be in for the next couple of days." Mr Blake looked rather awkward. "I'm afraid I might have been guilty of impersonation," he explained, "I wasn't sure what to say when he asked who I was, so I said I was his godfather. I don't suppose he'll mind, will he?" He took his mind off the crime by getting out his atlas of Great Britain and searching for Portsmouth.

"I do hope she'll be all right," whispered Mrs Blake as they waved her off at the station. "She's terribly young to be alone in a strange country."

"Well, we did what we could. Nothing more we can do for her now, I'm afraid."

Alexandria settled herself into her seat and let the train carry her to Portsmouth, where James Carlisle was about to get the fright of his life.

XVII

If I should die, think only this of me
That there's some corner of a foreign field
That is forever England.

Poor corner of a foreign field, thought Alexandria bitterly, as she surveyed the sorry scene around her. Portsmouth, she had decided, had to be the drabbest, shabbiest, greyest, most unwelcoming city in the entire world. "What a dump he lives in!" she thought in what was half sympathy, half accusation, taking out the piece of paper Mr Blake had given her with the directions from the station to the hospital. The sooner she found him and rescued him from this squalor the better. In fact, her idea of staying with him in England transformed itself rapidly during her sorry journey through the city she had dreamed about. She could not possibly stay here, she would insist that he take her back to Malta. It would be better that way anyway, she could go home with him and watch her father's jaw drop when they stepped through the door. If they had to stay in England, she might at least be able to persuade him to take her somewhere else to live. There had to be nice places in England somewhere. Where had Wordsworth and Keats and Rupert Brooke lived to write such lovely words and think such charming thoughts?

She paused outside the hospital entrance. It was no secret that she did not like hospitals very much and she had to practically hurl herself through the doors to get in at all. The smell of disinfectant conjured up memories of stitches and Plaster of Paris and splints and slings and monumental lies. *I fell down the stairs. I fell off a wall. I got beaten up by my brother. I walked into the wardrobe. The furniture in my house has a mind of its own. My father is a psychopath...* She wondered what would have happened if she had actually said that, but she had more immediate problems to deal with.

"I need to speak to James Carlisle," she told the lady behind the reception desk. "It's very urgent."

"And who are you, if I may ask?"

Alexandria did not like the woman's tone. She raised herself to her full, inconsiderable height and covered her left hand. "I am his wife."

She really did walk into it. "You can't be, his wife came to visit him an hour ago."

"That's nonsense," answered Alexandria, but she could already feel darkness roaring inside her head. "I am his wife."

"Run along, my girl, you're wasting my time."

Alexandria felt an icy hand clasping her throat and slumped against the counter for support, quite unable to catch her breath. "There now, there's no need for that. Pull yourself together!" But for the second time in two days, Alexandria simply could not comprehend what was happening to her. A mass of discordant noises blocked out the woman's voice and the background murmur of the hospital. She was caught in a nightmare, the same nightmare as before – trapped in a night without end, a night where the sunlight could not wake her. Darkness, silence. She felt herself falling...

When she came round, the first face to snap into focus was James's. She was lying in a hospital bed, a nurse held her wrist firmly between clinical, scrubbed fingers but James was at her side. Married James. "Oh my God, Alex, what are you doing here?"

"I- " The words froze in her throat. She was too torn between desire and revulsion to speak and found herself wishing that she could just scream. A long, desperate, animal howl roared inside her because there were no words left but she gasped and choked until it died. James heard only a tiny whimper and wished she could have spared him even that.

"Things were finished between us, Alex. What on earth did you come running here for? You must go home. You must go home at once, you're just a..."

"I've grown up," she snarled, with unexpected venom. Rage had won over whatever else she was feeling and her voice clattered like broken glass. "I grew up whilst you were away. You said it was just because I was too young." She peered at his left hand and saw the wedding band glistening in sickening confirmation. Her temples pounded with rage.

"Alex, I'm so sorry" – and to give the man credit, he probably was. It was difficult not to feel sorry for a girl lying half-dead on a hospital bed, thousands of miles away from home, jilted, rejected and he was not so heartless that he did not know whose fault it was. "I'm married."

"I know that!" But the whole terrible truth of the matter was only just sinking in. Could he have been married whilst he was courting her? No, perhaps not married but perhaps engaged or at least courting and he had gone to ask her father's permission to marry *her*. How had he thought he could get away with it, or had he been planning to break his English fiancée's heart when it came to it? Had she mattered a fraction more to him than the girl waiting for him in this distant country whilst he did his overseas duty? Just for a moment perhaps? Just for a heady Maltese summer?

"You have to go home," he said, reaching out to touch her arm. She recoiled violently, sickened by the sight of his hand reaching out to her. Pretend pity, she knew where that always led. "Look Alex, it's your home, you don't belong here. If it's the money, I'll pay for your ticket. It's the least I can do."

"I can't go home!" She attempted to sit upright but the room lurched like a fairground mirror and she fell back. "Remember my father? Did you think he'd magically disappeared or something? You know why I can't go back!" James looked so stricken with guilt she almost felt sorry that she had spoken to him like that but she was too consumed with hurt to resist a parting shot. "If you're afraid I might meet your little wife and tell her everything you can rest easy. I'll keep out of your way. You don't have to try and pack me off home in case I tell."

She had exposed his deepest fear. He looked from her to the nurse glaring disapprovingly in his direction and felt as if the whole world had conspired against him to create his worst-case scenario. She could not even be silenced with promises of help. He would have to rely on her discretion when he knew she had every reason to want to shame him.

"I think you had better leave," said the nurse, tucking the bedclothes in around Alexandria's motionless body. "I fail to see how your presence can aid this poor girl's recovery."

He resisted the temptation to try and touch her again and left the room. To make the situation about as terrible as it could have been, it was not as though he did not even love her – but that was something she would never understand. All she could hear was her father's laughter, her father who for all his faults had known all along that they would reduce her to this. A needle was slipped effortlessly into her arm but even sedation would not block out the cruel, mocking laughter of a man whose worst prejudices had been vindicated. Searing laughter and the breaking of dreams.

Whilst nurses rifled through her personal effects to try to find out her identity and next of kin, Alexandria surrendered to drugged sleep and drifted peacefully through a soundless ocean. She was being treated for shock, perhaps she was a little mad but there was something seductive about helplessness that she had learnt a long time ago and she wafted in and out of consciousness without even noticing the passage of three long days and nights.

If she had been destined for sainthood, this would have been a time of visions and enlightenment. She would have descended into hell with Dante and Virgil by her side and seen men metamorphosed into trees, thieves attacked by reptiles. In a Purgatorial circle she would have carried rocks on her neck, then, in the last ecstatic moments of her dream, she would have crossed the river into Paradise and the beatific vision.

Instead she remembered only tiny shards of consciousness. The presence of a nurse by her side, shivering with the cold, men shaking their heads and murmuring about scarring and untreated fractures, the sensation of slipping through swirls of cloud and black water. Then snatches of music she had learnt at home or at the convent. *Oh Mary we crown thee with blossoms today! Queen of the angels and Queen of the May!* The haunting rumble of The Last Post then a carol or a children's rhyme. *Xi shana, xi shana! Kulħadd ikanta magħna!* Words, words, words strung together from every year of her life and before. The last memory was of words and music woven in a thin discordant pattern around her.

Where have all the flowers gone?
Long time passing.
Where have all the flowers gone?
Long time ago.

Alexandria found herself walking slowly down a white corridor. The smell of disinfectant and bodies reminded her by degrees that she was in a hospital, but the drugs sliding dreamily through her body prevented

220

her from panicking, even when her vision snapped perfectly into focus and she saw doors on either side leading to rooms full of beds and cubicles. Somewhere, she could hear the twanging of a tuneless musical instrument and a man's thin voice singing plaintively, 'Where have all the young girls gone? Long time passing. Where have all the young girls gone…' By the time she arrived at the end of the corridor and saw a man sitting on an orange-backed chair playing a guitar, he had graduated, quite inexplicably to, 'lead kindly light amid the encircling gloom.'

The encircling gloom. There was something upsetting about the words that she could not make herself understand. 'The night is dark and I am far from home.' It was the drugs they had given her, she told herself, they were doing something strange to her emotions. She felt none of the raw sensation of grief that she had known. There was no heat, no intensity to it at all. She stood in front of this absurd stranger with his unkempt hair and gaunt, pockmarked, unlovely face, singing a Victorian hymn to the wrong chords and felt warm tears pattering against her cheeks.

He looked up at her, shamefaced, and stopped immediately. "I'm sorry. Where did you come from?" She closed her eyes, wondering if she could slip back into nothingness if she tried very hard, but she was hopelessly awake. If it was any consolation, and it probably would not have been, he felt exactly the same. "Sorry. Don't cry, love, it's only a song." Where on earth had this little girl come from? He had been happily wallowing in his own misery, when quite out of nowhere, this vision of innocence, swathed in hospital white, had appeared in front of him – crying. He had seen so many odd things over the past forty-eight hours or however long it was, that he could not rule out the possibility that she was an angel or a nymph who had come to offer him comfort. Except that he seemed to be the one who needed to offer comfort under the circumstances. "Do you want to sit down?"

She hesitated, bewildered by his well-spoken voice. "Where am I?"

The first of all questions. So, she did not know what she was in for either. "You're in the loony bin, sweetie." She looked blankly at him. She was not from these parts, evidently. "Do you speak English?"

"Of course." She had not said enough all at once for him to be able to place her accent. "I don't understand. Where am I? There's nothing wrong with my head."

"Doesn't have to be, nothing wrong with mine either." He reached out and placed a friendly hand on her arm but she shrugged him off very gently. It was the first time a girl had ever been afraid of him and he was too surprised to be offended. "Those are impressive scars." He had not intended it to be the next subject of conversation, but as he looked her up and down he noticed a web of lines running in all directions over her bare legs. She stepped back even further and he thought she would have made a scene if they had not sapped her energy. "It's all right, there's nothing to be ashamed of." She was faintly unsettled by his tone. She knew nothing about drug abuse and could not understand why he said everything in a half-whisper with barely any life in the words and why he sounded so educated and looked like a tramp. "I've got much more exciting ones than those."

She watched, half in fascination, half in horror, as he put down his guitar, rolled up his sleeves and revealed the most disgusting sight she had ever seen. On both arms deep red cuts showed up against the pallid flesh, running like embroidery all the way up to the elbow. She raised a hand to her head but the dizziness receded as fast as it had come. "But I did those myself."

He watched for a reaction, but she had recovered from the shock already and was not to be baited. "Why were you singing a hymn?" she asked. Her accent was delightful, something not quite Italian, not quite Arab.

"I'm a vicar's son," he said, swallowing laughter. "The one they don't talk about."

"Why are you here?"

"Well, you're not going to believe this, love, but it was like this." There was a little more energy in him now, he had something important to say. "I was walking down the street like as normal. The cars were rushing by, the sun was shining." He must be mad, she thought, sunshine hadn't been sighted on English shores for about a millennium. That was why they kept sailing all over the world pinching everyone else's. She switched her concentration on again. "So there I was, when suddenly, this great big tin of baked beans fell out of the sky, right on top of my head. When I woke up, I was in here."

He took a look at her to see if she could help explain it, but she was looking blankly at him, quite simply confused beyond words. "You know, pet, you shouldn't be in here. There's nothing wrong with you that they can mend."

She managed a smile before she turned around and began the long walk back in the direction she had come from, relieved to feel numbness creeping over her once again. No wonder they had to drug her, this was a mad, mad world they had put her into. How else would she survive without this tube in her vein? Oh she felt tired. Everything seemed to be such an effort, the putting of one foot in front of the other, the dragging of an IV stand. It was a cross between jumping into the cold sea and the day after a beating. There was no pain but she felt dazed and slightly nauseous, and there was a cloud of something like sadness all around her. 'The night is dark and I am far from home.'

It was either James or Malta. One moment, the words conjured up James as she would always remember him, tall and handsome in his uniform,

223

standing next to her watching the sunset on the first day they met. But at the same time as she was imagining him coming to find her – sailing into Grand Harbour in Valletta as she had hoped and prayed he would whenever she walked past it – she found herself watching her brothers huddled together, waiting for her to return to them through the dark, dark night they were all caught in and could never escape. Somehow, as she stood against the wall paralysed with despair, someone led her back to her ward and put her to sleep.

"It was nice of you to come and visit me," the shrill, acidic voice commented, somewhere on the outer orbits of Neptune. "*Marija*, what have they given you? You must be as high as a kite!" Auntie Josephine's voice could always pierce anything, even Edward's closed conscience, but Alexandria still could not accept that it was really her. Her waking dreams had been full of visions of home and it was quite impossible that it could be true. "Alex, sweetheart, when you have a moment you might like to open your eyes."

Alex was afraid of opening her eyes, that was when the dream died and she found herself alone with just her IV stand for company. "You're not really there!" she tried to shout, in a voice that rasped unexpectedly. Silence. She knew it was just an illusion. A sharp tug on her right ear opened her eyes immediately.

"Of course I'm here, you silly girl! Don't you think I'm a bit on the large side for a ghost?"

"Not as large as a tin of baked beans," said Alex, fixing her eyes firmly on the woman's face. Yes, it really did seem to be her. She was fatter for sure, almost as big as a giant tin of baked beans in fact and her hair (which she had hardly ever seen before) was grey and black like a badger, but it was definitely Auntie Josephine and she was not reacting to her as she should. "I'm sorry, auntie, I can't seem to get excited. I really am pleased to see you, you know."

"It's all right, you're drugged up to the eyebrows, the idiots. There's nothing wrong with you." Mental illness was not to be admitted, even by a nurse, even by a nurse who had just heard her niece claim that she was smaller than a tin of baked beans. "Sit up for Auntie, there's a good girl. You shouldn't be in bed at all."

Alex found herself being helped to sit up, a state of affairs that seemed to clear her head a little. "What are you doing here? Did my family send you?"

"No, you little troublemaker. Your family do not know where you are, nor do they greatly care I suspect." The girl looked crestfallen, it was time for apologies. "I'm sorry little one, I'm afraid this is all my fault. I thought it would come to this sooner or later. What happened?"

So Alexandria explained her last evening in Malta, how she had heard her father's threats as she stood on the landing, how she had robbed him, the journey, the Blakes and the terrible revelation at the hospital. Josephine sat by her bedside and listened, passing her grapes as she had once passed her pastries to ease the truth out of her. It was not unlike their meeting of years ago; her untidy hair and crumpled hospital garb made her look painfully young; when she sat beside her, she still swung her legs and they were still scarred, but Alexandria was a woman now and instead of cheerfully telling her the most disgusting things that had ever happened to her, she reached the end of her narrative and burst into floods of tears.

"Listen to me, Alex, I am going to do the right thing this time," promised Auntie Josephine, pressing a wet, shaking head against her enormous shoulder. "Your family don't love you. They must have known where you were going. They knew I was living in England and could have looked for you. Even if that cursed brother of mine didn't care, why didn't your mother write to me in secret to ask my help?" She hardly knew why she was thinking aloud, the poor girl sounded as though she would never stop crying, but she must have done a lot of crying since they brought her here and there would be much more to come. "Come and stay with me in London."

She should have said that at the start, the shaking fizzled out. Alex lifted her head and looked up at her. "Could I?"

"Well, I'm hardly going to let you wander round England begging on the streets, am I?" She always thought it a pity she could never sustain the gentle touch. "Come with me to London and we'll sort you out. You can't possibly go back to Malta just yet."

"How do I get out of this place?"

"Leave *that* to me."

XVIII

Well, shake it up baby now
Twist and shout
Come on, come on, come, come on baby now
Come on and work it on out
Well work it on out, honey
You know you look so good
You know you got me goin' now
Just like I know you would

Life with Auntie Josephine and her little house in
Stamford Brook. Alexandria wondered in middle age
whether the sixties had been quite as much fun as she
remembered them, whether she had really sung those
songs, thought her clothes fetching, longed to own a
Mini. She almost felt as though she were letting the side
down for her generation when she admitted to her
embarrassingly conservative daughter that she had
never seen The Beatles in concert, attended a protest
march or even once been offered a marijuana spliff.

She certainly did not feel footloose and fancy free to
begin with, but Auntie Josephine succeeded in guiding
her out of the morass of depression and bewilderment
she had fallen into as perhaps no other person could
have done. She approached the problem from two
angles. The nurse in her insisted on keeping the girl
busy so that she would be too preoccupied to think
about her wretched situation and too tired at night to lie
awake. So, before she went out to work, she would
leave Alex a long list of things to do, errands to run that
would keep her outside and on her feet for hours at a
time, little jobs and mathematical problems that would
engage her mind. She knew what her brother had not

deigned to know, that Alexandria Sant'Angelo was the golden girl of the family. The only problem was that she was a girl. If any of her brothers had shown such wit and precocity, they would have been helped into glowing careers. They would have read law at university as Alex had wanted to do. No expense would have been spared to get them to the bar. Edward would have spoken proudly about his son the barrister, his son the judge. But Alex was not his son, which was one reason among many why she had found herself living in Auntie Josephine's spare room, unemployed, exiled and, as they could only assume, scarcely missed.

Auntie Josephine had her own plans for little Alex but for the moment she wanted simply to get her back onto her feet and to have quite a bit of fun getting there. Part two of her plan was simple female genius: shopping and creature comforts. Alexandria had arrived in England with virtually nothing of any use on her and the spare room of her spinster's house was hardly the most inviting place for a young girl to sleep in. To start with, Alex borrowed Auntie Josephine's clothes but Auntie Josephine was about ten sizes bigger than her and her lithe figure disappeared in the folds of dull-coloured fabric. So on her first free day, the two of them went on a shopping trip.

It was difficult to say who enjoyed it more. Auntie Josephine was a woman who had given up the chance to have children she would dearly have loved and her life had suddenly, miraculously, been invaded by an orphan in need of adoption. Having spent her life looking after countless strangers in varying stages of decay, she found herself looking after a child of her own kith and kin, the closest she could ever have to her own daughter. The years of spinsterhood fell away as she hustled the girl around the busy shops she knew. She was Professor Higgins, transforming a downtrodden waif into a sixties sex kitten. She was young again,

Alexandria was her youth, the youth she had lost to war and duty.

She took her first to the hairdresser's and persuaded her to have her hair cut short in the latest fashion. The girl sat in patient silence whilst the work of a pair of skilled scissors aged her by a decade, turning her almost immediately from a schoolgirl to a woman on the threshold of life. Auntie Josephine helped her choose cosmetics that they spent ages trying on at home, different shades of eye-shadow, the loudest colour of lipstick. They went hunting for trendy clothes, Alex's first pair of high heels that she had to walk up and down the street in for hours before she could keep her balance properly, cheap and cheerful skirts and trousers, any style at all as long as they were bright. Greens and reds and blues, fountains of colour, colour everywhere. She was falling into a rainbow world. What Uncle Sam/Salvatore once did for his grieving, black-clad family far away in Sliema, Auntie Josephine did for Alexandria now.

She knew that the girl had to make a home for herself in England. In what had either been a fit of pique or a moment of divine inspiration, the girl had run away from home and she would never be welcome there again. Even if there were such a thing as forgiveness among the perverse Sant'Angelo clan, it would be quite simply madness to return to such a place. And if she was estranged from her family, she might as well be estranged from her country. Auntie Josephine knew that Alex had not yet fully appreciated the one-way nature of her escape and she had to be happy and settled in England before she began to feel the tug of homesickness or the yearning for her brothers and cousins.

She knew that she would be cold, so she made sure she had warm clothes to brave the outside world and thick blankets to sleep under. She brought colour into her life because she knew that she would miss the bright light of the sun and the shimmer of the sea. On one mad Saturday shopping excursion, they came home laden with tins of canary yellow paint and spent the rest of the day painting the walls and ceiling of the spare room. On another occasion, Auntie Josephine came home from work with reams of fiery red curtain material and they spent the evening hunched over the sewing machine. There was enough left over to make a bedspread and Alex spent the next week burrowing underneath it like a hibernating caterpillar, still child enough to find a yellow and red room delightful.

And perhaps there was a little guilt in Auntie Josephine's energetic outpouring of generosity. A debt owed to a child she had abandoned to her torturer such a short time before, for all her fine intentions. Perhaps even a note of fear in her determination to ensure the happiness of the girl at all costs. It had not been a freak accident that led her to the mental hospital. She knew what could become of a young mind so terribly abused, though she did not know the sum of what had happened, and she simply would not allow her to go down that road. The fact that she might be simply papering over cracks did not occur to her, nor did she ever question whether she was actually doing the right thing. In the spring and summer of 1963, she knew only that she had brought a shivering girl carrying her only worldly belongings in a suitcase, into her home and turned her into the kind of woman she would have liked to have been herself if she had ever been young.

She showed her how to cover thin jagged scars with powder as though it were that easy to make it all disappear. She gave her a secure, dazzling bright little room of her own where she could rest in safety, but Alex did not feel particularly at home in safety. The only life she could truly appreciate was one in a state of perpetual warfare and she had been pulled out of it too late for the transition to peace to come easily. She was a demobbed soldier, relieved to be out of uniform and away from danger but lost away from the clatter of guns. The only way she had ever been able to show love was through minor acts of heroism; jumping forwards to take a blow that was meant for another, owning up to one of the few misdemeanours that were not her fault, risking a lie to send an irate father off the scent. But Auntie Josephine did not need rescuing. She was strong and old, a woman of the world with a nurse's skin that was too thick for anything to break through. And Alex was the one who was being rescued.

Except that in her dreams she was back in the prison she had been rescued from and it did not seem like a prison from so far away. She did not dream that she was running away from the house bleeding or that she was locking herself in the bathroom, sweating and praying that he would lose interest and disappear. She did not even dream that she was standing in Mother Eugenia's study being told that she would one day leave Malta and make a life for herself somewhere far away. She would wake up with images of palm trees and little painted boats in front of her eyes, which even the yellow walls could not crowd out. In dream, she had the kind of Maltese childhood her friends had had. She scrambled in and out of rock pools with the sun on her back; she rushed to the *festa* of Saint Anthony in her best dress with sixpence in her hand for flowers; she packed a bag with *ħobż biż-żejt* and almond cordial and went on a picnic to Buskett.

She battled against homesickness by reminding herself of all the things she enjoyed in England: pop music as loud as she wanted to play it, make-up, long painted nails, short hair, trousers, anonymity. She told herself that she was young and safe, that she had fallen feet first into a glorious new world she only had to decide to like... "If Malta was that wonderful, you would never have left it," she could hear Auntie Josephine reminding her without ever prompting it. Or perhaps it was not Auntie Josephine at all, perhaps it was the voice of her own better judgement – the two sounded so similar she often muddled them up. Then it would pour with rain and she would stand for hours in the bus queue getting drenched, thinking: "How on earth did I find myself here? What did I do to deserve banishment to this miserable, Godforsaken wasteland?!"

"It's no good feeling sorry for yourself," Auntie Josephine explained, with typical empathy, when she brought the subject up over dinner one evening. "You'll never get over it until you stop pining to go back. You can't go back to Malta."

"I can't stay here, I feel like a fish out of water!"

"Then find yourself a different bowl." She had been dreading the moment Alex expressed the desire to go home and was letting panic make her aggressive. "If you wanted to leave your family, you didn't have to flee the country but you did. That ought to tell you something."

"I was looking for James." The name still caused a nasty sickly feeling to descend on her and even Auntie Josephine could not bring herself to ask Alexandria if she had truly believed the man would have accepted her back in his life, marriage or no marriage. "I thought maybe I could get a job there."

"With what qualifications? You didn't even complete your degree."

Alexandria had been thinking. "I thought maybe I could train as a teacher."

"Oh don't be silly, you could possibly..." But then a small light went on in Auntie Josephine's head. "I'm sure you could," she said. Alexandria looked at her with justifiable suspicion.

"Really? I thought maybe if I could find the money to go back…"

"No, no, no, you're going about it the wrong way round." A myriad of possibilities displayed themselves. She launched straight in. "Now that you're here it would be much better if you trained here. How would you support yourself back home without your family to turn to?" She knew that this had not been Alexandria's plan, but she had a foothold now. "Once you're qualified, you could always get yourself a job in Malta if you wanted, because you could support yourself."

It was almost fraud and Alexandria knew it. "Why don't you want me to go back?"

Because there can be no going back for you, she thought, because you have no idea what it would mean to be alone in your own country without a family to fall back on. Because my brother will find some way to destroy you, even if you are not in his house. "I want what's best for you," she said. "Of course you must go back if that's what will make you happy, but get yourself some qualifications first. Do we have a compromise?"

"If I have to stay here any more time at all, I must learn to love it," Alexandria told herself, as she sought out the addresses of teacher training colleges. "I was a prodigy once, I can learn anything. I will start with the easy bits." When she started travelling to college, she learnt to like bright red buses. She made herself warm to the colour, the accent of the man who worked the ticket machine, the blurred view of rows of town houses and shoppers.

At Hillfield College, she learnt to like green grass. She studied the sensation of it bending under her shoes, the damp, fertile smell of it after a downpour. Eating her lunch in the canteen, she learnt to think fondly of the array of different accents she learnt to distinguish across the table. Students who said 'innit?' were Londoners, 'luv' and 'pet' belonged to the northerners and anyone who spoke with the most lovely lilting tones of all was Irish.

And on one fateful day, she heard an accent she knew immediately. As she strode out of a seminar, she heard three men, two of them obviously identical twins, talking together in a corridor and knew that they were Maltese. A surge of homesickness erupted in her after months of battles against it and she paused for a moment, unable to bring herself to move away from the sound but too taken aback to approach them.

Nicholas looked up from his conversation and saw a lovely face, too lovely to be dismissed as simply attractive, looking in his direction. Naturally shy, he blushed a little and turned to his brother, feeling suddenly quite isolated from his male companions. A face that was young and old at the same time and made something stir in him that he did not understand. But the absence of words unsettled her and she turned hastily away, striding down the corridor with something like irritation. They were seminarians "and he's going to be another Father What-a-Waste!" she raged, feeling the beginnings of anti-clericalism stirring inside her.

"Amazing how much can hang on a moment like that, isn't it?" I muse, knowing how much the near miss has annoyed Benedict. It is almost worthy of *Romeo and Juliet*. I am left wondering what would have happened if they had struck up a friendship there and then, exchanged a few friendly words. I try to calculate just how much suffering would have been avoided if they had not been so young and awkward, if the moment had not passed. It is useless to speak like this.

"Why didn't they just talk to one another?"

"They were shy." A lame excuse for wasting a life-saving opportunity, but it is not for me to keep thinking up reasons why it should have had to happen as it did. I find myself wanting to apologise for not being able to intervene and make it all work out, for not being a Shakespearean mastermind able to step in and tie up the threads in time for the final bow. Their paths crossed too briefly to join together then. Nicholas did not have the painful joy of looking on her again and thinking her lovely and feeling as though they were alone in the world together until he was forbidden to think such things anymore.

I must leave him watching her retreating figure, knowing that he feels alone and that I cannot come to his rescue. Once again, I find myself wanting to reach across the years to say something, do something, because I know that I should be by his side. But I cannot reach him. I know that he will suffer and I am the cold, clinical reporter, witnessing carnage simply to entertain others. Except that I am not cold and I do not want him to come to harm. "I wish it had never happened!" I shout across the murmuring waves, "I wish it could all disappear!"

There is no answer, even from Benedict.

XIX

Nicholas sat in the library, battling to meet an essay deadline. His papers were disordered and dog-eared and he had begun doodling little stars along the margins to disguise the fact that his mind was elsewhere. It did not help that Seamus O'Reagan, the only other person in the room, was sitting on a windowsill reading *The City of God,* drumming his heels casually against the wall. Nicholas finally gave up altogether. "Why am I here?" he demanded, to the rows of bookshelves. "What am I doing here?"

"You could always go and study somewhere else if I'm disturbing you," suggested Seamus cheerfully, "like the kitchens."

"No, I meant *why am I here*?"

Seamus glanced up at the ceiling. "Well, first there were the dinosaurs, I gather, then various other complex life forms. Neanderthal Man made an appearance in approximately..."

"Stop that!" Nicholas knew exactly where he had got that response from. "I mean, why am I *here* here?"

Seamus was just starting to enjoy himself. "Well, as the Catechism tells us we're here to love God, to serve Him and be happy with Him..."

"But why am I being happy with Him HERE?!" Seamus had never had much of a reputation for taking life seriously, but Nicholas found his flippancy insufferable when he was on the verge of a crisis. He fidgeted with pens and pages of notes. "Why am I here? Why am I here? Is it such a complicated question?"

Seamus tried one last wisecrack. "I think there's something in the Gospel about taking up your cross."

Nicholas buried his head in his hands. "Don't try

that with me, my brother taught you that."

Seamus closed his book. "Nick, what's up with you? You've been out of sorts for days."

"I don't know," came a muffled answer. "I suppose I'm just having a funny five minutes or something."

"Is this all about Victor?" Nicholas flinched, refusing to lift his head. "It's all right, everyone's a bit upset."

"Upset?" he squeaked, sitting up with a start. "I've never been so unsettled! What did he just vanish like that for? After all these years?"

"It's just the way it's done." But that was cold comfort to Nicholas, who had woken up one morning the previous month and found that the room that had once been occupied by his friend Victor was empty and its occupant had disappeared into thin air. "He changed his mind about getting ordained, that's all. Lots of men do. Better that it happened sooner rather than later. So he left."

"But he didn't even say good-bye. One minute we were chatting in the common room, the next morning he'd *gone*."

Seamus shrugged. "It wasn't his fault, he wasn't allowed to tell anyone he was leaving. They don't want us to get any ideas." Nicholas stared miserably into space. "Or have you already got a few?"

Nicholas stood up abruptly and began clearing his desk. "Of course not, I'm just a bit shaken," he reassured him, scooping up books and papers into his satchel. "Everything's changing. The Church is changing, we're changing. I don't feel ready for this."

Seamus jumped off the windowsill and walked over to where Nicholas was standing. "You'll be fine," he promised, as if he knew. "Loads of people feel like this before ordination. You'll feel better when you get back to Malta. You said nothing ever changes there."

"But even that's changed!" Nicholas leaned back against a bookcase, feeling his pulse galloping. "Malta has just been granted independence and I wasn't there to see it happen. All sorts of upheavals have been going on in my absence, I won't recognise the place!"

Seamus was confused. "Independence is good, isn't it? We've been waiting to get rid of the fecking Brits in Ulster for centuries!"

Nothing seemed to perturb Seamus. On his ordination card, he had printed the saying that his mother had whispered to him when troubles visited them: *All shall be well and all shall be well, and thou shalt see that all manner of thing shall be well.* But the words of a medieval mystic would have meant very little to Nicholas as he tried to comprehend what was wrong with him to make well.

"Are you having a crisis of faith?" asked Gregory, as they packed their bags to return to Malta.

"No, certainly not," and he meant it. "Nothing like that. I just feel as though I've fallen off a roundabout."

"I don't know what you're talking about."

"I'm not sure I do either."

"You ought to talk to someone about this."

"I am, I'm talking to you!"

"You'll feel better when we go home."

"Where's that?"

It would not have helped Nicholas to be told at the time that he was suffering the same identity crisis that his mother had suffered when she was ordered back to Malta after settling in another country, or that her adopted brother had felt when he lost his family and struggled to make himself a part of another, that it was his turn to feel lost, uncertain, homeless. Except that he could not afford to feel lost. He was supposed to be a shepherd, a young religious at the cusp of radical changes in the Church he had been trained to serve. The young were not supposed to feel so uneasy.

I falter where I firmly trod

And falling with my weight of cares
Upon the great world's altar-stairs
That slope thro' darkness, up to God.

He was not supposed to want desperately for there to be some tiny part of his life that was settled.

"Life really wasn't meant to be this painful," remarked Gregory, looking out of the train window. "It's never easy saying good-bye to old friends, but we'll see them again."

"I know."

"We haven't been away that long in the grand scheme of things." He had the feeling he was dramatically missing the point somehow, but that he needed to say something. "I thought you'd be looking forward to seeing everyone again."

"Of course I am, you know I am."

"It'll be easier after we're ordained. You'll feel much more settled."

Nicholas had to accept that he was glad to be back in Malta when it came to it. It helped that, contrary to some dire warnings, the horrors of hunger, unemployment, riots and the breakdown of law and order had failed to visit. And the excitement of being back in the family home helped conceal the fact that they no longer belonged there. The long years of catching up – Pawlinu's marriage, the births of his children, Rosaria's transition from schoolgirl to journalist, the passing birthdays and Easters and significant dates – occupied them so that they barely noticed to start with that they were being treated like guests, honoured guests but still guests, and that they were using their very best manners to greet the people they most loved.

And on a bright, hot day in July, Nicholas and Gregory stood in their mother's sewing room, dressed in the vestments she had made for them. They were an impressive sight; dark, serious though clearly bursting with excitement, swathed in billowing gold and white silk. The last well-dressed priests of their generation. Carmelina could barely contain her pride: "My boys," she said, taking their hands, "my wonderful, wonderful boys! I haven't been so happy since my wedding day!"

She would never be as happy again, but they travelled to Valletta in high spirits, not knowing that it was the last time the family would gather together for a celebration. Carmelina, Rosaria, Pawlinu and his wife and children, stood in the beautiful, majestic cathedral in a sea of proud friends and relatives, watching the long procession of acolytes and ordinands walking to the sanctuary in a montage of colour and light.

Nicholas remembered the smell of the incense smoke uncurling around him as his hands were anointed by Archbishop Gonzi and associated it forever with the ecstatic, heart-stopping, inexplicable sense of knowing... knowing that he was a priest. He felt so overwhelmed that when the choir began to sing, their voices seemed to be coming from another world:

Panis Angelicus,
Fit panis hominum
Dat panis coelicus
Figuris terminum.

Carmelina only lost her composure when she knelt before her son for Holy Communion and made the mistake of looking into his face. Nicholas held the host before her but a sacrifice that transcended time made all other boundaries of time meaningless. The likeness was too strong; the features too familiar to her and nothing of significance could ever be relegated to history. That was how she understood anyway, how she exchanged a single glance with her priest-son and saw Lawrence as she had known him long ago. Lawrence Falzon, whose grave she had never visited, who had never grown old, who never saw his sons grow up, watched her through the face of their son. They stood together without the intervening years to divide them. *Corpus Christi.* The small white host touched her tongue and she shuddered with emotion.

A crusader cathedral. We stand in a side chapel, looking out at the intricately painted walls and the vast sanctuary lavishly decorated for Easter. We are meant to feel small and we do feel small in the midst of this cavern of history. Grand Masters worshipped God here. French revolutionaries looted it and brought the wrath of the people down on their heads. The British tried to gain possession of it. John the Baptist stoops, head almost severed, across the gloom of a Caravaggio canvas. Our little family drama seems a little dwarfed against the backdrop of centuries of spiritual warfare and art, but that is almost a relief. There is no one to immortalise the anointing of little Nicholas Falzon.

The moment flickered for a moment then faded into the unremarkable past, but all the same it is a moment I wish I had truly witnessed. Perhaps it is only because I wonder what it would have been like to see my father a priest. It is an odd kind of a privilege to be a priest's daughter, to feel so close to a way of life that most people simply do not understand, to be able to find my way around a breviary, to have taken my first steps holding consecrated hands. And at the same time to realise that my very existence caused scandal among the same sort of people with whom I have lived and worked.

Benedict stirs suddenly. He has seen his fair share of sumptuous churches since we arrived here and seemed to have barely noticed that we had stepped into yet another but he is wide awake. "Don't you feel a little odd being a Catholic sometimes?"

It is an interesting proposition. "Just sometimes?" I

ask. My eye catches his bare legs and I realise that he has stepped into church in his shorts. I drape my pashmina around his waist like a large red towel. "What brought that on?"

"Well, if your father was ordained a priest," he is still wrestling with the idea and failing miserably. "He wasn't supposed to have children." So far so good, I think. He looks desperately uncomfortable, as though he is struggling not to utter some obscenity. "Doesn't that mean that, technically, you have to accept that you should never have been born?"

"Yes, but then I would have to accept that God makes mistakes and I can't accept that."

"That's a cop out."

No, not a cop out at all, but perhaps the answer came too easily. He knows I have been thinking about it and perhaps that I have already been asked that question, but it does not matter. One of the perks of being a priest's daughter is the ability to alienate and be alienated by everyone. The dungaree-clad, muesli-eating spiky-haired remnants of the seventies who see the unauthorised offspring of clergy as an agenda to hide their frustrations behind; the Catholic-baiters who see us as just another embarrassing scandal to beat the pious with; the happily few Holier Than Thous who parade their manufactured worthiness before them and see us as nothing more than a repulsive mistake. But we are none of these things, mostly because a person with such an unlikely birthright can aspire to being something closer to what these groups desire to be: too radical to pander to the lost trendies of a past generation, too adult to stoop to self-righteous gloating and wise enough not to fall into blasphemy.

"I think there's a place for a priest's daughter in the Church," I say, because he does not need an elementary guide to Catholic politics yet. "God needs troublemakers as well as ladies polishing brasses. As it happens, I think

242

the Church is like a family."

Benedict sniggers with the weight of twelve years worth of secular education behind him. "That sounds like something out of one of those sugary missionary pamphlets."

"No, really," I insist. "Just like my family. Everyone not getting on with one another. Plenty of villains and people screwing up their lives... and lots of perfectly ordinary people to act as a buffer zone. And a few saints to stop us all falling into monumental despair."

"I haven't seen many saints yet."

"Well, do you expect them to go round wearing halos?!"

He jumps. "I wish you'd keep your voice down in here! There are people praying!"

I love it when heathens start telling me how to behave in church. "Don't stand there moralising in my pashmina!"

"You really do sound *foreign* when you take that tone!"

A kindly gentleman with a badge pinned to his lapel approaches us very courteously and asks us if we would like to continue our argument somewhere else. We stumble outside like naughty schoolchildren sent out of class, Benedict still decked out in red poly-cotton.

"Never in my life have I been escorted out of a public building before."

"Well lucky you that it's such a novelty." I never mean to sound so angry. The devil makes me do it.

I cannot even give him a scandal to sink his teeth into. I know he has waited patiently for this part of the story to get a few good lust scenes: the innocent young priest falling for the voluptuous sex kitten, the hypocritical prude breaking his vows in secret, a conception in a presbytery cupboard. Something suitably lurid that will entertain at the same time as appeasing a prejudice. But I am destined to be a disappointment, because the most that can be said about the whole affair was that it was deeply tragic. There was no scarlet woman, there was no scapegoat in a collar. I cannot manufacture anything stronger than that.

It all began when some one in their infinite wisdom decided to lend a young priest to a Catholic school in faraway London that was in need of a geography teacher and who thought it would be a good idea for the boys to be taught for a year by someone from overseas. And everyone thought that Nicholas would be the perfect choice, as he had spent so long in England and done his teacher-training there. The only problem was that no one knew how unsettled Nicholas was and he was not very good at voicing objections to his superiors.

"I've barely been back in Malta for five minutes and I've got to go back to England again!" he wailed, as he packed his only recently unpacked suitcase. "What are they trying to do to me?"

"Did you tell them that?" Gregory looked out the window to avoid the sight of his brother huffing and puffing about the room.

"Of course I didn't. Fat lot of good it would have done."

"Well maybe you should have done. You'll be a dreadful teacher if you're miserable."

"Thanks. You really know how to make a man feel better!" Nicholas stopped what he was doing and perched on the edge of his bed. He half-wondered whether he wasn't developing a talent for making life difficult for himself, but a nagging sense of duty hit him every time he felt the need to complain. "If we were in the army and our commanding officer sent us on a mission, we wouldn't just say 'oh I don't think I want to, it'll be uncomfortable', would we?"

"I wish you wouldn't use militant metaphors like that. We aren't soldiers."

"Then what are we?"

"I prefer shepherds."

Nicholas felt his temper flare. "That's because you think of shepherds as little boys in tea towels at the school nativity play! Or those ridiculous pictures of shepherds in green fields surrounded by fluffy, laundered sheep!"

"I think I may have seen a real shepherd once or twice."

"All right, let's say shepherds then. So if we were shepherds crossing rocky ground in the searing heat and we were tired and desperate for shelter but our sheep needed to be fed – would we just leave them and make ourselves comfortable? Or would we keep going until we found new pastures for them?"

"I fail to see how this relates to whether or not you spend a year teaching geography to English kids?"

"Just that I've been asked to go. So I think I must go."

But Nicholas was not the only one who felt wary about his move. The night before he left, an elderly priest who was staying with the community on a visit, watched him as he went about the mundane rituals of dinner and washing up and chatter in the common room after evening prayer. "You shouldn't be sending that young priest away," he said before he retired for the night. "He will come to grief."

"Nicholas Falzon is perfectly competent," he was assured, "and very popular. That's why he was recommended."

"He is more vulnerable than you realise. You should not be sending him so far away." But it was far too late to change carefully laid plans by then even if they had wanted to listen to the old man. Without any sign of a reprieve in sight, Nicholas boarded the plane and travelled alone to a new community and a fresh set of avoidable disasters. As he waved good-bye to Gregory and the rest of the family, he realised that it was the first time in his life that he was going somewhere without his brother. It felt terribly wrong somehow, like a bad omen, but he hated superstition. "I am a grown man," he pronounced to the swirling cloud and the blue arc of sky, but if that was the case he wondered why he had such a strong desire to bury his head and weep.

XX

I cannot hold the time back. The fragments of people's lives rush past like vague landmarks seen from the safety of a high speed train. It is how our own lives will pass and be seen by those who come after us long after we are dead. Only the salient points will remain. All the rest, the infinitesimal moments we shared and loved will burn away to nothing. *Leaving not a rack behind.*

Forward all the same, forward without a backward glance, past Alexandria buying her own flat, past Nicholas teaching children about rivers and volcanoes, past Gregory working as a parish priest, past Carmelina finally giving up on keeping up with the changing fashions and locking up her sewing room once and for all, past Rosaria enjoying her first job as a journalist.

I feel heartless to march on in this way, as though Rosaria's achievements as a writer meant nothing, as though it is not worth pausing to comfort Carmelina as she drapes an old sheet over her faithful mannequin and packs away her boxes of pins and spools of thread, wondering why no pretty women buy their clothes made to measure any more and why the priests are willing to forgo her intricately beautiful vestments for plain white albs with prints of butterflies stencilled all over them. It is no good her telling herself that she is old, because no one ever really thinks of themselves as old. She is on the margins of another generation's story and her heartache must be quietly forgotten.

Nicholas had had the sinking feeling that he would not be away for just one year and accepted the request to stay on for one more year without complaint. Getting used to London life had been more complicated than he had expected. It held nothing at all in common with his happy experiences of England: the fresh air, the stunning landscapes, the vast green spaces, the camaraderie of a rural community. In his early months there he felt as if he had been sent to some enormous penal colony, living out his days hemmed in by tall buildings, the murderous roaring of cars and buses and an alien, chattering people.

His school was infested with miniature barbarians, seeking out his weaknesses to provide easy ways to torment him whilst showing no interest in his subject whatsoever. "Next time a child asks how to make a Maltese cross, I'm going to throw him out of the window," he complained loudly to his colleague Richard Mason as he stood in the queue for lunch. "They always think they're the first person to have thought of it!"

"You really mustn't take it personally," came the usual answer. "They can sense it if you do and they'll never give you a moment's peace."

"And have you seen the test papers I got back from Form Three? Anyone would think I hadn't taught them anything all term."

The test papers in question had been very nearly the last straw for Nicholas. He had given them a basic map of the world and asked them to label different parts of it, the Pacific Ocean, for example, the USSR. The thirteen-year-olds in question had proven so oblivious to the world around them that fewer than half had been able to label the five continents correctly or even name them, one idiot at the back of the class had muddled Italy with Ireland and some little runt whose spatial awareness stretched only as far as the outer reaches of the Northern Line had not realised that he had the world upside down and so he managed to get the North and South Poles wrong along with absolutely everything else.

"I suspect I am making reparation for some heinous crime from my past," he suggested with morbid cheeriness in a letter to Gregory.

"Hope it was fun," came the reply.

"Can't remember. Maybe its purgatory in advance of something I'm going to do."

"Don't be silly."

The night before the new academic year began, Nicholas sat in the staff room with the other boarding staff, discussing the decision to appoint the school's very first female teacher. It was not some brave new idea in a brave new world of emancipated sexes, rather necessity after the head of maths had submitted his resignation on grounds of ill health, just weeks before the beginning of term.

"I don't know that this is wise at all," complained one of the older housemasters. "I mean, no offence to the lady in question, but this is a boys' school."

"We needed to fill the vacancy quickly," came a weary explanation from the corner of the room. It was not the first time the subject had come up since the headmaster, Fr Anthony Doyle, had made the decision and he was beginning to tire of having to defend himself every five minutes. "We could hardly have started the term without a maths teacher, could we?"

"I hear she's very young."

"Well, we won't hold that against her. She'll get over the affliction in time."

"Don't think I'm being old-fashioned or alarmist or anything..." a snigger failed to be stifled between the pages of *The Times*. "I just don't think we should put gunpowder too close to the fire, that's all. Some of our boys might start getting ideas..."

"Speak for yourself," came an uncharacteristically curt interruption from beside the bookcase. It was Nicholas, the world's safest vocation. "If she's a teacher she'll be the enemy whatever she's like."

"How charmingly naive of you, father. There are certain dangers regarding these matters that you may not yet be aware of."

"You read too many cheap novels, Master Nicholls," Nicholas explained, with a smugness he would come to regret bitterly. "It doesn't happen like that."

"I have never read the sort of novel you allude to in my entire life. I'm sorry to hear that you have."

Fr Doyle gave an irate signal for Nicholas to restrain himself and changed the subject.

O happy irony! O necessary sin of Nicholas! Next morning, Alexandria Sant'Angelo, wearing a dainty white dress covered in strawberries, flounced into the staff room on a wave of Chanel. Fr Nicholas Falzon's fate was sealed. Time stood suspended as they glanced at one another from across the staff room, the other people melting into misty indifference. They were aware of nothing else. It was as though their whole lives had been a preparation for this moment of reckoning and they were simply drawn together, vows and promises crashing to pieces around them.

It is a pity it did not happen quite like that. Their eyes did not meet across the crowded room, time did not stand still. He watched her walking in and recognised her face immediately. That much happened, he remembered her. And yes, his heart gave an unfamiliar quiver at the sight of her, but he was a priest and the idea of loving her or wanting her simply did not come into the equation. He knew – or thought he knew – that it was impossible. And Alexandria glanced at him as he sorted out his teaching notes for the day and somehow managed to drop half of them on the floor and remembered him from teacher training college. She remembered that he was Maltese and felt a cheering of the heart to know that there was a compatriot of hers on the staff.

That lunchtime, they introduced themselves to one another properly and passed an enjoyable hour exchanging stories from home. He was a little put off by her social background and managed to deflect any questions about his by mentioning that his father had died when he was a child. It had the desired effect and she did not ask him any questions about his parents. They left the table friends.

And that was how it should have remained. A quick chat during morning break, a hurried exchange of ideas for a class project, a moan about writing school reports. The senior staff worried about Alexandria's voluptuous presence in this all-male environment, but it was more the influence she was having on the boys she taught than anything else that bothered them.

Hoards of bored adolescent boys suddenly found a beautiful woman in their midst, talking in husky dulcet tones about long multiplication and πr^2. By an odd coincidence, mathematics became the most popular subject on the timetable. The boys adored her, leaving little presents waiting for her in her desk every morning and flirting outrageously. Letters of complaint from parents appeared periodically in Fr Doyle's pigeonhole, wondering whether it was entirely healthy for their little boy to be taught by a woman who had all the allure and charm of a supermodel. But still more arrived wanting to know the secret behind a none-too-bright son's rapid improvement in his normally weakest subject. She stayed.

And in the meantime, whilst attention was diverted in entirely the wrong direction, Alexandria and Nicholas became close friends. The fact that they were both Maltese gave them a certain immunity from gossip, as if their shared national identity offered an alibi for any other attraction. They both began to look for reasons to meet the other without even realising that they were doing it, the two of them so naïve that it never occurred to either of them that they were spiralling into a situation that could only end in tears.

It was one evening in early November that should have woken them both up. Nicholas went round to Alexandria's little apartment to discuss a play she had put herself down to help him produce next term. It should have given her enough warning that something was afoot as she had never shown any interest in amateur dramatics whatsoever, but she had quite inexplicably felt the urge to sign up when Fr Nick had asked for volunteers. And so there they were, Nicholas sitting at the kitchen table drawing up a timetable of events whilst she prepared a tasty dinner. There would be auditions the following week, he already had a basic idea of who would be suitable but it needed to look fair. Then two rehearsals a week with the dress rehearsal after half term to give the boys time to learn their lines. They could reset the play in the present day to avoid complicated costumes.

He talked incessantly about the play all through dinner, apparently ignoring the lighted candles she placed around the room and the way she had managed to cook his favourite food for him, drawn from the knowledge she had built up about him over the past few months. She was amazed what she had learnt: that his favourite soup was pea and ham, that he was fond of English puddings, particularly apple crumble, that he liked Neapolitan folk songs but found opera overbearing, that he was one of life's innocents, innocent in every sense of the word, that he had the worst haircut in the world.

When the dishes had been washed up the idea came to her. "I'm going to change your hairstyle," she said, primly, sitting him in a chair. "I know you're a celibate, but you could make some effort."

He protested, more out of shyness than the thought that there was something odd about it, but before he knew it, she was lowering his head over a basin of warm water and washing his hair. He felt her fingers weaving in and out of the wet curls, the gentle pressure of her hands caressing his scalp and felt his face reddening. There was a fire in him, but it was not the desire he had been warned about. There was no burning, flaming furnace of passion in him at all, just the warm, wonderful-terrible glow of being close to someone who seemed to him, in the soft scented light around them, to be perfection itself.

"If I had ever married, it would have been her," he told himself, as he slipped into his starched bachelor bed that night. There was a conspicuous absence of alarm bells even then. "If I had met her a few years ago." He even felt a tug of what must have been regret as he switched off the light, but at that moment there was something pleasing about the sacrifice. For the first time, he understood what the sacrifice of the priesthood meant and he smiled in the darkness in the knowledge that he had indeed been tempted and had not been found wanting. He had left her house with damp hair and a clean conscience, and so it would remain. All was well with the world.

Oh Nicholas. But it was nearly the Christmas holidays and he had plenty of time whilst she was away to learn the miserable, unromantic loneliness of falling in love too late. But it was to be many months before he dared to call it love.

XXI

It was very nearly the happiest Christmas Alexandria ever remembered. She went back to Auntie Josephine as soon as term ended, laden with news and presents. Josephine let her talk as they pinned paper decorations up all over the house and assembled the Christmas crib. She looked delightfully well and was in such good spirits that it almost seemed a shame to have to wreck things for her.

"You mention the name of Fr Nicholas rather a lot," she observed, as Alex walked around the sitting room placing the Three Kings in the farthest places she could reach – at the back of the sideboard, on the highest bookshelf and in the corner of a windowsill. She watched carefully as Alex stiffened and turned around.

"Well of course, we work very closely together." She had mastered the art of covering her tracks at a fairly young age and thought she sounded very natural.

"You change when you talk about him."

"I do not!" But she was unable to stop herself from blushing. "Really, you've made me embarrassed now!"

"You do change. Your voice changes." She sat down in her armchair and watched for the next reaction. Alex realised she was being watched and turned her back on her as if she had suddenly realised that Melchior looked a bit out on a limb in between the pot plants.

"I don't know what you mean. He's a friend from home, that's all. Of course I'm fond of him."

That was enough of an admission. Josephine let it pass for a moment. "Where is he from?"

"Sliema, would you believe? I probably passed his house on the bus to school. And he's got an identical twin brother. I always wondered what it would be like to be a twin."

Josephine asked two or three more questions. She was getting to know the man very well indeed. She quickly found out where he went to school, what subject he taught, that his father had died when he was a child, that his mother had lived in America. When there was a pause in the conversation, she drew a sharp breath and asked the question. "Are you in love with him?"

Alexandria could not have been more indignant. How could she think such a thing of her? Of course not, what a ludicrous suggestion, how very typical. Why was it that you couldn't be seen in the company of a man for five minutes in this Godforsaken little country without someone suggesting something like that? Josephine backed down, knowing that the answer was most certainly 'yes' but that there was very little she could do about it.

"I just don't want you to get hurt, that's all," was all she said before letting the subject drop.

"Don't talk to me about getting hurt."

And in the tight community of the school, Nicholas was facing his own struggles. Unlike Alexandria, there was no escape for him, very little to divert him from her absence and he found himself becoming bad-tempered and increasingly irritable as the holidays wore on. His companions had changed from being his friends to an insufferable nuisance.

It was fortunate that Richard Mason, who saw him the most over the Christmas period, misunderstood the problem spectacularly. Richard had family accommodation on the school site and Nicholas celebrated Christmas that year in the eccentric little apartment on top of the library which Richard shared with his wife Janet and their two young children. "You're becoming a workaholic, old man," Richard observed after lunch on Boxing Day whilst they did the washing up. "Out of term you should be relaxing and enjoying yourself, going sightseeing or something, and instead you fidget about the school looking for things to do."

"Well, I do have classes to prepare."

"Rubbish. You shouldn't be so earnest by now." A small child ran into the room. He scooped her up, a little impatiently. "You've no idea how lucky you are," he said, "I sometimes really wish I had your freedom."

You can have it, thought Nicholas miserably, wondering whether he was not just suffering from the tired old delusion that the grass is always greener on the other side of the fence. He did not want to be free because it meant being alone. He thought that he would have been happy to live out the rest of his life in the happy servitude of a family if it had been with her.

I stretch lame hands of faith and grope
And gather chaff and dust, and call
To what I feel is Lord of All
And faintly trust the greater hope.

Nicholas's life from that moment turned into an assault course of days to be battled through. If the remaining days without her were bad enough, her return to school at the beginning of term was unbearable torture. He found himself torn between yearning for their break time conversations and the need to stay away from her, wanting to see her even if for just a moment and the knowledge that the sight of her was feeding the very feelings he was supposed to be snuffing out. He spent long hours in the chapel praying for strength to overcome the temptation whilst at the same time he found himself praying that there could be some solution that did not involve being separated from her.

He knew that if he could just fight his way through to the end of the academic year he would be sent back to Malta and they would never see one another again. He would be saved. But he did not want to be saved. Whenever he thought of never seeing her again, he realised he actually preferred the torture of being near her than a life in far away safety. There were moments when he seriously wished that he could wake up and find that he was back at home in Sliema and this was all a futuristic nightmare. Or that everything could just stop, could just end for him.

Then, on a crisp, bright morning of the half term break, Nicholas looked out of his window to see Alexandria parking her car. She waved up at him. "What are you doing here?" he called down. She was dressed for a day out, warmly swathed in a long coat and hat. He knew she had come for him.

He hurried down the stairs and stepped outside. "It's all right, I've come to rescue you," she explained cheerfully. "Richard says you're turning into a hermit and I'm to get you off school property."

"I really don't think I can," he began with the half-hearted tone of a man who knows perfectly well he will. "Where are we going?"

"Get into something a bit more suitable and I'll tell you. Somewhere out of London."

It was madness. He told himself not to go as he changed into his civvies and tried to control his excitement. It was possible to break a compulsion – any compulsion. Did he imagine he was the only man who had ever fallen in love and had to get over it? How many millions had fallen in love with women they could never have: other men's wives, women who were not interested in them, women from the wrong clan, the wrong country, the wrong creed? History was littered with broken hearts and he somehow believed that he was entitled to have his love requited.

Nicholas climbed into the passenger seat and let himself be carried away on a mysterious journey.

If Benedict sniggers again I am going to kick him under the table. Hunger has come to get us and we are sitting in a café eating *pastizzi*. It has a slightly secretive feel to it as it is underground and we are seated right in the corner. A charming lady about my own age does battle with the coffee machine. "Give me one good reason why this is funny?"

"I'm not laughing," he promises, scattering flakes of pastry, "but he was clearly fighting a losing battle. You can't fight a natural instinct." I affect a loud yawn. "Well, you can't. Celibacy's unnatural."

"So is wearing clothes, but I've no desire to see everyone in the altogether."

"It's not the same thing. Sex is something fundamental to human nature."

"Is it really? I really needed a scientist to tell me that." I simply have to take him down a peg or two. I aim for his weakest point – his propensity to get embarrassed. "You and I don't seem to do too badly."

He responds with admirable restraint. "Yes, but that's because we know we'll eventually get married."

"What's that got to do with it? You're not exercising your 'natural instinct' yet, are you?"

I note a slight pinkening of his cheeks. Victory awaits. "Yes, but that's different, I'm just postponing..."

"Don't find yourself staggering around with your knuckles dragging against the floor, do you?"

Pink becomes scarlet. "No-no, stop that!"

"Don't have to be dragged from my arms to the safety of a cold shower very often, do you?"

"Please oh please would you please keep your voice down!"

"Well stop talking such patronising nonsense then! If we don't behave like over-sexed bunny rabbits, we shouldn't assume everyone else does."

He whispers: "Ssssh. Please, please, be quiet!" He waits long enough for the other customers to resume their eating and drinking. "I love you Kris, I respect you. Please don't get the wrong idea about me. But perhaps we shouldn't assume that everyone has our self-control."

I cannot bring myself to laugh, but never in my life has anyone accused me of possessing the slightest shred of self-control. There is so much I still do not understand about his world. We are the ones who for centuries have been owned by other people, all the great colonial powers one after the other. His forefathers on the other hand were the masters of their fate and everyone else's and yet he does not seem to want to be free. It is as though it is safer to be the powerless victims of impulses beyond our control, the slaves of our genes, our histories, our failed human condition, rather than to be free to make the wrong decision and have to accept responsibility for it. I cannot offer him the Calvinistic fairytale of human actors walking helplessly through their scripted lives, predestined to success or failure. I know that none of this need have happened. I know that Edward did not have to abuse his children, Luigi did not have to give way to a depraved temptation, James Carlisle did not have to betray my mother, Leonardo did not have to cheat on his wife, Elizabeth Wilson did not have to surrender her life for someone else's shame. Even our most mundane choices are still choices that may or may not be made – I did not have to tell this story, Benedict is under no obligation to listen. And I suppose, Nicholas and Alexandria did not have to flee London together that day. I would rather accept the decision they made than deny their power to make it.

They drove as far as the coast. Nicholas began to relax as soon as the outposts of the city gave way to open countryside. "Where did you learn to drive?" he asked, over the roaring of the open windows.

"My aunt taught me," Alexandria bellowed back,

259

"but actually she's the worst driver in the whole world."

The fact was flagrantly obvious as they hurtled their way down narrow roads, bumping into the kerb whenever they turned a corner. "I thought there had to be some Maltese connection with it somewhere." It occurred to him that he did not know how to drive, but there seemed to be a good many things she did that he did not know how to do. He watched as she placed a cigarette between her lips and lit up. His mother had always discouraged them from smoking, convinced that it had contributed to their father's early death.

He could hardly believe that they came from the same world. He let his thoughts wander until they settled entirely on her and he could not find the motivation to rectify the matter. "I miss the sea terribly."

"I thought I should tell you to bring your swimming things but that would have given it away," she said, chirpily. "Anyway, I don't imagine you'd be able to break through the ice."

"I can't swim," he confessed. "I stopped going near the water after my father died." He thought it too morbid to tell her that he had always half-feared that he would dive down and find his father's body lying among the weed and rock formations. It was knowing that he had died at sea that did it, even though he had not been buried at sea. He knew he was treading on dangerous ground, but found himself saying: "I miss him."

She sounded cheerfully callous. "Oh I think fathers are a little overrated," she lied, when she knew perfectly well just how much she would have liked a real one. It was just that she could not understand why he could not see what a perfect deal he had had. She was sure that, had he had the choice, he would rather have had a good father for a short time than been plagued by a bad one forever, but he had never had that choice. He took her comment as a reminder that he should not have been so self-pitying and slipped into silence.

Nicholas had to accept that it must be quite a nice beach in good weather. A long strip of sand stretched out into the distance for over mile without a break. On one side there were dunes interspersed with bracken, on the other the sea, wild and eternal clawing at a languid sky. Except that the rain had only just stopped and the beach was a muddy swamp that they squelched and skidded their way through and the sea and sky had merged into an unpromising haze of grey. The air was heavy with a dank smell of rotting seaweed.

"How did the two of us end up in this country?" he asked with a laugh, throwing a flat stone across the water. It bounced four times before being swallowed up. "They could have sent me anywhere – Ireland, Africa, India!"

"God has a sense of humour, as Mother Eugenia used to say." I bet even Mother Eugenia could not have predicted this, she thought with the slightest shudder, or she would definitely have let me stay in the convent.

"That's funny," he remarked, "that's the first time I've heard you mention God."

She stiffened. "Well I'm not the theologian, am I?" It was impossible for a moment for her to conceal her hostility. "Apart from Midnight Mass, I haven't set foot in a church since I arrived in England and I haven't felt a great deal the worse for it."

He felt wounded but knew it was not the time to show it. His mother would have reminded him that an angry person was an unhappy person. "There's no need to be cross, I was just remarking." She was looking directly ahead of her and had speeded up her pace. "Am I allowed to ask why?"

"Because it didn't feel right here," she said and she still sounded irritated with him. "It meant nothing to me here."

"You're very annoyed about something that means nothing to you."

She snapped to a halt and faced him, as though she had just been called to attention. "Look, I didn't invite you here to take that preachy tone with me," she said, causing him to take a step back. "You might be as pure as the driven snow but those of us who've messed things up don't feel quite so welcome."

He had never seen her like this before and began to wish desperately that he was not alone with her. "I'm not sure I know what you mean," was all he could think to say.

"Why are all the saints virgins and martyrs?" she demanded. It sounded like a non-sequiter to him but he knew he had to give her an answer.

"They're not. Mary Magdalene, Elizabeth of Hungary, Augustine certainly wasn't. Most of the early saints weren't..."

"Don't give me a shopping list!"

They had stopped walking and were standing on a dry patch of grass sheltered by overhanging cliffs that had appeared from apparently nowhere. Alexandria was flushed with temper and she was breathing a little too quickly. Nicholas realised that she was familiar with the place, because she sat down in the alcove with the confidence of a person who had known it was there for them all along. He sat down beside her. "What happened?"

"You don't have to know, you're too nice." She sounded less aggressive now, but still annoyed, though he was not sure who the target was now. "I don't want to lose your friendship."

"You won't," he promised, "I'm a priest. You mustn't be afraid to tell me anything."

She actually growled. "I don't care what you are!" She noticed him flinch visibly and did not care any longer what he took her for. "I suppose you would be shocked if you knew I wasn't a virgin, wouldn't you?"

He was, but his years of pastoral training hid it graciously. "No, of course not." He had also been taught not to ask for details in case he appeared to be prying for the sake of it, but asked: "When did it happen?"

"I can't." She sounded almost sleepy. Without thinking, he slipped his hand over hers. She felt protected by it somehow, as though he were holding her close to him. "It was when I was a child." She felt his reaction that time, the predictable tightening of muscles, the slight start. "There, I knew you'd be shocked."

"Yes, but not with you," he said quickly. "How old were you?"

His hand was holding hers again. She knew she could tell him anything. "I was nearly seven the first time."

He had never felt so appalled. He felt his stomach churning and tightening with repulsion. He knew he could not admit to her that he had not even known things like that happened to children that young or she would never trust him to understand her. "But it wasn't your fault," he blurted out, "you were a child. You weren't even at the age of *reason*. It was –" he struggled with the word. "It was rape."

"I don't think so," she replied. "I feel as though I could have stopped him if I'd wanted to." She sounded weary again, almost in a trance. "He said I'd wanted him to."

"That's nonsense, he would say that. And you couldn't possibly have stopped him."

She turned on him with savage rage. "How do you know that? What do you know about any of this? You know *nothing* about such things."

He felt as hurt as if she had slapped his face. "I know that much," he said quietly. "I want to help you."

She faltered, loathing herself for attacking him.

"You priests talk as if you knew everything, but let me tell you something. When my father attacked me, I cried and struggled until I learnt that there was no point resisting and didn't bother any more. I never struggled with *him.*"

She was right, he was hopelessly out of his depth but he knew he could not abandon her now. "It has nothing to do with it. How were you supposed to fight something you didn't understand?"

"He never did that to his own children. I used to play with them. They would have told me. If it wasn't my fault then why was it me, why wasn't it someone else?"

"Perhaps he thought they might give him away. He must have known you had no one to turn to." Nicholas noticed something glistening in the corner of her eye, then a tiny trail of moisture appearing down her face, which he reached out instinctively to wipe it away. Her cheek felt hot and wet. He felt the old shiver of emotion again and let her lean towards him and press her head against his open hand. It seemed to fit so perfectly. "It's all right. There. It's all right."

He drew her into his arms, feeling the weight of her head transferring to his shoulder, and stroked her hair. He thought to himself that it was how he would have comforted his sister if she had been in distress and that there could be no harm in it. He felt the faint shuddering of a woman struggling with tears and held her a little closer, whispering all the while that it was all right, that her troubles were over now because he could not have known that more were coming or that he would be the cause.

She felt his cheek pressing gently against her forehead and reached up to kiss him. She waited for him to push her away but he drew ever closer to her until all she could see was him and even the little daylight that was left was blocked out. The hiss of the indignant sea

264

seemed so far away that they both forgot for a moment that there is no such thing as a hidden love and they felt blissfully alone. Nicholas could almost have made himself believe that for those few guilty minutes, God had looked away and left them to misbehave in secret.

"I suppose it's too much to ask for an explanation?" After a silent journey back to London, Nicholas had walked straight to Richard Mason's home and was standing in the sitting room whilst Richard blinked at him from the comfort of his armchair. "I'm not sure what I'm supposed to explain, old man," he answered, sincerely perplexed. Nicholas certainly had an improved complexion after his trip to the seaside – Richard had never seen the man more rosy-faced – but he hardly looked like a person who had spent a pleasant afternoon in the company of a charming young lady. "I said that you should get out more and suddenly Alexandria Sant'Angelo appears like an answer to prayer."

The spiritual reference jarred horribly. Nicholas felt dirty, as though his fall was somehow imprinted all over his face for the world and his wife to stare at. "I think you knew what you were doing."

Richard shrugged his shoulders. The truth was that he had never possessed the strongest set of convictions and it had not really occurred to him that someone else might find his conduct morally objectionable. "Well, I knew perfectly well that if I didn't do a little matchmaking the two of you would never get your act together."

"There was nothing to get together, I'm a priest!" Nicholas shouted. "Couldn't you at least have respected that?"

Richard was not unmoved but refused to be steered away from the main point. "But you do fancy her, don't you? I knew I was right about that."

Nicholas felt his hackles rise. 'Fancy.' What a word. "You don't know anything, you smug complacent Englishman!"

Richard had never entirely registered their difference in nationality and could not take the insult seriously. "There's nothing wrong with being English," he said, shuffling in his chair. Nicholas groaned in exasperation and turned his back. "Listen, there's no point in huffing and puffing at me. I just created the circumstances."

Silence engulfed the room. Richard waited for Nicholas to drop his hands down from his face and turn around but he stood, frozen, like a personification of grief carved onto a cenotaph. He did not attempt to break the silence himself, afraid that it was all that was holding his friend together and that a single word might break him like an earthquake. He truly had never intended to cause so much hurt.

Finally, Nicholas stood up straight and lifted his head out of his hands. He turned around and Richard noticed that he was whiter than he had ever seen him before. "If that was all you did," he said quietly, "then I shall just have to create another set of circumstances."

XXII

He could not bear to think about what he was doing. He had the feeling that if he could just get himself onto a flight home, if he could board a plane and close his eyes until he was safely airborne, there was still a chance that he could save his vocation. He could not allow himself to focus on the details of his plan, most of all he could not think about her and how much she would loathe him for this. It had all been his fault. He should never have gone with her, he should never have allowed himself to get so close to her. It seemed to him, looking back at the whole sorry affair that there had been so many moments when he could have drawn back, but he had let them all pass and now they would both suffer whatever he chose to do.

There was too much noise in his head. He could not listen to it anymore. He strode through the maze of corridors to the headmaster's officer with his mind in a helpful blur and knocked on the door before he could lose his nerve. His entrance surprised them both.

"Send me back to Malta, father," demanded Nicholas, before the door had completely closed behind him. He felt a monumental sense of relief to have said it. He repeated: "Please send me back, I can't stay here."

Fr Anthony regarded him with detached intensity, making Nicholas feel as though he had known all along that this meeting would take place sooner or later. The suspicion was confirmed. "I knew you'd come to ask me that," he said, softly. "We've been very worried about you, Nicholas."

Then why did you not do something? thought Nicholas, staring straight ahead of him, but there he was expecting everyone else to have done things and not done things again. He struggled to catch his breath. "How did you know? I really was very careful."

"It's not that easy to hide feelings as strong as that," he explained. "Details betrayed you. It's difficult to explain to you because you can't see yourself and you are still so young."

That at least is not my fault, thought Nicholas, miserably, but the knowledge that his guilty little secret had been screaming at the senior members of the school all the time that he had been so carefully hiding it was the final insult. He began to understand why Alexandria had responded to him the way she had to begin with, though he could not find enough anger in him to speak to Fr Anthony quite like that. "I don't understand how you could know about such things."

Fr Anthony chuckled. "Come now, I said you were young but you should be old enough not to fall into that error. Do you imagine that there is any human situation I haven't seen in forty years as a priest?" He noticed Nicholas turning away and realised he was antagonising him. He returned to the original subject. "It's just the way you are when you're in the same room as her. Your body language gives you away. Why don't you sit down? "

Nicholas pulled a chair towards him and sat. He felt grateful for the chance to do something. "How could you know what I felt before I did?"

Fr Anthony weighed his words carefully before making the admission. "We all thought you felt strongly about Alexandria Sant'Angelo, but I couldn't be sure until now." He watched Nicholas getting up and walking towards the window.

"After all that." He was almost angry. Every gesture, every word of his over the past six months had been carefully considered. He had tried not to even let himself think of her in case it showed on his face. Dear God, he might as well have just got on with it!

"Have you broken your vows?"

It was a hard question to answer correctly. "Yes, but not in the way you're thinking," he explained.

"What do you mean by that?" Nicholas was reddening again. He stared fixedly down at his clenched hands. "Forgive me for asking, but have you made love to her?"

"Not technically. That is–" he choked with mortification, scrambling for the words. "What I mean is we haven't done *that*."

"But?"

"But we could have done. And I–" Let it go, he thought, falling into the last circle of despair. If he could see through him so easily, let him hear it all. "I wanted to. We both wanted to. That's why I know I must go."

"I understand."

Nicholas glanced out of the window at the empty playground below. For the rest of his life despair was always symbolised by a grey concrete football pitch with a fine dusting of moss gathering around the edges and two rusted goal posts. This was what it meant to be lonely; to return to Malta on the back of some lame excuse that would have to be repeated to everyone except his confessor. His friends could not know, his mother in particular could not know – he even wondered whether there were some things he could not share with Gregory. And all the time to live with the real reason... and without it. "I've let everyone down."

"Can I make a suggestion?" asked Fr Anthony finally. "I think it might help to soften the blow a little. May I suggest that we send you back to Malta for a couple of weeks? I can arrange for staff to cover for you. Then you can have a think about where all this is going. You haven't known each other very long; it might peter out when you're away from the environment."

It won't, I know it won't, thought Nicholas but he

was prepared to accept almost any offer that took him away. "What if it doesn't?" he asked.

Fr Anthony's response was typically phlegmatic. "Then you must discern where your life is going once and for all or you will drive yourself mad."

***

Alexandria drove home through a whirl of emotion. This was love. This was more she had ever felt in her life, even for James Carlisle on the summer night in the garden under the stars. She drove with the windows down in spite of the chill and the pollution, singing on the top of her voice: *All you need is love!* By the time she neared home, her forced good spirits had deteriorated and she found herself changing her route and travelling in the direction of Auntie Josephine's house.

She was supposed to be happy, she told herself. She had been held in the arms of a man who loved her. He had told her that, over and over again as they curled up together like lost children on the windswept beach. She could still feel the shudder of ecstasy she had felt at the sound of his voice, the tiny details of the moment: the sense of intense heat as she shivered with the cold, the coarse sand rubbing against the few gaps in her winter clothing, the crack between the hem of her trousers and her sock, her fidgeting hands. She remembered the smell of him, which she fancied was like polish and candle smoke.

And she remembered how he had broken away from her without warning and leapt to his feet, protesting: "This is wrong, I can't do this!" Then they had argued and made up and argued again and finally ended up back in one another's arms, so that now she did not know how to remember it all and hurtled between ecstasy and icy resignation between the road and the front door, behind which Auntie Josephine was soon to struggle with the temptation of saying 'I told you so.'

Instead she remarked: "You really do have a talent for getting into quandaries, don't you?" It was almost as insensitive, but Alex was in combative mode by now and would have argued with her whatever she said.

"I really didn't ask for this, it's like some sick joke!" she complained. "It's typical, isn't it? The first truly decent man I fall in love with – honest, honourable, gentle, handsome, everything I could possibly want – would turn out to be a bloody priest, wouldn't he?"

"What are you going to do?"

"I don't know!" Even now she could not steady herself. A voice snarled in her ear that if she couldn't have his love she didn't care whilst another lamented that she could never live without it and yet another contemplated that it would have been so simple if she could have met him whilst they were both young and uncommitted. "It's the Church's fault!" Well, it was. The entire might of the Faith, past, present and future, had conspired to destroy her one hope of happiness. It was an evil papist plot. The Church that had given her courage and security in childhood had now come back to exact its revenge.

"Don't be silly, Alex, you know better than that." She meant to be sympathetic, why oh why did she hear herself sounding exasperated? "No one forced him to become a priest."

"How could he possibly have known what it meant? The only women he'd ever met before were his mother and sister." In her mind she was thinking by now that they were free. No one could force him to stay a priest, the Inquisition was not going to come and drag him kicking and screaming back into his collar. "You talk just like him! He's an adult, he can do what he likes."

It had been Josephine's firm conviction in the past that there were only so many disasters that one family could be forced to deal with in a lifetime, but at this stage in her life she had lost most of her convictions and beliefs. "You know nothing about the life he leads, love. The priesthood isn't just a job he can drop and trade for another."

Alexandria felt a nail sticking out of the side of the kitchen table and squeezed it to control her rage. "I don't see how much you know about it either. You haven't been a practising Catholic for years."

"That's a libel!" she retorted. "I always go at Christmas and Easter. Anyway, you don't have to be the Blessed Mother to know that this is *wrong*." Alexandria looked away. "Look, it can't end well for you. You'll have to let him go sooner or later so you may as well do it now when it won't hurt so much."

But it would still hurt. She could not see what the timing had to do with it. It would hurt to give him up now or tomorrow or at the end of the year... she jumped, startled. "You don't suppose he'll do something silly, do you?"

"Like what?" Being a nurse, she immediately thought of suicide and was fairly sure that such a man would not run to that.

"He said we would have to stop seeing one another." She got to her feet. "How could we manage that working in the same school unless he went away?" Josephine motioned for her to sit down again. "He'll disappear! He'll leave, I know he'll leave!"

"Just calm down." Josephine, who was not feeling particularly calm herself, got up and put the kettle on. She needed a job to do, anything to conceal the fact that she was thinking about the next move. Whenever she had felt the smallest yearnings for the pitter patter of little feet during her childbearing years, she had consoled herself with the thought that young children were basically a nuisance: unreasonable, unpredictable, largely uncontrollable. But she had come to realise that

272

the younger generation were always like that, even when they were twenty-something young professionals. "This is going to sound terribly middle-aged," she said, from behind a cloud of steam.

"Never mind, I thought it would," answered Alex, tartly. Just sometimes and only just sometimes, Josephine had to admit that Alexandria reminded her of her brother. "I know what you are going to tell me to do. But if you imagine I'll let him walk out of my life without a word of explanation you must think I'm mad."

"Is there very much to explain?"

Alexandria spent the rest of the day agitated and undecided. It was the simplest solution, to let him slip away so that he could go back to being a priest and she could go back to life as she had known it. Except that she had hated life as she had known it. She had never asked to be a teacher, she had certainly never asked to be alone and it had never occurred to her that she would find herself banished indefinitely in a strange draughty country a million miles away from anything that gave purpose and sense to her life. And she was sure that he could never go back either. When she imagined him trying to walk away, she could never quite imagine him getting onto the plane. He packed his bags, left his room, boarded a bus to the airport, but he always stopped at the last minute, just as he was about to put his foot on the first step. Her imagination did not stretch far enough to seeing him leave her behind.

She held back from ringing him, that day and the next day, though she could barely believe afterwards that the time she crossed had been so short. Then on the next morning, she lost her nerve and rang the school. The curt voice of a secretary informed her that Fr Nicholas Falzon was not there and no, she could not take a message. Alexandria hung up then thought of another way in. Disguising her voice as best she could, she asked: "Could I speak to Mr Mason, please?"

"Is it a school matter?"

"No, I'm his sister-in-law." What a bloody stupid lie, she snarled at herself, as if it weren't easy enough to find that one out.

"Oh I see, well you can't speak to him on this number, he's got a telephone line of his own."

A phone of one's own, mused Alexandria, taking down the number. She hung up and tried again. A man's voice answered this time. "Richard?"

"Yes, speaking."

"Where's Nicholas?"

There was a muffled cough at the other end. "Hello there Alexandria," he said. She knew he had expected her to ring. "How should I know?"

"If you're going to be a liar you might at least put your back into it," she retorted. "They said he wasn't here. Where is he?"

"Why are you asking me?" Having made the mistake of bringing them together in the first place, Richard was now determined to do the decent thing and keep his mouth shut. "I can't think why he'd tell me if he was up to something."

"Because you were his friend and one of the only people he trusted. He's gone, hasn't he?"

The female voice was unrelentingly direct. He felt as though he were being cross-examined. "Yes, but I don't know – I really don't know where he's gone! No one's supposed to know."

"I know you know where he is." Christ, she'll be putting the thumb screws on me next, he thought, seriously contemplating putting the phone down. Except that she would simply come round and confront him face to face which would be a fate worse than death.

"Look, I promised I wouldn't tell you."

"I'll tell him I held you at gunpoint. Now, where is he?"

"He's taking the 14:40 flight from Heathrow back to Malta."

"Thank you. Didn't hurt, did it?" He heard the crack of the phone being slammed down and struggled to catch his breath. If one of his pupils had excused themselves from a misdemeanour with the old excuse 'I really didn't mean to' he would have commanded them to grow up.

XXIII

Upon my bed by night I sought him whom my soul loves;

I sought him, but found him not; I called him, but he gave no answer.

"I will rise now and go about the city, in the streets and in the squares;

I will seek him whom my soul loves." I sought him, but found him not.

The watchmen found me, as they went about in the city.

"Have you seen him whom my soul loves?"

Scarcely had I passed them, when I found him whom my soul loves.

I held him, and would not let him go...

"You know, if that wasn't in the Bible you'd be disgusted with it," Benedict informs me. We have returned to the family home and scurried up to my room, so that Benedict can sprawl on my bed and I can search for inspiration among the books and artefacts scattered around the room for packing.

I am reminded that it will soon be time to leave. I knew when I came out that I might not come back to Malta again for a long time after this visit and arranged to pick up the bits and pieces that I have accumulated here during my many childhood visits. I have thrown away a great deal; a ludicrous inflatable crocodile I bought when I was twelve, other assorted relics of childhood beach holidays; sand-encrusted shells, a faded towel, a hat I deliberately dropped into the water because I hated the colour of it.

Other things remain, mostly of a religious nature and

almost all belonging to Nanna Carmelina because she was one of the few members of that generation I really missed when she was gone. With a touch of mischief, she left me a set of priestly vestments she made when she was still sewing, joking that I might have a son one day who would be a priest. There are other things, all very familiar, a rosary, an icon, her missal, bulging with holy pictures and prayer cards. "What's disgusting about that?" I ask. "It's the Song of Solomon."

"Yes I know, but it doesn't really fit in with the whole RC image, does it?"

"I don't know. My Nanna's marriage guidance would have made a gynaecologist blush."

I wonder what she would have made of Benedict if she had met him. She would have been pleased that I was marrying an Englishman – and oh such an English Englishman – and I think she would have approved of his gentle, careful manner. She would have seen his doubts as an irritating phase he was going through and expected me to charm him back to reality again, if she had not had a good try herself first. All in all, the impression would have been favourable and she would have avoided the tiresome habit of telling us how much more fortunate we were than they had been.

I know how fortunate we are in some ways. Benedict and I came together in a fairytale year in an academic playground, surrounded by beauty. Old universities always have a hint of the romantic about them, a whisper of a bygone age and we fell into one another's arms in a world of gowns and candlelight and oak-panelled rooms. There were no obstacles, no complications; there was no one to hurt. So yes, we were fortunate, much more fortunate than those who came before us, but we did not ask for it to be the way it was.

Nicholas had come to hate any building that denoted travel. He was as unsettled and miserable about the process of moving from one place to the next as he had ever been, except that now there was no hope for him at either destination. He had been unhappy in England but leaving it meant leaving behind the only person who offered him the prospect of happiness. He should have been glad to be going back to Malta at last, but he almost wished that he could have been sent anywhere else. Some neutral, unknown place perhaps, large and anonymous enough to hide in forever. A place with no memories, no history. If he could have made a place for himself to live in, it would have been a vast, crowded habitation that had sprung up in a single moment, superficial, new and full of dark corners where he could simply disappear.

He bought a paper, but found it impossible to read. Even in his civvies he felt as though the world knew he was a priest in disgrace. He searched out the quietest most private corner of the entire airport to sit in during the excessive hours he had to wait, then used the newspaper as a shield to block out the outside world, not glancing at a single word. It was all part of the same sensation of life spinning out of control, what he had meant when he told his brother that he felt as though he had fallen off a roundabout. He knew there had to be some end to it somewhere and he simply had not found it yet, he just had to reach out and find it.

Alexandria found him first. He felt a hand touching his shoulder and a sudden charged silence around him. The paper fell from his hands but he could not look at her, glancing without focus ahead of him. He reached up and took her hand. "Why did you come?" he asked, at last.

"Why are you running away?" she responded. He felt the urge to rest his head against her arm. If he was supposed to be running away he was too tired. He wanted to curl up in her arms and find stillness there. "What are you afraid of?"

Nicholas remembered why he was there like the return of a stabbing pain and forced himself to stand up. She refused to be put off and ruffled his hair. It was too intimate a gesture to be explained away. "What are you afraid of?"

He still could not look at her. "Ho paura di me," he said.

She hesitated, confused. "You can't fear yourself." This was hardly the moment for Nicholas to explain that he was quoting a line from a Puccini opera and that it was an admission of his own weakness. "How could you think of running off like that? Didn't I at least deserve a good-bye?"

He looked at her with such a sudden, sharp movement that she disengaged herself from him. "I didn't want to say good-bye," he explained. "I didn't want to say good-bye to you. Do I have to spell it out to you?"

She had never thought she would be glad to hear a man angry. She said: "You don't have to say good-bye to me if you don't want to. It doesn't have to be like that."

His head was going round again. He felt as though everything was turning around, the other passengers, the kiosks and counters, everything except her and she stood in the centre of it all, waiting for him to steady himself. He did not give the answer she had hoped for but she had left no detail out of her plan. He said: "I have to get on that plane. I'm supposed to be going back to Malta to think through this. I have to make a decision."

"I know, I was told," she answered, rather taking the wind out of his sails. "I'm coming with you."

He could not have been taken more by surprise. "That's not really the idea," he began, "I'm supposed to…"

"I don't care whose idea it was for you to make a

decision that involved me without telling me!"

Just pick up your case and walk away, a voice instructed him. Turn around and walk away. He knew it should be easy, even if she made a scene. If he truly wanted to end it, he had simply to disengage himself from her and go. If he could bring himself to walk away from her a second time. "It's not meant to be like that," he began, but she was holding his hands again and he felt bound to her.

Alexandria waited for him to resist, but he was rooted to the spot. She knew she would never have another chance to say it: "I love you." They were standing close enough together that a passer-by might have mistaken them for lovers struggling to bid one another farewell. "This isn't going to go away, you can't just disappear."

She noticed that his eyes were red. "I have to think," he explained, but it all seemed so lame. "I don't know what to do."

She turned, still holding his hand and began to lead him to the gate. "Think," she ordered him, with considerable determination. "We must both think. We got into this mess together, so we'll get out of it together."

"I don't think you appreciate the full implications of this," he began, staggering to a halt. "I have to make a choice. I'm being dishonest with everyone if I don't. I'll bring shame on the priesthood."

She paused, looking down at the hands she held in hers so casually. It was the first time she had ever thought of them as consecrated hands and for a moment, she almost understood what she was asking him to give up for her – if it were possible for anyone to get their head around what it meant to participate in the greatest of all mysteries. She kissed his hands in a gesture of reverence she remembered from childhood and let them go. "I can't ask you to choose me," she said, stepping back, "but I will be there when you choose."

***

Gregory murmured an awkward thank you to Alexandria as she placed a cup of coffee in front of him and left the room. Apart from the cloud of tension hovering around the kitchen table, there was nothing particularly notable about the home he had so recently entered. An attractive young woman had led him into a tiled hallway and up a flight of stairs that led to a small apartment. They had exchanged trivial conversation as they stepped into a kitchen that could quite easily have been his mother's, with its containers full of olives and capers in vinegar, and its pin neat orderliness. The gossips he had been forced to deal with over the past weeks would have been surprised to find out that the Scarlet Whore of Babylon was so house proud.

And then, of course, there was Nicholas. It was no longer quite like looking in a mirror for him, his brother was casually dressed, he had let his hair grow a little longer and nerves had made him lose weight. "Are you going to talk to me?" he asked at last, without a hint of annoyance.

Gregory jumped, aware of his rudeness. "Sorry, I was just taking it all in."

Nicholas smiled. "That's all right, you're taking it very calmly if I may say so. Are you well? Is everyone well?"

"We'll be all right." He could not say that they were not at all well without making an accusation and Nicholas did not deserve that. By the look of him, he had enough to worry about. "Are you getting by? Do you have work?"

"Alex is working for a bank. I'm taking whatever work I can find." Nicholas faltered, toying with mistrust before adding, "I can't find a teaching job."

"I didn't think you would." Gregory peered into his cup, looking for his nerve. "Nick, why did you come back? Why couldn't you at least have stayed away?"

It was an unfriendly question. Gregory might as well have opened his front door and asked what the hell he was doing there. "We wanted to make our home here. Is that so strange?"

"Didn't you stop and think what it would mean?"

Gregory simply could not fathom how a man who had never intended to hurt anyone could have blundered into a situation in which he had enemies on both sides. On the one side there were the anti-clerical papers who felt undisguised loathing for the man because he was an ordained priest and had seized on the story of a cleric leaving his order for a woman as a stick to beat the Church with. In the absence of any lurid details they had simply made them up and had painted a picture of a disturbed frustrated man flinging his clerical collar over the bastions to liberate himself in the arms of a racy ex-convent girl turned temptress.

On the other side of the coin there were unsuspecting people like his mother, who felt bitter and repulsed by what they saw as a wicked betrayal of everything they stood for. Gregory doubted that either party would feel particularly vindicated if they entered this apartment. "You shouldn't have come back," said Gregory. "Scandal aside, it was hardly practical, was it? You'll never get a teaching job here again, or possibly any permanent job. What qualifications do you have that will count for anything now?"

"I was very good at moral theology," Nicholas replied, but the rejoinder was too weak for even him to laugh at.

"Even if you weren't a priest, I'd have told you not to come back. People are leaving; doctors, nurses, teachers. There's trouble coming."

"I'm not interested in the political situation."

"It might be interested in you." Nicholas flinched visibly. "Don't you read the papers?" No, in all honesty he didn't and he thought the reason obvious.

"Are you ashamed of me?"

The silence was so absolute that Nicholas regretted fishing for reassurance. "If I thought there was any way to save your vocation, I would ask you to reconsider what you're doing," said Gregory. "As it stands, I think you should try to sort out your situation."

"We are!" Nicholas jumped in, "I've applied to be laicised. We want to get married. I know it's all a bit of a mess, but we will sort everything out."

Gregory covered his face for a second, unsure whether he was suppressing laughter or tears. He had never heard such a shambolic state of affairs described in such euphemistic terms. His brother had left the priesthood, reneged on his vows, been demonised by anyone with an opinion and ostracised by his entire family, he had no career prospects at all and virtually no sympathetic contacts. A bit of a mess missed the mark by several millennia.

"Should I go and see mother?" asked Nicholas, awkwardly. "I thought that maybe if I explained everything to her..."

"Please don't," Gregory replied, far too quickly. It betrayed everything he had not said. "It wouldn't be good for either of you."

Gregory still could not reconcile the superficial normality of the environment with the heartache it had caused them all. As a man whose life seemed to be dedicated to dealing with other people's crises and life stories, he was beginning to believe that some stories held no heroes to speak of, and perhaps no villains either, just a lot of rather bewildered individuals thrown together by forces they could never begin to understand. For a generation born into the drama and horror of a world war, bewilderment seemed a poor offering to the world. It was certainly an inadequate consolation to a woman who had suffered and sacrificed so much in her life without complaint. Gregory knew that she would never understand what had possessed her son to walk out into the cool of the early morning one day and leave his religious order behind, very quietly, without a word of farewell.

But Gregory thought he understood why, even if he knew he would not have walked that way. "Take care," he said fondly as he got up to leave. "They'll come round eventually."

"I hope so," remarked Nicholas, walking down the stairs with him. "We feel so alone. It's like living under a curse."

Quite so. And it had yet to complete its work. It must be passed down to a new generation. He said 'all your descendants' on that bitter day many years ago before Alexandria and Nicholas were born and so it had to be. How could a mere two generations be enough to satisfy Leonardo Sant'Angelo's hate-ridden revenge from beyond the grave? I must come into existence but I can do so only as others are torn away. There must be more deaths before my presence is even known about, but it is as Leonardo knew it would be, almost as if he had had a vision of the misery he was unleashing as he said the words. And I will still be doubted by the only person whose good opinion matters to me, but perhaps that is all part of the curse. Perhaps playing the part of the doomed prophetess is the end of it. The Cassandra Curse to end all curses.

XXIV

Sorrow is but the guest of night,
Joy cometh in the morning.

I would like to believe that there is some truth in the old proverb, but if there is then we are far away from the morning yet and I will never record the dawn breaking. That is for other writers, other storytellers. I notice that Benedict is becoming restive, but I cannot tie up the threads as he would like it. He is not unsettled any more, the story is breaking him.

"You can end it wherever you want," he says, holding a hand out to me. That means he wants me to stop but we are trapped now, even if he does not realise it yet and there can be no escape. Perhaps I would never have started if I had stopped to think what a labyrinth we were entering but we cannot retrace our steps so far now and I cannot pretend it away as if I dreamt it all during a particularly gloomy night.

"What were you expecting?" I ask him. "Didn't anyone tell you that truth was stranger than fiction?" I try to be humorous but end up simply sounding bitter. "Let's see who we have had so far. We've had child abusers, adulterers, drunkards, suicides, wayfarers, bastards, aristocrats and various other sub-categories of protagonist. To complete the smorgasbord, how about..."

"Don't."

"Don't what?"

"Please don't."

I have shaken his sensibilities again, he looks positively disgusted with me. Quite understandable under the circumstances, he should be disgusted and perhaps he should be disgusted with me for not doing the decent thing and keeping my mouth shut, but I do not have any sympathy anymore. I find myself feeling irrationally angry. "Well what on earth did you expect? Happiness is hardly very gripping is it? If the Sant'Angelos had been nice, calm, pleasant people who had got along with one another, blessed their sons and lived in a state of mutual respect and affection and if the Buhagiar/Falzons had not had to bury half of their family members before they could grow to get on one another's nerves – *I would have had nothing to tell you!*"

"Yes, but-"

"And if I were to tell you that my parents lived out their quiet little lives without complications, my mother as a teacher and my father let's say a data analyst to be really boring, they had me and we all lived happily ever after in a quaint little farmhouse in Naxxar, would you really want to know about it?"

"It always has to be one extreme or the other with you people, doesn't it?" he exclaims, "is it too much to ask for a little – moderation?!"

I find the proposition disarming. Tragedy is all right if it is suitably discreet and happens infrequently enough to allow regular tea breaks. Yes indeed, it would all have happened quite differently in a colder climate. "If it helps, there is about to be a family reunion." I'm lying, but it will soothe him for a moment.

It was a family reunion of sorts. That is to say, Nicholas entered his mother's house again, rather sooner than Gregory would have recommended, but on that day he did not stop to think whether it was wise or not. He knew he had to go there the moment Alexandria erupted into the room in tears and shook him awake, not realising that she had woken him up when she left earlier and he was only dozing. "What is it, my darling?"

He reached out to hold her but she clearly had other ideas and chivvied him into sitting up. "You must get up!"

"What's going on?" He stifled a shudder as she dropped a rolled up newspaper into his lap. Nicholas had stopped reading them altogether when he found himself appearing among their unfriendly pages and found the sight and smell of a newspaper unsettling. "What's happened?"

"I'm sorry, my darling," sobbed Alexandria, placing a moist hand on his arm. "I can't say it."

Her reaction made him think that it was just some other story about them and he was taken completely unawares when he unrolled the paper and saw his adopted brother gazing cheekily back at him in black-and-white. He remembered nothing of the moment afterwards other than that he took a sharp intake of breath and knew that Pawlinu must be dead before he had even taken in the headline. The man had not been a public figure or held any great ambitions. He was not the sort of person who won awards and honours. Really good people who kept out of everyone's way were only ever noticed when something terrible happened to them.

He got to his feet amid a clatter of discordant noises. He felt as though he were caught in the middle of a battle. He seemed to hear distant explosions, the thunder and screech of shells dropping all around him as he dressed. The only black clothing he could find was the black suit he had worn as a priest, which even minus the collar was inescapably clerical. There was nothing to be done about it, he was in mourning, he had to wear black. He could not risk shaving as the ground was trembling under his feet and he could not keep still long enough to trust himself with a razor blade, so he stepped into the street, dazed and dishevelled, looking like a bewildered clergyman who was trying to find his way home.

I remember, I remember
The house where I was born.

Not once on the short journey to Sliema did it occur to Nicholas that he was making a mistake. He was beyond thought, unable even to take in the scale of the tragedy that had engulfed his family. He could grasp the fact that his brother was dead but had not even managed to stretch his imagination far enough to think of him like that. He let his mind slip into numb oblivion rather than risk picturing the moment it had happened, until he found himself walking down the street that led him home.

As he neared his mother's house, he noticed a group of boys he did not recognise playing football in the road. It was not quite as safe for them as it had been for him at that age. Cars kept disrupting them, sending them scurrying onto the pavements and then a door was flung open and an old woman told them off for making too much noise. Nicholas realised that she was the same woman who had told him off at that age. She was exactly as she had been when he was a boy, wearing the same clothes, her hair rinsed the same colour. Just a little more stooped, a little more lined.

He remembered the house as a place where he had learnt the meaning of love. As he pushed open the barley-coloured door, a wealth of memories settled on him, causing him to linger for a moment before crossing the threshold; the earliest moments of consciousness – the whirr of his mother's Singer sewing machine late at night, Nanna Buhagiar flouncing around the kitchen amid the smell of coffee and baking, complaining to herself about the quality of her daughter's cliental; Uncle Sam's explosive appearance, falling asleep with the murmur of the rosary washing over him... and the aching, empty experience of death entering their world.

Rosaria had seen Nicholas approaching from the

balcony and came downstairs to intercept him before her mother saw him. She startled him as he tiptoed into the hall, unaware that he was being watched. "Rosaria?" he whispered, "Zazi is that you?"

"Why have you come?" she asked, stepping towards him. He was unnerved by the tone of it. The shrill girlishness he remembered had been replaced by a rich resonance he did not recognise, but there was a great deal about her that he did not recognise. She had cut her hair short and it sat about her head it in an immaculate red-brown bob like a declaration of adulthood. Her face had lost the plumpness he remembered (she had after all been the youngest and always a little over-indulged) and she had a sharp, pinched look that would have made it difficult to place her age. He would have thought her very plain if he had not known a little of what she must have been through over the past twenty-four hours.

The transformation in Nicholas seemed to trouble Rosaria more and he watched as she brought her hands to her face and began to cry. It broke the invisible stand-off between them and he hurried forward to embrace her. She buried her face in the course fibres of his shirt and gave a stifled scream. He had forgotten how ugly grief was and quaked at the sheer animal misery of it as she gasped and wailed, clinging to him as if she could not decide whether she desperately needed him or wanted to tear him limb from limb. "Why did you come?" she choked, convulsing with noisy sobs. "Why are you here? Bad enough to lose one brother!"

He was my brother too, he thought, but knew better than to say anything. In any case he could hardly find the energy to speak; he felt winded. He had half-expected to arrive and find that it was a terrible mistake. As a boy he would gladly have given some other family the tragedy he could not take in, now he wanted to make it quite simply disappear. He wanted it not to be or at the very least to see some gap in the house where

Pawlinu should have been, some dark void somewhere at the top of the stairs where he had sat when he was a child or on the balcony where he had hidden to avoid household chores. He did not want his life to stop anymore, he wanted the world to stop, every person, every animal, everything to freeze as it had been the moment an ancient detonator cracked and sent three members of his family reeling into eternity. But then, he knew he was only wishing for what everyone craved at such a time. Their misery was not even fresh.

"I had to come," he whispered, "why did no one tell me? I found out reading the newspaper!"

She broke away from him and would have said something rash that she could have regretted at her leisure if a voice had not called from upstairs: "Rosaria, who are you talking to?"

Rosaria pushed Nicholas towards the door. "Get out! She mustn't see you in the state she's in!"

But Carmelina was already descending the stairs. "Gregory?" she called. The shock had confused her, Gregory was already at the church, but seeing him in the poor light dressed as he was it was an easy enough mistake to make. "Who sent for you?" she asked.

Nicholas could not think of an answer. He had not thought that he might have to explain his presence. "I came as soon as I heard."

"You had no business entering my house uninvited," she said, so coldly that he almost wished he could have been worth her anger. "I did not call for you."

Nicholas felt Rosaria's hand pushing him closer to the door but he braced, sensing a last opportunity. "I thought this was my home."

"It is not your home and you are not my son!" There was emotion now, but not anger, something closer to disgust. "You have made your own home now. Go back to that creature you chose above your duty!"

This was the worst, the very worst misery he had

ever felt. "She is not a creature," he said, but he had no strength left.

"Whore then. I don't care what you call her."

"You've no right to call her that!"

"I did not come down here to argue with a stranger." An invisible knife pierced him through. He leant back against the doorway to steady himself. "Rosaria, will you show this gentleman out?"

He let her lead him outside where the sudden searing heat almost knocked him down. Rosaria's eyes were still streaming. "I destroy everything I touch, don't I?" he said, pretending to shield his face from the sun.

"Yes," Rosaria agreed, without a trace of mirth, "you do." He hit his head against the wall of the house but it was not enough and he sank his fingers into his hair. She rested a restraining hand on his arm. "Do you love her?"

"Yes," he said, "and no, I'm not going to leave her."

"I wasn't going to tell you to," she promised. "You've made your choice; what good would it do to break her heart now?"

He let his hands drop down to his sides. "None whatsoever. I can't betray absolutely everyone."

Rosaria dragged him around by the arm so that he was facing her. "Be a man!" she commanded him in a half-whisper, sounding so like their mother that he could almost have smiled. "You've made your choice. You love her, she loves you. Stand by what you've done and to hell with everyone else. It's done now."

There speaks a woman, he thought. He said: "I wanted to go to the funeral."

She paused for thought. "I'm sure you'll find some quiet little corner of the church to hide in," she said, quietly. "There's room for all of us, one way or the other."

And so it was that Nicholas walked to his parish church ahead of everyone else and found himself a place to sit behind a pillar so that he could watch people as they arrived. He knew everyone of course; neighbours, family friends, casual acquaintances. Face after familiar face moved past him, unaware of his presence, like some spectral dance of a past life. He was the uninvited guest at the divine banquet, an impostor skulking in the shadows. He half-expected someone to suddenly recognise him and denounce him before the assembled congregation as the disgraced priest, that most loathed of human failures.

No one did, blinded by their grief and haste. Nicholas wondered how his father would have reacted to all this, whether he remembered enough of him to be able to guess what he would have said to him. He knew he was not remembering the real man after so long; Lawrence had become an icon of fatherhood to him through the lens of an early death, just like Pawlinu would do, the man who died trying to save his children. He should never have come home from America, thought Nicholas, his mind sliding drunkenly from one idea to the next. He would have been safe in a little corner of the New World where nothing ever happened. Perhaps he ought to take Alexandria out there? It was a land built on social misfits, men and women out of place in their own countries. Except that he could not bear the thought of packing up and moving again.

The organ began to play and he shuffled to his feet, keeping his face well hidden from the procession that was moving down the aisle. The priests came first, a dramatic sight in black and he knew them all. Gregory led the way, which Nicholas thought a mistake – he should not have had to deal with the strain of saying his brother's requiem Mass, but then he did not know that Gregory had tried to give him the Last Rites and had to drag his sister-in-law away when she arrived on the scene and he couldn't bear to let her look at it.

There were the others as well, Fr Jonathan and other priests he had known from his boyhood, interspersed with companions who had been ordained with him. He covered his eyes when he caught a glimpse of his family, too appalled to take in the sight of them struggling behind no fewer than three coffins.

It was too horrible, he told himself he did not need to see it, but his vision had blurred by the time he looked up at the sanctuary and he saw an impressionist painting of Gregory and his companions assembling behind the altar. A voice rang out: *The Lord be with you.* The congregation hesitated – Nicholas heard the rustle of heads turning – then they seemed to recollect where they were and responded. Gregory also paused, unsettled as if by some unexpected turn of events, then braced himself and continued. It was only when he resumed the words of the Mass that Nicholas realised that he, not Gregory, had spoken. He quaked with mortification and utter despair. The only thing more tragic than saying a much-loved brother's requiem Mass was not saying it.

Three hours later, Alexandria found Nicholas sitting alone in the church. He had no cause to hide anymore and sat in weary silence, unable to compel himself to move. She sat beside him and waited for him to come round, concealing a rankling fear that he would not acknowledge her existence at all. She had felt a sense of impending danger when he insisted on going to his family, all the more so when he said that she should stay behind. She had never met Pawlinu and could not share his sense of loss, only the blind, immediate horror of the news. Pawlinu's life was something that linked Nicholas inextricably to his family and to a part of his life in which Alexandria had played no part. She had imagined him going back to the family home and being warmly welcomed, grievances forgotten at such a time. Then she imagined them persuading him not to go back to her, poisoning his mind against her until his new life seemed worthless and he had no desire to return to it.

When he did not return, she became more anxious still, her panicked fantasies seemingly confirmed. In the half-light of the parish church, they were confirmed again by his silence. He should have noticed her presence immediately, turned to her, but he showed every sign of having slipped into a world she could not enter. "I'm here," she said, quietly, reaching out to take his hand. He had got up before she could reach him and she followed at a distance as he walked slowly in the direction of the Lady Chapel.

"I said, I'm here," she repeated, a shade too loud. "Can you hear me?"

He lifted a candle from the ledge where a row of squat white cylinders flamed stubbornly, swathing his face in light, "My brother's gone," he said, looking into the flame.

"I know, my love."

"And my mother. And everyone. They've all gone." He looked up at the icon of the Holy Family: the veiled, radiant Madonna staring in child-like ecstasy down at the sleeping infant in her arms, whilst a wistful Joseph looked on, calm, paternal – present. "In a country that values families more than any other, we have no family."

"A fat lot of good my family were to me," Alexandria retorted. "and if your family loved you that much, they wouldn't have abandoned you for any reason. We have each other, isn't that enough for you?"

"I think they think that I abandoned them," Nicholas explained, deaf to her bitterness. "It was the wrong time to leave the priesthood. Gregory said there are bad times coming." He lit a fresh candle. The wick was embedded in the wax and went out several times before bursting into life. "I want to do this properly, Alex, I want to marry you."

"That rather depends on the Vatican, doesn't it?" she answered. She felt a distance between them for the first time, watching him lighting votive candles whilst she stood in the shadows, wondering at the meaning of it all. She felt annoyed with herself for not caring more about doing things properly. "That is, of course your papers will come through." She wanted so badly to sound convincing. "I want to do what will make you happy."

"I want you to be happy about this."

She stepped forward and put her arms around his neck, protesting that of course it was what she wanted and they could be happy whatever happened around them. For a moment they could believe that all they needed was one another, like Edward had believed on his doomed wedding day, like any couple who have ever been in love have believed. It did not even seem to matter that she could not follow him into the mysterious sacramental world of faith and prayers and wonder that had been hers once, though she could hardly remember how she came to leave it. He would lead her back, she knew he would, because the only lesson she remembered from it all was that there really was such a thing as love.

"Take me home," he pleaded.

"You are home," she said, and led him through the silent church.

XXV

I have waited so long to come into being that it is almost an anticlimax now that the moment has come about. Like every human being that was ever created and will ever be created, the miracle occurs quite unnoticed in a tiny, darkly fertile corner of a woman's body. In an unrecorded minute of an uncharted night, I burst into life. The journey of growth and life with its confusion and anger and ecstasy that has brought me home, begins now with a single, microscopic cell.

What a piece of work is man! How noble in reason! How infinite in faculties! In form and moving, how express and admirable! In action how like an angel! In apprehension, how like a god! The beauty of the world! The paragon of animals!

I grow in secret, settling myself down into the safety of my mother's womb. I am as small and delicate as a raindrop, increasing in richness as cells multiply and knit together. Long before my mother or the doctors find me out, my heart begins to beat. A gentler rhythm than my mother's resonant, overpowering heartbeat, but there is another sound; I am not alone. A companion grows beside me, made of the same substance, nurtured by the same womb but separate. We soon have our own nervous systems, our own vital organs; in sleep we are caught in our separate dream worlds. I reach out to touch my brother curled up beside me in the darkness and the unsung first love that only twins can know begins.

Shall I give my brother a name? I would call him Pawlinu to carry on a dead man's memory, but he is not allowed a name. I should not even be recording him here. There is room for every other kind of human being there, but he was not a member of my family, no he was not my brother, his heart never beat the pulse of life. He must be forgotten, annihilated because he did not survive the course. I will risk revolution and give him a name, call him my brother. The human world of meetings and partings touches even the hidden lives we refuse to name or think too deeply about, and there had to be at least one parting that took place before we had even taken our first breaths.

Rumblings around us, the throb of a coming calamity. We search for one another but a curtain of blood appears to separate us. A moment before it falls, his mouth opens as if he would like to scream but his distress is known to no one except myself and I am powerless to part the blood curtain and drag him back to sanctuary and nourishment. He is gone. My brother. My brother is gone and I am alone in the cavern of life where death has trespassed. The pounding of my mother's heart grows faster like a frenzied drumbeat, but the sound brings no comfort with it any more. I am alone. Alone   alone ...... alone....

And all of this happened as my mother walked down a busy street in the late autumn sunshine, wondering why she was feeling so unwell. She had been feeling weak and listless since she got up, but blamed it on the sleepless night she had had. As she made her way towards the bus terminus, she felt the first spasm of pain, but she did not know she was pregnant and leant against the wall of a nearby building, waiting for it to pass.

"Are you all right?" asked a lady carrying a basket. "Is anything the matter?"

"I'm fine," she gasped, but the pain was suddenly so excruciating that she could barely draw breath. The world was breaking up into fragments of grain. She lifted her hand to her head and found it slippery with perspiration. "Help me!"

She bent double to try to stop the cramping and saw blood seeping through her clothing, then an invisible blow to the back of the head brought her down. She heard the clamour of raised voices around her and the sensation of the ground lurching beneath her. She knew it was judgement day; the world was collapsing all around her, it was all coming to its prophesied end – for her at least. That was what it meant to die. There was no end for her only for everything she had ever known. The buildings, the people, the liquid ground that could not hold her, it was all passing away.

From far away, a man's voice that she did not recognise rang out through the void. A cold, steely voice she felt that she ought somehow to know, though the words meant nothing to her. *My son, I put my curse on you. I curse your wife, I curse your marriage and I curse all of your descendants to the last of your race.* The curse rings across the generations, a father's revenge towards the son who married into the wrong family, another father's revenge upon the daughter he could never stop hating though he never knew why... just a curse, a family curse born out of a futile, meaningless hatred that need never have been, working its way from father to son and beyond.

She felt her head and shoulders being lifted off the dusty ground. Someone had slipped through the growing crowd of onlookers and was cradling her in his arms. "Make them go away!" she whimpered, because she seemed to have fallen into a nightmare again. She was trapped in the night without end that always came to claim her when disaster struck. As she lost consciousness, Alexandria found herself walking through swathes of icy mist. She could almost have been in England again and she was carrying a curly-haired child, the mist and darkness obscuring everything except the face of the child in her arms. She tripped and stumbled across invisible paths and crevices uncertain where she was going. She had the vague sense that she needed to hide the child somewhere, that there was a calamity ahead, but the air was thick and dark around her and she was hopelessly lost. She began to call for help, but her voice refused to carry, stifled by the close, oppressive atmosphere and she became afraid, calling and calling into silence with darkness everywhere and a child's white face looking up at her in mild reproach.

Then there were faces everywhere. She had almost preferred the macabre emptiness to the company that seemed to be gathering around her and her little one with an undefined sense of menace. And all the faces talking at once in screeching discord, uttering the words of a curse at her. Her companions seemed almost familiar: A fair, elegant woman's face like something out of an Edwardian photograph, a scowling old man, startlingly like her father, and others she did recognise, her mother, looking like a pre-Raphaelite goddess, her father as she had never known him, boyishly handsome and a little awkward. *I put my curse on you... and all your descendants.* Uncle Luigi aged, frail.

He knew Alexandria's eyes had focused themselves when she flinched and tried to push him away. A pulse began to thunder in her neck. "It's all right," he said quickly, rocking her gently back and forth. "It's all right, I'm not going to hurt you."

He had said that to her before and lied. She tried to push him away but the pain paralysed her. She felt sickened by her own helplessness. "Why are you here?" No answer. Energy returned to her voice. "Uncle Luigi, why are you here?"

He hesitated, feeling the presence of a crowd sent to damn him and wondered if there was still the chance to run away. But he had promised that he would make his peace with her if the occasion presented itself and there she was in his arms, vulnerable, bleeding, almost as though they had been called upon to relive an encounter

299

from long ago as it should have been. "I'm here because I have a debt to pay," he explained.

"Why do you come to me now when I'm dying?" She sounded halfway between accusation and fear.

"You're not dying," he said with calm authority.

He was as reassuring as she remembered him. She could almost have trusted him. "I'm bleeding to death!" she cried, "I can feel it!"

"It's a miscarriage," he explained, "did you know you were pregnant?"

He knew immediately that he should not have said it; she would have preferred to think she was dying than that. Tears appeared in the corners of her eyes. "This is a judgement," she whispered, but she at least rested her head against his cradling arm.

"It's not a judgement – not against you anyway," he insisted, stroking her hair. "You are the one among us who least deserved to suffer," he told her. She was slipping in and out of consciousness now and he felt the weight of her unsupported head in the crook of his arm. "We have all contributed to this, me most of all." He felt her trying to shake her head but she had no strength left to protest. "Listen, you must understand. I was worse than him. I knew what he was doing and I knew it meant that there would be no one for you to tell about me. I could have stopped him. I could have stopped myself."

Now she knew she was dying. Why else would he have expressed remorse to her then? She was not to know the long journey of soul searching and guilt that he had gone through in her absence and heard only a sudden, unexpected pronouncement, partially eclipsed by the growing darkness. As she slipped away, she felt the most overwhelming sense of injustice. She was sure that it was not meant to end this way, lying in a pool of blood in the arms of such a person, however repentant. "This is a judgement," she lisped and she was not awake long enough to hear his response. For a brief stretch of time, she was without hearing, without history and without a name.

Nicholas sat in the doctor's consulting room in a daze. So much had happened to him of late that he no longer believed any of it was completely real. He had not so much fallen off a roundabout as gone hurtling into some surrealist nightmare where everything he touched exploded in his face. "Did neither of you realise she was pregnant?"

"No." He fought off the temptation to blush and lost. "I'm sorry. She's never been very – regular. She might not have realised the signs. It was the first one, you see." His voice tightened. Oh God, he was going to cry in the middle of this clinical little room, in front of a member of the medical profession who could not have sounded less sympathetic if he had made the most supreme effort.

"She was carrying twins. She got here in time for us to save one of them."

Nicholas blinked, sure that he had missed something somewhere. "Are you saying that she is still pregnant? I didn't think it could happen like that."

"If they were non-identical, they would have separate amniotic sacs," he explained. "So yes, she is still pregnant at present."

The doctor used the tone Nicholas had used when he had been called to the bedside of a terminally ill patient who did not know that the end was coming. "What's wrong?" he asked, rising to his feet. "Please just tell me."

"I wouldn't bother standing up yet if I were you," came the response. "I hardly know how to say this but I'm amazed she was able to conceive at all, and I'm not sure she will again." Nicholas sat down again, noting the change in the doctor's tone. "Her body's a mess! It's little wonder she couldn't carry twins."

Nicholas felt himself breaking into a sweat. In his

confusion, he did not think of the obvious meaning and imagined that Alexandria had cancer or some debilitating disease that neither of them had known about. "Is she sick?" he asked in a small voice.

"Please don't play the innocent with me," snapped the doctor, "don't imagine for a moment that I don't know what that girl's been through. It should be in the hands of the police, except that she's not strong enough to go through a court case in her condition."

A light went on. "But it happened years ago," Nicholas began to explain, conscious that he was covering his back. "How can it make an impact now?"

"Any severe stress or ill treatment when the body is developing can make itself felt in adult life," came the explanation. Just in case Nicholas had not got the message, he added, "and it certainly has made itself felt."

"I need to see her," he said, after a long pause.

Alexandria was still unconscious when he approached her bed. She looked surprisingly peaceful considering the ordeal she had been through, blissfully unaware of anything that had happened or might happen. The presence of machines and tubes all around her made her look like a misplaced child, she simply did not seem to belong there. Everything was too clean, too sharp, too ordered to touch her.

He resisted the temptation to reach out to her, even though he knew he would never wake her in the condition she was in. She was a woman, he thought, who did not remember the day her childhood came to an end because she had never been a child. He had fondly imagined once that he could make it up to her somehow. Those years of growing up were so short anyway, only a tiny fraction of a lifespan. He had thought that he could make it all feel to her as though it happened in some other life or to someone else because if she was happy as a woman what had happened before would be of no consequence. It had never occurred to him that she had grown up damaged, weakened, that they could have had the power to rob her of motherhood, though he supposed that neither man had intended that.

The doctor had finally tried to put his mind at rest about it all. He had told him that there was an agreement between the Maltese and British governments for certain complex medical cases to be sent to London for treatment. It was not usual for pregnancy-related cases to be sent abroad, but given the number of complications and potential complications – the list had been too alarming for Nicholas to memorise – he hoped that she could be transferred to a London hospital as soon as her condition was stable enough for her to travel. It offered the best chance for her and the baby.

Nicholas had given a wry smile, thinking that they were going to be banished from Malta in spite of their efforts, but at least it would not be for long. He did a mental exercise in positive thinking and imagined them flying back to Malta carrying a tiny bundle. Alexandria, whose drug-induced nightmares showed a very different future, trembled in her sleep.

XXVI

As revenge went, it was as spectacular as a member of the Sant'Angelo family could possibly have arranged it. I know that Benedict is going to ask me why, as though there has to be a reason for every malicious, self-destructive act a person has ever committed. Three, two, one...

"But there has to at least be a motive," he explains, right on cue. "What did he have to gain from it?"

What did he have to gain from any of it? What did Edward Sant'Angelo, whose life might have been dedicated to destroying everyone he came into contact with, have to gain from persecuting his own daughter when she was a helpless child who depended on him? What did he have to gain now by trying to prevent the very same daughter from receiving the help that might have saved her life and that of her child? It is a valid enough question from a person too innocent to know the meaning of the word malice but it is blind absurdity to ask it after such a journey. Could anyone truly imagine that such a man would slip quietly away into the sunset when there was unfinished business to attend to? When he had not quite achieved his own destruction yet?

And there is something else that my flagging audience cannot understand. To curse your own offspring is to commit an act of self-destruction. So is child abuse, so is risking the life of your daughter and granddaughter. When a man destroys his descendants he ends his own memory because there can be no one left to remember him, let alone to remember him well. It is the most absolute of deaths pursued only by the most evil or the most insane.

So I will let this most gentle, this most forbearing of

men believe that this decades-long vendetta is all the fault of a madman if it is easier to bear. We are in the end times now, the final moments and it cannot matter very much if the truth is obscured just a little by wishful thinking. I cannot tell it in its entirety. An invisible hand covers my mouth. I find myself stifled at the moment when I have so much to say, when there is so much that needs to be told. I can only allow the tiniest glimpse into the room where the doctor, so confident shortly before, tries to explain to Nicholas that Alexandria will not be going to England because her father put in a personal plea for her to be kept where she was, claiming that he was worried that the travel might be too much for her.

I will draw a discreet curtain over his indignation that an ignorant man (or so he thought) should be listened to above the urging of a member of the medical profession with nearly thirty years of experience. I will not recall how he said there was nothing to be done because there was so much corruption in their precious country these days that it was hardly worth trying to talk sense because no one was listening, or how he cursed his democratically elected leaders for dragging an independent country so full of promise into the political gutter. Nicholas, who did not have a political bone in his body, would have been quite happy to ignore the water shortages, the unrest, the unnerving influence of Libya, the lack of decent cars, chocolate or toothpaste, every possible complaint that anyone could make about little Malta under its current administration if he could only have got Alexandria to London to ensure the safety of the only people in the world he had left to care for.

"Can we appeal?" he asked, when the doctor had finished ranting. "I don't know how he even knew this was happening – Alex hasn't spoken to him in years."

"Do you imagine it takes that long for news to get about? Of course we could appeal, if we only have the time. That's rather the problem."

In a fit of desperation, Nicholas plucked up the courage to seek out Alexandria's father himself. They stood on the doorstep of Alexandria's family home and engaged in a shouting match, Edward claiming in emotional tones that he was only thinking of his daughter whilst his almost son-in-law asked what exactly he knew or cared about her condition anyway. The circular conversation went round and round on the same loop until Edward lost his temper and demanded to know why anyone cared if she lost it anyway.

"It's called a baby," shouted Nicholas, not caring in the least that most of the residents of the street had come out to listen, "and unfortunately for the little mite you are somewhat related to it."

"It's not a baby, it's a mistake," Edward retorted, not missing a beat, "and it's a bit rich you taking that tone with me. Who's going to mourn the loss of a priest's bastard?"

Nicholas had never slammed his foot in a person's front door before and was convinced his toes had been shattered, but the door stayed open. "I'm not proud of the way things have turned out but at least I'm not a murderer," he said, and this time he meant to be overheard.

Edward fell unexpectedly silent and Nicholas in his naivety wondered whether he had jolted his conscience. He stepped away from the doorway and waited for the response. It was so quiet when it came that only Nicholas heard. "He said 'to the last of your race'. Better for the last of a cursed line to die before it can be born. I'm doing the world a good turn."

I beg to disagree, but unfortunately I do not have the capacity to protest. My father, as confused and shaken as ever, watched the door slam shut. He could not remember how long it was before he found the strength to walk away.

A flash of inspiration took him to Rosaria's office, just a short walk away. He had some idea that she would be able to help him but it was only when they began to discuss the situation that the plan began to make any sense. Rosaria, on the other hand, knew exactly why a man in a desperate situation would instinctively home in on a journalist and whisked him out of the building as quickly as she could. "This is my little story," she explained, as she guided him in the direction of a nearby café she used when she needed to have a private conversation with someone. The waiters were discreet and there were two or three niches where they could sit without being seen. "Tell me all about it."

So he told her everything, pausing only to allow her to order a couple of coffees and light up a cigarette – which he pretended he did not mind. She sat quietly in a cloud of smoke for several minutes after he had finished. "My goodness, but what a family you've got yourself muddled up with!" she exclaimed, finally. "Mind you, I'm sure there's more to it than that. Whoever's responsible must know there is something a little odd about the request. If the poor girl's in such a bad state she needs to go to England in the first place, one would think they'd smell a rat when her own father claims she's too ill to get the treatment she needs. Even the government aren't that thick."

"I don't want to start any trouble," said Nicholas hurriedly. "You don't have to go turning over any stones looking for dirt. I just thought that if people knew that she'd been prevented from getting the treatment she needed abroad it might put some pressure on the powers that be…"

"Sob stories aren't really my department," answered Rosaria, and her brother could have been forgiven for thinking her unspeakably callous. "I like turning over dodgy political stones."

"Do you have any other suggestions?"

She looked up at the painting hanging on the wall above Nicholas' head, searching for the source of her uneasiness. The picture was one of those nostalgic glimpses into a forgotten world put together for the benefit of tourists. The earth was a little too green and fertile and an old lady dressed in an *ghonella* stooped down to a small child in unrecognisable peasant costume who was handing her a loaf of bread. "If your situation became public, it could certainly make a difference, if the right people are embarrassed into doing something," she thought aloud. "And it's certainly in the public interest to know if the system's being messed around with." She looked down at her own reflection staring out of the coffee cup. "Nick, I don't know how to say this, but if you want a quiet life, are you absolutely sure you want this splashed all over the papers? I would have thought you'd had enough of that after all the gossip you've caused."

"We never asked to be gossiped about!" he answered. "This is different. As the good Maltese public were so very interested in our private lives just a short time ago, they might be interested in a story worth reading about now." He felt awkward now, as though he were wasting her precious professional time. "Look, I'm only asking you because I couldn't think of anyone else to talk to."

"Charming."

"If we fight the decision it will take too long to be of any benefit to her, she's already nearly four months pregnant. I want to jolt these people into doing the right thing but the one thing she doesn't have is time. If there's some other way, let me know what it is and I'll do it."

It was almost like asking a lawyer if he thought rough justice might be the preferable solution to long, expensive hours in a courtroom. One of Rosaria's more cynical mentors had joked once that journalists were the most powerful people in the world and he could not understand why anyone did anything else. Why bother, when you could be a politician, philosopher, fashion expert, sports commentator, teacher, activist, data analyst, policeman, prosecutor, judge, jury and executioner all in one job? "I'll come and see you this evening. Is Alexandria at home?"

"No, they won't let her leave the hospital."

They parted company outside the café and Rosaria began to move in the direction of her office. As soon as she realised that her brother was out of sight, she changed direction and slipped quietly through the crowded thoroughfare.

"She didn't exactly lie to him," I tell Benedict, desperate to defend Auntie Rosaria's honour. In spite of her unwitting (and I truly hope it was unwitting) role in my removal from a sunny climate to the chill of a London boarding house, I really loved Auntie Rosaria. She inherited her mother's understated spirituality and Uncle Sam's wild sense of mischief, gracing these seemingly irreconcilable characteristics with a good dose of sardonic wit and cynicism. At the age of fifty she was still being politely ejected from church for commenting out loud if she didn't like the homily, and thrown out of feminist meetings for accusing them of being post-colonial secularist neurotics in a nineteen seventies time warp. It was really very difficult to like – and not to like – Auntie Rosaria.

"She never promised she wouldn't turn over any stones."

"She knew he didn't want her to."

Oh yes, she knew, but I don't suppose she intended to cause quite the havoc she created and she was as good as her word. The feature appeared within the week and was much commented upon. Nicholas sat at Alexandria's bedside and said that it was only a matter of time before there was a change of plan. They began to talk as though it was going to happen.

Then the days and weeks began to pass. I continued to grow, undeterred by whatever shenanigans were going on in the outside world. For a mistake I am fearfully and wonderfully made. Cartilage becomes bone, fingernails and hair appear, I hear faraway sounds of life in some other universe. But I am losing the race somehow; I am not growing quickly enough.

"It's no good, they won't budge," said the doctor, one morning when Alexandria had asked if she could go out for the thousandth time and been told to stay still. He took Nicholas aside to explain the situation. "We're basically nearly out of time. The later it gets, the less sensible it is to move her. I think we may have to resign ourselves to the fact that she's not going anywhere."

"How premature can a baby survive?" asked Nicholas. He needed a defined point for them to aim at, even if it was late. "Surely she doesn't have to carry the baby all the way to forty weeks?"

"Nowadays, we would stand a chance of saving the baby as early as twenty-six weeks, theoretically earlier, but it's no easy matter. The baby appears to be a little light for this stage of development, which puts it at a disadvantage."

"So if it could hang on just a few more weeks? Maybe six or seven?"

I wait and wait, growing stronger all the time. I would perhaps have gone on waiting patiently in my underwater cavern until the proper time if I had been given a sporting chance, but even the protective environment of my mother's damaged body cannot save me from the dark forces waiting to overtake us.

It was a cruelty Uncle Luigi truly did not intend when he telephoned the hospital to speak to Alexandria and the hospital staff let her get up and take the call thinking it would do her good. After all, she had received virtually no visits from her family in all the long weeks she had been in hospital, which was most unusual. Normally, they were trying to stop indulgent families turning up at every conceivable hour of the day or night, laden with prohibited food, making a noise or a fuss that caused distress to the patient and inconvenience to the nurses. But in Alexandria's case it was almost a relief for them to discover that there was someone of her own blood who took an interest in her.

"I just wanted to check how you were doing," he said the second she picked up the phone, as though he feared she might slam the phone down when she realised who it was.

"I'm all right," she answered. "I wish they'd let me out of the hospital, though, I've been bored sick."

"I'm sure it's for the best." He heaved a sigh of relief; she was talking to him completely naturally. "I'm sorry about your trouble. I read about it."

"Well, they're doing their best for me here, I can't complain." She sat down, expecting a long conversation. She had never thought she would find herself saying it. "Thanks for being there when it happened."

"It's all right. I was glad to be there."

She hesitated. "You thought I was dying, didn't you?"

He clearly had not expected that. "I wasn't sure. I've wanted to say those things to you for so long, I thought I might not have another chance." Another pause and she knew that he was deciding in his mind whether to share something with her, but there was something even more urgent that she needed to know from him.

"Uncle, were you the only man there?"

"I don't think so," he replied, "quite a crowd gathers at the scene of an accident. We weren't alone if that's what you're asking." He sounded defensive, misunderstanding where the conversation was going.

"Did any of them – I know this sounds strange to ask – but did any of them curse me?"

"Certainly not! What an idea!" He sounded genuinely taken aback. "Who would do that in such a situation, you were in such distress!"

She felt churlish asking, but she knew someone had said it. "So you didn't curse me then?"

"What a terrible idea! I apologised, don't you remember? I confessed everything to you!" He sounded on the verge of tears. "Don't you remember anything that passed between us?"

"Yes, yes of course I do," she promised, feeling terrible for even suggesting it, but the need to find out the truth was stronger. "It's just I'm sure I remember hearing someone telling me they were putting their curse on me. It was definitely a man. I could hear him as clearly as I can hear you. He said something like-" She tried to remember the words in her head. "'I put my curse on you. I curse your marriage and I curse all your descendants.' I can't remember the words exactly, but you would remember if you heard." There was a long silence at the end of the line. "Are you still there?"

"Listen to me, *hanini*," he said slowly, "I know you've no reason to trust me, but you must believe me now if you never trust me again. It's just your memory playing tricks on you. You must have heard your parents talking about it and forgotten about it until then."

"I'm sure I never did," she answered, but she could feel an old, dizzying fear seizing hold of her. Stop it! She commanded herself. She said to him, "I never heard those words before then."

"You must have done."

"But why would I have done? What does it mean?"

He was tempted to put the phone down there and then, knowing it would be preferable to taking her any further down that dark road, but he could already hear the fear in her voice. "Alex it's a nonsense. Just something a poisonous old man said in a fit of pique. It means nothing."

"Who said it?" She leant forward, trying to stop the room swaying but she was five years old again and there was no one to turn to for help. "You must tell me now."

"It was your grandfather, on your father's wedding day. There had been a falling out, he didn't like his son's choice of bride. Look, it means nothing, it was a stupid argument!"

"Why did nobody tell me?"

Her voice sounded so far away. He had to reach out to her before he lost her again. "Because it was a nonsense! Because no one ever believed in it!"

"He cursed everyone didn't he? The voice said 'to the last of your race.'"

"There was no voice, you imagined it."

"But how could I have known if I hadn't heard it?"

"You heard it before, that's all. Please listen, it's not true. There's no such thing as a curse. Can you hear me? It's meaningless rubbish!"

He heard the clatter of the receiver hitting the ground and then nothing.

Her waters broke before they could find a trolley to carry her to theatre. "Stop this!" she shouted, the force of the contractions jolting her into the foetal position. "It's too early! You must stop this!"

"We can't, the amniotic sac has broken," said a nurse, taking hold of her hand. "The baby's coming now."

"But it's too soon! Do something!" She expected there to be a magic answer to the crisis, in her mind she had always imagined that doctors could do anything with their machines and medicines. She knew she could not give birth yet. The power of modern science had to prevail.

"Her blood pressure's out of control." The doctor's

voice, taking on the tone they always used when the worst case scenario appeared before them. "I'll have to operate or I'll lose them both."

Alexandria screamed for Nicholas but he was being kept well out of the way and could not hear her. "Don't!" she managed to shout, "Don't touch my baby!" But someone was holding her still and she felt a needle breaking into a vein in her arm. She was sure that they could not do this against her will. "I do not consent!" she shouted, but the syringe was barely empty before her head began to swim. The last thing she was aware of as the clouds of anaesthesia paralysed her was a kicking and turning of frantic somersaults inside her stomach and the knowledge that she had lost yet another battle.

They cut her open the second she lost consciousness, racing to drag out my slimy, pink, wriggling form before the anaesthetic could reach me. Contrary to the worst of predictions, there was no need for mechanical life support. My lungs filled with air without needing any persuasion and I gave an angry yell. "Nothing wrong with her lungs anyway," remarked the nurse who cut the umbilical cord. "What protesting creature has she brought into the world?"

My silent, unconscious mother has brought me into the world. For now, there is nothing more to say. My mother rests and recovers, my father is ecstatic and I – well for a moment I will just be.

XXVII

It came so close to a happy ending that I am almost tempted to end things here, with threads coming together and the promise of happiness and reconciliation. I could tell Benedict about how my father's papers came through shortly after my birth – too late for his name to appear on my birth certificate but freeing him to marry. I could tell him about the quiet wedding shared by just six of us – Nicholas, Alexandria looking a picture in a long pink dress, Rosaria and Richard Mason all the way from England as witnesses and Gregory naturally playing his rightful part. It was not quite the big romantic wedding Alexandria had dreamed of, but it still felt a little like a dream when they had all thought that it might never happen, particularly when they turned around at the end and saw Carmelina sitting at the back watching them.

She took them all back to the family home where they found the table laid out for them and Nicholas realised she must have been up late into the night cooking and preparing for their arrival. They were a family again, enjoying a special occasion, like any other family. He could almost have believed that they had never been apart and never would be parted again. Memories returned to him as they sat and ate together of other gatherings around the table long ago: Uncle Sam introducing them to bubble gum after dinner to Nanna Buhagiar's intense annoyance, Pawlinu explaining in hushed tones why he had decided to go to America after all, his father regaling them with exhilarating and highly improbable stories of his adventures in the Orient on the last leave before he died, and one of his earliest memories of all, sitting at the very same table amid the faint smell of dust and cordite because his mother absolutely insisted that it was to be business as usual, even if there was virtually nothing to eat and the house had almost been blown to smithereens with little Pawlinu in it.

"I owe you an apology," confessed Carmelina, as the meal drew to a close. She had moved to a nearby armchair and sat there, the picture of contentment, holding her grandchild whilst the others finished their trifle. "You know something, when I heard that Alexandria was with child, I actually wondered if it was yours, but this little mite is definitely one of us."

That afternoon set the tone for the next three-and-a-half years. My parents moved to Sliema and Rosaria, unmarried and unmarriageable, continued to live at home. They were happy, private years where little that was going on in the world was able to interfere. It was the peaceful and – they thought – just conclusion to an unlikely journey across countries and continents of which they were the weary survivors.

But life is rarely as straightforward or as just as that. As I said at the very beginning, for those of us who were born in the wrong country, at the wrong time or under the wrong circumstances, there can be no such warm sense of belonging, no comforting sense of being at home. No family is so private, so self-sufficient that it cannot be torn apart as they all should have known, except that anyone can believe that they have lived through their quota of suffering.

It is suddenly dark. There is no twilight here, no in between time, just light and then night falling in an instant. Above our heads, blinking lights herald the planes bringing people to Malta and away again. People who do not want to leave or perhaps who did not want to come. "Why did you leave?" asks Benedict, staring straight ahead. "You must have come to England before you were very old. You said you hardly remember a time before."

"We left because Auntie Rosaria couldn't help herself," I explain and I feel uncharacteristically phlegmatic about the whole thing. Let it be said just as it happened. "It was like she said, she liked turning over political stones," I tell him. "She suspected all along that there had been more to her sister-in-law's plight than met the eye and wanted to know what it was. So she let some years lapse, thinking that would be enough to ensure that no one was hurt and she started investigating."

"What did she find?"

"I don't know exactly. That's the worst insult." I could probably find out without too much difficulty because she must have published something. "I think it had something to do with her getting hold of some classified letters." I wonder if I just do not want to know. "Whatever it was, it must have been fairly damaging because the repercussions started almost immediately."

I just about have enough energy to tell him how my father came home one day in a state of turmoil because he had been dismissed from his job without a word of explanation, only to be followed by Rosaria who already knew. She gathered my parents together to announce that the four of us would have to leave the country before our passports were withdrawn.

"What have you done?" demanded my father, "I thought I told you not to take the story any further?"

"Yes but that was ages ago," came the poor excuse from a woman of words. "Anyway, this is a free country. I had every right to carry out my investigations."

"It's obviously not that free," answered my father, in case she had believed her own rhetoric. "How do you know our passports are going to be withdrawn?"

"Let's just say I've been tipped off, shall we?" she said, taking off her coat. "If I'm wrong, we can come back, but I don't imagine I am if you lost your job. In fact, I think it quite likely you'll never have another one here."

"I was told that last time," snapped Nicholas. Rosaria watched as he threw himself into a chair. "Why is it that whenever I get my life together someone has to come at it with a mallet?" he asked the world in general. "What did you find that's caused this? Couldn't you at least have kept us out of it?"

"I can't explain now, there isn't time."

Carmelina proved even harder to pacify. "What does it matter if they take your passports away?" she reasoned with impeccable logic, "they'll have to give them back sooner or later and you weren't planning on going anywhere, were you?"

"Mama, there's more to it than that," Rosaria explained. "For a start it's an insult. It's the sort of thing they'd normally do to a criminal. But in practical terms, if someone stops you leaving a country it's not going to be for any good reason."

She ended up resorting to well-intentioned lies, telling her mother that it would not be for long. It was a storm in a teacup, a few officious people sabre-rattling, they would be home again before she had even noticed their absence. It was the least she could do to ease the blow when she was taking away her mother's most precious possessions. Carmelina just wanted an explanation. "Can't you at least tell me what this is all about?"

"Not yet."

When it came to it, she was the most stoical of the lot of them. Whilst Alexandria argued with Rosaria that they could not just flee at a moment's notice after they had fought so hard to be accepted, she picked me up and took me home to start packing. She had learnt at a very

318

young age that life was full of catastrophes and heartbreaks beyond her control and dealt with this latest disaster with clinical efficiency. When we eventually left, she had even made sure that there was enough food in our hand luggage to last us in case we arrived in London too late to get an evening meal.

It was only after we had left her behind at the airport that I gather she gave way to emotion and was grateful for the presence of Gregory to remind her that she was not completely alone. "All my children," she murmured. "Pawlinu dead long before his time, my son and daughter refugees and I do not even know why. What will happen to you, I wonder?"

"It's all right Mama," quipped Gregory, disguising a lump in his throat as a cough. "I suspect I'm destined to be spectacularly boring." The humour failed, he noticed her eyes glistening. "You mustn't worry, she always over-reacted. They'll be back home soon and we'll think what a fuss we made."

Carmelina actually laughed; a laugh without a hint of mirth in it. "Indeed." She knew that we would come back again and that she would welcome us back into her home – but always as visitors.

And somewhere in a wild world that bears no resemblance to anything I have ever known, I find myself being carried through a maze of different rooms and settings, listening to the jabber of strangers speaking words I do not even recognise as another language. There is so much noise and movement; I am dizzy and lost amid too many people and places I cannot recognise. I find myself waiting for the moment when I will wake up and find myself safely in my bed, sweating with the stress of a dream, but this is an infant terror that I did not create. I wait for someone to explain but no one thinks to do so or to tell me that it is a madness that will pass. I am lost and I cannot find my way. I cannot find my way home.

Epilogue

Time for one last walk and then we must be gone. A walk along Sliema seafront, just Benedict and I, to take up the last hours before going to catch our flight. The sea is calm this morning, barely a patch of white as far as the eye can see. Behind us the high rise buildings and glitzy hotels and bars spread themselves along the coast like a stack of children's building blocks; gaudy, conspicuous, artificial but the monuments to a new age of tourism and commerce. The children in their designer clothing, racing up and down the promenade on micro scooters tell the same story of an island finding its feet in the modern world. An island nation where I do not belong.

Better that way. In a world of lost people, I cannot help but wonder whether it is possible for a country to lose itself in the process of changing and adapting. If it is, I am not sure that I want to see it, but if that is the case, I cannot possibly explain what brought me back in the first place. Why should I have wanted him to see it then? Why did I bring him here if it is of so little consequence that we can leave now and pretend that it never existed?

"I like your country," says Benedict, as if to remind me that he has not fled the scene. "We can come back again soon."

I am not so sure, and I know it is not my country, any more than England where divisions fester beneath a veneer of inclusiveness and the virtue of tolerance has morphed into a weapon to silence dissent. Better to be a stranger there than in a place that feels so familiar that it is impossible to bear it. I can take my leave of all of them: Edward Sant'Angelo, Leonardo, Antonia, Carmelina, Ġorġ Buhagiar, Lawrence, Sam/Salvatore, Nanna Buhagiar, Luigi, Pawlinu, Elisabeth, Rosaria, the whole array of them whom I have loved and hated and buried on the way. Who knows where they are now? I do not suppose it makes much difference, but those of us who remain wish them no ill, not even the ugliest amongst them. We will all stand before God one day and probably when we least expect it, when there are no more places of escape left open to us. Let them all rest now in their far away graves, in America, in France, at the bottom of the sea. Let them all be at peace as those of us who remain behind cannot and will not allow ourselves to be.

"Benedict?" I am aware of his presence beside me and realise that I am a little surprised to find that he is still there. "It was not a dream."

"I know."